Praise f— AL PESSIN and his
TASK F—

"If your thing is a … se,
and action galore, … .
Don't wait. Check it out. Now."
—**Steve Berry,** *New York Times* bestselling author
of the Cotton Malone thrillers

"Don't mess with the good guys. Reading Al Pessin's
Blowback is like saddling a rocket. Once it gets going,
hang on for one helluva ride!"
—**John Gilstrap,** *New York Times* bestselling author of
the award-winning Jonathan Grave thriller series

"*Blowback* is a realistic—and top-notch—boots-on-the-ground military thriller featuring the secret counterterrorism unit Task Force Epsilon. Author Al Pessin gives readers a front-row seat as über-resilient unit leader Bridget Davenport directs U.S. Army lieutenant Faraz Abdallah on a harrowing undercover mission to the Syrian terrorist camps in pursuit of the elusive Taliban mastermind al-Souri. The pages will fly by as you draw closer to the heart-thumping, action-packed climax. Pessin really knows his stuff, and *Blowback* proves it!"
—**Alan Orloff,** Thriller- and Derringer-Award winning
author of *I Know Where You Sleep*

"*Blowback* is a timely military thriller that pulls no punches. Al Pessin brings the war on terror to life as few authors can. Highly recommended for fans of Alex Berenson and Brad Thor."
—**Ward Larsen,** *USA Today* bestselling
author of *Assassin's Strike*

"The blistering and bracing *Blowback* is a thinking man's (or woman's!) action thriller, a scarily prescient take on current events that foretells the headlines instead of exploiting them. Al Pessin's second entry in the Task Force Epsilon series conjures comparisons to James Rollins's seminal Sigma Force in all the right ways while staking out his own turf in a crowded landscape. A riveting and relentless read."
—**Jon Land,** *USA Today* bestselling author

"Original, action-packed, gripping, and timely—*Blowback* kept me up all night. Al Pessin knows Washington and the war on terror. And Hollywood, take note, Al Pessin is the new Tom Clancy."
—**Tony Park,** international bestselling author

Sandblast

TOP-FIVE SELECTION, UNPUBLISHED BOOK OF THE YEAR, 2018 ROYAL PALM LITERARY AWARDS,
SHORT-LIST SELECTION, 2017 BOSQUE FICTION PRIZE

"Al Pessin escorts you through thrills and chaos, writing with the sure hand of authority. This guy knows his stuff."
—**Richard Castle,** *New York Times* bestselling author of the Nikki Heat thrillers

"In *Sandblast*, Al Pessin has crafted a taut action-thriller that really pulls you in. You'll feel like you're right beside the main character on an increasingly perilous journey filled with impossible choices that threaten to change him at his very core. The plot is highly original, and I felt like I was there. It's a great book."
—**Henry V. O'Neil,** author of The Sim War series

"*Sandblast* is the definition of a terrific military thriller—straightforward, precise, and devastating. This timely, realistic story—with its authentic and knowing voice, and courageous main characters—propels readers to the peak of white-knuckled brinksmanship and will be awarded top marks by fans of Alex Berensen and Vince Flynn."
—**Hank Phillippi Ryan,** Mary Higgins Clark, Anthony, and six-time Agatha award-winner

"*Sandblast* is tense, believable, and relevant. Pessin calls on his years in the Pentagon and White House press corps for the keen details that bring this tale to life. There's a high emotional content here, too, as we follow the almost impossible quest of a likable and massively outgunned hero."
—**T. Jefferson Parker,** *New York Times* bestselling author of *The Last Good Guy*

"So exciting—and so terrifyingly realistic—you won't be able to put it down. If you like complex international thrillers, keep Al Pessin on your short list of must-read authors."
—**D. J. Niko,** international bestselling author of The Sarah Weston Chronicles

"*Sandblast* is an aptly titled nail-biter of a thriller that opens at a pulse-rattling pace and only ratchets upwards from there. Al Pessin not only knows how to tell a story but his journalistic background imbues this tale of an Afghan-American Army officer infiltrating a terrorist organization with compelling authority."
—**Les Standiford,** author of *Water to the Angels* and many other books, director of the creative writing program at Florida International University

"Al Pessin brings a lifetime of frontline experience to a novel that could have been taken from today's headlines. Utterly compelling and a cautionary tale for our times."
—**Retired Admiral James Stavridis,**
former dean, Fletcher School at Tufts University,
former commander, NATO forces (including
those in Afghanistan), and frequent media commentator

"*Sandblast* vividly depicts a close-to-real scene, which makes the story more entertaining and educating."
—**Ali Ahmad Jalali,** Afghan Ambassador to Germany,
former interior minister of Afghanistan and Afghan
presidential candidate, and Distinguished Professor
at the Near East South Asia Center for Strategic
Studies (NESA), National Defense University
in Washington, D.C.

"The author writes with incredible authenticity . . . Exceptionally well plotted . . . complex and consistent . . . Each chapter adds a new hook . . . The story will appeal to a broad range of readers. We met the people, felt their anxiety, sweated with them in their decision process. This is a deeper story than it appears . . . The inner turmoil of the protagonists propels the story. The reader is pulled along, seeing lives lived, lost, and changed. Faraz is a heroic character of sequel deserving merit."
—**Statement of the judges,** 2018 Royal Palm Literary
Awards given by the Florida Writers Association

Books by Al Pessin

THE TASK FORCE EPSILON THRILLER SERIES

Sandblast

Blowback

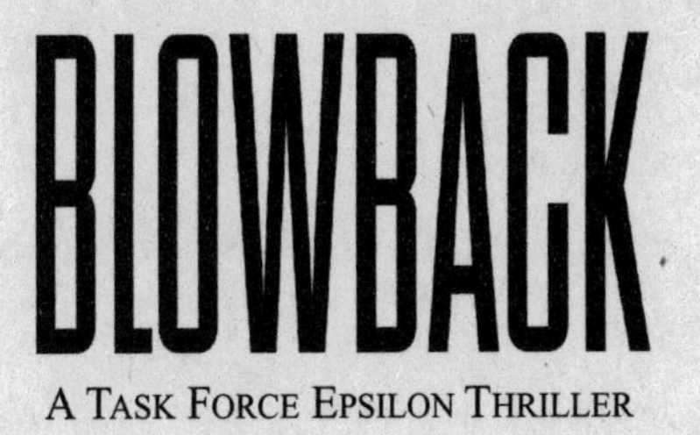

A TASK FORCE EPSILON THRILLER

AL PESSIN

PINNACLE BOOKS
Kensington Publishing Corp.
www.kensingtonbooks.com

PINNACLE BOOKS are published by

Kensington Publishing Corp.
119 West 40th Street
New York, NY 10018

ISBN-13: 978-0-7860-4673-7
ISBN-10: 0-7860-4673-2

First Pinnacle paperback printing: March 2021

10 9 8 7 6 5 4 3 2 1

Printed in the United States of America

Electronic edition:

ISBN-13: 978-0-7860-4674-4 (e-book)
ISBN-10: 0-7860-4674-0 (e-book)

For Sam and Steph

Part One

Chapter One

The six-man Special Ops team slipped into the village at two a.m., walking almost silently along the edge of the hard-packed dirt road past the ramshackle one-room houses, trying not to disturb the sleeping dogs. The men were all in black, with night vision goggles protruding from their helmets and M4 assault rifles at the ready. The thin mountain air was cold, and their breath, steady and even in spite of the long climb from the landing zone, turned to fog. Clouds obscured the moon—always a good thing.

GPS indicated their target was forty meters ahead.

Thirty-five hundred miles to the west, a young man walked along a very different road in a nondescript residential neighborhood of South London.

It was well into a cold, drizzly evening as he rounded the corner, twenty minutes from the Underground station where he'd gotten off the train. Mahmoud wore black jeans, a dark green T-shirt, and a black jacket. His baseball cap and backpack were gray, and the cap bore no team logo. He pulled it down to his eyebrows as he turned into the wind.

Mahmoud found the spot he had scouted between the light circles of two lampposts and checked his phone. Three bars, just as before. He turned into a dark alcove between two houses and wedged himself into a small space behind their dumpsters. He dialed the international number he had been repeating to himself all afternoon.

The distant phone rang once, twice, and the beginning of a third time. Someone picked up and blew a small puff of breath through the wires, satellite links, and cell towers into Mahmoud's ear. He understood—all was clear.

Mahmoud recited the saying in Arabic, as it had been recited to him on another call a few hours earlier. "If you do not recognize Allah, at least know him by his power."

The line was silent for a second, as if out of reverence—not for the wisdom of the words, but rather for their power at that moment.

Then the programmed response came: "*Allahu akbar*." God is great.

The sergeant leading the Special Ops team raised his right fist to signal Stop. He turned toward his men, checked his weapons, and adjusted his goggles. The others did the same. He looked at each man in turn, and each one gave a thumbs-up to indicate *ready*.

The sergeant turned forward again and resumed the advance.

* * *

Mahmoud touched his phone's screen to end the call, then removed the back and tossed the battery into the dumpster. He took out the SIM card and crushed it with his fingers as he resumed his walk, planning a circuitous route to a different tube station on a different line.

At a public ash can with a tall neck and a small opening for cigarette butts, he disposed of the SIM. He dropped the rest of the phone in a trash bin a few blocks away.

The rain was heavier now, dripping off his jacket and onto his shoes. He had another ten minutes of walking ahead of him.

The Special Ops team's target was sleeping on a homemade mat on the dirt floor of a small hut in the center of the village, a few steps off the road behind an animal shed. He was alone. Blood from his wounds had soaked through the makeshift bandages and stained his borrowed shirt. His dark beard was scraggly. His wool cap lay next to him. His traditional Afghan trousers and tunic were filthy from one interrogation, two gunfights, eight hours on the road—some of it walking—and a day in this hut.

His right leg jerked, and his right hand moved as if to raise a weapon. He woke up in a sweat and nearly cried out. It was the third time that night he'd had the same nightmare: The Taliban search party caught him. He was in a fight for his life. He lost.

Awake now, the young man heard footsteps. He reached for his AK-47, for real this time, and pointed it into the darkness.

Someone opened the door, slowly and quietly. The red lights of laser targeting sights swept the room.

A voice said in foreign-accented Pashto, “Lower your weapon.” He did, but he kept his hand on it. He thought he knew what was happening, but here, one could never be sure.

Three men entered with practiced speed. The first grabbed his AK. Another pointed a rifle at him. The third approached and shined a light in his eyes. He winced and turned away, then blinked and turned back, looking straight into the light.

The man behind it, apparently the team leader, twice compared the face he saw to a photo on a small tablet computer. “State your name,” he whispered in English.

The man on the floor swallowed. It had been a long time since he’d said his name, his real name. He took a breath, his tone and his identity strengthening as he formed each word: “Lieutenant Faraz Abdallah.”

“Code word and authentication, please, sir.”

“Sandblast, Whiskey-Alpha-5-9-0-Sierra-Sierra-Romeo.”

The team leader nodded and put the tablet back into his pocket. “Master Sergeant Murphy, sir. We’re here to take you home.”

A twentysomething Arab man didn’t stand out on the London Underground, especially not in this neighborhood. Mahmoud took a seat and played a game on his phone as he settled in for the long ride back to the safe house. He didn’t much like electronic games, but playing helped him blend in with the crowd. And it kept his eyes down under the baseball cap.

His backpack was lighter than it had been that morning. He had no more spare clothes. And he had three fewer mobile phones, having used each one once in far-flung parts of the city before dismantling and discarding them.

Mahmoud had been remarkably calm for most of the journey. But every time he thought about what he had set in motion, his heart raced and beads of sweat formed at his temples. The infidels would truly know Allah's power. And with His help, they would see the futility of their war on His people.

Less than forty-eight hours earlier, the enemy had scored what they saw as a great victory, a drone strike in Afghanistan. They had committed the cowardly murder of Ibn Jihad, leader of the newly unified global movement to end the occupation of the Holy Lands and establish Allah's law throughout the world.

Through the acts launched by his phone calls, the holy fighters would begin their revenge. The infidels would realize that their victory was hollow, that no drone could crush the believers, that time and right and numbers were on the their side.

Mahmoud's stomach grumbled. He hadn't stopped to eat all day, hadn't spoken to anyone or purchased anything. He had scanned a different travel card for each train and bus ride. He had changed his shirt, jacket, and baseball cap in public restrooms several times and trashed the used ones. He was certain that no one knew who he was or what he had done.

Hunger pangs were a small price to pay, especially compared to the price the brothers would be paying tomorrow. He still thought of them as brothers, maybe some sisters, too. Tomorrow, they would be martyrs, like the great Ibn Jihad, may Allah grant him the highest place in paradise.

In His blessed memory, tomorrow would be the greatest day ever for the jihad.

Faraz walked to the team's Black Hawk helicopter under his own power, surrounded by the Special Ops guys. It was a strange sight—American troops with blackened faces, body armor, helmets, M4s, and night vision goggles walking with an Afghan in sandals and traditional clothes.

It looked like he was their prisoner. But he had called them in to rescue him.

He had been undercover in Afghanistan for months, inside the Taliban, eventually close to its top leadership. He had participated in terrorist operations. He had almost been killed several times. And he had narrowly avoided the nightmare that haunted his sleep.

Most importantly, Faraz had accomplished his mission, called in the drone strike, setting the terrorists back, he believed, by months, if not years.

On the chopper, they had Faraz lie down on a gurney so a medical team could check him over. He protested when they lashed his chest and legs down, but they said it was for safety.

He threw a look at the medic when he started the IV. The man said, "Hydration, sir." But those were the last words Faraz heard before he went under.

The Black Hawk stayed low and banked hard, descending the Hindu Kush into Pakistan.

Chapter Two

Bridget walked along the hospital corridor, her navy-blue power suit covering her insecurity. She was about to take her boyfriend Will home to recuperate from having his left leg just about blown off in Afghanistan.

As the head of the Defense Intelligence Agency's new secret counterterrorism unit, Task Force Epsilon, Bridget Davenport had tracked terrorists, faced down four-star generals, and argued with the president of the United States. That seemed tame now, compared to taking Will Jackson back to her place for the long term.

She stopped to check her reflection in a window with a curtain drawn behind it. Bridget had finally made time to get her light brown hair cut above her shoulders. Her suit was tailored to her trim frame and matched her eyes, and her white silk blouse was unbuttoned just the right amount. She adjusted the lapel.

Bridget smiled at some wounded troops gathered at the far end of the hall who were clearly checking her out. Then she took a breath and knocked on Will's open door.

"Hi, babe." He was freshly shaved and his black hair was trimmed tight to his head. He wore jeans and a white

T-shirt that hugged his muscles and set off his skin. Will was sitting in an upholstered visitor's chair. He flashed a broad smile when Bridget came in, complete with his lone, right-side dimple.

"Babe?" She stopped just inside the room and cocked her head. "Is that a promotion from kiddo?"

"I guess it is. Now, come here so I can pin it on you."

Bridget walked over and kissed him. Their hug was awkward. He couldn't stand because of his injury, and no one was saying when he might be able to. She could only hope his SEAL training would help him power through.

After months away from Will during his deployment, Bridget had visited him most evenings since he'd arrived at the Bethesda military hospital a week earlier. Physically and mentally, he had good days and bad days. Now, minutes away from getting out of the hospital, this was clearly a good day.

A nurse appeared at the doorway with a wheelchair and a clipboard. She cleared her throat to interrupt them.

"Ah," Will said. "Here is the other woman in my life. Bridget, Nurse Gabby—tough, but unfair."

"Hi," Bridget said.

"Hello, ma'am. We are just a few signatures away from getting rid of Lieutenant Commander Jackson, and not a moment too soon." Gabby bent down to hand the clipboard to Will, and he signed his discharge papers. Even wearing flat nurse's shoes, Gabby was taller than Bridget in her medium heels. Thin, blond, and fresh-faced, Gabby looked maybe twenty-two, if Bridget had to guess.

While Gabby went over Will's rehab plan, Bridget scanned the room. It was immaculate. All the monitors were lined up along the wall, ready for the next patient.

Will's duffel and a small backpack waited by the door. Through the window, she saw several other hospital buildings, including the campus centerpiece, a World War Two–era, fifteen-story tower that held hundreds of patient rooms.

Will handed Bridget his copies of the paperwork, and she deposited them into her purse. Gabby helped Will put on his camo jacket and transfer to the wheelchair.

"I can take it from here," Bridget said.

"Oh, no, ma'am. I need to see him all the way out. Hospital rules."

"Ladies, ladies, please, don't fight over me." Will pulled the duffel onto his lap. "Let's just get out of here."

Bridget picked up the backpack. "Lead on, Nurse Gabby."

Eight floors below, the small phone vibrated in the pocket of Fatima's jeans. Her breath caught, and she nearly cut herself with the knife she was using to chop celery for the cafeteria's lunchtime salad. This was the signal she had prayed for, and also feared.

"Excuse me, chef," she said to her boss. "Bathroom break, please."

"Okay, but quickly."

"Thank you, ma'am."

Fatima stepped off the stool that made her tall enough to reach the prep table. As she left the kitchen, she wiped her left hand on her apron and used the right to tuck a stray lock of hair into her hijab. The traditional scarf, tight around her face, made her olive cheeks look chubby and accentuated the false smiles she offered colleagues as she made her way to the exit.

In the hallway, Fatima checked her watch. Three minutes before nine. The signal meant this was the hour that would change the world, cripple the infidels, and end her life in the most virtuous way. Her religious beliefs and personal grievances brought her here. Working with the military people these many months as she smuggled in the components, she had come to hate them more deeply than she thought possible.

Fatima awakened to the true calling of Islam not long after arriving at George Washington University three years earlier. Her parents spent their life savings to send her to GW from their modest home in Pennsylvania. They were immigrants from Jordan—nice enough, but clueless collaborators with the infidels.

And they weren't even her real parents. Her mother and father, may Allah protect them, had died in a Zionist air strike on their refugee camp in Lebanon when Fatima was only two years old. Her so-called parents in Pennsylvania would cry this night, but she long ago convinced herself not to care. It would only prove their treachery.

Fatima went into the ladies' dressing room, opened her locker, and knelt in front of it to block the view in case anyone else came in.

She removed the black rectangular metal controller from a cardboard box hidden under a pile of old magazines and pulled out its long antenna. The device was heavy, with a powerful battery inside—its weight matching the gravitas of what it would enable her to do.

Fatima flipped its power switch. The red light glowed. She caressed the bulb with her thumb, felt its warmth. She stared into the empty locker, letting her eyes lose focus, and breathed in a steady rhythm as she had been taught.

All fear was gone now. She was in Allah's hands. The task was simple and much rehearsed. Fatima glanced at the numbers counting off on the watch.

Bridget, Will, and Gabby were delayed in the small lobby on his floor. There was some sort of medical emergency. All the elevators had been put under manual control to get the right people to the right place as soon as possible.

A crowd gathered. Bridget checked her BlackBerry. Nothing urgent, but she knew that wouldn't last. It never did. She needed to take Will back to her apartment and get to the Pentagon before the next crisis hit.

She put her hand on Will's shoulder, and he put his hand on top of it. Neither of them was good at waiting, but it couldn't be helped.

Finally, an elevator arrived. Bridget, Will, and Gabby were the last to board.

Fatima thought about the others. She had never met them, didn't know who they were. But she knew they worked in different parts of the hospital complex. They had smuggled in their components, as she had. Now, they were crouching by their lockers or hiding in closets or bathroom stalls, ready to join her in the greatest strike of Allah's holy jihad.

As the seconds ticked off, Fatima moved her thumb to the small button next to the light. At 8:59:50, she said the

Shahada, the affirmation of faith, the words a Muslim is supposed to recite before dying.

"*La ilaha illa-lah, Mohammed rasulu-lah.*" There is no God but God. Mohammed is the messenger of God.

The time turned over to 9:00:00. Fatima took a breath, closed her eyes, pressed the button, and whispered, "*Allahu akbar.*"

Chapter Three

Bridget heard the first boom. Inside the brick and concrete shaft, it was hard to tell what it was. Then a huge explosion shook them and seemed to push the elevator against the shaft wall and back against the opposite side.

The crush of falling bodies tipped Will's wheelchair onto the legs of the man next to him. Bridget's head smacked into the door, and on the rebound, she fell onto Will. His chair collapsed, sandwiching him inside it. He cried out and dropped the duffel onto the floor. The lights went off, and people screamed in pain and panic.

The elevator seemed to hang in space, then plunged downward, accompanied by more screams from its passengers. The handle of Will's wheelchair pushed into Bridget's chest. Nurse Gabby was on top of her.

Then the braking system kicked in, and they came to a screeching halt, the handle digging into Bridget's ribs. Will's legs were crushed between the big wheels. The man under him cried out. Pieces of the ceiling came down—the light fixture onto Bridget's head, the ventilation fan and its motor onto Gabby, who rolled off Bridget in a tangled heap of arms and legs.

The emergency lights came on. Bridget pushed herself off the handle, easing the pressure on Will. He was holding his bad leg.

"You okay?" she asked.

"Shit. Leg hurts like hell."

"Don't try to get up. You have blood on your cheek."

Will wiped it away. "Yours, I think." He pointed toward Bridget's head.

She reached up and found blood soaking the hair on the right side. "Jeez." Bridget reached into her purse. There was nothing she could use on her injury except Will's discharge papers. She pressed them to the wound and winced.

"Please. Off me," the man under Will said. His voice was weak. He appeared to be in his eighties, and he'd borne the weight of three people, plus the wheelchair. Bridget helped Will disengage from the chair and slide off the man onto the floor.

Gabby was lying behind Will, bleeding from her head and not moving. A man and a woman in scrubs crouched down to take her vitals and assess her injuries. They ordered others to push to the sides, laid her out flat, and started CPR.

Bridget moved to help them, but the pain in her head spiked, and she felt dizzy. She steadied herself against the wheelchair, one hand still holding the papers to her head. She rubbed her chest. Broken ribs, she figured.

A navy captain in fatigues was trying to open the gray steel doors, and Bridget turned to help him. No go.

They heard two more distant explosions, then another, much closer, that rocked the elevator again. Everyone reached out to hold onto something.

An older, red-haired woman in the back of the elevator was crying. "What's happening? What's happening?"

Bridget answered. "Try to calm down, ma'am. They'll get us out soon."

"Good question, though," Will said.

"Must be an attack, so many explosions." Bridget took stock of what happened. She had heard half a dozen explosions in the last minute or so.

"Hey! Help us!" the captain shouted. Others joined in. "Help! Help!"

There was no response.

"They won't hear us, but they'll know we're in here," Bridget said. "From the sound of it, they have lots of other priorities."

The man in scrubs—Dr. Carlton, according to the stitching on his pocket—knelt over Gabby and performed chest compressions. "One . . . two . . . three . . ."

A woman in a nurse's uniform sat next to Gabby's head, stroking her hair and delivering the breaths at the proper intervals. Their actions were professional, practiced.

"Let me help you," Bridget said, moving into position on the other side of Gabby.

"Ma'am, you should sit down with that head wound," Dr. Carlton said.

"I'm fine."

"No, you're not." Carlton resumed his work.

Bridget felt a wave of dizziness and sat on Will's duffel. Bridget's head hurt like hell, and she got shooting pains in her chest with every breath. She reached up to wipe away a bead of sweat running down her cheek and realized it was blood.

A high-flying counterterrorism expert, now a terror

attack victim. She didn't like the sound of that. And she especially didn't like being trapped and unable to spring into action. She reached for her purse and took out her phone. No signal. "Damn."

"One . . . two . . . three," Dr. Carlton continued.

Will was talking quietly with a young blonde, also on the floor, who had ceiling debris in her hair and tears streaking her makeup. She was saying something about coming to the hospital to visit her boyfriend. Will was telling her it would be all right. The older man who had been crushed under them sat with his back against the wood-paneled wall, holding his left leg.

Dr. Carlton and the nurse stopped working on Gabby and stood up. They bowed their heads. The doctor bent down and put a handkerchief over Gabby's face.

Bridget reached out to take Will's hand. "Oh, God," she said. Bridget had seen death before. Too much of it. But it was not supposed to happen here, not like this.

Will held her hand. "We'll get those bastards," he said. "We have to."

President Andrew Martelli was having breakfast with the congressional leadership in his private West Wing dining room. The waiters in black pants and vests, white shirts, and bow ties were removing the remains of bacon and eggs with croissants and fruit salad. The time for small talk was almost over.

The House minority leader was finishing a story about one of his down-home constituents, probably not a real person, designed to illustrate why the president was wrong about trade policy. Martelli was preparing a polite but dismissive response.

Two Secret Service agents and Chief of Staff Greg Capman came through the door to the president's left with an urgency that drew everyone's attention. The minority leader stopped mid-punchline.

Capman whispered into Martelli's ear. "Protocol One, sir. No drill."

"No drill?" The president's eyes widened.

"Yes, sir."

"Ladies and gentlemen," Martelli said, "I have to go." He got up.

The others pushed their chairs back to do the same. "What's happening?" the minority leader asked.

The president was halfway to the door, flanked by the agents.

Hurrying to keep up, Capman answered for him. "We're not sure yet. We'll keep you posted." By the time he finished talking, they were already in the hallway.

Martelli turned toward the Situation Room, but Capman grabbed his arm. "No, sir. The bunker, for now." A Secret Service agent was already indicating the way, and another was holding the elevator open at the end of the hall.

Martelli exhaled, turned, and moved quickly. Over his objections, they made him practice this on a monthly basis.

Bridget rested her aching head in her right hand. Her left hand was still holding onto Will. She hated surrendering to her situation. Hated the pain. Hated the awful people who would do this. She wiped the continuing trail of blood on her face and fought off another wave of dizziness. The air was already getting stuffy.

The red-haired woman slid down the wall, knees to her chest. She started keening, rocking forward and back. “I need to get out of here. I need to get out of here.”

Bridget struggled to her feet, with one hand on Will’s wheelchair for support. She leaned toward the woman and took her hand. “It’ll be all, right ma’am. We all want to get out. And we will. It’ll just be a little longer.”

“I can’t breathe.”

“I know it’s tough. Just go slow. In . . . out. Nice and easy.”

The woman complied.

“Good. Now, close your eyes, take yourself somewhere else. It won’t be long now.”

Bridget turned toward the front of the elevator, her eyes passing over Gabby. How could this happen? It was her job to prevent such attacks. Well, it had been her job until two days ago. Now it was her job to respond.

When Martelli and Capman came out of the elevator thirty feet under the White House, the small military staff on duty in the secure command center had the TVs on and the video link open to the team upstairs.

“What the hell’s going on?” the president said to the empty room.

“Attacks in at least three cities around the world,” came the voice of National Security Council duty officer Jay Pruitt from the Situation Room. He turned toward the camera to face the president, adjusting his dark-framed glasses and bow tie. “They hit Bethesda Naval Hospital big-time, sir. Over half a dozen bombs. Unknown number of casualties." He took a piece of paper from someone off camera and glanced at it. "Reports of multiple bombs and heavy casualties in London and Paris, too. All around the same time. Within the last few minutes."

The president sat heavily in his leather chair at the head of the table. "How the hell . . ." His voice trailed off, and he looked at the ceiling.

He was back on task about two seconds later. Martelli looked into the camera next to the TV screen. "All forces on high alert, maximum security everywhere . . . bases, airports, everywhere. All resources to Bethesda, and whatever help we can provide in London and Paris."

"Yes, sir," came the voice of the president's chief military liaison, a three-star general. Martelli saw him on another screen, hunched over a laptop computer at the far end of the Situation Room.

"And get me the hell out of here," the president added.

"Working on it, sir," the general said. "We need to be sure there are no further threats."

In London, Mahmoud was also staring at a TV screen. It was a mid-afternoon talk show. Rich women discussing rich women's problems. It disgusted him. He turned down the sound.

A minute later, the News Alert banner came onto the screen, and Mahmoud turned the volume back up.

"BBC News. A large explosion has rocked Whitehall in Central London. We have few details, but damage seems to be widespread and the ambulance service is responding to numerous casualty reports. Police are asking people to avoid the area to make way for emergency vehicles. Stay tuned to BBC for further updates."

Mahmoud jumped to his feet and punched the air. "*Allahu akbar! ALLAHU AKBAR!*"

Some thirty-two thousand feet up on an arcing course not far south of Mahmoud's apartment, the C-17 cargo plane fitted for medical evacuation rocked gently in the backwash of its refueling tanker.

The nurse assigned to the only occupied bed watched Faraz roll onto his back, shivering, and she heard him let out a moan. It was cold in the plane's cavernous interior, particularly with so few people on board. Even the highest-level VIPs rarely got one of these giants to themselves.

She administered a booster dose of sedative through the IV and Faraz relaxed. He hadn't opened his eyes. She tightened the blankets around him. If he was still feeling the cold, he was too far gone to know it.

The nurse looked at her watch. They'd been airborne for eight hours. Six more to go.

Mohammed Faisal Ibrahim, known to his allies and enemies as "al-Souri," the Syrian, sat on a well-worn carpet on the ground with his trusted man Nazim under a camouflage shade in the desert northeast of Damascus. A small radio played classical Arab music.

Al-Souri's body ached from injuries the infidel Americans had inflicted on him in Afghanistan a week earlier. Their grenade had sent a window shard into his side,

causing blood loss and internal damage that should have killed him, but for Allah's grace and the unexpected medical skills of his protégé, Hamed.

Oh, Hamed. How could you have been an infidel spy?

In fact, al-Souri should have died twice last week, but Allah had saved him so he could issue the order. It took only a few words to change the course of history—a saying, conveyed from the mountains of Afghanistan to the jihad's communications hub in London, and from there to the fighters around the world.

After that, al-Souri had relinquished command and, against the doctor's orders, traveled three thousand kilometers west by road and small airplane. As he traveled, the brothers and sisters across the world said their final prayers before their martyrdom.

"The Syrian" was home now, ready to begin the greatest work of his life. He would participate in the global jihad, of course, but his priority was to defeat the Shiite dictator Assad and begin the task of spreading sharia across the world.

First, though, he would hear of Allah's victory. The infidels would know Allah's power in the heart of their capital cities.

Al-Souri shifted his position, trying to get comfortable in spite of his wound. It was not prayer time, but he prayed silently. His eyes were half closed, and he rocked gently forward and back.

Nazim reached for the radio.

"Leave it," his boss said in Arabic. "Allah will provide."

"I cannot stand the waiting."

"This waiting will not be the greatest test Allah gives you. Quiet, now."

A voice broke into the music—news of the bombings in the United States, Britain, and France—the three most hated infidel invaders.

"Victory," Nazim whispered.

Al-Souri smiled a rare smile and went back to his prayers.

Chapter Four

They were praying in Bridget's elevator, too. The larger particles from the ceiling had settled to the floor, but the small ones still hung in the air. Everyone looked gray in the low wattage of the emergency light. The odors of sweat and blood were unavoidable. People protected their airways with their hands. The captain at the front was coughing.

"Try to breathe slowly, sir," Bridget urged.

It seemed they'd been in there for hours, but her watch said it had only been twenty minutes. The woman in the back was rocking again, and her lips were moving, apparently in prayer. The young woman who Will had comforted was sitting next to the nurse, who held her hand and whispered in her ear. Dr. Carlton was making his way through the crush of people, checking each person as he went.

Bridget helped Will into a sitting position and stood up the folded wheelchair to make a little more space. He leaned against her legs. She picked a piece of ceiling tile out of his hair and tried to look anywhere but toward Gabby.

Then they heard running outside the elevator.

"Help!" the captain shouted. He coughed again. "We're in here!" Others picked up the chant.

"Fire department," came the voice they'd been praying for. Then two knocks from the outside. "You in there?"

"Yes!"

"We're here!"

"Help us!"

Bridget stood and took charge. "Quiet, everyone." She held onto the captain for support and raised her voice. "We have fourteen people in here, several injured, one . . ." The word caught in her throat. "One fatality."

A man's voice came from outside. "Thank you, ma'am. Please stand clear of the door as best you can."

Bridget shooed people toward the back.

The curved end of a crowbar came through, high up between the doors, and some considerable amount of force was applied to the other end. The doors moved slowly at first. Then the mechanism kicked in and the doors opened as they normally would, with their familiar hiss.

Bridget looked up to see three sets of firefighters' boots. The elevator was between floors, but there was a four-foot overlap they could get through.

The captain went up first to help with the pulling. Next was the young woman, with a boost from the nurse. That made room for the red-haired woman to reach the front, so she was next.

"Stand back, please." One of the firefighters eased himself into the elevator.

"This man next," Dr. Carlton said, pointing at the older man with the injured hip. The firefighter and the doctor lifted him into the arms of the men above.

Bridget and the nurse helped Will hobble to the door. The two women and the firefighter pushed on Will's good leg while the men above pulled his arms. Will let out a yell, but he made it into the hallway above.

Dr. Carlton turned to Bridget. "You're next, ma'am."

She was going to argue, to say others should go first, but she was in position and the firefighter was on one knee, his hands intertwined to provide a step. Bridget put the flat underside of her left shoe onto it, and he lifted her out of the elevator. Her ribs screamed with pain.

"Thanks," she said.

Bridget looked for Will. He was sitting against the wall across from a nurses' station, a few steps from the elevator. She joined him and put her arms around his neck.

"You should have someone look at your head," Will said.

"I'm okay. Look at this mess."

A stream of doctors, nurses, and firefighters moved past them, some carrying wounded. Most of the ceiling tiles were on the floor, along with loads of other debris. One man in a bloody shirt staggered by, then sat heavily on the floor, stared off into space, and cried softly.

Bridget released Will, and they watched in silence as the firemen lifted Gabby out of the elevator and carried her body into one of the patient rooms.

Will squeezed Bridget's hand. She leaned her head on his shoulder for a few seconds, "I should really get out of here." Bridget stood with difficulty, one hand on the wall.

"Where do you think you're going?" Will said, still on the floor. "We're stuck here, and you need to see a doctor."

"I will, but not now. I'm not a priority, and I don't have time to wait."

"Don't have time?"

"I have to get to work."

"Really? In the middle of this?"

"Especially in the middle of this." Bridget looked at her phone. Still no signal. She surveyed the carnage. "We'll never get you to my place. You okay here for a while?"

"Yeah, sure, leg is killing me, but you really—"

Bridget held up her hand to stop him. She reached into her purse. "Here's my apartment key. It's all set for you. If you end up staying here, that's fine, too. Call me later, okay?

Will stared at the key in his hand. "Okay, yeah, whatever. At least let me look at your head."

Bridget knelt down and turned so he could see the wound.

"It's still bleeding, and you seem a little shaky."

Bridget crossed to the nurses' station and found a rolled bandage on the floor. She returned to Will and knelt down again. "Okay, let's see that SEAL first aid training."

Will doubled and tripled the bandage over the gash, then brought it around before tying it tight.

"Ouch."

He admired his handiwork and seemed to approve. "Stand up slowly. How do you feel?"

"Yeah, not bad. I'll make it. I'm sorry to leave you here, but . . . Jeez, now that I think about it, the Pentagon seems awfully far away."

"It is. Maybe wait—"

"No. That just means I have to get going." She looked up and down the hallway. "This is on me."

"On you? C'mon, Bridge."

"On me to fix it, anyway."

"This?" Will swept his hand across the chaos. "I know you're Superwoman, but how you gonna fix this?"

Bridget exhaled. "Yeah. There's no fixing this." She turned to face Will and whispered, "But like you said, we will hit those bastards, and that will be on me. Partly, at least."

She knelt down and kissed him. "I'm sorry, Will. I really have to go."

"Sure, sure. Go ahead. Just take care of yourself, okay?"

"I will. Thanks." She cupped his cheek.

"Go on. I'll be fine."

Bridget gave a half smile. She turned and walked to the stairway beyond the elevators. When the door slammed behind her, she wished she'd turned back for another look.

The stairwell was crowded, and the air was full of particles. The going was slow, with injured people blocking the way. Bridget held the handrail with her left hand in case the dizziness returned. Her right hand was on her chest. She got stabbing pains with every step.

More people flowed onto the stairs at each floor. Bridget passed the fifth floor one agonizingly slow step at a time. It would take her a goddamn hour to reach the ground at this rate.

"Make a hole!" someone shouted behind her, and everyone pressed to the wall as medics passed carrying an unconscious woman in a waiting room chair.

Bridget made a snap decision. She fell in behind them and stuck with them, earning several looks of admiration tinged with resentment. She ignored the pain in her ribs, but the fast descent and constant turning made her dizzy again.

The cool air from the open emergency exit door hit her one flight up, and that helped. At the doorway, the mid-morning light blinded her, and the pain in her head spiked. Bridget shielded her eyes and continued behind the medics toward a parking lot jammed with ambulances and fire trucks.

She stopped against a tree to steady herself and catch her breath. She had no idea where she was in the sprawling Bethesda complex. Sirens wailed from several directions. People shouted orders. Others called for help. Medical teams and volunteers carried injured people to a lawn that doctors were using as a triage area. From there, the victims were being directed to undamaged parts of the hospital or put into ambulances.

Bridget turned and looked back toward the building she had just left. People continued to emerge from the stairwell, some holding onto friends, colleagues, or strangers.

Most of the buildings she could see were damaged. At least two were on fire, and water flew high from firehoses, arcing down into the rubble. The medical center's tower was gone—the upper floors destroyed, whatever was left below obscured by a plume of black smoke.

To her left, more than a dozen bodies were laid side by side and covered with towels and bedsheets in a makeshift morgue. No one had had time to put up a tent or barrier for privacy.

A paramedic came up behind Bridget and touched her arm. "Ma'am, let me help you."

"No. I'm okay. Where are we, exactly? Which way to Wisconsin Avenue?"

"Ma'am, I have to dress that head wound."

"No, it's okay."

"Ma'am, your field dressing is soaked through." The fully geared-up, six-foot-three medic tightened his grip on Bridget's arm. He was not taking no for an answer.

"All right," she allowed. "But quickly."

He took her to the back of his ambulance and went to work. He removed what Will had done. "Sit." He indicated the step below the vehicle's back door.

Bridget complied. The medic used water to clean most of the blood from her hair and dried the area with a sterile towel. He sprayed saline solution and put on a fresh bandage. Bridget's eyes were directly opposite his name tag.

"Thanks . . . Kearsy," she said.

"No prob."

Bridget touched her chest and winced.

"Broken ribs?"

"Seems that way. Nothing to be done, though."

"You'll need an X-ray."

"Sure, in my spare time." Bridget checked her phone again. Nothing. "Do you have any comms?"

"Only for medical emergencies. Regular service is down. This is big."

"No kidding."

As Kearsy was applying the last piece of medical tape, two other members of his team arrived with a man on a gurney.

"Traumatic arm injury and cardiac arrhythmia," one of his colleagues said.

"Load him up," Kearsy ordered. "All the local hospitals are already overfull. We're heading to GW."

"GW?" Bridget asked. "Downtown?"

"That's right. No use waiting in line out here when we can get faster service hauling ass to GW." Kearsy helped lift the gurney into the ambulance, and the other medics hopped in after it.

"I have to go with you."

"Sorry, ma'am."

Bridget pulled her ID out of her purse. "Look, it's a matter of national security that I get to the Pentagon."

Kearsy read the ID. "It's against regulations, ma'am."

"You going to quote regs to me in the middle of this?"

Kearsy looked around, seemed to realize the regs didn't necessarily apply. He looked back at Bridget. "Okay, ma'am. Hop in the front. We'll take you as far as we're going."

Kearsy was already heading toward the driver's seat. Bridget ran the three steps to the passenger side, causing more sharp pains through her ribs. She opened the door and climbed in. Kearsy had the truck moving before she could shut the door.

The siren blared as they made their way through the jumble of emergency vehicles and out onto a road Bridget didn't recognize, with policemen waving them ahead.

They turned south on Wisconsin, and Bridget saw that the road had been cleared of all nonemergency traffic. She reached for her seat belt and caught a glimpse of a stage and bunting that had been set up on the hospital's front lawn for some sort of ceremony. The platform was now a casualty staging area with torn and singed red, white, and blue banners.

Kearsy pushed the accelerator, and Bridget headed to work on city streets at sixty-plus miles an hour.

About halfway to downtown, her phone came to life, pinging out of control with texts, emails, and messages. "Where the HELL are you???" was top of the list, from Jay Pruitt at the White House. "We need you here NOW!!!"

Here? At the White House? Shit.

Bridget hit Reply and thumbed: "I was at Bethesda. Terrible mess. Heading toward you now." She hit Send.

Her other messages were similar to Jay's. It seemed everyone was looking for the head of Task Force Epsilon. She wrote back only to Liz at her office to say where she was going, and to her mother, who knew she had gone to Bethesda that morning and was understandably freaking out.

Bridget looked up from her phone to see the tony apartment buildings of northwest D.C. flying by. As they approached Massachusetts Avenue, she saw dozens of people flocking toward the National Cathedral. It was eerie not to hit traffic as they sped through Georgetown. The few people walking in the empty road scattered as the ambulance approached.

Kearsy slowed to take the left turn onto M Street, then veered right onto Pennsylvania Avenue to cut the angle for GW. He pulled into the ER driveway as another ambulance cleared the way. The staff was on them in a second, helping the crew move their patient and starting treatment before they'd passed through the sliding doors.

Bridget got out, a bit unsteady again. A nurse came over to help, but Bridget waved her off. "I'm fine. There are lots of folks worse off."

The nurse protested, but Bridget shooed her toward another ambulance pulling in behind them.

Through the open vehicle door, Kearsy said, "I've gotta move this thing." He held out a business card. "Call me anytime."

Bridget took the card and got back in. "Take me to the White House," she said. "Please."

"I thought you were heading for the Pentagon."

"Change of plans. It's urgent. Please, Kearsy."

"I have to wait for the crew and get back to Bethesda."

"It's only a few blocks. You'll be back in five minutes."

Kearsy looked toward the building. His team was still inside. He looked back at Bridget. She made sure he saw her put his card into her purse. "Okay, five minutes," he said. Kearsy gunned the engine and swung the truck left at the end of the driveway to get back onto Pennsylvania Avenue.

At 18th Street, they came to a wall of city buses across the road, flanked by police cars with lights flashing. Bridget saw SWAT officers take cover behind the vehicles and point rifles at them.

Kearsy hit the brakes.

An officer ran toward the ambulance with gun drawn and his left hand up. "Stop! You can't come through here! GW is that way." He gestured behind them.

Bridget reached out of the window to show her ID. "DIA. They're expecting me at a meeting in the White House."

"Sorry, ma'am. No one gets through without specific orders." He turned toward Kearsy. "You have to move this thing right now."

"I'm getting out," Bridget said. She showed the officer

both her hands. "I'm unarmed." She opened the door, stepped down, and closed it behind her. "Thanks, Kearsy."

"No prob," he said. "Just don't let them shoot me." He turned the wheel hard left and made a slow U-Turn.

"Ma'am, you can't be here," the officer said.

Bridget moved off the road toward a small park and took out her phone. "I'll get out of your way. I'm calling for authorization."

"All right, ma'am. But walk across the park and go into that restaurant. You can't be out here."

"Understood."

Ten minutes later, Bridget covered the last two blocks to the White House on the back of a police motorcycle. The chilly November air blasted her face and tousled her hair below the borrowed helmet. Holding onto the police officer hurt her ribs, and the helmet hurt her head, but she still felt a rush as she approached the West Wing entrance.

A uniformed Federal Protective Service officer waved them through the gate. Bridget saw that the unarmed marines in dress uniforms had been replaced by an assault team in dark green jumpers and body armor brandishing semiautomatic weapons. She noticed snipers on the roof, too. They were always there. But today, they were making themselves visible.

When the bike stopped at the door, Bridget dismounted and handed over the helmet. She instinctively shook her head to loosen her hair. That was a mistake. The dizziness hit and she staggered, grabbing the policeman with her left hand and her head with her right.

She felt some blood that Kearsy had missed and

thought about what she must look like. Her skirt and jacket were bloodstained and coated with white ceiling tile dust. She had a large bandage on her head, and her face was probably dirty.

"Ma'am, we'll have the doctor take a look at that," said the intern Jay had sent to escort her. The earnest young man was running toward Bridget from a side door, his red tie flying behind him. He grabbed her arm and looked at her with what seemed like exaggerated concern.

Bridget steadied herself and brushed some dust off her suit. "I'm okay," she lied. "Quick ladies' room stop, then to the meeting."

They breezed through the ID check and metal detectors, and she let the young man hold her arm as he led her along the labyrinth of blue-carpeted corridors.

In the bathroom, she wiped the last of the blood from her hair—what she could see, anyway—and splashed water on her face. She couldn't do anything about the stains on her suit. She bent down to wipe off her shoes. She thought about Bethesda—Will, Gabby, all the bodies outside. Her ribs ached.

Bridget stared at her reflection in the mirror. She looked like she had been through . . . well, exactly what she had been through. She shook it off and turned for the door. Bridget would never go to a White House meeting, or any meeting, not looking her best. But today was not a day to worry about such things. She had come this far and was not stopping now.

"Bridget! Oh my God!" Jay greeted her as she came into the Situation Room. "You're injured."

"It's nothing. What's going on?"

"It's not nothing. What happened to you?"

Bridget told him the short version. As she finished, the dizziness hit again. She reached out for support. "Jay, sorry, I need to sit down."

Jay swiveled one of the leather chairs so she could sit. "Can we get the doctor over here?" he called out.

The next several minutes were a blur. Bridget tried to scan the room, see who was there, check the displays on the large screens, but she couldn't focus. A navy corpsman got there first and knelt in front of her. She slumped into his arms and vomited a little.

"We need a gurney," the medic shouted in the general direction of the security staff. He sat his patient up, but Bridget winced from the pain in her ribs. "She should not be here, sir," the corpsman said to Jay.

That seemed to rouse Bridget. She was not going to let them kick her out of the Sit Room. "I'm okay. I need to be in this meeting."

Bridget could tell that her voice sounded odd. The room moved around her. She felt the medic's hands protecting her head as she slid out of the chair onto the plush carpet.

Chapter Five

Faraz stirred. He felt the chill of the air-conditioning on his face, the only part of him not firmly tucked in under the sheet and blanket. He licked his lips, then opened his eyes—and shut them immediately against the light of an overhead fluorescent.

He blinked a few times, and the room came into focus. The walls were beige from the floor to a wide wooden rail in the middle, then white to the acoustic tile ceiling, with air vents and lights in a checkerboard grid. There were two metal visitors' chairs with brown cushions. A cart heavy with medical equipment stood to his left. To the right were a rolling hospital tray, a cabinet built into the wall, and a small fridge humming in the corner. He was facing the door, but rolling his eyes up in their sockets, he could see a window across the top of the wall behind him and a sliver of blue sky.

He twisted his body to get his right hand out from under the covers and wiped his face. Where the hell am I? How did I get here?

Memories flooded back. He couldn't answer those two questions, but he remembered what came before. The air strike. The escape. The carnage at the farmhouse. He covered his eyes with his free hand, as if that would block the images.

He remembered the rescue, too. The relative safety of the village. The late-night visitors. The walk down the mountain to the landing zone. The roar of the Black Hawk. Then . . . nothing.

Curiosity got the better of him. "Hello," he said. His voice was hoarse. No reply.

Faraz coughed and swallowed. "Hello!"

The door opened and a nurse walked in, all in white, from her old-school cap to her below-the-knee dress, tights, and shoes. She was a blue-eyed blonde, five feet two inches tall and about half as wide, with a smile to match. Faraz was out of practice at guessing a woman's age, but she seemed older than he was—thirty-five, maybe.

"Lieutenant Abdallah, glad to see you're awake. How are you feeling?" The nurse checked the readings on the equipment and the flow of the IV.

Faraz had not seen a woman with her face and hair uncovered in nearly a year. He hadn't seen blue eyes or blond hair, either, and had hardly spoken to a woman in all that time. He'd also been sleeping, it seemed, for a long while, so it took him a few seconds to say anything. "Where am I?"

"Sir, you are in the U.S. Navy Lawrence T. Nicholson Medical Center. And you didn't answer my question." Her voice was confident, with a hint of Southern accent and a clipped efficiency that indicated she expected specific answers to specific questions.

"Sorry." Faraz blinked his eyes to clear the cobwebs. "What was the question?"

She spoke slowly, like he was a child, but there was a tease in her eyes. "It was, 'How are you feeling?'"

"Oh." Faraz mentally took stock of himself. "Okay, I guess."

"Let's have a look at your arm." The nurse pulled back the covers on his left side and checked the bandage covering his bullet wound. "Any pain?"

"No, actually. Thanks."

"Good."

The nurse continued through Faraz's catalog of injuries, checking the gunshot wounds to his right shoulder and left side. That last was just a graze. He had been kicked hard in the chest, too, but that was . . . he wasn't sure how many days ago. No matter now.

When she finished, she tucked Faraz back in.

"Um, and where is the Lawrence . . . whatever medical center?"

"U.S. Naval Station Guantanamo Bay."

Bridget was in a smaller but much fancier medical facility: the White House clinic. The floor was a pattern of presidential seals. The walls were packed with high-tech medical gear and glass-fronted cabinets stocked with supplies. The plush chair where she sat was intended for the president of the United States.

The highly skilled surgeon who worked on her head was a one-star admiral. His uniform pants gave way to a white hospital coat with his rank insignia on the sleeve.

The nurse was navy, too, and he passed instruments to the doctor with practiced efficiency.

"How's it look?" Bridget asked.

"It'll be fine," her admiral doctor replied. "But you definitely needed more attention than you got at Bethesda."

"They were pretty busy with more serious injuries."

"I'm sure they were."

Bridget saw the bandage Kearsy had applied, now blood-soaked and lying in a basin.

"That dressing was put on by an ambulance driver," Bridget said.

"Looked like he was driving when he did it."

"Got me here, anyway." Bridget was silent for a few minutes while the doctor continued to close her head wound with stitches, but she was getting anxious. "Sorry, doc, but I need to get into that meeting. How much longer?"

"Well, let's see." The doctor patted the wound with a fresh bandage and showed Bridget that it came away clean. "You're just about done." The doctor took a fresh bandage from the nurse and put it in place. "All set now. But take it easy, and go see your regular doctor ASAP."

"Yes, sir," Bridget said.

"Stand up slowly, please." The doctor offered his hand.

Bridget took it and stood without dizziness. "Thank you, doctor."

"You are most welcome. I believe there's a corporal outside the door to take you to your meeting."

"Guantanamo?" Faraz thought he must have misheard her.

"*Si. Bien venidos en Cuba*," she drawled, extending the last word to make it *Cooooba*. She smiled at him with perfect teeth, looking him straight in the eyes, as no woman in Afghanistan ever would.

"Excuse me?" After speaking Pashto for so many months, Faraz's brain was not ready for Spanish.

"Welcome to Cuba, Lieutenant. And don't worry. You're at the naval base, not in the detainee facility." She giggled at her bad joke. All Faraz could think was that he looked a lot more like those detainees than he did like this nurse.

"What am I doing at Guantanamo Bay?"

"You are getting the best care the United States Navy can offer. Beyond that, Lieutenant, I do not know." She gave him another smile and reset his covers. "You rest, now."

"I don't want to rest. I want some answers. Why am I here? How did I get here? What the hell day is it?"

"I can tell you it's Tuesday. The rest is well above my pay grade. But we've let the powers that be know you're awake, so perhaps someone will come by who can answer your questions, or at least 'not answer' them from a higher level." There was that giggle again.

Faraz started to ask another question, but realized it was useless.

The nurse filled a plastic cup from a pitcher on the rolling tray to Faraz's right. "Here's some water, and we'll get you a meal. You must be starving."

Faraz hadn't thought about it, but now that she mentioned it, he was. "Thanks."

"You're welcome, Lieutenant. We are navy, but don't mind feeding the army now and again." She gave him a wink, which unnerved him a little. She tied a cable with a handle and red button to his bed rail. "My name is Julie. If you need anything, push this button. See you later, Lieutenant."

Faraz watched her skirt, stretched tight across her ample bottom, as she walked to the door. He hadn't seen anything like that in the last year, either.

Faraz stared at the button. It wasn't so different from the detonators they had used in Afghanistan. He took it in his hand, ran his finger along the side of the handle, pretended to push the button, and whispered, "Boom."

Bridget slipped back into the Situation Room through a doorway behind the president's right shoulder and took the first available seat along the wall. She saw the president in profile, and he looked terrible. She had met him a couple of times, and even in a crisis he was usually cool, confident, smiling. Not today. He looked older. His thin face was drawn. His color was poor.

The CIA director, a five-foot-five, bookish admiral, was in the middle of a brief on the Europe attacks. His laser pointer shined a series of red dots onto a screen displaying a map of greater Paris. "We had bombs at these three French military facilities. This one is a training center for new recruits. No firm casualty figures yet, but we expect that to be in the hundreds."

"New recruits on-site?" Martelli asked.

"Yes, sir."

The president shook his head. "Please continue."

The screen changed to an aerial shot of Northolt Royal Air Force Base in West London, a facility used for

VIP flights, including the ill-fated final takeoff of the late U.S. secretary of defense. "Sir, the Northolt control tower has fallen, and at least dozens died in explosions at a barracks and a dining facility."

"I've been there half a dozen times."

"Yes, sir." The screen changed again, this time to a map of Central London. The admiral wielded his pointer to focus on a building just south of Trafalgar Square. "And here, a truck bomb blew the façade off RUSI, the Royal United Services Institute. Numerous casualties in the building and outside. It's a busy area, and it was lunchtime."

Bridget gasped. She knew people who worked there, had been there several times herself. RUSI was the British military think tank where justifications for the wars were crafted. It was on Whitehall, a half-mile-long road that connected Trafalgar Square to the defense ministry, 10 Downing Street, the Houses of Parliament, and Big Ben.

Bridget hadn't known there were other attacks. A wave of dizziness hit, and she felt queasy. She thought she might have to leave the room again.

"Anything further?" Martelli asked.

"No further attacks, sir. Level five security is in place as you ordered at all U.S. and allied military facilities, as well as key civilian sites, especially transport hubs." The admiral sat down.

"Thank you." The president looked around the room, as if to see whether anyone had anything to add. He noticed Bridget. "Ms. Davenport, what happened to you?"

"I was at Bethesda, sir. I'm all right." It seemed she had been telling that lie all day.

"Well, thank God for that. Has the medical staff had a look at you?"

"Yes, sir. Thank you."

"Good. We need you and your team for what's coming. Jay will brief you up." He turned to the room. "Anything else?"

No one responded.

"Very well. This is a dark day, and it's up to us to restore the light. It's a multipronged response—military, intel, and especially finance. If we can stop the money, we'll choke them to death. Now, let's get to work."

He stood, and so did everyone else. Marines opened the double doors behind the president, and he left with his senior staff.

The meeting broke into a dozen conversations. Bridget sat back down. Jay walked directly to her and sat in the next chair. "Feeling better?"

"Yes, thanks. And worse. Somehow, I hadn't known about the other attacks."

"I was about to tell you when you fainted on me." Jay was a thin, balding, fifty-something career diplomat in an impeccable pin-striped charcoal suit who had served decades in hellholes and posh capitals. Now he ran the White House's Central Asia policy. He and Bridget had worked together before. She knew that analysis, strategy, and negotiations were his strong points. Blood and trauma, perhaps not so much.

"Yeah. Sorry about that," she said.

"Here." He handed her a two-page summary of what had happened. "It's the latest as of half an hour ago. This would seem to be the 'strategic blow on all our enemies' your operative warned us about."

Bridget skimmed the top page. "Yes. I guess so. An apt

description of what happened, unfortunately. I wish he'd been able to get more."

"Me, too. But I'm glad he's out alive, at least. Anyway, we'll see how 'strategic' this turns out to be. It's our job to make sure *they* suffer the strategic setback, not us."

"Right." Bridget felt herself slumping in the chair, as if carrying the burden of the attacks on her shoulders. She sat up straight. "I obviously missed most of the meeting. Is there a claim?"

"Not yet, but an attack of this scale could only be Ibn Jihad's organization."

"Automatically triggered by his death?"

"Maybe. Or maybe ordered by our surviving 'friend,' al-Souri."

"Oh, shit."

"We were so close, Bridget. Your man was so close."

"Damn. We'll get him, Jay. I swear we will. What do you need me to do?"

"I was getting to that. The short version is, we hit every terrorist target we can, starting today. Long term, we use covert ops and financial sanctions to shut them down."

"Shut them down? Isn't that what we've been doing since 9-11?"

"Yes. But we're taking it to yet another new level. Well, you are."

"Me?"

"Yes, you and Epsilon. Your success hasn't gone unnoticed. You're the point person for long-term intel and covert response. When the president says 'shut them down,' he means for good."

"All right." Bridget rubbed her wounded head.

"Best take care of that. First draft's due in seventy-two hours."

"Seventy-two hours? Not sure what we can—"

"Bridget, I like you, and I know you're hurting, but this is a 'yes, sir' kind of day."

"Right. Sorry. Yes, sir. You'll have our first draft in seventy-two."

Jay looked embarrassed to have pulled rank on Bridget. But with her head clearing, she understood. Like he said, it was that kind of day.

"Thanks," he said. "You can't beat these guys for symbolism, though."

"What do you mean?"

"The election is one year from today."

"Oh, jeez. I hadn't noticed."

"In this building, it's impossible not to."

"As if there wasn't enough pressure to respond."

"The president has been pretty good at balancing politics and policy. Let's just get results because it's the right thing to do. Take care of yourself, Bridget. See you soon." He touched her shoulder and moved to intercept a general on his way out of the room.

Bridget looked back at the papers. The combined casualty toll already rivaled 9-11, and it would surely go up. Was it really only two days ago that they were toasting her in the secretary of defense's conference room?

Now, she was a statistic among the wounded on the worst day of terrorism in history. Before even reading the terrorists' gloating, Bridget knew they'd see it as their best day.

Worst or best, it was just another day in the endless war. Endless so far, that is. The President of the United States had just made it her job to end it.

Chapter Six

Bridget had classified attack details on her computer and frantic news coverage on three TV sets bolted to the top of the wall above her desk. At least a dozen bombs had gone off in each city. Casualties were still rising. Disruption to transportation and business stretched around the world.

Her small office on the secure DIA hallway in the Pentagon's second basement felt more claustrophobic than usual.

Like an elevator.

The fluorescent light was white. The gray carpet was industrial grade. The discolored acoustic ceiling tiles looked like they might come down at any moment. But her door was open and she had a window into the shared workspace where some of her staff members worked.

Everyone was head down, working to figure out what they'd missed or what was coming next. Bridget thought she should call them in for a pep talk—have them sit around her small table or lean on the credenza or literally poke their heads through the doorway if the room was full. She should tell them it wasn't their fault, that they were only part of a much larger team, that they were the best in the business, and that if there had been any indications, they would have seen them through their vast surveillance network. She should tell them the country was depending on them to get back at it, stop the next attack, and plan the retaliation.

But Bridget didn't have it in her. Not right now, anyway.

She had washed up and changed into her emergency set of clothes, which was always ready in a garment bag hanging on a wall hook. But it didn't make her feel much better. She got up to put on her suit jacket. Her office felt unusually cold—maybe another side effect of what she'd been through. She checked the TVs.

Between horrifying footage from the attack sites, pundits were calling it a "massive intelligence failure." CNN had turned that quote into a banner that ran continuously under their coverage. MSNBC called the attacks the November Nightmare. On Fox, they named it after the president—the Martelli Massacre. The euphoria over the hit on Ibn Jihad—now barely fifty hours earlier—was forgotten. Indeed, some commentators were saying these attacks were retaliation and blaming the president.

Bridget knew such a large-scale event couldn't have been organized so quickly. But that didn't stop the criticism.

Her head and ribs hurt. The attack, the pell-mell ambulance ride, and the White House visit had drained her of adrenaline. She was having trouble keeping her eyes open. And it was barely noon.

Bridget picked up her desk phone and dialed the Bethesda hospital's main number for at least the sixth time. The call still wouldn't go through. She wanted to check on Will. More than that, she wanted him to know she was thinking about him. But it would have to wait.

Her secure phone rang.

"Davenport."

"This is Major Harrington responding to your email, ma'am."

It was not a day for pleasantries, and she knew Gerald Harrington wasn't much of a pleasantry kind of guy. He was an army intel officer known for managing the toughest operations. Bridget had met him only twice, but she remembered him well—short, bald, muscular, all business. She was one of the few who knew his real name. For the agents he ran, he was only "the major."

Bridget rechecked her secure computer messages. "Major, for some reason I can't get an update on the evac of my operative from Afghanistan. How is it that I have clearance for just about everything except that, especially considering that I authorized the evac?"

"Operational security requirements, ma'am. The mission was in progress. I can now tell you that he has arrived safely at his destination."

"Thank God. He was supposed to be in D.C. hours ago. Wait, he wasn't at Bethesda this morning, was he?"

"No, ma'am. He's at Guantanamo Bay."

"What? What the hell is he doing there?"

"Ma'am, Operations determined—"

"You mean *you* determined."

"Yes, ma'am. We determined that he could be a security risk. He's been living as a jihadi for months, doing the terrorists' bidding—"

"For us."

"Yes, ma'am, for us. But that is likely to have messed with his head. He's young, he's a first-timer, and he's been through a lot. Did a helluva job in the end, but it's best for him, and for us, if he has some secure downtime and a full psych eval. Gitmo provides that."

"Secure downtime? You put him in—"

"No, ma'am, of course not. He's in a secure wing of the base hospital. He can't leave. He's in news blackout and he has no comms, but he's an honored guest. He's getting all the care he needs, whatever he wants to eat, and psych evals starting tomorrow."

"Still sounds like you've taken my man prisoner."

"He's our man, actually, and he's not a prisoner. Ma'am, you've dealt with enough returning soldiers and operatives to know this was a good decision."

Bridget couldn't argue. As long as they took care of Faraz, maybe it was for the best. She sat back in her chair and found a position that didn't hurt her ribs.

"All right, Major. I want medical and psych updates daily. And make sure he knows he's a hero, not a prisoner."

"Yes, ma'am. We'll be in touch."

"Good-bye, Major." Bridget hung up before he could reply, irritated and facing a million things to do and now only seventy hours to do them. She had no time, and possibly not the pull, to fight the major on this. And maybe he was right. Faraz would need to decompress. Heck, she could use a few weeks of secure downtime herself. Maybe a psych eval, too.

No time for that, either. She'd have to rely on her usual self-medication. Bridget picked up her mug and headed for the office coffee machine. She had the germ of an idea and some research to do.

* * *

By mid afternoon, Bridget had to admit that she needed to go home. She was tired and feeling a little light-headed. She'd never ended a workday that early, but she thought if she didn't go right then, she might not make it.

She read the draft plan on her screen one more time. She was reasonably pleased with it, but she didn't trust her judgment at that point. Bridget opened a secure email and sent the plan to Liz Michaels, her young expert on all things jihadi.

"Appreciate your eval on this, and back-office capabilities to execute," Bridget wrote. "Heading home. Talk tomorrow." She hit Send and stood up to gather her things.

She was about to leave when the phone rang.

"Davenport."

"Hi, babe."

"Will! How are you? Where are you?"

"I'm okay. Still at Bethesda and stuck here for several more days, at least."

"Oh, jeez. How's the leg?"

"Not good. Wound opened, ligament stretched. Almost detached, apparently."

"That doesn't sound good."

"No. Hurt like hell, too. But they gave me the good stuff."

"I may need to borrow some."

"Ha. How's your head? Did you make it to the White House?"

"Head is okay. I got to the White House in time to get stitched up by an admiral, no less, and have a shitload of work dumped on me. But I'm feeling a little iffy, so heading home."

"Wish I could be there."

They were silent for a few seconds.

"That was rough this morning," Will said.

"Yeah. So sad about Gabby."

"And so many others. She was a sweetheart, though."

More silence.

Bridget felt light-headed again. "Listen, Will, I really have to get home before I pass out."

"Okay. I'll call you tomorrow. Take care of yourself."

"Hey, Will."

"Yeah."

"I wish you could be there, too."

Faraz was sitting up in bed, working on his lunch—baked salmon, boiled potatoes, and overcooked vegetables. A square of lemon cake beckoned him from the corner of the tray.

Major Harrington walked into the room without knocking. "Good afternoon, Lieutenant. How are you?" Although the words were friendly, the tone was matter-of-fact, like he was required to say them before getting to the point.

"I'm well sir, thank you." Faraz knew the major from the training for his first mission. He saw that the man still wasn't wearing a nameplate on his uniform. "Why am I here, sir? And what happened? Was there an air strike?"

"I can tell you your mission was successful. You are to be congratulated. Further details will come later. As for why you're here, a little transition time, R & R, debrief.

Just routine." Harrington seemed to lie easily and smile with difficulty.

Faraz looked at his forced expression. He was catching on to what was happening to him. "Psych eval, behavior modification, loyalty test, maybe?"

"Nothing so dramatic." Another easy lie. "Take time to rest. Eat some good food. It'll help you get back into the swing of things."

Bullshit, Faraz thought. But he wasn't going to say it. He was reacclimated enough for that, at least. But if the major could give him false cheer, he could return false sincerity. "Great. You got shuffleboard here?"

The major laughed like he thought it was a good one. "I'll check for you. Meanwhile, get some rest. And enjoy that dessert. Let us know if there's anything else you need."

Faraz looked around the room. "Actually, sir, a prayer rug would be nice."

It was presumably hard to surprise the major, but that seemed to do the job. He recovered quickly. "No problem, Lieutenant. We'll get right on that." Harrington patted Faraz's good shoulder, gave him his best fake smile, and turned to leave.

"Major?"

Harrington stopped at the door and turned back to face Faraz. "Yes, Lieutenant."

"I want to go home."

"Of course. That's what every soldier wants coming off a deployment. We'll talk about it."

"When?"

"When, what?"

"When can we talk about it? When can I go home?"

"We can talk about it when you've had some time to adjust, to gain some perspective."

"But Major—"

"Lieutenant." Harrington was giving orders now. "You need to work through this process. Then we can talk about the future. I can't say exactly when that will be. It depends in large part on you. But we will talk about it at the proper time." He looked Faraz straight in the eyes to be sure his point hit home.

Serving in both the army and the Taliban had accustomed Faraz to taking orders, so he stifled his urge to argue. "Yes, sir," he said.

Harrington turned and left, and Faraz heard the door's lock click. He pounded the bed with his fist. Damn that major. Damn the army. Damn everything! Faraz had felt like a prisoner when he was with the Taliban. Now he was a prisoner of the U.S. military.

He pushed the tray away, sending the lemon cake careening to the floor.

This was over the line. His whole mission was over the line. That's what had been eating at him all this time. To protect his mission, the army had faked his death and told his parents that their only son died in a training accident.

Damn them. He had rejected the mission. Then they sent some woman named Kylie Walinsky to mindfuck him. She had convinced him the mission was so important that it justified the lie, justified ruining his parents' lives.

Why had he listened to her?

All he had wanted to do was honor his cousin Johnny, who died in the first days of the Afghan war. He hated himself for agreeing to that lie.

Maybe, if he could go home, explain it all to his parents, put their world back together, maybe then he could find some peace. That locked door and that by-the-book major stood in his way.

A sudden fierce anger rose inside him. His face turned red, and his breathing quickened. He crushed the bedsheets in his fists.

Faraz forced his breathing to slow. He was a U.S. Army officer. He had to rein in his emotions, evaluate his situation in a professional manner.

He leaned back onto the pillows, rolled to his good side, and closed his eyes. Breathe. Breathe and sleep. Freedom will come in Allah's good time.

The dream crept up on him. He was running, out of breath, bleeding, lost, surrounded. A desert wind roared in his ears. He called for help but didn't hear himself. He turned and came face-to-face with Karch, his pursuer. The man was double his actual size, but somehow Faraz killed him with one swipe of a sword. Then another Taliban assassin came, and another, and finally al-Souri himself, Faraz's terrorist boss, smiling, holding out his hand to stiff-arm Faraz to a halt, hurting his chest, then raising the hand to his throat and choking, choking. Faraz's arms were somehow pinned to his sides, and al-Souri was choking and Faraz couldn't breathe, and his throat hurt, and his chest hurt like the pain might kill him.

Faraz bolted upright in bed and gasped for breath, sweat pouring down his face, his eyes wide, his hands on his neck to ward off the attacker.

As his mind cleared, he saw only the closed door to his hospital room and heard only the soft beeps of the monitors. He breathed in heaving gulps, then slowly settled.

He felt weak. He struggled to pull off the covers and got out of bed, holding onto the headboard for support.

He stretched the IV tube and sensor cables to their limit, leaning on the bed most of the way to the door.

He had to get out of there, had to get to safety.

Faraz reached the doorknob.

Locked.

He put all his depleted strength into it.

Nothing.

He leaned against the door, defeated, out of breath, then slowly made his way back into the bed, got his legs under the covers, put his head in his hands, and cried.

Chapter Seven

The next morning, Julie brought Faraz's breakfast—coffee, juice, fruit, scrambled eggs, white toast, and, the nurse reassured him brightly, "turkey bacon." Then she smiled a smile that said "Aren't we clever?" and left the room.

No one in the U.S. military had ever worried about serving Faraz pork before. This was odd. His mission, his cover identity, had spilled over into real life. He wasn't sure whether that was good or bad. He also wasn't sure whether he would have eaten real bacon. Before this mission, he wouldn't have given it a second thought.

No matter. He was ravenous again, and he cleaned his plate.

After breakfast, Julie gave him underwear, hospital scrubs, and slippers, then pulled a curtain around his bed. While he was changing, he heard furniture being moved. When he opened the curtain, he saw they had brought a small, square table into the room and set metal chairs on three sides. He also saw stacks of books and magazines on a side table.

The major came in with two men, one in a suit, the other in a hospital coat.

"Good morning, Lieutenant," Harrington said. He had a small, rolled-up piece of carpet in his right hand. "Okay if I put this over here?" He stood the prayer rug in the corner of the room, under the windows.

"Sure. Thanks."

"This is Dr. Ellison. I won't be introducing the other gentleman."

Faraz figured the doctor was a shrink and the other guy was a spook.

"Please, join us," the major said, pulling out a chair for Faraz.

The major and the suit sat across from Faraz. The doctor sat off to the side in the room's one comfortable chair and took out a notebook.

"What? No bright light shining in my eyes?" Faraz asked.

"I told you, it's not like that," Harrington said.

"Yes, you did," Faraz said, with more than a little sarcasm. Then he corrected himself. "Yes, you did, sir."

The major and the suit tag-teamed asking him about life in the Taliban, every detail he could remember about the people he met, the operations he participated in, how and why he fled, how he managed to evade the Taliban dragnet. Sometimes, it seemed like they were genuinely interested in the intel he had gathered about Taliban operations. Other times, it felt like a cross-examination—like they were suspicious, didn't necessarily believe his story, weren't sure they could trust him.

The doctor said nothing but took copious notes.

It didn't take long for Faraz to get angry. Screw these

guys. I just came off one of the most important covert ops ever undertaken by the United States of America, and I did it alone. None of you could have done it. No one else could have done it. If you don't believe me, you can go fuck yourselves.

But he didn't say that. He stared straight ahead and answered their questions.

When they asked about his break with al-Souri for the third time, Faraz lashed out. "Okay, goddamn it, I didn't escape. Al-Souri sent me to spy on you, to plan the next attack, okay? Move me over to the prison or take me outside and shoot me."

"Now, Lieutenant—" the major started.

The doctor cut him off. "I think we've done enough for today, Major. Thank you, Lieutenant. We'll see you tomorrow."

Faraz was surprised that the major deferred to the doctor, who stood and led the others out of the room.

Alone, with the late morning sun streaming through his high window, Faraz felt like he was being punished.

He padded over to the windows and stood on tiptoes to look out. Below was a sidewalk through a narrow passageway of immaculate white stones that ran along the hospital's outer wall. In the distance were palm trees and the blue water of Guantanamo Bay. In between was a double fence, ten feet tall and topped with rolls of razor wire. Video cameras capped the fence posts.

Damn it. Where is that anger coming from? Gotta keep it in check.

* * *

Liz appeared in Bridget's office doorway looking much too energetic for 0730. "This certainly has it all," she said, holding up a printout of Bridget's plan. "It's the long-term companion to the short-term bang-bang they're doing."

Bridget had hired Liz a little over a year earlier after reading her PhD thesis on the emerging new strategies and tactics of terrorist organizations. She brought fresh perspective, good analytical skills, and excellent Arabic. To Bridget, Liz's calf-length, pin-striped pencil skirts, Oxford shirts, flat shoes, and curly brown hair falling well below the shoulders made her look like she belonged back in a sorority house, not at the DIA planning covert ops. But she had already proven both her toughness and her smarts more than once.

"It'll tick pretty much all the president's boxes," Liz said. "If it works."

"You don't seem all that confident." Bridget sounded more like a bureaucrat than she wanted to. "Can your team handle the back-office part?"

"Sure, but who's the agent?"

"Leave that to me."

The next afternoon, well short of the president's deadline, Bridget sat in the middle of one side of the conference table in the secretary of defense's office suite. Liz sat against the wall behind Bridget in case her expertise was needed. They stood when Secretary Marty Jacobs came through the door with Jay Pruitt from the White House.

The right sleeve of Jacobs's gray suit coat was pinned

to his shoulder. Bridget was with him when he lost his arm on a fact-finding mission to Afghanistan a year earlier.

"Good to see you, sir," Bridget said. "How are you?" She'd learned to offer him her left hand.

Jacobs shook it. "I'm well, thanks. But you're the one with fresh injuries. How's the head?"

"Better, sir, thank you."

"Glad to hear it."

Bridget introduced Liz, and they all sat down.

"All right," Jacobs said. "I've seen the summary, but lay it out for me."

"In short, sir, we convince the terrorists to invite one of our agents into their organization. We turn one of their most effective recruiting tools against them—their program to radicalize Muslim youths in the West and lure them to the war zone."

"We'll create a sand cat," Jacobs said.

"Exactly, sir."

That's what the militants called their foreign recruits.

Sand cats—*Qat al-ramal*—thrived in the deserts of the Middle East and Central Asia. They were known for being cute and cuddly when young, ruthless killers when they grew up.

The terrorists aimed to make these soft rich kids into hardened combatants in terror cells across the Middle East. Except the women. The women would be married to fighters and have their children. And a select few might be useful as suicide bombers.

Bridget passed a piece of paper across the table. It was marked "Blowback: CLASSIFIED."

"Our man's name will be Karim Niazi. Liz's team will create an online profile—a bored gamer living in his late parents' basement in Detroit. Initially, he'll be curious about Islam, looking to find out more about his faith, to find meaning in life beyond the video games.

"Karim will link over to some militant sites that promote the radical interpretation of the Koran and rail against the evil deeds of America. He'll make a few comments at the end of articles and become increasingly angry at the deeds of his own government, the lies they've been telling him for his whole life."

"The lies we've been telling him."

Bridget smiled. "Yes, sir—the occupation of the Holy Lands, the war against Islam. We have to make it believable."

"And if he gets recruited, then what?"

"The mission will be to learn the innerworkings of the terrorist network, the locations of its key bases and commanders, its attack plans, capabilities and weaknesses, and its sources of funding and logistical support. Of course, the agent will also be on the lookout for anything on an MTO." MTO was government jargon for Major Terrorist Operation, like the one they had just suffered.

Jay spoke for the first time. "Mr. Secretary, that's the kind of information that could shut down the terrorists for a long time, maybe for good—exactly what the president wants. Current military operations are having an impact, but as you know, they can't go on forever."

"I understand that. But speaking of forever, what's the timeline on this mission?"

Bridget turned to Liz for the answer. "Well, sir, yes, not forever, but our experience indicates we'll need two to three months to establish a believable identity and get the invitation."

"That is forever in this war," Jacobs countered.

"Yes, sir," Bridget said, deflecting the pressure from Liz. "But we also need time to recruit and train the agent. If we start now, and both processes come together, we could have intel flowing by, well, the summer." In that split second, Bridget decided not to say "in time for the election." But her message seemed to get across.

Jacobs sat back in his chair. "All right. I'll take it to the president. I think he'll appreciate the name, anyway."

Bridget smiled. "Yes, sir, I thought he might."

Over the years, many of the United States' most well-intentioned efforts in the war on terrorism had ended poorly. Training Afghan and Iraqi forces led to "insider" murders of U.S. troops. Western programs to expand access to media and Internet provided the militants with new avenues to spread radicalization. Millions spent to promote democracy and "get out the vote" resulted in the election of governments hostile to the United States.

It happened so many times, the intelligence community had a word for it.

Blowback.

This mission was designed for the terrorists to experience some blowback of their own.

Before she went home that night, Bridget received the official authorization.

All she needed now was a sand cat.

Chapter Eight

After five days of debriefings, Faraz was out of patience. Some days, he got angry, and they walked out. Other days, he faked the anger to get rid of them.

He was allowed some time outside in a courtyard. He would lay on the ground and stare up at the Caribbean sky, imagining it was the sky of Afghanistan. Sometimes, Faraz walked the fence line and watched the ships go by.

He asked to see the major.

"Sir, how long is this going to go on? I think I've earned the right to get back to my real life. Frankly, sir, it's boring as hell in here."

"I appreciate that, Lieutenant. But we need to keep you here a while longer. We'll see what we can do to make your time here more enjoyable."

Faraz shook his head and turned away so the major couldn't see him purse his lips. Still, the message was clear.

"Hang in there, Lieutenant. Help is on the way." Harrington left and locked the door behind him.

* * *

Apparently, the major's "help" was a TV, a stack of old DVDs, and a DVD player, which Faraz found installed in his room after that afternoon's courtyard break. He still couldn't get live programs, but at least he could watch something.

So after a surprisingly good dinner of roasted chicken and mashed potatoes, with more lemon cake for dessert, Faraz changed into his pajamas, put on a movie, sat in the comfortable chair, and put his feet up on a tray table to watch a DVD.

But he had trouble enjoying the movie. It was another stupid waste of time, burning more days of his life on a mission that was over, a mission he shouldn't have accepted. He turned the TV off and threw the remote control across the room.

Faraz closed his eyes, and he was back in Afghanistan.

He was walking through a village market with a bomb in a satchel on his shoulder. He saw women and children eating lunch, faces he remembered. He didn't want to do it, but he had to plant that bomb. It was part of his mission—the mission the U.S. Army had sent him on.

A voice in his head screamed DON'T DO IT!

Faraz moved faster. He passed two policemen, who turned and gave him a look. The danger sent a shot of adrenaline through his body. The hairs on his arms stood up. He made a turn to evade the police.

His senses were on high alert. Escape or die. It made him feel alive.

Faraz gripped the arms of the chair as if he were on a roller coaster, which, in a way, he was, and had been for these many months.

A knock on the door made him jump, his eyes wide open, his breaths in quick, shallow gasps.

"Wait," he said. Faraz stood up, wiped his sweating forehead with his sleeve, and straightened his scrubs. "Come in."

The woman who entered was petite, brown-skinned, and not wearing a nurse's uniform. Her sparkly gold minidress showed a generous amount of cleavage and stopped well above her knees. High heels accentuated her shapely legs. Her chestnut hair was streaked with blond, and her long, painted nails matched the dress.

"Hi," she said. "I'm Jazmin."

"What? I . . . I think you have the wrong room," Faraz stammered and averted his eyes.

Jazmin closed the door. "No, this is the right room. They told me maybe you could use some company."

Faraz looked back at her. She gave him a coy smile and a sideways look. She hung her small purse on the doorknob.

Jazmin let him take her in and did a slow twirl. "They told me to call you Joe. So, what do you say, Joe, can I stay a while?" Her eyebrows rose in question. Her tongue traced her lips. She had a voice that was high and sweet, with an accent that by turns said New York and San Juan.

Faraz scratched his head and sat down. It took him several seconds, but finally he figured out that Jazmin—not the DVD player—was what the major meant when he said help was on the way.

Where the hell did the military get a hooker to make a house call at Guantanamo Bay? And how did they get the authorization to do it? Faraz exhaled and shook his head. If they could put an American soldier into the Taliban on the other side of the world . . . yeah, they could get Jazmin to Gitmo.

He gestured to a chair, and she sat, pulling it uncomfortably close to him, until they were knee to knee. Her short dress rode even farther up her thighs. She leaned forward. "They didn't tell me you were so darn cute, Joe." Jazmin put her right hand on Faraz's left knee, then raised her eyes to meet his. She half smiled, her lips parted, her pale pink lipstick shimmering. She winked. The invisible cloud of her perfume engulfed him.

Faraz's body responded, and the process accelerated when she slid her hand a few inches up his thigh, rubbing a small circle with her thumb. Faraz hadn't been with a woman for a very long time.

"The major sent you?" Faraz asked.

"Oh, I don't know the ranks, Joe. I can only tell you they put me in a cold, noisy airplane for several hours and told me to keep you company. And I'm glad they did." She smiled again and moved her hand farther up his thigh.

He reached down and removed it, using his right thumb and forefinger around her wrist, as if she were a hazardous material.

"I don't know about this," he said.

Jazmin sat back and put her hands in her lap. "Okay, Joe, we can take it slow. You got anything to drink in here?"

Faraz was glad for the safe subject. "Water and soda in the fridge."

"That will have to do."

Faraz couldn't take his eyes off Jazmin as she crossed the room, bent over to get the drinks, pushing her rear end in his direction, and came back with two cans of diet soda. "Can you open them? I don't want to break a nail."

Faraz complied and gave the first one to her.

She raised it in his direction. "To you, Joe. And to a fun evening."

Faraz was grateful for the soda. His mouth had gone dry.

"Where you from, Joe?"

Faraz wasn't even sure what answer he should give. "Let's talk about you."

"Well, I'm from the Bronx."

Jazmin wove a probably false story about a failed career at beauty school. She kept finding reasons to touch Faraz's leg or arm, and he kept finding reasons to break the contact. Part of him wanted to throw her onto the bed. But the bigger part of him thought that would be yet another sin, and he should avoid failing this test from Allah.

Test from Allah? What was he thinking? Who was he? Damn.

The next time Jazmin touched his leg, he let her hand stay. She leaned forward to massage higher and higher up his thigh and pushed her cleavage toward him.

He put his hand on her leg but then removed it. If he had ever felt anything quite like that, he couldn't remember.

"It's okay, Joe," she said as she took his hand and put it back on her leg. She pressed on it gently and moved it from side to side, as if teaching him how to caress a woman.

Faraz leaned into the task and let her scent seduce him.

Jazmin stood and bent forward, bracing herself with her left hand on the back of Faraz's chair and letting her breasts press against his chest. She breathed into his ear as her right hand reached his crotch. He let her stroke him through the pajamas. It felt so good.

And also, so wrong.

Faraz closed his eyes to surrender, but all he could see were the virtuous women of Afghanistan, covered in their chadors, working from dawn to midnight cooking, cleaning, farming, minding children—enduring everything their domineering husbands, hard land, and demanding God threw at them.

The words of the Koran came to him: "Do not come to fornicate, for it is shameful and evil. Follow not in the footsteps of Satan."

Jazmin continued stroking and purred softly. "Mmm. That's good, isn't it, Joe?"

"Yes," he said, his voice raspy, his shoulders slumped in surrender. But in his mind, another voice said, "For men . . . and women who guard their chastity . . . Allah has prepared . . . forgiveness and a great reward."

Faraz needed Allah's forgiveness for much that he had done. The images of the market came again. He closed his eyes harder, hoping they would go away, but they only got stronger.

Jazmin reached under his shirt and turned her hand down so her fingers slipped behind his waistband. His breathing quickened.

He wanted her.

He wanted Allah's forgiveness.

He needed the touch, the tenderness, the release.

He needed the validation his faith provided.

Faraz brought his hands up quickly, knocking Jazmin off him. She fell back onto her chair. He jumped to his feet. “No, I will not!” he bellowed. As he heard the words, he realized he had said them in Pashto.

Jazmin recoiled, wide-eyed. Faraz grabbed her shoulders and pulled to her feet. “Out! Get out!” he shouted, in English now. Then more softly, and with a level of disdain that surprised him, “Fucking whore.”

He pushed her hard toward the door. She stumbled in her high heels and fell into his hospital tray, sending it and herself crashing to the floor.

On hands and knees, with Faraz towering over her, Jazmin crawled toward the door. “Help! Hey, get me out of here! This guy is crazy!”

The door opened, and two MPs rushed in, placing themselves between Jazmin and Faraz, while a third helped her stand and leave the room. The two MPs confronting Faraz backed out behind her. The door slammed. Then it opened, and a hand came in to grab Jazmin’s purse. The door closed again, and the bolt slid into place.

Faraz was left alone, panting and sweating. The erection pushing against his pajamas was fast receding.

He threw the chair Jazmin had used at the door. He braced to fight if the MPs responded. But they didn’t.

“Come on!” he screamed. “Fight me, you assholes.”

Faraz knocked more furniture around the room, daring the MPs to come in. He opened the wall cabinet, hoping to find something to throw.

His breath caught. There, on the bottom shelf, were the clothes he wore when he left Afghanistan. The sand-colored baggy trousers and tunic were washed and folded, but still stained with his blood. The sandals were caked with the sand and mud of his parents’ homeland.

Faraz reached into the cabinet, placed his right hand

under the clothes, put his left on top, and removed them with great care. He caressed the low-grade cotton. It brought him to another time, a time of danger and stress, but also a time when he was closer to Allah. His breathing slowed. He felt a surprising calm.

He put the clothes on his bed, stripped off his army pajamas, and put on the traditional Afghan outfit he'd worn for all those months.

He hugged his midsection, pressing the fabric against his skin as if it might somehow enter him.

Faraz pulled his blanket to the floor and folded it to look like a Taliban bed mat. He lay down. Even through the blanket, the floor was cold, like the earth of Afghanistan.

He brought his knees to his chest and rocked back and forth until he fell asleep.

Chapter Nine

Bridget's alarm woke her at 0500. She had an early flight to catch. Her cell phone rang before she could get out of bed.

"You may want to cancel your trip today, Ms. Davenport." It was Harrington, calling to tell her what had happened.

"You did what?" Bridget got out of bed and headed for the bathroom.

"The intent was—"

"You hired a hooker? A hooker! And foisted her on him without warning—a man in a fragile state of mind who has been living as a devout Muslim for months?"

Harrington was silent for a moment, then continued. "The docs are calling it post-traumatic stress, not adding 'disorder' to the diagnosis, at least not yet. But no point in you coming down here."

Bridget put the phone on the vanity and turned on the speaker.

"Unbelievable, Major. What the hell kind of operation are you running down there?"

"Ma'am—"

"I will be on the flight as scheduled. Try not to cause

any more disasters in the meantime." She ended the call and reached for her toothbrush.

Bridget never met Jazmin, but they would have agreed on one thing. The flight from D.C. to Guantanamo on a C-130 cargo plane was brutal. The four propeller engines issued a guttural growl for six interminable hours. The bare, windowless interior packed with supplies was uncomfortable and frigid.

Bridget's doctor had removed the White House bandage from her head and replaced it with a smaller one she could hide under her hair. Her ribs still hurt, but not as badly as they had on that awful day a week earlier.

A crewman gave Bridget earplugs, a snack box, and a small bottle of water. She had a side-facing canvas-and-metal seat near the front, with the wall to lean on. A narrow pathway led through the crates and steel containers to a small garbage can fitted with a toilet seat near the back, more or less hidden from view by a green plastic shower curtain.

Lucky for Bridget, unlike Jazmin, she had known what to expect. She wore long johns, top and bottom, wool socks, heavy khaki pants, and two layers of sweatshirt topped by a leather bomber jacket. Winter gloves were in her backpack. She'd fished her combat boots out of the back of her closet. Most of it would come off as soon as she hit the tropical heat of Gitmo.

"More water, ma'am?" one of the crew members offered.

"No, thanks." Bridget preferred to pass out from dehydration, if it came to that, rather than have to sit on that garbage can.

She tried to focus on the book she'd brought, but her mind kept wandering. Will was arriving at her apartment today, while she was away. Her visits to Bethesda had been brief. He was pretty drugged up most of the time. But she was looking forward to their delayed reunion tonight.

Bridget also thought about Faraz. The full report she received before boarding prescribed a twelve-week program of decompression, healthy food, exercise, and psychiatric therapy, and that was just for starters. Meanwhile, what he knew and how he was feeling made him a security risk, so he would be kept where he was.

Twelve weeks put him well outside the Blowback mission parameters. Liz reported that the sand cat "Karim" was establishing himself on jihadi websites. With luck, they'd need a warm body to play the part soon.

Bridget had to make her own assessment of Faraz's condition. He was her best hope for Blowback—or had been, until last night. If the mission was going to be delayed, or impossible, she would have to explain it to the secretary of defense.

She knew she should maintain professional distance, but Bridget couldn't help feeling a special responsibility for Faraz. She was the one who had sent him to Afghanistan. She was the one, in her Kylie Walinsky cover identity, who convinced him to do it, against his own better judgment. She was the one who let him believe he could go home when it was over.

Bridget owed him a visit to say thank you and well done, and she had news that had to be delivered face-to-face.

This would be a tough meeting, maybe nothing more than a long, wasted day. But she had to try.

* * *

Upon arrival at the base, Bridget was checked in and issued a temporary ID. The terminal had all the charm of a 1950s small-city airport with a dash of military austerity. The yellowed ceiling tiles and ancient check-in desks framed a scene of men and women, mostly in camouflage uniforms, carrying bags and equipment to and from large piles on the floor. Security was tight, as it would be at any base, but it seemed even stricter here, no doubt because of the detention center.

Bridget made her escort wait so she could use a proper ladies' room and shed some of her layers. Then a driver took them the short distance to the ferry. An assortment of cars and military trucks crowded the flat-top boat for the trip across the mouth of Guantanamo Bay to the main part of the base.

She got out of the car and found a spot along the rail to breathe in the salt air. As a first-timer, Bridget was awed by the blue Caribbean, the broad bay, and the mountains to the north. Most of the passengers were military, but half a dozen civilians stood chatting not far from Bridget.

"Who are they?" she asked the escort, a navy ensign, who looked to be about Faraz's age.

"Teachers for the base school, back from leave. They're off a civilian flight that came in same time as you."

"Civilian flight?"

"Yes, ma'am. Couple of times a week from Florida."

"Naval base, terrorist prison, civilian flights. Doesn't seem to compute."

"Gitmo's like that, ma'am."

Bridget felt the ferry slow down as a U.S. Navy destroyer and a Panamanian freighter crossed in front of it. She knew what that was about. The freighter would be heading for the Cuban port city in the upper part of the bay. Under the terms of the U.S. lease, American warships escorted civilian freighters through the naval base's waters into and out of the port. It was one of the strangest maritime arrangements in the world, and it was rejected by Cuba's post-revolution leaders, who were powerless to do anything about it.

As the ferry pulled in, Bridget looked to the east. Somewhere down the coast was the prison that held hundreds of men who were the worst of the worst global terrorists, so the U.S. government said. It was hard to imagine as her escort narrated a brief tour during their drive.

"Navy Exchange is there, ma'am." He pointed to the right, where Bridget saw a supermarket, kiddie arcade, fast food restaurants, and an assortment of stores. "Good place to buy souvenirs."

Bridget saw some bad-taste T-shirts in the window of one shop: "Released from Gitmo." "Attitude Adjustment Instructor." That was a firm no. Well . . . if she had time, maybe she'd stop later to get something appropriately tasteless for her navy boyfriend.

They came to an intersection with a U.S. Post Office, an American brand gas station, and an Irish pub.

"Fun spot, if you're staying overnight," the ensign said. A sign outside read, "Best Burgers in Cuba," and Bridget didn't doubt it.

"Thanks, but I'm planning to catch the C-130 on its return leg this afternoon."

They turned left and passed officers' houses that might

as well have been airlifted from the Northern Virginia suburbs near the Pentagon. It always amazed Bridget how overseas U.S. bases often looked more like American suburbs than military facilities.

Before she could finish the thought, they came into the circular drive in front of the white, two-story hospital with a large red cross painted on its sloping roof.

Major Harrington was waiting for her outside in the shade of an awning. He offered his usual firm handshake. "Good afternoon, Ms. Davenport. Smooth flight?"

"Hello, Major. How's our man?"

"Not well. But better that we talk inside." Harrington led Bridget to the door. She saw the rest of the major's team waiting in the lobby—two navy doctors in uniform trousers and white coats, and a man in a suit whose haircut and demeanor said he was security or army intel.

The blast of over-air-conditioned air was no cooler than their greetings.

They led her to Dr. Ellison's office, with its view of the bay and wall full of diplomas and certificates. He was the hospital's chief psychiatrist, with the rank of navy commander. The doctor sat behind his dark, wood-grain desk and got right to the point. "Lieutenant Abdallah is in a delicate state. We don't recommend that you meet with him at this time. We made that clear in our report."

"I understand, doctor, but this is a high priority. My orders are to see him, make my own assessment, and report back to the secretary of defense." It was a stretch, but not much of one.

Dr. Ellison was thin and balding, with a complexion far too pale for a tropical deployment. He folded his bony fingers in front of him. "Yes. I'm sure your assessment will be valuable. Ours is that meeting with you could further set back his recovery and delay any timeline for his return to duty."

"You made that clear in your report, too. But this is our call."

"You know about the incident," Ellison said.

"Is that what you're calling it? The incident?" The men were silent, avoiding her gaze.

"That was a miscalculation," Harrington said.

"You gentlemen have quite an anodyne vocabulary—'incident,' 'miscalculation.' Monumental screwup is more like it. Is that part of your regular treatment plan, doctor?"

"It was not our call," he said in a tone that was half apology, half accusation.

"Well, it is your hospital. I suggest you take a stronger role in what happens to your patients."

Ellison looked back at her, clearly struggling to slough off the insult. "Still," he said, "the result is what it is. The major's effort to speed the lieutenant's recovery demonstrated that he cannot take on the stress of a mission at this time."

"We'll see. I'll make my report, after which it will be your job to fix this ASAP."

"Of course, we will do our best to help Lieutenant Abdallah recover from what he's been through, but no promises, and no timelines."

Bridget got up to leave, but the men stayed where they were. "Let's go," she said.

"I understand that the lieutenant has met you before in a cover identity," Ellison said.

"Yes, he knows me as Kylie Walinsky."

"And you'll be keeping it that way?"

"Yes."

"Well, this should be interesting."

"What do you mean?"

"He has been asking to see 'Kylie Walinsky.' And he is insisting that we call him 'Hamed.' I gather that was his cover identity in Afghanistan."

"Yes. That wasn't in your report."

"It is a new development. As of this morning, he would only answer to Hamed. And you'll find him in his Afghan clothes."

Out of the corner of her eye, Bridget could see the major smiling as he stood. "So, Ms. Walinsky," he said. "Shall we go see Hamed?"

Bridget ignored him and spoke to the doctor. "Am I supposed to humor him, call him Hamed?"

"No. It's best if we don't feed his neurosis. But he may retreat into it if he's not happy with what you want to talk about, which I think seems likely. I warn you, he can become quite agitated. Rapid changes of mood are typical of his condition."

Bridget sighed.

The doctor continued. "You see now why we oppose this visit. Would you like to reconsider?"

"I came here to see for myself."

"Well, I can't stop you, but I ask you to keep it short and be careful not to do anything that will delay his recovery."

* * *

Upstairs, Bridget went into Faraz's room alone and closed the door behind her.

He stood at the foot of the bed, hands on hips, head cocked to the right. "Hello, Ms. Walinsky. Are you the one who can get me out of here?"

The man Bridget saw seemed a lot older than the one she had met a year earlier at a training site in Mississippi. He had a scraggly mujahideen beard. His olive skin was darker from the sun of Afghanistan's deserts and high mountains. And there was something else. His eyes, maybe. Certainly his attitude. In Mississippi, he had been about as green as they come, almost too green to be approved for the mission. He seemed to have acquired a decade of seasoning since then.

"Not exactly." Bridget hesitated, unsure what to call him. She decided to avoid names or ranks. "But I might be able to help. You're looking good."

"Really? You like my outfit? My beard? Why does everyone here lie to me?"

"I'm not lying. You look healthy, strong. That's all I meant."

"Right." His tone was hostile.

"Let's sit, shall we?"

"Sure."

They sat, and Bridget took a notebook out of her purse. "So, tell me, how are you feeling?"

"Greeeaaat."

To Bridget, the message was "stupid question."

Bridget's Kylie Walinsky identity had known him by his real name, had been sympathetic to him, had become his friend. She would use that. "Listen, Faraz—"

"Call me Hamed," he said. His tone escalated from

hostile to angry. “Do I look like Faraz? Is that who you want me to be?”

Bridget thought maybe she should back off, change the subject, maybe leave the room. But if he was going to be able to get back to work in any reasonable time frame, she would have to push through the anger, and so would he.

“That’s the wrong question,” she said. “The question is, who do *you* want to be?”

“Now you sound like those so-called doctors.” He waved a hand to dismiss her and looked away. “You mindfu—” He stopped himself. “You messed with my mind before. Not again.”

Bridget stuck with the “friend” approach. “Look, I know you’re not happy being held here. I wouldn’t be happy, either. The mission was even more difficult than we anticipated. You’ve been through a lot.”

He looked back in her direction. “Yeah, thanks. You seem to be the only person who gets that.”

“I’m sure that’s not true.”

“I’m sure it is. The interrogation team seems to be intent on painting me as a traitor or a lunatic. And that major is the worst. Everything he says is a lie. He’s a real piece of work. You know what he did last night?”

“Yes. I’m sorry about that.

Faraz pursed his lips and looked away again.

Bridget leaned forward to take him into her confidence. “I understand it’s frustrating to be here. But that attitude is not going to help you get out.”

He had no response.

“Being ‘Hamed’ is not going to help you, either.”

He looked down at his Afghan clothes. Now he appeared more sad than angry. “Then what will?”

"You need to work with the doctors, work through your issues. Find a way forward."

"I want to go home."

"So they told me, and I get that, too. But it can't happen immediately."

"When, then? You told me I could go home when the mission was over."

"I believe I said I would *try* to make that happen. But you can understand there's no way the major will let you go home in this state of mind."

Faraz raised his voice and leaned forward, forcing Bridget back. "What the hell state of mind do they expect me to be in? I'm sure you've read the details of what I went through."

"Yes, I did. You did an amazing job. We asked a lot of you, and you delivered."

"Then give me a medal and send me home. Isn't that what's supposed to happen? That's the only way I can get my head together."

"I'd like to help you. I really would. But I'm afraid it will have to be the other way around. First come to terms with what happened, then maybe go home." This was the opening she had been angling for. It seemed futile now, but she couldn't go back to Washington without raising the subject. "Or maybe prep for another mission."

"Another mission?" Faraz pounded the table and jumped to his feet.

The sudden display startled Bridget.

"Sorry," he said. "Sorry." He looked down at the table and sat. Then he said slowly, "I just want to go home."

Bridget let a few seconds of silence pass. That was a no on her first agenda item. She had one more thing to discuss with him. The doctors would not approve, but it could help convince Faraz to work through his problems. It could also cause the setback the psychiatrist had warned her about.

"I have to tell you something that's going to upset you. But it will help you understand some of the complexity of going home."

Faraz looked up at her.

"I'm very sorry to tell you that your father passed away about a month ago."

He looked at her in disbelief. "My father?"

"Yes. We understand he had a heart attack. They determined that he died almost instantly."

"Oh my God." Faraz put his head in his hands. "My father . . . *Allahum aghfir laha. Allahum taqwituh.*" Faraz mumbled the Muslim blessing for the dead. O Allah, forgive him. O Allah, strengthen him.

Faraz stood and staggered back, away from the table, knocking over his chair. Was it anger in his eyes, or fear? His back hit the wall and knocked over his prayer rug. He unrolled it with a gentle kick, knelt, put his forehead to the carpet in the general direction of Mecca, and moved his lips in silent prayer.

Bridget looked away out of respect.

Then he raised his head. "You did this."

She turned back toward him. "Faraz—"

"Don't call me Faraz! You killed Faraz. You told my parents I died. You said they would get over it. Now you've killed my father, too." Faraz stood, his face turning red.

Bridget stood to face him. "I know this is a shock, but you need to calm down."

Faraz glared at her across the room. "Don't tell me to

calm down! My father is dead. My mother . . . Oh, good God, my mother thinks she has lost both of us in the last year." His voice cracked. "We need to make this right. I need to go home right now."

He moved toward her. She blocked his way.

"Please, sit down. Let's talk it through. Give yourself time to grieve, to understand the situation fully."

"The situation is that my father is dead, my mother needs me, and I'm getting the hell out of here right now."

Faraz pushed Bridget out of his way. Her back slammed into the wall, sending sharp pain through her ribs. She narrowly avoided hitting her injured head.

He found the door locked, as usual. He pounded on it. "Hey! Let me out of here! Hey! Open this door!"

A voice from outside said, "Stand back, please."

Faraz stepped back. "Okay, okay. I'm back."

The door opened, revealing the doctor, the major, and two MPs.

"I need to go home, right now."

"That's not going to happen," the major said. "We've discussed this, Lieutenant. You need some time."

"Time's up, Major. I need to go."

"Sorry, son." The major's false sincerity seemed to trigger something in Faraz. Calling him "son" at that moment was undoubtedly a bad choice of words.

Faraz pushed past the major and tried to make a run for it, but the MPs stopped him. They each got him by an arm and marched him back into the room.

Bridget stood against the wall, out of their way, hardly believing what she was seeing.

Faraz calmed down, and the MPs loosened their grip. Bridget took a step toward him, "Faraz—"

"You did this!" he screamed. He lunged toward her with hands out, as if to grab her by the throat. The MPs held him. Bridget staggered backward, out of danger but breathing hard.

"You ruined my life! You'll never let me out of here."

From outside the room, the doctor shouted down the hallway, "Restraints!"

Faraz's tirade continued while the MPs wrestled him onto the bed. Once he was strapped down and had stopped shouting, Bridget moved to his side. "Faraz, I want you to know you have my deepest condolences."

Faraz stared at the ceiling, fists clenched. He was mouthing a prayer.

Bridget decided to make her final points, whether he was paying attention or not. "You should also know that your mother is doing all right, coping. The shock of you returning could make things worse for her. As I said, there's a lot to think about. We'll talk again when you're feeling better."

Faraz turned toward her and yanked at the restraints, shaking the bed and startling Bridget. He seemed to take some satisfaction in scaring her. "Just get the hell out of here," he said through his teeth. Then he turned toward the ceiling again and would say nothing more.

Bridget left the room and walked straight into Major Harrington and Dr. Ellison. She held up a hand to shut down the "I told you so" speech, even though she deserved it.

"My report will be in agreement with yours," she said. She walked past them, down the stairs, and out of the hospital into the searing afternoon sun.

Harrington followed her out. "Ms. Davenport, I have

some other candidates for your mission. I'll be in D.C. later this week, if you want to discuss."

Bridget couldn't look him in the eye. "Call my office to set it up," she said.

Back on the ferry, Bridget stared at the scenery but didn't see it. All she could see was Faraz in restraints, seething. He was truly alone now. He'd have to work out his problems with the shrinks and the major. Meanwhile, she needed to focus on her own problems. Chief among them was that she'd have to find someone else to shut the terrorists down.

Bridget slipped into bed next to Will at nearly one a.m., dislodging Sarge, her cat. She was exhausted from the trip but had grabbed a quick shower and put on her usual oversized T-shirt. When she touched Will, he jumped.

"Hey," she whispered. "It's just me."

"Mmmm."

She pressed her body against his, put her right arm around him, and kissed his shoulder blade.

Will started to turn toward her but winced with pain.

"Easy, sailor." Bridget could feel the large bandage on his thigh.

He completed the maneuver, and they kissed. It was a deep, longing kiss with a full-body embrace.

When the kiss ended, Bridget asked, "What do the docs say?"

Will sighed and pursed his lips. "Extra weeks of rehab. Can't say how many. No promises long term."

"I'm sorry, Will."

"Yeah, thanks. But, um . . ." Will smiled that one-dimple smile that she loved. “I’m cleared for all other activities.”

They kissed again. Will tried to roll on top of her, but the pain stopped him. “Damn.”

“Let me.” Bridget pushed him onto his back, sat up, and took off her T-shirt.

Chapter Ten

There was no more pretense of Faraz being an honored, hopefully short-term patient. He was a prisoner, and he'd be there for a while.

MPs came into the room whenever the nurses or doctors did. He was watched closely during his outside recreation. He was convinced they were putting some sort of drugs in his food.

At least in Afghanistan he'd had options. He could talk to people, make plans, come up with strategies. Most of the time, he could have escaped, if he'd had to, although he probably wouldn't have gotten far. Here, they had him covered from all angles.

The evenings were the worst. He'd been through the DVD collection. He was left to turn his situation over and over in his mind. He thought about his mother a lot. He needed to be with her, but he seemed unable to take the pathway home that the shrinks dangled in front of him, if that was even real.

Faraz had faced the same despair in Afghanistan, and yet he'd found a way out. It involved an AK-47 and the deaths of dozens of people.

Here, he could see no way out.

"How was your dinner, Lieutenant?" Nurse Julie summoned the same level of cheer near the end of her shift as she did at the beginning. The MPs guarding the open doorway were decidedly not as cheery.

"Fine." Faraz held out his tray, piled with empty plates. With little else to do, he had been eating everything they put in front of him. He was regaining some of the weight he'd lost in Afghanistan and losing some of the muscle he had built.

He sometimes bantered with Julie. But tonight, he had no stomach for it.

Julie seemed to notice. "All righty, then. You have a good evening, and I will see you tomorrow." She took the tray and left him alone.

Sitting in bed with the head raised, Faraz felt under the covers with his right hand and found what he had put there during dinner. It wasn't exactly what he needed, but it would have to do.

The dinner knife was dull, with only a short serrated section near the tip. He pressed his thumb against the small points on the knife and rubbed back and forth. Nothing. He pressed harder. Then harder still. Finally, he drew blood. He pulled his hand out and tasted the drop on his thumb.

This could work.

Another drop of blood seeped out of the small cut and ran down his thumb. In his mind, the red streak spelled out the word Exit.

Faraz took a tissue from his bedside table, wrapped it around his thumb, and leaned back on his pillow to think.

It didn't take long to make the decision. There truly was no escape, except maybe this one.

He felt a pang of guilt. He would be abandoning his mother. But they were never going to let him see her again anyway. And she already thought he was dead.

Faraz sighed. No one would mourn him. There was no one to say the blessings, to cry at his graveside. That had already been done.

Maybe Kylie Walinsky would mourn him. But he didn't care about her. He'd be pleased to make her feel even a fraction of the pain and guilt he felt.

Faraz got out of bed, picked up the prayer rug, went into the bathroom, and locked the door. He put the rug on the floor and the knife on the vanity. He washed his hands at the sink, stood facing east, and prayed. He knelt on the rug and leaned forward, putting his forehead to the floor. "*Allahu akbar*," he repeated. God is great.

After his prayers, Faraz rolled up the rug, undressed, folded his Afghan clothes, and placed them neatly on a shelf under the sink. He caressed the top layer, as he once caressed the army beret his late cousin Johnny had given him all those years ago, the one with the insignia of the unit they both joined, the Screaming Eagles. Johnny had been Faraz's closest friend, his mentor. Against all reason, Faraz convinced himself Johnny would approve of what he was about to do.

Faraz turned on the shower and made the water as hot as he could bear. He took the knife, stepped in, and sat on the tub floor.

He stared up at the shower light as steam rose around him. The hot water stung the cut on his thumb. It was pain he deserved. And he deserved more.

He raised the knife.

But this was a sin. Suicide is forbidden. Ah, but in jihad, it is allowed. This would be his personal jihad, his personal strike against Walinsky and the major and the shrinks. Damn them to hell.

Faraz put the knife against his left wrist. He said the *Shahada*: "There is no God but God. Mohammed is the messenger of God."

He took a breath, closed his eyes, pressed as hard as he could on the knife, and ran the sharp edge into his skin.

Even though he was expecting it, the pain startled him. Faraz opened his eyes. He was bleeding, but not the gush he expected. He settled himself and slashed again. He cringed but recovered. He raised his right hand a few inches above his wrist and slashed down as hard as he could several times.

Now the gush came. Faraz was becoming accustomed to the pain. The hot water kept the blood flowing. He felt light-headed.

It wasn't his wrist anymore. It was Walinsky's.

Faraz slashed again. And again.

He closed his eyes and leaned against the wall. He thought of his mother, felt the warmth of her embrace. He opened his eyes to look at her. But she was gone. His whole life was gone.

Julie looked at the clock above the nurses' station in the secure wing. She had fifteen minutes left in her shift. Normally, she would leave it to her relief to check on Faraz before his bedtime. But something told her to do it herself—something in Faraz's attitude, maybe his lack of banter after dinner.

She went to his door and knocked. The MPs turned, ready to accompany her inside. "Lieutenant Abdallah," she called out in her brightest singsong.

When there was no response, she opened the door a little and called again. Nothing. Julie poked her head inside and saw that Faraz wasn't there. Then she heard the shower. She went to the bathroom door and raised her voice to be heard. "Hi, Lieutenant. It's Julie. Just checking on you. I'll be back when you're finished."

She found it odd that Faraz didn't reply. Maybe he couldn't hear her over the water. Maybe he was in a bad mood. Some steam escaped through the space under the door. Julie shrugged and returned to her desk.

Ten minutes later, she tried again. This time, Faraz's room was filled with steam, and she was surprised to hear the water still flowing. When she knocked on the bathroom door, he still didn't answer. "Lieutenant," she called out.

She pounded her fist on the door. "Lieutenant. Lieutenant!" Her voice was suddenly desperate. She turned to the MPs. "We need to open this door."

The men looked at each other, not sure what she wanted.

"Now!" she screamed. "Break it down!"

The larger MP stepped forward, raised his left foot, and kicked. The door held. He kicked again. No movement. Then both men put their shoulders into it. Julie heard a crack. A couple more hits and the doorframe gave way.

They saw Faraz slumped in the back of the tub, his blood spiraling into the drain.

Chapter Eleven

Bridget opened her apartment door and found Will on the sofa playing a special forces video game, his bad leg resting on two pillows stacked on the coffee table. He didn't look up when she opened the door.

"Hi," Bridget said.

"Yeah. Hi." He twisted the controller, setting off explosions on the TV. The volume was uncomfortably high.

Bridget hung her coat on a hook by the door and kicked off her heels. She went and sat next to him. "Fun?"

"Closest I can get to the action," Will said, still not looking at her. He hit a button to throw a grenade and blow up an enemy position.

Bridget winced, but she took hold of Will's arm and put her head on his shoulder.

He pulled away. "I need both arms for this." He raised the controller and pushed furiously at the buttons. His avatar attacked but got blown away by a hidden bomb. "Shit!"

"Sorry. Was that my fault?"

"Whatever." He tossed the controller. It bounced off

the coffee table onto the floor, sending Sarge the cat diving for cover.

"How was your physical therapy today?"

"Sucked, as usual."

"What do the docs say?"

"They say it's going well. I say, at this rate, I'll be cleared for action just in time to retire."

Bridget feared the same. She couldn't imagine Will in another career, or stuck behind a desk. She had served nine years in the army and knew the allure of action and the camaraderie and satisfaction that life provided.

"We should go somewhere, get away, you know?"

"You wouldn't be able to work fifteen hours a day if we did."

"I'm sorry about that. I had hoped this would be different. But you know what's going on."

"Actually, I don't. How's it different from what's been going on since 9-11?"

"My new job, for one thing. We're under a lot of pressure."

Will scoffed. "Pressure is busting down a door and not knowing what's on the other side. A deadline for a memo is not pressure."

"Is that what you think I do? Write memos? We work in the real world, just a little differently than you did."

"Than I *did*. Thanks."

"Than you did and will do again. Okay?"

"Are you humoring me now? Great seeing you for our daily five minutes."

Will used both hands to ease his leg off the table, then pushed himself up, leaning on the sofa arm and the cane they'd given him.

"You know," Bridget said to his back, "another thing that's different is that instead of being halfway around the world for months on end doing your job, you're here throwing guilt at me for doing my job."

Will hobbled to the bedroom and slammed the door.

Bridget's first thought was to go after him. He was prickly these days, but that was clearly the wrong thing to say. She should go after him, hold him.

Maybe later, when he cooled down.

Bridget went to the kitchen to zap a frozen dinner. By the time she got into the bedroom twenty minutes later, Will was asleep, his cane leaning against the night table.

Bridget was up, showered, dressed, and making coffee by the time Will came to the kitchen doorway, looking sheepish.

"Sorry about last night," he said, leaning on the cane. "I blame the bourbon." He pointed at an empty bottle, now in the recycling bin.

"I'm not sure that goes with your meds. But hey, I'm sorry, too. I know this is tough for you." She walked over and kissed him. He put his free arm around her, and she hugged him as hard as she dared.

The coffee maker beeped. "Saved by the bell," Will said.

Bridget looked up at him. "Maybe I don't want to be saved."

"That's nice, but you're all perfect for work, and I have a session with the shrink this morning. Post-combat-injury stuff. Should be fun."

"Oh, sorry to hear that. I had some post-tour sessions. No fun at all, but useful, actually." Bridget went to pour the coffee.

"You figure I could use some head shrinking?"

"C'mon, let's not start. I'm just saying."

"Yeah, okay." Will took his coffee and kissed her. "Sorry, babe. Maybe I need the shrink as much as the PT. You know the SEAL motto—'The only easy day was yesterday.' "

"That's really dark, when you think about it."

"I'll ask the shrink."

Bridget gave a half laugh. "Hey, how about if I make sure to be home for dinner tonight? We have steak and fries in the freezer. I seem to remember you do a pretty good job with that."

"You remember right. It's the only meal I can cook besides combat rations."

"Well, I'm done with those. Shall we say steak fries at seven?" Bridget put her travel mug in her purse.

"I'll believe it when I see you come through the door. But yeah, that would be great."

When Bridget walked into her office at 0730, the secure phone was ringing.

"Davenport."

"This is Major Harrington. Lieutenant Abdallah made a suicide attempt last night, but he's alive."

"Oh, sweet Jesus." Bridget dropped her bag and sat down heavily in her desk chair.

"He used a dinner knife. Made a mess of his left wrist,

lost a fair amount of blood. But he'll recover." The major's tone was neutral, his cadence even, as always.

"What do we do now?"

"We? We don't do anything. The docs will continue to work on him, mind and body. He'll be on suicide watch. His days working for us are over for the foreseeable future."

Bridget exhaled. There was no arguing.

"I'll see you this afternoon to present the other candidates. I should be in the building by 1700. That work for you?"

"Sure." Bridget didn't hide her disappointment. Even after her visit to Gitmo, she had been hoping Faraz would pull through and take the mission. Had the doctor been right? Did her visit set back his recovery, drive him to this?

Bridget knew no one factor ever triggered a suicide. But that didn't do much to ease her guilt.

Faraz woke up back in his bed with lots of tubes and sensors in him leading to a collection of monitoring machines. His restraints were on, and the door was open. None of it made sense. He saw the call button tied to the rail near his right hand and pushed it.

Julie appeared in the doorway. "Lieutenant Abdallah, you have no idea how glad I am to see you awake. You gave us quite a scare."

Now Faraz remembered. "Oh, shit," he said.

"Shit, indeed, Lieutenant. We will not have any more of that." Julie checked his vitals on one of the machines.

Faraz looked at his wrist, wrapped in a bandage that

covered most of his hand. His fingertips were yellow from disinfectant. "I guess it didn't work."

"And thank goodness for that. I'm afraid you'll be eating with a spoon for a while. No more knives for you. Nor forks, either. The doctor will be in to see you shortly." Julie leaned in and put a hand on Faraz's shoulder. "Seriously, sir, stick around. We'd hate to lose you." She squeezed his arm, then left him alone.

Promptly at 1700, Harrington sat in Bridget's office, feet on the floor, back straight, looking freshly dressed and shaved after his flight. "Abdallah is awake and has no permanent injuries," he reported. "The doctors predict a long road back. You should have it in writing shortly."

"All right. What do you have for me?"

Harrington presented his candidates, all Arab Americans, using old-school paper files with eight-by-ten glossies of each man and a one-page career summary. "Top man is Staff Sergeant Daoud Osmani, age twenty-six. Palestinian origin, decent Arabic. He's Three -Five-Foxtrot, same as you, so he knows the basics." The military designation for intelligence analyst was 35F.

"No combat experience or training," Bridget said, perusing the info sheet.

"Abdallah didn't have any deployments, either. I say give this guy and the two others a try. Let's put them through the grinder, same as we did for Abdallah, and see who comes out the other end . . . unless you have any better ideas."

"No, unfortunately, I don't. Okay, start with these three, and let's see what happens."

After Harrington left, Bridget could easily have filled several more hours with work, but she was determined not to break her promise to Will. So she pushed back from her desk and left, feeling guilty about going home for a romantic evening while Faraz lay injured in a hospital bed and the file for her highly touted Blowback mission, also in bad shape, sat idle in her safe.

Will served the steak and fries, and Bridget made sure he knew she was impressed. He had opened a bottle of Bordeaux and found a couple of candles to put on the table.

Bridget picked up her glass and took another sip. She looked across at Will, his clean white T-shirt stretched across his chest. He cut himself a generous piece of meat, looked up at her, and smiled before popping it into his mouth. Sarge rubbed along Bridget's ankle and curled up under the table. "This is nice," she said.

"Nice? You're too kind." It sounded like a typical Will wisecrack, but it might have had some of the previous night's tension behind it.

Bridget stood and walked around to his side of the small table. "I mean really nice." She put her hands on his chest from behind. He turned to look at her and reached up, put his hands on her back, and pulled her in for a kiss. Her hands slid down along his chest.

Bridget pulled back and slapped him playfully on his back. "Finish your dinner, sailor. You've got to get your strength up."

"I don't recall any complaints about my strength."

She moved to his side and pointed a finger at him. "Let's keep it that way." She kissed him again, then licked her lips. "Hmm, I do love that wine." Bridget returned to her chair and looked across at Will.

They were both grinning so hard they could barely eat.

Chapter Twelve

Early evening in Washington was the middle of the night at the small base in northeastern Syria that the Americans called Outpost Brennan. U.S. troops weren't supposed to be in Syria. But after the attacks ten days earlier, President Martelli had ordered them in anyway.

Major Ed Reister was finishing a surprise two a.m. walkaround. He was pleased that his Syrian militia trainees were at their posts and keeping their eyes on the dark terrain outside the base, rather than smoking and chatting as they used to. These men had joined up years ago for the seemingly impossible task of fighting both the Syrian government and the militants.

This was Reister's third deployment. He was about to miss yet another holiday season with his wife and son.

Reister finished his circuit at the west observation tower, where he found Staff Sergeant Rodney Jenkins and a Syrian militiaman. The Syrian snapped to attention. He looked to be in his fifties, thin with sunken cheeks and graying hair. He gave the Americans a British-style salute, his palm toward them. Reister figured this guy had seen more than his share of fighting various enemies over the decades. He noticed that the man's hand shook a little.

"You all right, Haitham?" Reister asked.

"Yes, sir."

"Up you go, then."

Haitham saluted again and started climbing the tower steps to take over duty scanning the perimeter through the sights of the large, fifty-caliber machine gun. Jenkins stayed on the ground to talk to his boss.

"You teach him to do that?" Reister asked.

"Oh, sir. You know that's not my style. That's all him."

Jenkins was the best trainer in the American team of twelve. He was also the opposite of Reister in many ways—brown skin, black hair, and an infamous player at any coed base he visited.

"Your men seem to be coming along nicely," Reister said.

"Better be, sir. And if they're not, they'll hear from me."

"And this guy?" Reister asked, pointing up the ladder.

"Haitham? He's okay. Handles the weapon, follows orders, salutes every two seconds. But you know, sir, I hate to turn my back on any of these guys."

"Roger that."

The trainee who was relieved from tower duty came down.

"Good job, Abed," Jenkins said. "Get some sleep, now."

"Yes, Sergeant." The man nodded toward Reister and trotted off toward his tent.

"I'm going to do the same," Reister said. "See you in the morning."

"Good night, sir."

"Night."

* * *

The woods half a mile from Outpost Brennan were lush for this part of Syria, watered by a stream that ran during the rainy season along the edge of the hill behind them.

Standing under the first row of trees, al-Souri took the binoculars from Nazim and surveyed the target from left to right. From here, on the moonless night, the base shined like a beacon, even with its lights dimmed. The men looking back at him from the towers would have no idea he was there.

It was unusual for al-Souri to go on an operation. At age fifty-five and still recovering from his injuries, he had to admit his best fighting days were behind him. In recent years, he'd drawn his gratification from being the puppet master, making plans and sending men, and indeed, women and children, to their deaths in service of his cause. Allah's cause, he'd say.

But he wanted to be there for this one. He wanted to escape the relative safety of his base, to feel the adrenaline of the attack, to show his men that, old and injured though he was, he was still a fighter.

Through the binoculars, al-Souri saw the main gate and the illuminated signs starting a hundred meters out that read, in English and Arabic, "STOP," "LIGHTS OFF," "WAIT FOR SIGNAL TO PROCEED, LETHAL FORCE AUTHORIZED." He also saw the concrete barriers that forced approaching vehicles to slow down and zigzag around them.

The driver and his partner had practiced that maneuver

on the road outside al-Souri's camp to ensure they could do it at the maximum possible speed.

Al-Souri made a sharp exhale through his nose, a scoffing sound, and handed the binoculars back to Nazim. "Is it time?"

Nazim checked his watch. "Yes, Commander. The shift has changed."

"Keep a close watch," al-Souri said. Although he'd been home for several weeks, it still felt strange to be speaking his native Arabic rather than Pashto, as he had for decades in Afghanistan.

He left Nazim and walked past two rocket launchers and his team's SUVs to the large van they had brought with them. The chassis sat low, weighed down by its cargo. Several of the men were finishing the job of covering its windshield, windows, and tires with metal plates. A senior fighter made the final inspection, using a wrench to ensure that the bolts were properly tightened.

Behind the vehicle, al-Souri found two young fighters on prayer rugs on the ground while four others stood guard. He waited for the men to finish.

When they got up, he could see the fear in their eyes. He put his hands on their shoulders in an embrace. "*Allahu akbar*," he whispered.

"*Allahu akbar*," they responded.

"*Wal aa tah-saban* . . ." al-Souri began the Koranic verse, and they joined him. "Do not think of those that have been slain in God's cause as dead. Nay, they are alive." Then he led them in the *Shahada*.

The man who had moved to the top of the United States' Most Wanted list of terrorists kissed each fighter on both cheeks and led them to the van. The driver got behind the wheel and peered through the narrow slit in the plate covering the windshield, finding the right angle for the best view. His partner got into the passenger seat, tasked with helping the driver find his way and taking over if he got injured or if he panicked.

"Seat belts," al-Souri ordered. They were likely in for a rough ride. There was no point having them thrown from their seats or hurt and unable to finish their jobs, if it could be avoided.

"You are ready, my brothers." Al-Souri closed the driver's door.

He looked toward Nazim, who signaled "all clear." The guards stepped back as the driver started the engine, put the van in gear, and moved forward. Al-Souri and the others walked alongside.

At the edge of the woods, the driver stopped, and al-Souri heard him through the metal plates, faintly at first, "*Allahu akbar*." Then he shouted it. *"Allahu akbar!"*

The tires threw up dirt and leaves as he floored the accelerator and the vehicle leaped forward out of the woods.

Sergeant Jenkins was doing his own walkaround to keep the militiamen on their toes. He stopped to speak to each man on watch, using all of his severely limited Arabic.

Jenkins was at the far end of the compound when he heard the rumbling. He turned toward the main gate and took off at a sprint.

"What do you see? What do you see?" Jenkins shouted at the men in the observation towers.

"Nothing, sir," came the response.

"Hit the lights!" Jenkins reached the stairs to the nearest tower and took them three at a time.

The perimeter floodlights came on with the clunk of a large circuit breaker. Only then did they see the van approaching at high speed.

"Fire! Fire!" Jenkins screamed, and they did. But it kept coming. Jenkins could hear their bullets pinging off the steel plates as the van navigated the barriers at impressive speed.

The fifty-cal gunner, Haitham, joined the firing, but Jenkins saw he was way off.

"Hit the target! Hit the target!" Jenkins screamed at him.

The man turned toward Jenkins. He had a strange look on his face—arrogant, satisfied, far from the obsequious manner he'd put on a few minutes earlier. Haitham swung the gun around to spray the compound, hitting two Americans who were running from their posts to help at the wall.

It took Jenkins a split second to realize what was happening. By the time he raised his weapon, the big machine gun was pointing at him. Jenkins only had time to think "fucking asshole" before a burst of large bullets cut him down.

Major Reister had bolted out of bed as soon as Jenkins started yelling. He pulled on his pants and stepped into his boots just in time to hit the floor when the fifty-cal rounds swept through, piercing the walls of the trailer that served as his quarters.

He got up, grabbed his M4, and opened the door.

The van smashed into the gate and exploded. The blast

threw Reister back against the footrail of his bunk at an awkward angle, injuring his right side. The rifle flew out of his hand.

Reister retrieved the weapon and limped back to the doorway. He saw several of the outpost's rudimentary buildings on fire. The charred remains of the van had continued into the camp after the explosion, spreading fire and debris. The site of the main blast was a three-foot-deep crater of vehicle parts, what was left of the gate and guardhouse, and bodies.

He dove to the ground at the sound of the first incoming mortar. The shell hit at the back of the compound and destroyed a storage building. Reister knew the gunners would adjust their aim. "Defensive positions!" he shouted to whoever might still be alive to hear him.

His surviving men and a few militiamen were already running to sections of the wall that were still standing. His two medics, an American and a Syrian trainee, had their bags in hand, and each was crouched down by a wounded, or more likely dead, comrade.

The only good news was that the explosion had knocked Haitham and his weapon to the ground. But he took an M16 from one of the dead Americans and resumed firing.

"Take cover!" Reister yelled. He stood, bent over, and ran to get behind the sandbagged walls of the clinic. Breathing hard, he emerged, spraying gunfire in Haitham's direction.

More mortars landed, crisscrossing the camp in a standard pattern. Haitham was still shooting. Reister saw several Americans fall, along with more of the Syrians. He fired toward the gunman again and forced him to hit the ground. Reister fired one more burst and saw Haitham's prone body jump. Got you, you bastard.

The mortars were still coming, and a terrorist ground assault could be on the way. Their only hope was air support. Reister ran for the comms shack. Power was out, but the backup battery was good. He grabbed the mic and squeezed the transmit button. "Mayday, Mayday. Outpost Brennan truck bomb, incoming fire. Air support Echo Papa. Repeat, air support Outpost Brennan, Echo Papa, Echo Papa."

"EP" were the initials for Emergency Priority, a request that takes precedence over all others. It would indicate to command that his troops were in imminent danger.

Reister released the mic button and listened to the static. Another mortar shook the building.

"Roger, Brennan," came the remarkably calm voice on the radio speaker. "We copy air support Echo Papa. Over." Reister took a moment to catch his breath before rejoining the fight. The voice on the radio returned. "Outpost Brennan, be advised, command reports air support ETA eight minutes."

Reister's shoulders slumped. Headquarters would consider eight minutes an excellent response time. But he knew it was a death sentence.

Al-Souri had watched the attack through the binoculars with Nazim at his side. The men did well, keeping to the road as gunfire bounced off the metal plates. Praise Allah, one of them hit the detonator button as the van broke through the gate.

"*Allahu akbar*," he whispered. Nazim and the other

men mumbled the same in response. Then the teams on the mortars had started their work.

Now, al-Souri called a halt and scanned the target one more time. No one was firing at them anymore. He turned to his men. "One more barrage. Then we go."

"But, Commander," Nazim objected, "the assault team is ready."

"No. We have struck a great blow for jihad. Now we must preserve our resources."

Nazim's men fired their mortars, as ordered. Then they picked up the remaining shells but left the launchers, which were too hot to handle. They were inside the vehicles in seconds. Their drivers carved a path through the woods and turned onto the road, lights off, heading away from the outpost and staying as much as possible in the shadow of the trees.

By the time the helicopter gunships swooped low over the tree line, the terrorists were gone. And Outpost Brennan was, too.

Chapter Thirteen

Bridget woke up the next morning pleasantly sore from the long, passionate night they'd had after dinner. Will was still sleeping, so she threw on a T-shirt and went to make coffee.

She smiled when she saw the dishes still in the sink and remembered why they hadn't been washed. Will's mobility was improving, providing them with more options, and his energy level was better. His physical therapist was definitely getting a Christmas present.

Bridget measured out the grounds and the water, turned on the machine, and hit the TV remote.

It was all the newscasters could talk about. Twelve Americans and twenty-seven friendly Syrian militiamen dead, a remote outpost ambushed and destroyed, senior officers criticized for not providing enough protection or rapid air support, and of course, a failure of intelligence to detect the threat. It was one of the largest U.S death tolls of the war on terrorism.

And, the analysts asked, what were U.S. troops doing in Syria without congressional authorization?

Bridget wasn't sure how the White House would answer that one. Martelli's approach these days was "seek forgiveness, not permission." But there wasn't enough forgiveness in the world for this one.

She leaned back against the fridge and hung her head. This kind of thing always hit her hard. These were her people. Bridget had been out there as an army officer. She was supposed to be helping protect them as an intelligence official.

Bridget saw Will limping toward the kitchen. He was smiling until he saw her. "What's wrong?"

She gestured toward the TV.

"Jesus Christ."

"Yeah," Bridget said. She stepped toward Will, and they embraced. "I gotta go."

"I'm getting that on a T-shirt for you."

She snorted a laugh. "Too many T-shirts. I'd have more use for a new travel mug." She tilted her head toward the coffee maker dripping its magic into the carafe.

"Sure," Will said. "I'll take care of it." He pointed toward the sink. "And that, too."

"Thanks. Sorry." Bridget headed for the bathroom.

In the shower, she was hit by a cold blast of water. She had no time to wait for it to warm up. She'd face more pressure for quick results from what was supposed to be the long game she was playing. The secretary was going to want to know what was happening with Blowback.

The cinder-block building half a world away was nondescript. It sat well off the road in a field of sand and rocks. Three white SUVs were parked outside. Dirt from the woods near Outpost Brennan was still on their tires.

One room in the back had been converted into a television studio. It had gray walls and two large lights shining into a windowless corner, making the room even hotter than it usually was.

There was an old carpet on the floor, and that's where Nazim invited al-Souri to sit. He wore a dark gray long-sleeved kaftan that covered his body completely as he sat cross-legged and faced the camera. In place of the turban he'd worn for decades in Afghanistan, al-Souri had a *takkiye*, the white knitted skullcap favored by imams.

"It is very bright," the commander said, squinting as his eyes adjusted.

"It is for television," Nazim explained. "But we will turn it down a little."

A fighter lowered the lights, then checked the focus on the video camera atop a small tripod. Another man took photos. Nazim handed al-Souri a microphone.

The commander reviewed his notes one last time, then set the paper aside. "I am ready."

"Will you cover your face, Commander?"

"No. Let them see me."

The video al-Souri made was carried far from the makeshift studio, then sent over a secure internet connection to a relay point, from which it was passed on several more times before being posted on a militant website. The light was harsh and the quality was poor, but that enhanced the authenticity.

Bridget's team sent it over, and Liz ran into her office to provide a rough translation as the video played.

"In the name of Allah, the most gracious and merciful, bless the martyrs of the Muslim Caliphate of the Levant. They have achieved our first victory, and we shall continue until all the occupied lands are free under Allah's blessed law. Occupiers! End the illegal war against the faithful. If you do not, we vow in Allah's name that you will not be safe—not in our lands and not in yours."

"Cable news will love it," Bridget said.

"Yeah. Pretty chilling."

"I wish I could say the threat isn't credible, but that looked like al-Souri to me."

"For sure." Liz reached over and replayed the video, then froze the frame. Al-Souri's black eyes were open. He looked directly into the camera. His beard was mostly gray and stretched from high on his cheeks to past his collar. "We haven't seen a good pic of him in years, but, yeah."

"So this confirms he survived the air strike on Ibn Jihad. And that means he probably ordered the November attacks."

"Yes, and yes." Liz sat in the visitor's chair.

"'The Syrian' is back in Syria. Damn. I wish we'd gotten him that night."

"He was lucky, and he wasn't the primary target."

"Seems shortsighted now." Bridget sat back in her chair.

"Yeah. Al-Souri is among the most radical. He holds a lot of sway, kind of a warrior scholar with all the right contacts." Liz gestured toward the freeze-frame. "And charisma to burn . . . if you're into that sort of thing."

"And now, with Ibn Jihad gone and the November attacks to his credit, he's a key player—maybe *the* key player."

"Yes again."

"And the Muslim Caliphate of the Levant?"

"First time anyone has ever heard of it."

Bridget lowered her chin, rolled her eyes to the tops of their sockets, and fixed them on Liz.

She got the message. "Right. On it." Liz spun in the chair and launched herself out of the office.

Bridget stared at al-Souri, staring back at her from the screen.

How did you know our guys were there? Did you have a man inside? Was he one of yours, or did you kidnap his family?

Bridget shook her head. They'd probably never know.

The video was a challenge, a dare from the man himself. I'm here. Come and get me if you can.

Bridget called Liz. "Make sure the recruiter knows our Karim wants to go to Syria."

"Good thought. Al-Souri's move makes Syria the new nexus. Have you seen the email I just sent?"

"No."

"The Caliphate manifesto was attached to the video file."

"Tell me."

"Immediate goal—impose shariah in Syria, Lebanon, Jordan, and Palestine."

"Meaning Israel."

"Right. Then they take over Central Asia and Europe. Standard stuff, but al-Souri could make a better run at it than we've seen before."

Bridget was reasonably sure that wouldn't happen. But until the U.S. stopped him—until *she* stopped him—al-Souri would kill a lot more Americans.

Chapter Fourteen

"Can I ask you a question, sir?" Faraz was nearing the end of yet another session with Dr. Ellison and wanted to turn the tables.

"Sure."

"Where do I go from here?"

"It's up to you, Lieutenant."

"That's your favorite phrase, isn't it?" Faraz thought he'd heard it about a million times since the suicide attempt ten days earlier.

Ellison didn't reply. He never replied to anger, always forced Faraz to calm down. If he didn't, Ellison left the room.

Faraz took a couple of breaths to ease his anger. "Sorry, sir. Okay. Where do I think we go from here? My wrist heals. I behave. You clear me. And I go home. That's where we go from here, if you ask me."

"There's more to heal than your wrist, Lieutenant." The doctor put his pen in his lab coat pocket and closed his notebook.

"Yes, sir. But I need to know there's a way out. That's why I . . . you know." Faraz held out his bandaged wrist.

"As you can imagine, your future is not entirely in my hands. But what we do here, together, is certainly a prerequisite for whatever comes next."

Faraz took another breath and let it out. "I'm just so angry all the time."

"That's part of what we're trying to deal with."

"But I have a right to be angry. They lied to me. They made me lie. I abandoned my parents, and now my father is dead."

"You may well have reasons to be angry. The goal is to move forward in spite of it."

"Walinsky said I need to 'understand the situation fully,' or something like that."

"Yes, not a bad way to put it." The doctor stood. "This was a good session. We'll talk more tomorrow."

After the doctor left, Faraz sat under the unblinking eye of the newly installed suicide-watch camera and considered his options. He had tried the only escape route he could think of, and they clearly were not going to let him do that again. They were not going to let him go home anytime soon, either. And he didn't want to stay in this hospital forever or, worse, get transferred to some sort of locked-down loony bin.

Maybe the only way out of this mess was straight through it.

Damn them. They were forcing him to think exactly the way they wanted him to. If he satisfied the docs that he wasn't crazy and convinced the major he wasn't a security risk, Walinsky would pressure him do another mission.

That was the last thing he wanted to do. Well, second to last. The last thing he wanted to do was to stay here.

* * *

The C-130 supply run from Washington to Guantanamo was starting to feel like a regular commuter flight to Bridget. She was none too happy about it, but she needed to talk to Faraz. The docs said he was improving but hadn't budged from their minimum twelve-week estimate.

"You're not going to upset him again, are you, ma'am?" Dr. Ellison asked in his office on the hospital's main floor.

"I might, frankly. Or I might get him to snap out of it."

"That's not the way it works."

"I know. I'm just saying I need to have this meeting. Maybe it'll help him. If not, we'll be no worse off than we are now."

"You may be no worse off, but he might be."

"It's a chance we have to take. That's why I came with an armload of authorizations."

Bridget handed over a classified file that had letters from the chief of navy medicine and the deputy director of National Intelligence. "Satisfied?"

"I suppose I have to be."

Bridget found Faraz in workout shorts, running shoes, and a gray T-shirt with ARMY across the front in blue. He'd had a haircut.

He stood behind his table, sweat towel in hand. "They told me you were coming."

Bridget couldn't read his tone. "How are you feeling?"

"Better. Officially, better."

"And unofficially?"

Faraz gave a half laugh. "Also better."

"Really? Last time I was here, you almost put me through that wall."

Faraz looked away. "Yes, ma'am. I'm sorry about that, truly I am." He turned back to face her. "I didn't know what I was doing at that time. Now, I've got my head screwed on straight. Well, straighter, anyway."

"Glad to hear it, Faraz. Can I call you Faraz?"

"Yes, ma'am. Sorry about that, too."

"Let's sit." They sat across the table from each other. "So, what's your plan?"

"That's what the shrinks keep asking. My plan is to get back in shape, convince them I'm not a security risk, and go home."

"Well, you've at least got the sequencing right."

"Yes, ma'am."

"Good. Keep at it. You will get through this."

"Thank you, ma'am."

"Now, the reason I came down here is that I need to show you a photo. We think we know who it is, but you are the one person who can confirm it." Bridget took a still photo from al-Souri's video out of her bag. "Can you tell me who this is?"

Faraz sat back and seemed to stifle a gasp. "That is Commander al-Souri."

"That's what we thought. Thank you for confirming it." She put the photo away. "Are you all right?"

Faraz's eyes were wide. He looked upset. "He's alive?"

"Yes. And back in the game in a big way."

"Wow."

"Yes, wow. That's why I came down here last time. I thought you could go after him again. But you're clearly in no condition to do that, even with your improvement. I appreciate the positive ID. We may need you to help with other intel as we go along."

Faraz was looking off to his left, through the high window, toward an undefined point in the sky. "You say he's back in the game. What did he do?"

"Right. You're still in a news blackout. Major attacks right after you came home. Another one a week ago. It seems he fled home, to Syria."

"Damn."

"And he's not done yet, or so he says in the video that pic came from. I'll get you cleared to read the details."

"I will do what I can to help you get that son of a bitch. Sorry."

"Don't worry about it. For now, focus on your recovery."

All the way home, Bridget wondered whether she'd set Faraz's recovery back, or whether she had given him something to live for.

Over the next several days, Faraz opened up to the doctors. He found that talking about things actually helped.

He went through his participation in terrorist attacks, the guilt he felt seeing people killed and maimed, the gunfights he'd been in. The most difficult topic was his parents, but he got through a discussion about them, too.

He got approval to go for a run outside the hospital compound, accompanied by MPs. They ran along a path by the bay and circled back along the main road. The blue of the water and the green of the tropical vegetation worked on Faraz like an elixir. He ran farther than he had planned, and then farther still the next day.

"I have good news for you, Lieutenant." Julie more or less sang the announcement as she came in to pick up his tray. "You are cleared to have Thanksgiving dinner tomorrow in the main dining room with the other patients."

"With actual people?"

"Mostly sailors. But yes." Julie let out a high-pitched giggle.

"That's good, I guess."

"That's great, Lieutenant, considering where we were a couple of weeks ago. Think of it as your homecoming, your mind catching up to your body."

"Thanks, Julie," Faraz called as she swung out of the room.

Julie was impossibly optimistic, but also right. Faraz was feeling somewhat like his old self. Well, more like a new self—one that had put his grief, anger, and guilt in a box and was working hard to keep it there. Some days, it leaked. Someday, it might explode. But for now, he had it under control.

He had to convince himself of that, as much as he had to convince everyone else. It was the only way out of here.

After his jog the next day, Faraz got out of the shower to prepare for Thanksgiving dinner and saw that his clothing shelf was empty. He looked in the cabinet under the sink in search of a fresh set of scrubs. What he found were his Afghan clothes, folded as he had left them before he'd tried to kill himself.

The sight of them stopped him cold. He stared at the outfit for a long time and rubbed the bandage on his left wrist. That tunic and pants could unlock his box of emotions. Faraz took a breath and let it out. He bent down, picked up the clothes, and threw them hard into the trash can.

He wrapped a towel around himself, went to the door of his room, and raised his voice. “Can I get some clean scrubs in here, please?”

Chapter Fifteen

"Lieutenant Abdallah is continuing to make progress, but his emotional state remains fragile. Our team is still assessing whether his presented demeanor is genuine and long-lasting, or a fiction created to gain his freedom."

It was the Monday after the holiday, and Bridget was reading her now-weekly progress report on Faraz. "I guess that's good news," she said.

"Ma'am?" The workman stopped what he was doing.

"Nothing. Sorry." Bridget was appalled that she had said it out loud. "Please, carry on."

"Yes, ma'am."

The man and his colleagues were replacing her wall-sized map of Afghanistan with an equally large map of Syria. They had stacked most of her chairs on the small conference table to make space to maneuver in the cramped office.

Bridget rolled her desk chair into a corner and turned her screen so she could work.

Her next email held a welcome surprise. Her old boss, Major General Jim Hadley, was coming back to DIA as director, cutting short his tour in Afghanistan. It was a big job, and for the first time she'd have a connection to the head of the agency.

She emailed congratulations, and about a minute later, her phone rang.

"Davenport."

"See the new boss, same as the old boss," Hadley said, his voice attenuated by the distance and the secure scrambling.

"I'm not complaining."

"Well, maybe you should be. We didn't always see eye to eye, as you may remember."

"Maybe the appropriate cliché has to do with the devil you know."

"I'll take that. Listen, I've read in on your Blowback Op. How's it looking?"

"We've slowed down the online profile's progress toward recruitment. Our army intel liaison, Major Harrington, says the candidates need work. I'm heading out to California next week to see for myself."

"I'll go with you, or maybe meet you there. It's on my way home—could be, anyway."

"Sure, sir. Let me know your travel plan, and I'll set it up with Harrington."

"Good. See you next week."

Bridget looked at her new map of Syria. Al-Souri was out there, somewhere. With the whole world to worry about now, why was Hadley asking about the operation designed to get him? Old habit, or pressure from above? In the wake of the Brennan attack, likely the latter. Either way, Bridget's threat radar was pinging.

* * *

Exactly a week later, Bridget stood with Hadley and Major Harrington on an observation platform at the desert training ground in California. Bridget had flown out on a commercial flight from Washington and had her overnight bag next to her. Hadley was en route from Kabul to D.C. to take up his new post on a quick stop to pick up fuel and a fresh crew. He still had his camo fatigues and combat boots on, dusted with Afghan sand. His blond hair was trimmed to combat zone length. At six foot three, he towered over Bridget and Harrington.

"Show me," Hadley said.

"Over there, sir, along the tree line." Harrington pointed to the left.

Bridget and Hadley peered through high-powered binoculars in the direction Harrington indicated.

Around them, the landscape of sand and rocks, decorated here and there with dead or dying bushes, was as close as the army could come to simulating northern Syria. The wooden platform, a sort of primitive suburban deck painted in desert camouflage, sat on an outcropping and provided them a long view, with the rising sun behind them.

They saw two men wearing heavy packs struggling to walk along a dry creek bed. One staggered and fell. The other helped him up, and they continued.

"Third man washed out?" Bridget asked.

"Yes, pretty quickly, too," Harrington said. "I'd give these two a C, maybe C-plus, but we can get that up if we have some time."

"How much time?" Hadley asked.

"Hard to say, sir. Four to six weeks, maybe."

Hadley grunted his disapproval and handed Harrington the binoculars. "We don't have that kind of time."

"I'm always the one demanding more speed, sir," Harrington said. "But we also know that sending out operatives who are not fully prepared usually has a negative outcome."

"I know that." A general's irritation was a powerful thing, enough to shut up even Major Harrington. "Well, it is what it is, I guess. Do your best, Major." Hadley saluted and turned to Bridget. "You're flying back with me, right?"

"Yes, sir."

"Let's go."

"These yokels are not cutting it," Hadley said in the car on the way to his executive jet at the airfield. Three stars and an agency directorship gave him access to a pool of aircraft to take him anywhere he needed to go at any time. "And I don't believe for a second that one of them will be ready in six weeks."

"If anyone can whip them into shape, it's Harrington."

"I'm not so sure. A can-do guy like him never says 'maybe' unless he means 'fubar.' " Fouled up beyond all repair.

Bridget hesitated, then said, "I've got another maybe for you."

"What's that?"

"Faraz Abdallah."

"Tell me."

"I don't know if he can beat six weeks, but he's made great strides. Of course, the docs are still skeptical. They say he needs more time. And Faraz only wants to go home."

"Every soldier wants to go home. Every trainer and every shrink wants more time."

The car stopped at the foot of the plane's stairs. Hadley got out, saluted the airfield commander, and started the obligatory courtesy chat.

Bridget headed straight for the plane, second-guessing herself. Maybe she shouldn't have mentioned Faraz. She had hoped that showing him al-Souri's picture and letting him read about the attacks would provide him new motivation. But she also remembered what happened the last time she pushed him too hard.

Bridget had a first-class seat in the silver-and-blue cabin of the C-40B, a military version of the Boeing 737 with posh décor and extra fuel tanks for long-distance travel by top government officials and their staffs. The pilot announced they would cover the twenty-four hundred miles to Washington in exactly four hours, with full internet and live TV service throughout. Pretty good snacks, too, Bridget decided as the flight attendant delivered a fancy soda water and bowl of trail mix, accompanied by a cocktail napkin with the air force insignia.

A few minutes later, she returned. "Ma'am, the general needs to see you."

Bridget walked back to Hadley's cabin and knocked on the open door. The cabin spanned the width of the plane, narrowing toward the tail. One side had a banquette that turned into a bed. On the other side was a desk with a leather chair and a TV high up on the wall. Hadley's camo jacket, with his new three-star insignia, hung on a hook on the door.

"Come in. Have a seat." The general was reading something on his computer.

A slim white intercom handset on his wall buzzed. Hadley picked it up. "Yeah . . . Good . . . Do we need a fuel stop? . . . Excellent . . . Yes, make the change. Thanks."

Hadley hung up and swiveled his chair to face Bridget. "Listen, the secretary got a serious ass kicking from the president last night. He obviously doesn't want to get hit by another attack. And the political clock's ticking, too. They want results yesterday."

"Political clock," Bridget said with some attitude.

"Look, it's not only that. We have a situation on our hands. Al-Souri has done a lot of damage in the last few weeks, and I'm damn sure more is coming if we don't prevent it."

"What are you saying, General?"

"I'm saying Abdallah is our best option. Unless he's foaming at the mouth and dancing around the room, we need him. He knows how to do this, and he knows al-Souri."

"You want to push him out before he's ready because the election is . . . what? Eleven months away?"

Hadley stared at her.

"Sorry, sir. Let me set up a call with the docs. Their latest still has warning lights flashing."

"And always will. They'd keep him on sick call for a hangnail."

"He doesn't have a hangnail, sir."

"You're the one who raised his name."

"Maybe I shouldn't have. That's a big responsibility you're taking on if you overrule the docs."

"I'm not overruling them, but I am pushing for a balanced approach to get the right man into the right position to prevent the next terrorist attack. It's not a small thing, and it's not politics. And I expect you to be with me."

"Sir, I've been hoping he'd be able to take this mission, but let's see what the docs say."

"I'll do you one better than that. You got anything urgent in D.C. today?"

Bridget smiled. "Only Christmas shopping."

"Well, it'll have to wait. I just confirmed with the flight crew. We're going to Gitmo."

It turned out generals get helicopters, too.

A few hours later, with the December sun hanging low over the Western Caribbean, Bridget and Hadley walked from the plane to a small navy chopper, where the pilot handed them temporary IDs and took off as soon as they had their seat belts fastened.

Five minutes later, they touched down at the hospital helipad and walked into Dr. Ellison's office.

"He's not ready," the doctor declared. The man looked nervous, but although he was four ranks below Hadley, the medical caduceus on his lab coat gave him license to speak his mind. "Lieutenant Abdallah needs several more weeks of therapy and evaluation, at least."

Hadley leaned forward, putting the stars on his uniform a little closer to the doctor. "Commander, your report says he's made—what's the phrase?—'significant progress,' right?"

"Yes, sir, but—"

"You've allowed him some freedom of movement, let him mix with other patients. Looks like the more you loosen the bonds, the better he does."

"Yes, sir, but—"

"No more buts, Commander. We'll go see him. If he's doing as well as you say—as *you say*, doctor—we'll talk to him about the mission."

"Sir, with all due respect, I do not advise it."

"Understood. Let's go."

"Sir," Bridget said. "He knows me in a cover identity. Should we come up with one for you?"

"Nah. At this point, he's either in or he's out. Either way, he might as well know who he's talking to."

Bridget and Hadley waited outside Faraz's room while Nurse Julie knocked on the door. Bridget wondered which Faraz they would meet on the other side of it—the angry one from her first visit, or the contrite, helpful one from her second.

"Come in." His voice sounded friendly enough.

"You have some visitors, Lieutenant." Julie opened the door and stepped aside.

"Ms. Walinsky," Faraz stood up, clearly surprised. He was clean-shaven, wearing fresh green scrubs. He came to attention when he saw Hadley.

"Hello, Faraz. This is General Hadley. We need to talk to you."

"As you were." Hadley offered a hand. "It's good to meet

you, Lieutenant. I want you to know that we recognize you did a helluva job on your last mission. You have my congratulations and my thanks, and now that you're feeling better, we'll arrange a ceremony to get you the medals you've earned."

"Thank you, sir." Faraz stood at ease, feet apart, hands grasped behind.

"Let's sit," Hadley said.

When they were settled, he got right to the point. "Lieutenant, we have a mission for you, if you feel you're up to it."

Faraz looked away and let out a breath. Then he looked back at Hadley. "Al-Souri?"

"Yes."

"I'm in."

Bridget thought he agreed too quickly. She had planned to let Hadley do the talking, but she spoke up. "Really? Until now, all you wanted to talk about was going home."

"I would like to go home, ma'am, but I read what al-Souri did. I kick myself every day for not taking him out when I had the chance. If he's the target, and if the docs will let me out of this place, I'm in."

"You let me deal with the docs," Hadley said. He had a satisfied smile.

"Thank you, sir."

Hadley stood to go, but he stopped. "I want to be honest with you, Lieutenant. The doctors are skeptical. They think it's too soon. But I say let's get you into some mission-specific training and see how it goes. Think you can handle it?"

"Yes, sir."

"All right. Good luck, Lieutenant." Hadley shook his hand again and led Bridget out of the room.

Bridget sat alone on Hadley's plane, pretending to read something on her laptop. She wasn't comfortable with what she'd witnessed. But people with stars on their uniforms operated differently than mere mortals. They were results oriented, and usually had the juice to get the results they wanted.

That disturbed her. Faraz's transition seemed too easy, definitely too fast. Bridget understood what the doctor meant when he had questioned whether Faraz's new attitude was genuine and long-lasting. She wondered whether Faraz even knew.

But maybe the general had a point. If the stress of training didn't crack Faraz's new veneer of confidence, he might actually be able to do the mission. Either way, they needed to know.

Bridget sent Liz a secure email. "We may have our sand cat."

Chapter Sixteen

Ten days later, Bridget was back on the observation deck in the California desert, watching Faraz walk along the creek bed toward the survival exercise finish line.

"He's doing well," Harrington said, "making much faster progress than he did first time around. Definitely better than our other candidates."

"That's good, I guess," Bridget replied. "I worry that he's too gung ho."

"You won't be surprised that I don't believe there's such a thing as too gung ho. He's getting high marks from all concerned, including pretty good marks from the shrinks. Barring setbacks, he'll be ready to fly in a week or so. He made me a believer, and that's not easy."

"I hope you're right. I'd like to meet with him this afternoon."

"No problem. The exercise ends at noon. We'll get him cleaned up and fed, and you can have him by 1400."

Bridget and Faraz sat on opposite sides of a table in a small conference room. She could already see he looked even better than he had at Guantanamo. He seemed stronger and much more relaxed. She could even detect a hint of the fresh-faced California boy she'd first met a little more than a year ago.

"How are you feeling?" Bridget asked.

"Good. A bit worn out from the exercise, but a decent night's sleep and I'll be ready to go."

Bridget smiled. "The timeline isn't quite that tight, but you will be leaving soon. We have a new identity for you to study. That, and the mission details, are here." She handed over a sealed envelope. "This material does not leave this building."

"Yes, ma'am." Faraz held the envelope with both hands. "I guess I'll have a chance to fulfill my promise."

"What promise?"

"That SEAL commander who was injured in the assault on the villa, he wanted me to kill al-Souri that day. I promised to do it another time. I thought the air strike had taken care of him. Now, I'll have a second chance."

Bridget felt a chill. That SEAL commander was Will. She'd watched the incident live in the Ops Center on a grainy infrared video feed from the nose camera of a drone.

She shook it off. "Maybe we'll arrange a reunion with that SEAL for you someday."

"So he's okay?"

"He's great." Bridget caught herself. "Last report I saw, anyway."

"Glad to hear it."

"And Faraz, since we're going to be working together for a while, I think you should know my real name."

"I figured . . ."

Bridget stood and held out her hand. "I'm Bridget Davenport, and you are now officially a member of Task Force Epsilon."

Faraz got up and shook her hand. "Thank you, Ms. Davenport. It's good to meet you."

Back in his room, Faraz sat at the simple metal desk. He broke the seal on the envelope and pulled out the papers.

He would be Karim Niazi. Karim and Faraz were the same age, twenty-five, and both were the American-born only children of refugee parents who fled Afghanistan after the Soviet invasion in 1979. But that's where the similarity ended. Karim's parents settled in Michigan, and they had died in a car accident several years earlier.

Faraz paused on that one, looked away, then forged ahead.

Karim had not been to college. The money from his parents' life insurance and the accident settlement was running low. He spent most of his time in their small house in Detroit playing video games and exploring online chat rooms.

He had attempted suicide last year. Faraz paused again and rubbed his wrist. Well, they had to explain the scars. Karim had taken to going to the gym as part of his rehab. That would explain why he was in better shape than a video game basement rat would be.

Faraz leaned his chair back and put his feet on the desk as he got to know his new identity.

Karim had only a basic knowledge of Islam and very little Arabic, mostly slang expressions and swear words, and a few Koran quotes. Now that suicide hadn't worked, he had no plan for how he would support himself when his parents' money ran out. His online explorations over the last few months had led him to believe that his life was a lie—that his true destiny lay elsewhere. In service to Allah.

When the invitation came to go to Europe, "Karim" had hesitated, allowing time for Faraz to prepare for the mission. Once he was ready, they would send Karim's final request to the recruiter, to join the jihad in Syria. Nowhere else.

Once the recruiter agreed, all Karim would have to do was go to Detroit Metro Airport, pick up a prepaid ticket, and board a flight to London. From there, he would be taken into the militant world, probably flown to Turkey and smuggled into Syria, where he would join other Muslim young people from around the world.

Of course, the jihadis could screw them, send Karim somewhere else. But that was a chance they'd have to take.

The last page of the mission brief had two of what the military called "caveats."

> Operative is to avoid contact with AS.
> Operative is to break and report immediately any intel on an MTO.

Avoiding contact with al-Souri made sense. The man would likely shoot him on sight. Immediate reporting on any Major Terrorist Operation made sense, too. But it was a mystery—what the planners called "operational discretion"—how he was to find out about an MTO, learn where al-Souri was and how he got his money, and get all the other high-level intel they wanted while avoiding the commander and his headquarters.

The briefing papers said, "Caliphate secrets believed to be distributed and compartmentalized," meaning they thought he could get enough from the network's periphery to get the job done.

Faraz wasn't sure they were right about that, but there was no turning back now. He had nowhere to turn back to.

The packet contained a username and password for Faraz to use on the base's secure network. He had thousands of words of chats to read, loads of details about Karim and his life to memorize, and several months of relevant news to absorb. He also had to learn all the Arabic phrases Karim had used in the chats, and a few more for good measure. And he would have to brush up his video game skills. The secure network had been set up for that, too.

Faraz pulled his feet off the desk and headed for the computer room.

The next day, back at the Pentagon, Bridget was still thinking about whether Faraz was truly ready when she received a summons to Hadley's office. It was upstairs, not far from the secretary's suite. Hadley had a large wooden desk, plush chair, carpet with the DIA seal, flags on poles in every corner, and a conference table that could easily seat a dozen. And it had windows. Ah, windows. Even a view of the Washington Monument.

Bridget knew that two weeks earlier, his office had been half of a converted shipping container surrounded by sandbags.

Hadley invited her to sit in a wood and leather chair in front of his desk. He pointed at his computer screen. "Your report on Abdallah looks good."

"I'm still concerned, but I guess that's my job."

"Your job is to get stuff done. Speaking of which, this mission has a lot of high-level attention. We need to keep closer tabs on him than last time."

"I can't see how."

"Well, I can see two ways. One is to have some of our other assets in Syria check on him as needed. We have a few locals, anyway, who feed us info."

"Yes, sir. Risky, but possible, assuming we know where he is."

"This could be how we find out where he is."

"Maybe. What's the other way you want to keep track of Faraz?"

Hadley took a breath and leaned forward. "The other way is to have you in Baghdad to exert real-time control over this operation—keep as close a watch on him as you can, move agents, drones, Special Ops, whatever it takes to push this mission to a successful conclusion in the shortest possible timeline."

"You want me to move to Baghdad?"

"Travel orders are here." Hadley picked up a folder from his desk and handed it over.

"Oh, General." Bridget read the orders. "I can do all this from here."

"No. You can't. We both know there's a big difference between being seven hours behind and six thousand miles away, sending your orders by email, versus being onsite, walking into someone's office, and making something happen."

Having had two combat zone tours as an intel officer, Bridget couldn't argue with that. She sat back in her chair, then looked away from Hadley and scanned the military service emblems hanging in a row on the wall.

"I need you to do this, Bridget."

"You know I got out of the army to avoid deployments," she said, still not looking at him.

"This isn't a deployment." Hadley reached over to point at the top line of the piece of paper Bridget was holding. "It's a 'temporary change of duty station.' The sooner this job gets done, the sooner you come back."

Bridget was silent, now staring at the orders, trying to think of something to say, knowing Hadley was right.

"Or I can find someone else," he said.

Bridget looked up. "To run my mission?"

Hadley stared her down.

"It's like that?" she asked.

"Yes, it is. You and Task Force Epsilon are the new hot thing, but you're not going to stay that way without results. We all understand these are long-term missions, but we need this intel in weeks, maybe a couple of months, not years or whenever it's convenient for you and Lieutenant Abdallah."

"Seems to me expectations are too high for both results and speed, sir. We don't want to set Faraz up to fail."

"That's why you're going over there—to make sure he succeeds."

* * *

That evening, Bridget made sure to be home for dinner. She ordered Chinese and got home at the same time the delivery arrived.

She put the food on the kitchen counter while Will finished an on-screen battle. Then she went to sit next to him.

"Let's eat. I'm starving," he said when he got the "Mission Over" message.

"In a minute." She took his hand. "I'm going to Baghdad."

"Your usual overnight trip to wherever the boss wants to go?"

"No. I'm sorry, Will. It's a temporary deployment."

"A what? Oh, shit."

Bridget couldn't tell whether he was sad or angry. "Yeah, exactly."

"How long?"

"Unclear. Several months, probably."

"Jesus." He pulled his hand away. "We can't seem to stay on the same continent for more than a few minutes, can we?"

"No, I guess not. This was supposed to be our time."

"Damn straight." Will leaned back into the cushions and looked at the ceiling. "So now you go off to where the action is while I sit here watching TV and playing video games, with physical therapy sessions the highlight of my week. Oh, and let's not forget emptying the cat litter."

Bridget sighed. "I'm sorry, Will."

"It's not your fault, Bridge. But this sucks!" He slammed his fist onto the arm of the sofa.

"Yes, it does." She took his fist in her hands, opened

it, and kissed his palm. "I'd swap places with you if I could. I know you'd be much happier that way." Bridget leaned in and kissed him. "I'll miss you, Will. But it's not forever. And you'll be back at it soon."

"Yeah, maybe. Probably just about the time you get home."

Bridget smiled. "That would fit our pattern."

"Well, our pattern sucks, too."

She kissed him again and he responded, but something didn't feel right. They made out for a minute or so, then Will broke it off.

"It's okay. It is what it is," he said.

"Yeah, sorry."

"C'mon," Will said, reaching for his cane. "Let's eat."

That night, Will lay with his back to Bridget. She snuggled up to him and reached her hand around to rub his chest.

He removed it. The move was gentle, but the meaning was clear.

Bridget felt like she was abandoning Will during the most vulnerable period he'd ever been through.

So now, aside from staying alive and keeping Faraz alive—and stopping the next major attack on America—Bridget had to worry that she was blowing the best relationship she'd had in more than a decade.

Part Two

Chapter Seventeen

Faraz got off the red double-decker bus at Marble Arch in a steady drizzle midmorning on the Monday after Christmas. If he'd walked east, along Oxford Street, he would have passed under the holiday decorations of the fancy department and specialty stores, and he could have browsed the tacky tourist stands. But he went north on Edgware Road, and into one of the city's most dense strips of Middle Eastern shops and restaurants.

He'd been in London a minute ago. Now, the city looked and felt more like Syria, or so he imagined. All of the shop signs were in Arabic. The aromas of Middle Eastern spices wafted out of grocery stores and competed with the smell of grilled shawarma on display in the restaurant windows. The newsstands offered a variety of Arabic papers, alongside *The Times* and *Evening Standard*. The vendors shouted in a blend of Arabic and some sort of twangy, colloquial English.

The road was crowded with buses, black cabs, and delivery trucks, and the sidewalks were equally busy with shoppers and a few wayward visitors.

Faraz was wearing jeans, a black T-shirt, and a black

zip-up jacket. He had on beat-up running shoes and a Detroit Tigers cap, and he carried a backpack over one shoulder with some clothes and toiletries. He had regrown his Taliban beard.

As he waited to cross a street, he exchanged silent greetings with some men sitting at tables under a restaurant awning, puffing cherry-flavored smoke from shisha pipes and arguing in Arabic, as far as he could tell, over soccer.

Faraz saw the coffee shop in the middle of the next block. The sign read ABU-TAWFIQ COFFEE PASTRIES BAKLAVA.

The light changed, and he moved ahead with the crowd. At Abu-Tawfiq's, he stopped to look at the cakes on display in the window. Peering past them, he saw a man behind the counter making a Turkish coffee. A couple of men sat at a table talking. In the back, a beaded curtain covered a doorway.

Faraz went in, jangling the bells on the door. The counterman turned, gestured toward a table, and spoke to him in Arabic, "*T'fadal.*" Please, have a seat.

When the man came to take his order, Faraz asked for a coffee and said, "Do you have any baklava with walnuts?" An unusual request—one nobody would make, unless they had been told to do so.

The man raised his eyebrows before saying, "I will check." He went behind the curtain and emerged a few seconds later. "I think we have what you want in the back. Please, follow me." He led Faraz to the curtain, parted it, and let him walk through.

It took Faraz's eyes some time to adjust to the dim light of the back room. When they did, he saw a small table with two chairs, a man who looked to be in his early thirties sitting in one of them. "Please, sit," the man said in English.

He looked Faraz over. "You seek baklava with walnuts?"

"Yes," Faraz responded as instructed by the recruiter's emails, "like my mother used to make."

"What is your name?"

"Karim Niazi."

The man held out his hand. "I am Mahmoud. You are welcome here."

Bridget's flight to Baghdad arrived that same morning. After check-in, security brief, orientation, and room assignment, she grabbed a quick shower and put on her civilian war zone work clothes—khaki pants and shirt with combat boots—then tied her hair back and set out to find her new desk.

At the open double doorway of the cavernous two-story-tall ballroom in Saddam Hussein's former Al-Faw Palace, an MP checked her new ID, still warm from the laminating machine. The room had once hosted lavish receptions and sometimes served as the backdrop for presidential speeches. Now, it had about as much charm as the Pentagon basement where she usually worked, with desktop décor of family photos and coffee cups.

The room's floor-to-ceiling windows were covered with heavy curtains for security. Soft tubes covered with silver foil, installed by U.S. Army engineers, hung from the ceiling to distribute a constant flow of cool air. A large, artificial Christmas tree still stood in one corner, with assorted decorations throughout the room.

The military and civilian members of the U.S.-led coalition who worked there supervised a variety of missions, ranging from fighting militias that opposed the Iraqi government to building schools.

Bridget asked a young corporal at the info desk to point out her workstation. He walked over with her, rattling off rules about noise, security, and food, and pointing out the emergency exits that led to concrete bunkers, in case of incoming rockets.

"Good to know," she deadpanned.

Bridget's cubicle was in a back corner, separated from the others by a six-foot partition rather than the usual desk-height ones. The handwritten sign thumbtacked to the partition read, "Davenport, DIA." The chair was broken. The keyboard shelf was hanging down under the desk. And the keyboard itself seemed to be missing.

"I'll find a chair for you," the corporal said.

"Thanks."

"Welcome to Iraq," he said before leaving. He pronounced Iraq like eye-RACK.

Bridget had spent nine years in the army. She knew the condition of her workstation was par for the course. She sat on the desk, tossed her day pack into a corner, and logged her phone onto the nonsecure network.

As she scanned her personal emails, Bridget got a visit from a woman in formfitting fatigues, with a sidearm on her hip and the rank insignia of an army major. "Hey. You the new kid? Welcome to paradise. I'm Robin, logistics deputy, which means if it's broke, I get someone to fix it."

She held out her hand, and Bridget took it. Robin's name tag read "Stern."

"Hi. I'm Bridget. I love what you've done with the place."

"Been here before?"

"Um, no. The other war."

"Ah, well, I'm sure you'll love it here." Robin had a surprisingly bright attitude for a war zone, but maybe that was how she got by.

"Not so far," Bridget said, kicking her broken chair.

"No prob, we'll get you fixed right up. You'll be . . ." Robin looked at the sign. "Doing whatever it is you do, in no time."

"Thanks."

Robin moved off and shouted at someone in the distance, "Torres, can we possibly get a working chair over here? First impressions are important, you know."

"Yes, ma'am," came the distant reply.

Bridget smiled, something she hadn't thought she'd be doing today.

Faraz sipped his coffee and put on, without difficulty, a mix of excitement and apprehension. He answered all of Mahmoud's questions, grateful for the repeated grilling Major Harrington and the other instructors had given him.

Mahmoud asked, "Why have you come here, Karim?"

Faraz sat back, as though he had to think about what to say, but he was ready for that one, too. "Because I am tired of being lied to, tired of doing nothing while crimes are committed in my name. I've had an easy life, but ultimately boring." The perfect answer. Too perfect, maybe?

Mahmoud put his hands on the table and stood. He was of medium height and build, but something about his manner said he was as likely to kill you as offer you another cup of coffee. His eyes were black and constantly moving. He had dark hair and facial fuzz that was struggling to be a beard. "Wait here," he said.

Mahmoud went out the back door, and two large men came in. They grabbed Faraz and pushed him to the floor.

"Wait! Please!"

Mahmoud returned, threw Faraz's baseball cap to the side, grabbed his hair, and pulled his head up. "If you are lying to us, we will kill you. Slowly."

"Yes. Yes. Please. I'm not lying." Faraz was breathing heavily, even though the instructors had done this, too.

Mahmoud dropped Faraz's hair and smacked him on the side of the head. The men picked him up and rushed him out the back door into a van. Mahmoud followed. The door slammed shut. Mahmoud held a cloth to Faraz's face, and everything went dark.

Robin delivered, as promised. Within half an hour, Bridget was sitting in her new chair and tapping the keys of her new keyboard. Her secure email appeared, and she opened the one labeled BLOWBACK CONTACT.

The team watching Faraz reported he had entered the coffee shop and did not come out. It also reported that a van sped out of the back alley and disappeared into the winding lanes of the neighborhood. They had not followed, as instructed.

Chapter Eighteen

Faraz woke up with a bad headache on a cold concrete floor, with a canvas bag over his head and his hands cuffed behind him.

He took a couple of deep breaths and assessed his situation. He had no idea how long he'd been unconscious or where he was. He assumed it hadn't been more than a couple of hours and he was still somewhere near London. He also knew it could have been days, and he could be anywhere in the world.

This was most likely a test of "Karim's" authenticity. There was, of course, that chance that they had figured out he was a fraud.

Only one way to find out. He sat up and called out, "Hello?"

"Stay there," said a voice. It sounded like it was on a loudspeaker, but he couldn't be sure. The echo certainly made it seem like he was in a large room.

He heard footsteps approaching from some distance, tapping on the hard surface. Two or three people, he figured.

Someone ripped the bag off his head. Faraz winced and turned away from the brightness of the room. When his vision cleared, he saw that the space was indeed cavernous. The ceiling was maybe thirty feet high, criss-crossed with steel rafters. The cinder-block walls were topped with a row of windows. It seemed to be part of a warehouse. A security camera and a loudspeaker hung high in one corner.

Three men stood in front of him. One pointed an AK-47 at him. Another held a cricket bat. Mahmoud squatted between them to face Faraz.

"Do you remember the last thing I said to you?" His accent was Middle Eastern with a hint of South London.

"Sorry, no, actually." Whatever had been on that cloth was still clouding Faraz's brain.

"I said that if you are lying to us, we will kill you."

"Right. I do remember now."

"Good. So, we shall begin." Mahmoud sat on the floor in front of Faraz. "What is your name?"

"You know my name."

The man with the bat put it down, walked two steps to Faraz, and hit him across the face with the back of his hand. He stayed there, towering over Faraz.

"I suggest," Mahmoud said, "that you answer the questions and not argue about them."

"Yes, sorry. My name is Karim Niazi."

"What is your real name?"

"Karim Niazi is the only name I have."

The man hit him harder this time, and Faraz toppled over. He sat back up and looked at Mahmoud. "Please, my brother, that is my name."

A third slap came.

"You have not earned the right to call me brother," Mahmoud said.

This time, Faraz was slower getting up. He tasted blood from a split lip.

"But all right. For now, we will call you Karim."

Mahmoud launched into his interrogation about Karim's background, probing for names of teachers, friends, relatives. Faraz had answers for everything, answers he hoped would hold up to any investigation Mahmoud and his organization might mount.

Whenever Faraz hesitated or was confused by a question, he got another slap. But the man never picked up the cricket bat.

Mahmoud grabbed Faraz's left hand and turned it so he could see the scars on his wrist. "Tell me about these."

"I was lonely, depressed, decided to end it. That actually led me to Allah's path."

"How?"

"They put me in counseling, got an imam to talk to me. He taught me about the Koran. That gave me a new way to look at stuff."

"What imam?"

According to Faraz's briefing papers, there was an imam in Detroit who would vouch for him.

"Imam Hussein," he said. "I'm not sure jihad is what he had in mind, but that's where it started."

Mahmoud got up to leave. "You say all the right things, Karim. We shall see whether your story is true."

Left alone, Faraz surveyed his surroundings. The room was bare except for a couple of chairs in one corner. All he could see through the high windows was a cloudy sky. He walked over and sat in one of the chairs.

The door across the room opened again, and Mahmoud's colleagues came in with a tray of food and a bottle of water. They crossed the room. One of them reached behind Faraz and took the cuffs off. "Eat," he said. "Do not try to escape."

The two men turned and left. Before they closed the door, they tossed in a blanket, prayer rug, a bucket, and some rough paper towels.

Faraz had experienced such treatment before, not so many months ago. Assuming he was still in England, that would have been about thirty-five hundred miles to the east.

He used some of the water to wash his hands and face, then sat down to eat. The food was terrible, dry pieces of chicken with rice and soggy vegetables. When he was finished, he used the bucket and left it by the door. The sky had turned dark. The warehouse lights came on.

Faraz considered it a positive sign that they had not come back to kill him. He prayed in a spot where he was sure the security camera could see him. Then he laid out the blanket in the far corner and went to sleep.

Sometime in the middle of the night, the door flew open with a bang. Mahmoud and the interrogation team ran in, and the man with the bat dragged Faraz to his feet.

"Liar!" Mahmoud screamed, almost nose-to-nose with him. Mahmoud pushed him hard, and he fell backward. The man with the bat picked Faraz up and shoved him against the wall. The third man pointed the AK at his head.

Mahmoud put the bat across Faraz's throat and pushed. "You lied to us! Now you will pay!"

"No, Mahmoud . . ." Faraz struggled to speak. "I . . . I . . ."

Mahmoud threw him to the floor and put a foot on his crotch. "Liar!" he screamed. "We know the truth!"

If they did, Faraz was dead. He was not going to admit anything.

"Tell me!" Mahmoud demanded.

The man with the AK moved closer.

"I have told you the truth," Faraz said through the pain. He was shaking, drenched in sweat. "Everything. I swear it by Allah."

Mahmoud stared at him. He removed his foot, bent over, and slapped Faraz, but not very hard, it seemed. Faraz looked at him, confused. Mahmoud slapped again, more gently. Faraz saw the other man lower his AK and smile.

"You are a brave man, Karim," Mahmoud said. "We need men like you." He helped Faraz to his feet.

Faraz put his hands on his knees to steady himself and catch his breath.

"Bring it," Mahmoud called toward the door.

The door opened, and another man came in with a copy of the Koran. Mahmoud took the book and handed it to Faraz. The men around him stepped back and stood with their feet together, hands folded in front of them. Mahmoud said, "Repeat after me."

Faraz repeated the oath, phrase by phrase.

"I, Karim Niazi, a son of Islam, swear by almighty Allah, the merciful and beneficent, that I commit my body and my soul to His jihad, to ending the infidel occupation of the Holy Lands, and to establishing His law for all mankind. This I swear upon my life."

"*Allahu akbar*," the men responded.

"*Allahu akbar*," Faraz said.

Mahmoud embraced Faraz. "Now you may call me brother," he said.

Faraz smiled. "Thank you, my brother."

Each man embraced him in turn. Then they led him out of the room and into their bunkhouse, where he spent the rest of the night sleeping on a cot—his first night as a sand cat.

Chapter Nineteen

It was pushing seven p.m. on Bridget's second day in Baghdad, and she was secure chatting with Liz Michaels at the Pentagon about mission plans and efforts to build the Task Force Epsilon team.

Robin came by Bridget's cubicle. "I see we've got you properly seated and even online," she said.

"Yeah. Thanks."

"Don't mention it. But we do hope for a five-star rating."

Robin had the casual banter of someone working in advertising or sales or some other normal job in a nice, safe, stateside office building—not what one might expect of a field-grade U.S. Army officer in a war zone. But Bridget knew that was normal. Even in a sandbagged facility that used to be a brutal dictator's dining room, with bomb shelters outside the door, and even with a sidearm perched on her hip, for Robin, this was just another day at the office. That had been Bridget's life, once. Now it was her life again, minus the sidearm.

"We'll see about that rating," Bridget said.

"Wanna grab some chow?"

"Thanks, but I've got a pile of work to do."

"C'mon, it's New Year's Eve. Unless you have a date, of course, which would be impressively fast."

Bridget laughed. "No. No date."

"Come on, then. The contractor hired these women from Bulgaria or Croatia or someplace, and they are making their specialty, chicken Kiev. It is to die for."

"Bad metaphor in a war zone."

"You be the judge.

"All right. But you've probably raised my expectations way too high."

Their trays weighed down by chicken, mashed potatoes, and assorted add-ons, Bridget and Robin found a free table in the dining facility's annex, a large tent with wooden floors and plastic windows that made it look like a greenhouse. The chicken Kiev was amazing, and the mashed potatoes were passable.

The desserts were large and, except for the water, the beverages were sugar-heavy. This was a meal designed for muscular men who were burning a lot of calories making war. Bridget would have to be careful, and also find out where the gym was.

"How long have you been here?" Bridget asked.

"Coming up on eight months, four to go," Robin said. "Hardest part is being away from my kids."

"Oh, jeez. How many kids do you have?"

"Three. Youngest was a year old when I left."

"That sucks."

"Tell me about it. She thinks Mommy is a character in an online TV show. The other two are just mad at me."

"They're with your husband?"

"Yes. Jeremy. Saint Jeremy. Former chopper pilot. He got out two years ago, but I was too pigheaded. My mom helps out, and his, too."

"Wow. My hat's off to you, and Saint Jeremy." Bridget raised her water bottle in a toast.

"Yeah, well, it's probably a huge mistake. How about you?"

"Oh, well, yeah, no kids, no husband, saintly or otherwise. Boyfriend shot up in the other war is recuperating at my place outside D.C."

"You meet him in Afghanistan?"

"No, after. I was academy, intel, two tours. That was enough for me. Got out, got the PhD, got a nice normal job at the Pentagon—well, as normal as that place can be. Then my boss decided to send me here."

"Well, congratulations. I'm sure it's a huge honor." Now Robin toasted Bridget.

"Oh, absolutely." They laughed.

"And I guess there's no point asking what exactly you do," Robin said.

"No, sorry."

"Don't worry. I don't know what most of the people here do." Robin leaned in conspiratorially. "And between you and me, I don't think they know, either."

"I'm starting to feel at home already," Bridget said.

A tall man with broad shoulders, a barrel chest, and a shaved head, wearing nonmilitary khakis, came from behind Bridget and stopped at their table.

"Good evening, Robin. How's the best-looking major in the army?" he asked in a Georgia old-boy drawl that Bridget thought he had to be faking. Then he turned his larger-than-life smile on her and asked, "And who is your equally ravishing friend?"

Robin rolled her eyes. "Be careful, Carter. You do know my gun is loaded."

"I do, indeed, as you have pointed that out on numerous occasions."

"Bridget, this large Georgia Bulldog is Carter Holloway, of Spotlight Security. He is to be avoided at all costs. Carter, this is Bridget Davenport of . . . may I say?" Bridget nodded. "Of the Defense Intelligence Agency. And this is her second day, so be nice."

Carter moved back, as if offended. "When am I ever not nice, Major? Okay. Don't answer that." He extended his thick hand toward Bridget, and she shook it. "Ms. Davenport, welcome to Baghdad. Lord knows we can use some intelligence around here." He said "here" like "heeah."

"Spotlight has quite the reputation," Bridget said. Spotlight's reputation was for blasting through missions with little regard for rules of engagement or civilians in their path. The firm was useful, taking on everything from convoy security to special ops–style missions when the U.S. military didn't have the assets or the stomach to do them itself. But Spotlight's approach to its work made a lot of people uncomfortable.

Carter parried the jab. "We have a reputation for being very good and occasionally very bad." The look in his eyes said he was not talking only about paramilitary operations.

Bridget ignored it. "What do you do for them?"

"I do whatever the army tells me to do . . . or the navy, or the marines, or the air force, I guess, and certainly whatever the DIA tells me to do." He gave her a cocky smile and a half wink.

"You sound quite versatile," Bridget said.

"I try, ma'am. I do try. And now, before Major Stern reaches for her sidearm, I shall try to get some of that chicken Kiev, lest the army grunts eat it all. It was a pleasure to meet you, Ms. Davenport."

"Bridget, please."

"Bridget. Robin, I'll see you around the campus, and I do hope you will continue to resist the urge to shoot me."

Carter gave them a nod and moved toward the service area.

"He's quite a character," Bridget said.

"That he is," Robin replied. "But he's far from the worst of them."

"Good to know. I'd forgotten what it's like."

"Oh, yeah. So many men, so few women, so little else to do except work. What happens in Baghdad stays in Baghdad. It's Vegas without the slot machines."

Bridget laughed. "Sounds just like Kabul. I could tell you some stories."

"I could tell you some back, and everyone knows I'm married with children."

Chapter Twenty

For Karim Niazi, still wearing his American clothes and carrying his U.S. passport, the New Year's Eve red-eye to Istanbul was uneventful. The plane was only half full, with a mix of international tourists and Turkish businessmen. When most of them headed into the city or changed to flights for Ankara or the beach, Karim strolled as casually as he could toward the gate for the flight to Diyarbakir in the east.

He was traveling alone, but he had the sense that eyes were on him. Probably two sets, at least—one from Mahmoud's organization, one from Bridget's.

Diyarbakir's small airport was not the closest one to the Syrian border, but it was a safe choice, frequented by journalists, aid workers, and a few intrepid tourists, which is what Karim claimed to be at the security check.

Diyarbakir was the center of Turkey's Kurdish region, with language and cultural ties to Kurds in Iran, Iraq, and Syria across the nearby borders. The Turkish government was wary of anything that could lead to support for Kurdish independence, so the airport had extra security. Mahmoud had assured Faraz that an American with a return ticket, tour book, and dollars to spend would breeze right through.

Faraz put his ticket and the American passport of Karim Niazi through a slot in the bulletproof glass that protected the security officer.

"How long in Diyarbakir?" the officer asked in stilted English muffled by the barrier.

"One week. You see my ticket."

The officer took his time with the papers. "Yes. Okay. Welcome." The man slid the paperwork back to Faraz.

Diyarbakir's small airport provided the typical mob of overaggressive taxi drivers. Faraz surrendered to one of them and gave him the address of the guesthouse where Mahmoud had booked a room for him.

He had trouble sleeping. The next day at noon, he would reenter the world of jihad.

In the morning, Faraz left early, pausing only to drink a small cup of Turkish coffee and pay his bill.

Tour book in hand and the rest of his belongings in his backpack, Faraz walked through the gate into the old town to savor his last few hours of freedom.

He admired the architecture of the stone houses with rounded windows and white abstract decorations. The streets were quiet at that hour. A few shopkeepers were just sliding up their security gates or dumping buckets of soapy water onto the cobblestones. They looked like a cross between Arab and Turk. The women favored colorful long skirts and blouses, with hijabs placed casually over their heads and necks, as if only for show.

It was colder than London, but dry, a welcome relief.

Faraz was glad Mahmoud had given him a sweater and a lined denim jacket.

He noticed a heavy police presence, men in Western-style uniforms carrying automatic weapons pointed at the ground. He had to trust that his new friends knew how to avoid the authorities when the time came.

Faraz stopped for a breakfast of scrambled eggs with tomatoes, homemade bread, and more sweet coffee. Then he browsed souvenir shops, where he politely declined "the finest quality merchandise at the lowest possible price."

With prayer time approaching, Faraz checked the map in his tour book and set a course for his rendezvous.

The Great Mosque of Diyarbakir looked more like a market from the outside, two stories high with a series of doors topped by rounded windows. In the middle was a taller section, crowned with a minaret. This was not anything to compare to the grand mosques of Istanbul or Arabia or anywhere else.

The inner courtyard was somewhat more impressive—columns topped with rustic engravings of Koranic verses. And inside the building, arches held up the high ceiling over pale blue carpeting designed to look like individual prayer rugs. At midday, light flooded in through the transoms.

By the time Faraz got there, it was about half full. He had been told to find a spot near the back, so he waited, pretending to admire the engravings, until the room filled up. As the imam started to chant the prayers, Faraz took a place in the next-to-last row and began to say his prayers.

When the service ended, he greeted the men on each side, as was customary, but did not follow them to the exit. He went the other way, to the back wall, and again feigned fascination with the décor.

A young man approached him. "*Salaam aleikum*, my brother."

"*Aleikum salaam*," Faraz replied.

"You are a visitor?"

"Yes."

"Welcome." Then the stranger added the code phrase Faraz was expecting. "These carvings are from the sixteenth century. They have survived many invaders."

Faraz gave the required response. "They're beautiful, but difficult for me to read."

The man smiled. "Perhaps you will have lunch at my father's house."

"It is my honor," Faraz said, and the young man led him out of the mosque.

Sadly, there was no lunch at the man's father's house. Instead, there was an alley with two men and a small, windowless van. They checked Faraz's backpack and frisked him.

Faraz thanked the young man from the mosque and got into the back of the van, where he found wooden floorboards and crates to sit on. There was a paper bag with a small oval Kurdish bread and a bottle of water. Faraz noticed an AK-47 under the front passenger seat. The driver closed a curtain so Faraz could no longer see or be seen and put the van in gear.

While Faraz was heading into the Turkish countryside, Bridget was on a call with Will. He had just woken up and sounded sleepy.

"Maybe I should call back later when you're awake," she said.

"No, I'm fine. Cat woke me half an hour ago. Anyway,

I have a packed day of video games and physical therapy ahead. Won't have time for chitchat." The sarcasm came through the connection loud and clear.

"Sounds like your world sucks as much as mine."

"More. At least you're where the action is."

"Only action we have here is mealtime and the occasional shelter drill."

That got a laugh out of Will. "That's not how I remember downrange tours."

"Me, neither. But I'm a headquarters rat now."

"Poor you."

Bridget felt resentment in that one. She didn't have an immediate response. Cue the awkward silence.

Will filled it, softening after his jab. "I miss you, babe, wish I could be there with you."

Real feelings. Dangerous territory. The last thing Bridget needed was to add "lovesick" to her list of frustrations. She was sad that they were separated but felt that being an adult meant dealing with it.

"I think we have to keep working on the nickname," she said.

Will didn't answer.

"Sorry," Bridget said. "Bad answer. I miss you, too, of course. I guess I feel like saying it only makes it worse."

"Yeah, maybe," he said. "I don't know. Any word on how long your deployment will be?"

"No. This thing's just getting started."

"Hey, Bridget." Robin's voice came from two cubicles away. "Want to get some chow?"

"I'm on a call," Bridget shouted back.

"Who's that?" Will asked.

"Just a friend asking if I want to get some food."

"A friend?"

"Yes, a friend."

"What's his name?"

"Will! C'mon, you want a list of the people I've met over here?"

"No. Sorry. Okay, so I'm a shithead."

Bridget made him wait a couple of seconds. "Apology accepted. Look, shithead, I know it's hard being left behind. You did it to me, remember?"

"Yeah."

"Her name is Robin, by the way."

"Thanks. Give her my regards."

"Sure. Let's talk later."

"Okay."

Bridget hung up and stared at her locked computer screen. She and Will had had a long-distance relationship for longer than they'd been in the same place at the same time. Having him at her apartment had been nice, but the memory had a feeling of unreality about it. Now that they were apart again, this seemed like the norm. A totally unsatisfying norm.

After an hour, the men stopped the van and went into the back. They removed some of the floorboards, revealing a crawl space.

One of the men looked at Faraz. "*Kontrol noktasi*," he said.

Faraz returned a blank look.

The man looked at his colleague. They seemed to be trying to remember the word. The driver provided it. "Checkpoint." Then he added, "You, down."

Faraz had to bring his knees to his chest to fit. The men tossed in his backpack. When they put the boards back on, there was not an inch of spare space.

The van started moving again. Faraz felt every bump in the road as he lay on the bare steel of the vehicle's floor. His tomb had a limited supply of air and an ample supply of exhaust fumes.

They slowed to a stop, then moved a bit several times. Faraz heard the driver speaking to someone. The driver's tone was bright. But Faraz's fluent English and Pashto and limited Arabic did little to help him understand the Turkish conversation.

Faraz tried to breathe evenly. The dust from the road made him need to sneeze. He managed to get his hand to his face so he could rub his nose.

He heard the rear doors open, and there was more conversation as, Faraz imagined, IDs were being checked. Questions were asked and answered, but Faraz didn't know what they were. Again, he stifled the urge to sneeze. He felt a cramp forming in his left calf and raised his toe as high as he could to fight it.

Finally, the doors slammed, and the van started moving again.

Faraz breathed through his mouth, still massaging his nose. It seemed like a long time before the men removed the floorboards. Faraz sneezed immediately, and the men laughed. He also reached down and pulled his left toe up to ease the muscle that was still threatening to cramp. The men helped him out of the hole.

Chapter Twenty-one

After two hours, Faraz felt a slight turn to the right as the van went off the paved roads onto a dirt trail. He held onto his seat as they bounced along for another ten minutes.

When they stopped, someone outside opened the rear doors. The flood of light blinded Faraz, but after a few seconds, he saw a man and a woman smiling in front of an old house surrounded by overgrowth. There were farm fields in the distance.

"Welcome, mate." The man shook Faraz's hand and helped him out of the van. "I'm Trevor. You made it this far, so let's celebrate, eh?" The accent was Australian, and the enthusiasm seemed fit for a gathering with shrimps on the barbie, as did his jeans, cotton sweater, and flip-flops. He was thin, and his beard was ragged.

"*Ahlan wa sahlan*," the woman said, offering the traditional Arabic welcome with a decidedly Down Under accent. She put her hand on her heart in greeting but did not offer to shake Faraz's hand. She was tall and wore a calf-length skirt over jeans, a long-sleeved shirt, sandals, and a snug hijab that framed her face. One wisp of red hair escaped.

"Thank you, my brothers," Trevor said to the men in the van.

One of the men tossed Faraz's backpack to him and closed the doors. The vehicle started moving immediately.

"I'm Karim," was all Faraz could think of to say as he adjusted his backpack on his shoulder.

"Oh, we know who you are, all right," Trevor said. "Been expecting you. You'll be with us for a night or two until we can sort out your travel." Trevor put his arm around Faraz's shoulder and moved him toward the farmhouse. It was an old wood-frame, with peeling white paint and homemade furniture on the porch. But Faraz noticed small security cameras mounted on the overhang. "Let's get you settled and feed you a decent meal. Still stale bread and water on the journey, I'm guessing."

"Yes, thanks," Faraz said. They mounted five wooden steps to the porch, and Trevor opened the door. The woman went around to a side entrance. Trevor switched to a whisper. "That's Melissa. She's a quiet one, but not a bad cook. That's why I married her."

Faraz forced a laugh.

"Smart as a whip, too, by the way. She's the one who helped me find the path. She's a gem, really."

They went along a hallway, skirting around a small gray safe on the floor with a digital lock.

"Seems like an odd spot for that," Faraz said.

"Good central location, though, don't you think?" Trevor slapped him on the back.

They went into the last room on the left, next to the back door. It was a normal bedroom with twin beds that must have once belonged to a family's children.

“Make yourself at home, mate. Loo’s across the hall. Come to the kitchen when you’re ready.”

“Thank you.”

“Um, you’ll find the back door locked. Just a precaution, you know. Some folks catch a bit of panic when they get this far.” Trevor stood facing Faraz and looked him over. “How you feeling?”

“Fine, fine. I’m glad to be here. Yeah, nervous about what comes next, but that’s what I came for.”

“Excellent,” Trevor said with his outback enthusiasm. “No place to run, anyway. We are right far out in the sticks here. If you turn the wrong way, you could run into lots of Syrians with guns. Not friendly fellows.”

“Ah, okay. I’m not going anywhere. See you in the kitchen in a few minutes.”

“Good.” Trevor grinned. He gave Faraz another slap on the back. “We’ll keep you inside until after dark. Then you can get some fresh air. Never know who’s watching.” Trevor pointed out the window toward the sky, chuckled, and left.

After a dinner of goat meat over rice with stewed vegetables, Faraz and Trevor sat on the porch while Melissa cleaned up.

“She won’t join us?” Faraz asked.

“Like I said, not a big talker. Also, she feels it’s not right to fraternize with strange men. Leaves that to me. She takes charge when the girls come through.”

“Girls?”

“Yeah. Good number of them, too. Allah bless them, they’re as committed as the men.”

"Hmm. I'm surprised there's no security team here."

"Don't need it. We're flying under the radar—a couple of converts to Islam homesteading in the countryside. We have some tech, but no need for guys with guns. Only drawback is, I actually have to do some farming. For appearance's sake, you know. But, hey, we're doing our part in the jihad, eh."

Trevor woke Faraz a little after two a.m. "Sorry, mate. Your ride is here. No time to provide our full hospitality service, but Melissa will pack you a snack."

When Faraz came into the living room five minutes later, Melissa handed him a cloth bag. "I wish you a safe journey," she said. "*Allah yukhaleek*." May Allah protect you. She offered a shy smile and left the men alone.

Trevor took Faraz outside to an ancient Ford SUV with blackened windows and a generous coating of backroads mud. Two men sat in front, and the driver signaled them to hurry.

"They'll take you to the fellows we call the guides, Trevor said. "Next stop, the Syrian Arab Republic."

"Thanks for your help." Faraz held out his right hand, and Trevor shook it.

"Don't mention it. I mean, really, when they catch you, interrogate you, torture you, don't mention it."

"Excuse me?"

Trevor burst out laughing. "Sorry, mate. I've got to get my entertainment where I can. Have a safe journey."

* * *

The ride was short, and the two men in the SUV didn't seem to speak much English. The last several minutes, they were driving through tall vegetation.

The driver stopped where the rough two-track ended in a clearing barely large enough for him to turn the vehicle around. The man in the passenger seat got out and whistled three notes, two short and high, the third long and low. The same signal came back. He whistled again, this time short-long-short. And again, the response came.

The man opened the van door, took Faraz by the arm, and led him into the overgrown field.

Two men appeared, wearing black cotton pants and black padded jackets, with traditional kaffiyehs on their heads and AK-47s in their hands. They kissed Faraz's escort on both cheeks and greeted Faraz with handshakes, but no one spoke. One of the guides set off in the direction they had come. The other wagged his head for Faraz to follow and took up a position behind him.

There was no fence or marker, but somewhere along the narrow, winding, path, Faraz's short stay in Turkey ended. After twenty minutes, they climbed an embankment to a road, and Faraz boarded a van with Syrian license plates.

Chapter Twenty-two

Faraz imagined that many sand cats were shocked when the van doors opened on the ramshackle camp. But to him, the scene felt both familiar and depressing.

The compound was small enough that he could see most of it from where he stood. It was surrounded by a wooden wall with guard towers on each side of the main gate. The road went straight through to a rear gate, with pathways and driveways leading off on both sides.

A building near the front gate seemed to be the headquarters. Past that were smaller buildings to the right and left for storage or sleeping quarters for senior fighters. Tents toward the back of the camp bore United Nations logos, apparently pilfered from refugee supplies. To the far right, smoke wafted from a chimney. Beyond it was another barracks building. Whatever latrine or sewage system they had was not functioning well. The whole place smelled like a ballpark men's room.

It was barely six a.m., but the camp was busy with people crossing in all directions. The only surprise for Faraz was that there were women among them.

A man who looked to be in his late twenties came out

of the large building, walked down two steps, and held out his hand. "I'm Nic," he said in American-accented English. "You, I assume, are Karim. Welcome to the jihad."

"Thanks. It's good to be here."

"Well, that's a lie. This place is a shithole. At least you don't have the deer-in-the-headlights look we usually get. You'll do fine. Come on, I'll show you your tent and give you the grand tour. Won't take long."

Nic led the way as they walked through the open center area. He wore a threadbare brown sweater, tan cotton pants, and old running shoes. He was shorter than Faraz, with a few extra pounds around his midsection. Nic pointed out the clinic, showers, and toilets. "That's the kitchen," he said pointing to the building with the chimney. "The women have a barracks and some tents on the other side of it. That's a no-go zone for us, obviously."

"Right," Faraz said. He got brief greetings from several people as he and Nic turned left into a cluster of small gray tents arrayed near a side gate, probably meant for taking out the trash.

"This is yours," Nic said. "It's a two-man, but you're alone for now."

Faraz bent over and went inside. It was little more than an overgrown pup tent. There were two sleeping mats, with only about two feet of space between them. Two wooden crates were the furniture, providing storage space and a surface on which to put things. Faraz put his backpack on the mat on the right and came back out. "All moved in," he said.

"Good. Let's wash up and get some food."

The two men walked back along the same route, then crossed the compound toward the kitchen.

"Where are you from?" Faraz said. "Wait, can I ask that?"

"You can ask anything you want. I'm from San Diego."

Faraz nearly said "me, too." But he stopped himself. That was the truth he had been trying to push aside for weeks—for more than a year, really. The last thing he wanted to think about was San Diego.

"I'm from Detroit," he said. He was trying to figure out Nic's ethnicity. His skin was a light shade of tan, but his accent indicated he had grown up in the U.S.

"How did you find yourself here?" Faraz tried.

"Usual story, really. Short version is my grandfather was Egyptian, used to take me to the mosque. Years later, I fell in with the wrong crowd, got strung out, found my way back through Islam. Turns out, what I was trying to escape through the drugs was the oppression and lies of a society where I didn't belong. Sorry if I sound like one of those websites, but it's the truth."

"You feel better here?"

"Yeah, actually."

"Well, that's good to hear. My story's something like yours, but both parents Muslim, and without the drugs."

Nic stopped near the entrance to the kitchen, turned, and gestured toward the rest of the camp. "You know, this is not exactly what anyone expects, but it's good to be on the right side of the fight."

"You fight?"

Nic seemed embarrassed by the question. "Um, no. Not yet. But soon. Maybe. We all make our contribution."

He turned and led Faraz up a few steps through the door to the buffet line. Nic took a plate, put a pita on it, and took a large dollop of hummus and two hard-boiled eggs. At the far end, he poured himself some tea and went out through a different door. Faraz followed suit and found himself in a small open area dotted with tables and chairs.

Nic introduced Faraz to several men and a few women—Jamal from Kenya, Ismail, a Moroccan from France, Latif, a quiet kid from Pakistan, and Tasha, a black former gang member who found Allah at the largest U.S. women's jail, in Los Angeles. They all seemed to be in their late twenties or early thirties, aside from Latif, the only teenager in the group.

The men were in jeans or cotton pants. The women wore ankle-length skirts and hijabs. Everyone had long-sleeved shirts and fall or winter jackets.

Along the camp's outer wall, Faraz and Nic came to a picnic table where two women were sitting.

"Ah," Nic said. "These are Cindy and Amira, also fairly new arrivals. Ladies, this is Karim, fresh off the bus. May we join you?"

"Sure," Cindy said.

Nic sat at the far end of the table from the women and indicated Faraz should do the same. He was figuring out the behavior protocols—it was more relaxed than at the safe house but still designed to avoid physical contact or excessive familiarity.

"Welcome," Cindy continued. "Or should I say *ahlan wa'saaaaaahlan*."

Faraz thought her accent was Australian, or maybe South African. She had olive skin, brown eyes, and bits of dark hair dangling from her hijab. She was thin and head-and-shoulders taller than her colleague.

"Amira and I arrived the same day. What was that, six

weeks ago? Yeah. A bit of a shock at first, but wouldn't want to be anywhere else. Where you from, Karim?"

"Detroit," Faraz said. The lie came naturally now. "And you?" he asked.

"Joburg. My grandparents thought it'd be good to get out of Iran before the Shah had them thrown into prison. So they snuck out to seek their fortune elsewhere. That turned out to be a convenience store off a highway in the bad, bad African suburbs. Dead end at the dead end of the world. My dad took it over, but I was not sticking around for my turn."

"What about you?" Faraz asked, looking at Amira.

"London," she said. Her accent was down-market. Her skin was darker than Cindy's, and her eyes were black.

"Hard to get more than two words out of her," Cindy said. "But she's all right." Cindy smiled at Amira, who returned a smile that, to Faraz, showed more sadness than anything else.

"Time for us to get to work," Cindy continued, sliding off the bench seat. "Got to check the schedule. What'll it be today? Folding bandages, painting walls, preparing lunch. Hmm. Let's go, Amira, and leave these guys to eat in peace."

"Nice meeting you," Faraz said, raising his tea in salute.

"You, too," Cindy said.

Amira just gave him that smile. She took her tray and followed Cindy toward the kitchen.

The warm teacup felt good in Faraz's hand in the chilly morning air. The smell of the tea reminded him of home. Another memory to suppress.

Chapter Twenty-three

After breakfast, Faraz and Nic walked into the central part of the camp just as someone in a guard tower shouted, "Open it up! Open it up!"

The gate slid to the side, and four SUVs sped in, spattered with dirt from the road. Three men ran out of the main house. One opened the driver's door of the lead vehicle and said, "What happened? You're late."

A large man emerged, dark haired and bearded, and spattered with blood. "Get the doctor," he said. He sounded angry and was clearly exhausted. He leaned on the car door.

Faraz saw a man and a woman were already sprinting from the clinic, both carrying satchels of supplies. They went up to the large man, but he shooed them away. "It is Matthieu. Third vehicle."

Several men removed Matthieu from the cargo area and laid him on the ground so the medical team could work on him.

Faraz, Nic, and the others approached but kept a respectful distance. "Who is that?" Faraz asked, pointing at the man still holding onto the door of the SUV.

"That's the commander, al-Jazar. They were out on a mission, expected back before daybreak."

Faraz looked at his new boss, trying to read the lines on his face, his body language. Al-Jazar looked like a hard man who had had a rough morning. He was tall, maybe six feet, in shape with sunbaked skin and a full but trimmed black beard. He wore a plain shirt and khaki pants, and a camouflage-pattern baseball hat. He had no equipment belt or bulletproof vest. His AK was on the vehicle's seat.

Al-Jazar walked to the third vehicle, stopping to check on other wounded fighters along the way.

The people from the clinic cut off Matthieu's shirt. Faraz could see that he had a bad chest wound, probably unrecoverable even under the best of circumstances. He also saw Matthieu's face. Faraz hoped he was older than he looked, because he looked like he was about sixteen.

The doctor and his assistant worked on Matthieu for several minutes as the growing crowd of perhaps three dozen stood in silence. It wasn't long before the woman put her right hand over Matthieu's face and closed his eyes. The man stood, his hands and shirt bloody. "Matthieu is a martyr of the jihad," he said. "*Allahu akbar*."

Al-Jazar and everyone else mumbled the same in response, and there was an impromptu moment of silence. Faraz heard some of the women crying behind him.

The commander recovered quickly. "Prepare him," was all he said before turning and mounting the steps to the main building.

Faraz lingered as the crowd dispersed. Several men picked Matthieu's body up and carried it toward the clinic.

Nic took Faraz's arm and led him toward the middle of

the camp. "It's not always like this. But honestly, I can't say it's the first time, either."

"I've never seen anything like that," Faraz lied, trying to affect shock and sadness.

"At least you didn't know him. I did. Nice guy, very dedicated to the jihad. It's sad, but . . . I don't know. He wanted to be a fighter. And I think that's the way he wanted to go. As a *shahid*." A martyr.

Faraz sighed. "And you? You want to go that way?"

Nic turned to face him, irritated. "Look, man. If you're not prepared to be martyred, maybe you shouldn't be here. Hopefully, we won't all die out there, but it's part of the package."

"Yes, yes, I know. Sorry."

"Okay. I know it's your first day. Let's see what my work assignment is, and you can tag along. Not a good time to meet the commander."

Faraz spent the day with Nic hammering together panels that would become the camp's next building. Nic introduced several other foreign Muslims who had joined the jihad, plus a few of the Syrian fighters.

"I had no idea there were so many of us," Faraz said.

"Sand cats? Yeah, this is a pretty big group, but we're spread out across the region."

"The Syrians look like a tough bunch."

"The commander attracts that type. Some of them are okay, but a lot of them resent having to train us. They think we're wimps, frankly."

"But you said Matthieu wasn't the first martyr. You'd think that would convince them."

Nic shrugged. "Time to wash up. The funeral's in half an hour."

There was no time for showers, so they joined the queue on the men's side of the building waiting for a few minutes at one of the sinks.

A Syrian fighter approached them, his AK-47 slung over his shoulder. "Karim Niazi?" he asked.

"Yes, that's me."

The man cocked his head to the side, turned, and walked back in the direction from which he'd come.

"Time to meet the boss," Nic said. "Enjoy."

Faraz followed the fighter to the main building. They went up the steps and through the front door. The man held up a hand for Faraz to wait while he went into an office on the right. He came out a few seconds later and held the door for Faraz.

The commander's cap was on the desk, exposing his black, wavy hair, still greasy and unwashed. At close range, Faraz saw a few gray wisps in the beard. Al-Jazar's bloody shirt was gone, replaced by a black T-shirt.

The man stood and held out a large hand. "I am Jazar. *Ahlan wa sahlan.*" His voice was strong, but he sounded weary.

Faraz shook his hand. "It's an honor, sir."

"You are from Detroit," Jazar said, rolling the R with the tip of his tongue. "Automobiles, Motown, murder." He laughed. His accent was heavy, but his English was pretty good.

"Yes, sir," Faraz said.

"You are a tough guy?"

"No. Well, yes, I hope to be."

Jazar laughed again. He seemed to enjoy intimidating the new recruit. "You know what is *jazar*?"

"No, sir."

"In English, you say 'butcher.' I am al-Jazar, the Butcher. It is not a nice name, but I earned it. You understand?"

"Yes, sir." Faraz's voice seemed to be getting smaller with each answer.

"I no longer use the name my father gave me," al-Jazar said, still looming over Faraz from across his desk. "My father was a weak man. He drank alcohol. He bowed to the Shia dictator who oppresses our people. He wanted to be a 'modern man.' He became a corrupt man, not worthy to be counted among the followers of Allah."

Al-Jazar walked around the desk and stood right in front of Faraz. "I use the name I earned in jihad. Here, you will learn to be committed to jihad. You will do what you are told. You will learn to fight. Maybe someday, you, too, will earn a new name."

"Yes, sir."

"Today we lost a brave martyr. You saw?"

"Yes, sir."

"Maybe we will lose you one day. Are you prepared for that?"

Faraz paused and swallowed. "If it is Allah's will."

"Correct. If it is Allah's will, you will be a martyr. If it is His will, one day I will be a martyr. We do not know His plan. Meanwhile, we make His jihad against the infidels and the false Muslims."

"False Muslims?"

Al-Jazar pointed to a poster on his wall. It showed the Syrian president smiling with a group of children. It had a red X painted over it. "The ones who claim to work for

Allah, but do not truly know Him—the devil Assad and all the Shia blasphemers." He turned back toward Faraz. "And some of our own Sunni people, usurpers, who came late to the fight and claim to be the leaders."

"Usurpers?"

"You will learn more in the coming days. Now, we must send our *shahid* Matthieu on his way."

Al-Jazar walked past Faraz and left the office. Faraz followed, and other fighters fell in line. When they came outside, Faraz saw that a crowd had gathered in front of the building. Matthieu's body was wrapped in a white sheet and lay on some wooden boxes. There was no casket.

Faraz went down the steps and stood near the front. The air felt notably colder than when he'd gone into the building a few minutes earlier. Clouds had rolled in, and night was falling.

Al-Jazar addressed the camp from the porch in a mix of English and Arabic, but Faraz wasn't paying attention. He was thinking about what the commander had said. "Usurpers who came late to the fight." Al-Souri had returned to Syria recently and created the new organization that was getting a lot of attention, claiming a leadership role. It made sense that some might bristle at that.

Faraz filed the thought away for future reference and focused on what al-Jazar was saying.

"Today, we say goodbye to our friend Matthieu. He came to us from Paris, not so long ago, it seems. He loved Allah. He found a place for himself in Allah's jihad. He achieved a greatness he never dreamed of. Some of you are sad, today, but I am not. I am happy for my brother who fulfilled his destiny, a destiny he sought with bravery and faith. He is already reaping his reward. Now, follow as we return his body to the earth."

Al-Jazar descended the steps, trailed by his crew of fighters wearing stern expressions. They waited as Nic, Jamal, Ismail, and three other sand cats lifted Matthieu's body onto their shoulders and led the way to a small cemetery outside the camp's rear gate.

Faraz fell in toward the back of the procession. He noticed that several women were helping one who was weeping. He also saw Cindy with a stoic look on her face, alongside Amira, whose cheeks were wet and eyes red. Cindy put her arm around her friend as they walked.

At the graveside, the smell of turned-over soil hung in the air. The men placed Matthieu's body on the ground next to the open grave and the pile of earth that would refill it. The only member of al-Jazar's Syrian entourage who was not holding a weapon stepped forward and offered the traditional prayers.

"*'Aeudh biAllah*," he began in Arabic. "I seek refuge in Allah. All praise is due to Allah, the entirely merciful . . ." Faraz knew the prayer from family funerals back home, starting with his cousin Johnny's.

He felt the danger more sharply than he had since leaving Afghanistan, which, it dawned on him, was not so very long ago.

"*Allahu akbar*," the prayer leader concluded.

"*Allahu akbar*," they all responded.

The pallbearers lowered Matthieu's body into the grave. Al-Jazar stepped forward, picked up a shovel, and dumped the first load of dirt on top of the young man. The prayer leader went next, then the security team, then the rest of them.

It was darker now, and getting colder by the minute. The only sounds were the shovel against the pile, the earth landing in the grave, and the women softly sobbing.

Chapter Twenty-four

The scene at al-Souri's camp a dozen miles away was quite different. His fighters were celebrating. They had repulsed the attack by the ungrateful one they called the Butcher.

Nazim fired up the crowd. "He could only have earned that name from slaughtering a goat, the coward!" The men cheered and fired their weapons into the air.

Al-Souri watched his men enjoy their victory with considerable satisfaction. He had returned to his homeland to help defeat the dictator and the invading infidels. He had brought skill, money, international contacts, and leadership. He offered the chance to take their fight to a new level, to finally gain the advantage.

But some were unhappy. Some, whose knowledge began and ended with themselves, saw him as a usurper. Nonsense. The smaller they were, the more they thought they should lead. The weaker they were, the more they thought they were strong.

Al-Jazar had had the temerity to attack his camp, to try to derail al-Souri's advance toward his natural position as leader of the Syrian opposition. Tonight, al-Souri had shown him, and all the others, that he knew how to defend his camp, how to be merciless against those who would question him.

Maybe now, al-Jazar would accept the new order of things. Maybe not.

Al-Souri called a halt to the celebrations and sent his men off to rest. He went into his small office with Nazim, newly promoted to officially be the great man's second-in-command.

"The men did well tonight," al-Souri said. "A credit to your training."

"Thank you, Commander," Nazim replied. "Allah was with us."

"Yes. But we must be prepared for larger attacks. Al-Jazar, and maybe others, will not be placated. They will continue to distract us from the real enemies."

"They have placed themselves among our real enemies."

"True." Al-Souri stared out the window. He thought of Nazim as a son, although the two could not have been more different. The commander was tall, thin, and had light olive skin, his balding head hidden by his *takkiye*. Nazim was five foot five and stocky. His dark skin revealed a Moroccan, or maybe a Turk, somewhere in his lineage. And his kaffiyeh couldn't hold his overgrown black hair.

In fact, Nazim was the son of al-Souri's great friend Omar, who had gone with him to Afghanistan decades ago, leaving the baby Nazim and his mother behind. Omar died soon after, and al-Souri had supported them ever since.

When al-Souri returned to Syria, Nazim welcomed

him, pledged loyalty, called him "commander" rather than "uncle," as he had in letters over the years.

"Tomorrow, we will have a visitor," al-Souri said.

"Oh?"

"A very important man. We must welcome him properly. He holds the key to our future."

"May I ask who he is?"

"We shall call him al-Malik." The King.

The next morning, al-Souri watched through his office window as al-Malik's entourage swept into the camp. There were two black SUVs packed with heavily armed fighters. The man himself rode in a Mercedes sedan with dark windows in the middle of the motorcade.

As the dust the vehicles churned up settled, al-Souri came out to greet his guest.

"*Ahlan wa sahlan*, my friend," he said, and he kissed al-Malik on both cheeks.

Al-Malik was not a king, but he represented one, or more likely several, and perhaps some princes, too. They were rich Sunnis from the Gulf who had pledged to help al-Souri defeat Assad in return for his promise to keep pressure on the infidels who, in other forums, the Gulf Arabs pretended were their friends.

The visitor embraced al-Souri and turned to acknowledge Nazim and other fighters who had lined up in greeting. Then, without a word, he headed toward the building, with al-Souri hurrying to keep up.

In the office, al-Malik fell into the one comfortable chair. His paunch strained the buttons of his Western-style shirt and the string that held up his traditional trousers.

His charcoal gray suit jacket was open. He took off his red-and-white kaffiyeh, the style favored by Saudi princes, and mopped his bald head with a large handkerchief.

Al-Souri handed him a small glass of sweet tea. Al-Malik accepted it without thanks. He sipped and gave a disapproving look, then put it on the desk. He took a hard candy from his jacket pocket, unwrapped it, and popped it into his mouth. Belatedly, he took out another and offered it to al-Souri, who declined.

"You are looking well," al-Souri said in Arabic.

"I look like a fat old man. I am happy to be a fat old man, and I hope to get both fatter and older." After a moment, he remembered to add, "*Inshallah.*" If it is God's will.

Al-Souri forced a smile.

"You had a battle last night," al-Malik continued.

"We were attacked. We defeated them easily."

"This is a waste. This is not what they want." He always spoke of "they." Al-Souri had never heard al-Malik say "his majesty" or "their majesties." The man was paid for his discretion, as much as for his willingness to travel to such places and deal directly with the pawns in the great game his masters were playing.

"I did not seek the fight," al-Souri said. "I seek only to lead us to victory over the Shia and the infidels."

"I tell you, you must solve this problem." Al-Malik's tone was matter-of-fact, but it was clear he expected to be obeyed. He crunched the candy, swallowed it, and lit a cigarette.

"These men—" al-Souri started, but al-Malik cut him off.

"Just solve it. No distractions. No waste."

The commander didn't like taking orders, but he couldn't afford to say no to al-Malik and his masters, or their money.

Al-Malik scanned the room with a look of disdain. Its Spartan appearance, decorated only with framed Koranic verses, clearly did not impress him. He flicked some ash onto the floor, looked back toward al-Souri, and stared through the spiraling smoke before continuing.

"I also am sent to remind you that the Shia and the infidels in Syria are not your only enemies. You must fulfill the other part of our . . ." He searched for the right word. "Arrangement."

"My friend, I have told you that such things take time. We had a great victory in November. Our operatives have had to remain quiet. We shall strike again when the time is right."

"No, my friend. You shall not strike when it is convenient for you. The West is off balance. They must be hit again, and soon. Martelli must suffer the political consequences and lose the election. We cannot afford another four years of him."

Al-Souri thought about that. He knew the Gulf Arabs didn't like Martelli. He was too smart for their taste, easing tensions with their enemy, Iran, making progress on Israeli–Palestinian relations, developing new sources of energy to reduce America's oil imports. And the president was pressing his new counterterrorism offensive more effectively than they had expected, hitting groups they secretly funded.

"It will be costly," al-Souri said. He knew that wouldn't deter al-Malik but thought he might be able to get some extra money out of him.

"You know that will not be a problem," al-Malik said, "if the plan is right."

"Have no doubt, the plan is right." Al-Souri leaned across his desk and lowered his voice. He outlined his idea for the financier. He had been working on it since Afghanistan.

As he spoke, al-Malik's eyes widened, and he leaned forward in his chair. When al-Souri finished, his guest sat back and let out a low whistle. He dropped what was left of his cigarette and stepped on it. "You think very big, my friend."

"As you know, my priority is Syria and the Levant. But if we are going to pursue the larger struggle, we must think big. We cannot do anything small after November. The fighters have already scouted their targets, started training their teams. But we have done as much as we can without more money."

"Of course. I shall present your plan for approval. I do not foresee any problems. When can you strike?"

"With money, soon. I cannot say exactly. And funding for our efforts here?"

"Yes, that is nothing compared to this."

Al-Souri nodded. Nothing in monetary terms, maybe. Everything in his apocalyptic vision.

"You will hear from me soon," al-Malik said.

"Will you stay for dinner?"

"Ha!" al-Malik spat his reply. He used both arms to heft himself out of the chair. "I must return to Damascus before dark and get a decent meal."

"Of course," al-Souri said, trying not to sound ironic.

* * *

That evening, al-Souri summoned Nazim to his office. "Will we attack al-Jazar tonight?" Nazim asked.

"No. We must find a way to unite all the factions. Otherwise, the dictator and the infidels will defeat us."

"Unite under your leadership?"

"Of course."

"Al-Jazar will never accept it. Others will oppose you, too."

"You are right. But there is a way. You must arrange a meeting of faction leaders. There, we shall settle this. And if we can't . . . Well, then you may get your wish."

"Yes, Commander."

Chapter Twenty-five

Faraz, Nic, and all the foreign men were in the field outside al-Jazar's camp for intensive combat training. They went through a series of exercises, then some basics of hand-to-hand fighting.

"This is strange," Nic confided during a water break. "Usually, we have to beg for this sort of thing."

"So, why the change?" Faraz asked.

"Unclear. But the boss is unhappy with last night, and there's no point in training fighters if you don't plan to use them. I'm down with it, though. You?"

"Yeah, sure. It's what we came for, right?" Faraz finished his cup of water and walked back toward the training area.

He allowed himself to excel—without breaking his cover. He needed to show he could be a fighter. He'd never accomplish his mission working on the camp's construction crew.

As the week went on, Faraz became known as one of the best at one-on-one fighting, with quick hands and fast-moving feet. He also scored high when they were given their first chance to fire AKs. He claimed he'd gone hunting with a friend in northern Michigan a few times and honed his skills on video games.

Al-Jazar noticed. Faraz was among three foreigners called into the commander's office. They would accompany the fighters on a mission, but hang back and observe.

Shortly after dark, in a new, all-black outfit but with no weapon, Faraz mounted an SUV with Ismail, the French Moroccan, and Jamal, the Kenyan. A Syrian fighter drove, and another rode shotgun. They were in the last vehicle of four as they sped along desert roads. The recruits had not been told where they were going or what the team would be doing.

They stopped on the edge of a town. A fighter opened the back door of Faraz's SUV and motioned for them to get out. All the men gathered as al-Jazar emerged from the lead vehicle and spoke. "Tonight, we strike a blow at the infidels. There is a hotel in this town where the foreign workers stay—men and women who bring Western ideas and immorality in the guise of education. Tonight, they have a celebration. But it will not go as they plan. This is the night your lives have been leading to."

Three of the fighters stepped forward, holding out vests for the foreigners to put on.

"What? What are we doing?" Jamal asked, backing away.

"We are performing Allah's jihad," al-Jazar said. Two of the men held Jamal.

"I am ready," Ismail said. He stepped forward and held out his arms. The men put the vest on him and clipped it closed.

"And you, Karim?" al-Jazar asked.

Faraz could see no way out. If he refused, he might be

forced to comply or, if not, relegated to a support role where he would never learn anything about planned operations. If he accepted, his mission could end in a few minutes.

But something didn't feel right. Suicide bombers normally went through extensive preparation—prayer, training, indoctrination. They would record videos to be used later. They would know every detail of their mission. If this was a test, he had to pass it. If it was a real suicide mission . . . well, it's where he had been a few months ago, anyway.

"I'm ready," Faraz said, and he let them strap him into a vest. It was heavy, weighted with explosives and metal pieces or, he hoped, with only rocks. He was sweating in the cool night air.

"You are the only coward," al-Jazar said to Jamal.

"Commander, I . . . I am not ready," Jamal said.

"But you are here. You have been with us for months, far longer than Karim. If you are not ready, maybe you will never be ready."

Jamal had no response. He looked at the ground. Al-Jazar signaled the fighters who were holding Jamal, and they forced him to his knees.

"Please, Commander," he pleaded.

Al-Jazar slapped him hard. Jamal fell sideways, and the men pulled him back to his knees. He spat blood. Al-Jazar held his AK against Jamal's forehead. "We have no time for cowards," he said.

Faraz could only watch. Would Jazar kill him as an example? If that's what he wanted to achieve, doing it at the camp, in front of everyone, would seem to be a better plan. Faraz smelled something. Jamal had peed himself.

The young man looked down in shame as the urine soaked his trousers. "Please, Commander. I love Allah and His jihad."

Al-Jazar flipped his rifle and slammed the butt into Jamal's face. The young man fell back into the gully by the side of the road, his nose broken and bleeding. He curled into a fetal position. "Please, Commander."

"Tie him," al-Jazar ordered, and two of the men bound Jamal's hands and feet. "Put him in the vehicle." The men lifted Jamal into the cargo area of an SUV and slammed the hatch.

Faraz breathed a sigh of relief. At least they hadn't killed the guy. Maybe that meant there was hope for him, too, and for Ismail. Or maybe al-Jazar was planning to deal with Jamal back at camp, after Faraz and Ismail had done their suicide bombing.

Al-Jazar turned to them. "Now," he said, "you two will do Allah's work." He stood in front of Faraz and Ismail, looked into the eyes of each one in turn, and asked, "Are you ready, my brother?"

"Yes, Commander. I am ready," they each responded.

"Good. Now we go." Each fighter stepped forward in turn to hug the two foreigners and kiss them on both cheeks. Then they formed two lines, with Faraz and Ismail in the middle, and walked toward the town.

Faraz could see the lights of what he assumed to be the hotel dining room. He heard rock and roll wafting across the desert. Through the windows, he saw people dancing.

He needed a plan. Taking the vest off could trigger the explosion, but he'd have to take that chance. Faraz would drop the vest and make a run for it. He would shout a warning, if the aid workers could hear it over the music.

If worst came to worst, his bomb would be the warning, from well outside the building. He and Ismail would be the only ones to die, or if he was lucky, maybe he could take al-Jazar and some of the others with him.

But not yet. He had to play this out as long as he could.

Faraz wiped sweat from his temples. He looked at Ismail walking next to him. The guy was about his age, a couple of inches shorter, with a baby face and a prominent nose. While Faraz worried his own face might show his fear, Ismail was stoic, walking with purpose. He was clearly convinced that this was his destiny.

Faraz touched the front of his vest. He could feel no button or lever. He hadn't been given a handle on a wire. Maybe it was a test after all. Or maybe the wire was clipped to the back of the vest, and they would give it to the bombers only at the last minute. Or maybe al-Jazar would detonate the bombs by remote control.

Faraz's heart was beating hard. It felt like it had moved up in his chest, making it hard for him to swallow. Adrenaline surged. Tunnel vision took over. His ability to reason was failing. They were getting very close to the hotel. He was near the point of fight or flight.

At a bend in the road, al-Jazar led them down an embankment into a gully. This was the final farewell. This was where he would find out how the rest of the mission would go.

The fighters gathered around the foreigners. Al-Jazar stood in front of Faraz and Ismail, stared at each for several seconds as if looking for any sign of weakness. The inspection seemed to last forever. Finally, al-Jazar spoke. "You will not be *shahid* tonight. We have other plans for you. These vests, they are for practice."

Faraz couldn't help letting out a sigh of relief. He bent at the waist, nearly threw up.

Ismail stood tall. "I will do it, Commander." He sounded disappointed.

"Not tonight, my brother. But you will have your time to fight for Allah, and to be a *shahid*, if it is His will. Now, you two will stay here." Al-Jazar cocked his head, and most of the men followed him into the town. Two fighters stayed to guard the foreigners.

Faraz regained his composure. He had come so close to blowing his cover and getting himself killed. He didn't think about what would happen next until Ismail said, "Look, there."

Faraz turned his attention toward the hotel. He saw the team approach. The fighters sprayed gunfire through the windows into the celebration. The *rat-tat-tat* sounded particularly severe. He thought he saw several people inside fall. He lowered his head.

"Do not turn away," one of the fighters ordered. "It is Allah's work."

Anger rose in Faraz. He wanted to jump the man, beat him to death. But that was not an option. Faraz balled his fists and looked back toward the hotel. The team moved closer, firing directly into the room from two sides. Even from a distance, the gunfire was loud, as were the screams. It was a bloodbath, without the need for suicide bombers.

Faraz felt sick. Once again, he had participated in a terrorist attack. Once again, he had done nothing to stop it.

He talked himself down. It would have happened even if he hadn't been there. Letting it happen was part of his job. If he succeeded, he would stop much wider carnage. But that didn't make it any easier.

The fighters broke off their attack and ran back toward Faraz and the others, who joined them in sprinting to the vehicles. They were speeding toward camp only five minutes after the shooting had started.

Faraz stared out the window, working hard not to appear as upset as he was. The fighters were whooping and congratulating each other. He heard Jamal moaning in the back.

When they came into the camp, there was a festive atmosphere. The fighters spilled out of the vehicles to hug and high-five each other. Faraz and Ismail stood apart, still wearing the vests. Ismail was smiling, having passed the test and witnessed a victory. Faraz should have smiled, too, but he couldn't.

Al-Jazar approached them. "We can take these off now," he said, reaching to unclip Ismail's vest. "You two did well tonight. We need brave men."

"What will happen to Jamal?" Faraz asked.

Al-Jazar grunted. He shouted something, and one of the fighters got Jamal out of the vehicle. His face was bloody, his nose askew.

Jamal collapsed at the commander's feet. When he looked up, Faraz saw the panic in his eyes. "Please, Commander, please," was all Jamal could say.

Some of the other foreigners had been roused from sleep and came out to join the celebration. They held back when they saw Jamal.

Faraz got his vest off and, moving slowly, he put it on

the ground. He assumed it didn't have real explosives in it, but he wasn't taking any chances.

"Gather 'round," al-Jazar said. He waved his hand toward Faraz and Ismail. "These two men did well tonight. They showed their commitment to Allah and His jihad." There was a round of polite applause.

Then al-Jazar turned toward Jamal, still cowering on the ground. "But this coward was weak," the commander shouted, then kicked Jamal in the ribs. "We have no room for cowards." He threw his arms out and turned in a circle, as if asking whether there were any other cowards in the group.

Then he turned back toward Jamal and spat. "All of you must be prepared to perform Allah's will at any time. All of you! At any time! Tonight, we moved against an easy target, infidels from your countries who come here to spread immorality. Soon, we will again move against a much tougher enemy, and you must all be ready. This enemy is a usurper, a man who left us at the mercy of the dictator Assad for decades, and now returns and claims to be our leader. We will not allow it!"

The Syrian fighters cheered, and a couple of them pointed their weapons into the air, ready to fire in support of what al-Jazar had said. He held up a hand to stop them.

Al-Jazar continued. "This sand cat will be punished. But he will have another chance. We need all the manpower we can bring to this fight. But I warn you all. Do not fail me. The time for second chances is over. The time for action is here. Rest now. We shall double our training schedule starting tomorrow. No more building and painting. You are all fighters now."

* * *

Alone in his tent, Faraz realized that al-Jazar's speech was confirmation that the rift among Syrian terrorist groups was deeper than Washington suspected. It also meant al-Jazar was now not so much a rival to al-Souri as an enemy. Al-Jazar would not know al-Souri's plans. Faraz was in the wrong place to accomplish his mission.

Damn those idiots for sending him here, risking his life on a wild-goose chase.

Faraz took deep breaths, as the docs had taught him. He directed his thoughts to something else, anything else.

He thought about his mother. That was a mistake.

It was past midnight in Syria, but approaching dinner-time in San Diego. *Mohr* would be eating alone in the kitchen. Or maybe she was having dinner with her sister, Johnny's mother.

That sounded better. He would go with that. They still had each other to lean on, to cry with over their sons.

Faraz focused on his breathing. He had to keep it together, or al-Jazar would get him killed, and it would all have been for nothing.

Chapter Twenty-six

The next afternoon in the base gym, Bridget was wishing she could get an update on Faraz. Better yet, that he or someone would deliver the intel they needed so she could get a ticket home. She was feeling the strain of trying to run her new Washington-based task force from Baghdad.

Meanwhile, the conversations and emails with Will seemed more and more stilted. Bridget could tell he was going stir crazy sitting at home and doing rehab and not much else. She suspected he was drinking too much.

She blew past four miles on the treadmill and turned up the speed, punishing the machine with her frustration. The gym was almost as big as the workspace and had been the dictator's diplomatic reception room. The crystal chandeliers were impressive. The faux gold décor was good for a laugh. The room was crowded with people who had few other recreational options.

As the digital counter turned over to six miles, Bridget slowed to cooldown pace and stepped off, still breathing hard. Her racerback top was soaked through. The tip of her ponytail was wet from the sweat on her back.

Bridget wiped her face with her towel and headed for

the exit, eager for a shower and some chow. She nearly bumped into Carter as he was coming in.

"Hello, Ms. Davenport," he said. "You look like you've had a good workout."

"Hi, Carter. Not my best look, I guess. And I told you, call me Bridget."

"I think it's a fine look," he said, making Bridget wonder what her sweat-wet T-shirt was showing. "Perhaps we can grab some suppah laytah, once I've had a chance to at least trah to match your dedication."

Bridget wondered again if that accent could possibly be real. "I don't know . . ." She started.

Carter cocked his head to the side. "Aw, come on. Give a Georgia boy a break. It's only a meal with several thousand chaperones in the D-FAC." The D-FAC was the dining facility—what they used to call the mess hall.

Bridget exhaled. "All right. How much time do you need?"

"Shall we say an houah, if that's not too long?"

"Sure. Meet you at the entrance."

"Yes, ma'am. Operation Suppah shall commence at . . ." He looked at his watch. "At 1850 at the main buffet."

"Operation Suppah?"

"Too much?"

"Yeah, a bit."

"Apologies. See you in an houah, then?"

"Sure." Bridget's limited enthusiasm for this venture had already dropped several points. But hey, there's a war on.

Bridget didn't like loitering outside the D-FAC and being checked out by the hundreds of men streaming in for dinner. It was her own fault. Her obsession with being on time meant she was always early, and this was the downside. As a bonus, she probably looked too eager when Carter came ambling up the path, freshly showered and shaved, wearing pristine khakis and a sand-colored T-shirt that showed off his just-toned biceps.

"So sorry to keep you waiting," he said. "Am I late?"

"No. Right on time."

"As we at Spotlight always strive to be." He gave her a broad smile.

Bridget returned a weak one. She didn't want to encourage him. Mentioning Spotlight was not a good move on his part. Bridget was no fan of security contractors. It was true, they got some things done that needed doing, but they were difficult to control and tended to be arrogant. They didn't have to kowtow to most of the military and government people they met. The company's name was exactly what it worked hard to avoid, the spotlight. Perhaps their notorious founder had a sense of irony.

"Shall we eat?" Bridget suggested, trying for a tone that said "let's get this over with."

Carter seemed to understand. "Absolutely. After you."

At the end of the chow line, Bridget grabbed a bottle of water. Carter took a can of nonalcoholic beer from a cooler and showed it to her.

"It's sad, but one must make sacrifices for the cause."

"You won't catch me drinking that stuff. I'm holding out for my next glass of Bordeaux."

"Not within a thousand clicks of here, I'm afraid."

"Now that is sad."

Carter laughed, and Bridget regretted making the joke.

She didn't want to appear to be flirting. On the other hand, she was stuck with him for half an hour or so. Might as well make the best of it.

They found seats in the annex tent, and Carter scanned the crowd. Bridget couldn't tell whether he didn't want to see any of his colleagues, or whether he did want to see them, or whether scanning his surroundings was an occupational tic.

The pepper steak in sauce with rice and mixed vegetables was not at the level of the chicken Kiev, but it was pretty good. Carter asked about her background, and was duly impressed with her West Point degree, combat zone tours, and PhD.

"So, tell me about Carter Holloway," Bridget said.

"Oh, the usual. Country boy makes good, joins the marines, gets out before they kill him, G.I. Bill to UGA, degree in law enforcement, gainful employment. But the petty crimes of Effingham County, which saw fit to hire me as a civilian investigator, simply could not hold my interest. Certainly not compared to all this." He swept his hand over the room.

"Effingham County?"

"Yes, ma'am. Accent on the 'Effing.' " He stopped himself. "Sorry." Bridget gave him a "don't be silly" look. "Effingham County is on the Alabama border, about as far from my home as you can get without crossing state lines. But it was no improvement. Let's just say, when Spotlight came a-callin', Baghdad sounded like an upgrade."

Bridget couldn't help laughing at that. "Hard to imagine, but I'll take your word for it."

Some men came by carrying trays of food.

"Good evening, sir," said a short, stocky man with brown skin, black hair, and a bushy moustache.

"Hi, guys," Carter replied.

"Aren't you going to introduce us to your friend?" the man said.

"Bridget, this is Ben Castillo, my number two. Good man, even though he's from New York. And these guys are . . . irrelevant, actually."

That got a round of grumbling.

"Gentlemen, this is Ms. Davenport."

"Well, ma'am, it's very nice to meet you," Castillo said. "But I recommend you watch out for this guy."

"I have already been warned," Bridget said, getting a laugh from the men.

"Don't you men have something else to do?" Carter asked. "If not, I'm sure I can find something."

"Not necessary, sir," Castillo said. "You two have a nice evening." He smiled at Bridget and led the men to a table on the other side of the room.

"Those are your guys?" Bridget asked.

"Part of the team. Good men."

"Yeah, they seem okay."

"You sound surprised."

Bridget smiled. She was surprised. So far, the Spotlight guys she had met did not live down to their reputation.

For the rest of dinner, the conversation flowed more easily than Bridget had expected. Robin was right—Carter was far from the worst of the men Bridget had met in war zones. He had a surprisingly philosophical view of war, especially this one. He was amusing, unfailingly polite, and not bad looking, for a jarhead. And he had gray eyes that grew crow's-feet when he smiled. Bridget was surprised she hadn't noticed that before.

Carter offered to walk Bridget back to her trailer.

"Oh, thanks, but no. I think I can find it. See you around, Carter."

"I'm glad I ran into you. I hope we'll do this again soon."

"Sure." Bridget turned for her trailer and stopped suppressing a smile. That had been remarkably pleasant. Just to have dinner with a man, a bit of banter, some laughs. It was just dinner, but it was amazing how big a difference "just dinner" could make to one's outlook.

Bridget diverted to the office to check the secure email. She ended up working for over two hours. When she leaned back to stretch, she noticed that even pushing ten p.m., the room was half full. She decided to call it a night.

A notification popped up on her personal account—a message from Will. "Miss you. Have time to talk?"

Bridget sighed, and her shoulders slumped. Now she felt guilty about her dinner with Carter. But that was silly. It was just dinner. He was just an acquaintance, a colleague of sorts.

Anyway, she was tired, not in the mood for a talk about Will's injuries and how awful his day was, or even how much he missed her.

Bridget had only been in the crucible of the war zone for a couple of weeks, but she already felt that familiar detachment from the real world—the feeling that this was the only world that was truly real. She'd only called her parents once, falling back into her old pattern. Her father called it the Black Hole Effect.

She got up and went to her trailer. Tomorrow, she'd tell Will she had already been in bed when his message came in.

Chapter Twenty-seven

Al-Jazar either had plans for a big operation or was working out his anger on the male recruits. He had the foreigners learning weapons handling and attack tactics and running rings around the outside of the camp in the midday sun.

Faraz pretended to be in as much pain as his comrades, collapsing after the last lap and breathing heavily.

"It was never like this," Nic said between gulps of air.

"Something has changed," Faraz said. "It seems al-Jazar is in a hurry to get us ready to do something."

"Yeah. I'd like to say I didn't sign up for this, but I guess I did."

Faraz pushed himself to his feet and offered Nic a hand. "Well, you seem to have lost a few pounds, at least."

"Thanks a lot."

"Anyway, I hope al-Jazar knows what he's doing."

"Why would you say that? Are you some sort of expert all of a sudden?"

"No. But even in a video game, emotion can overwhelm strategy and tactics."

"Yeah, well, this ain't no video game, is it?"

"No, it's not. Let's get cleaned up. I'm starving."

* * *

After dinner, Faraz lingered at one of the picnic tables, trying to figure out how he could escape. For now, there was no way. Maybe al-Jazar's eagerness would make him reckless. Certainly, the man was arrogant enough to do something stupid. That would be Faraz's chance. For now, he would have to wait, see how things developed.

Faraz was about to go to his tent when some of the women came out of the kitchen. Having finished their work cooking and serving the men, it was their time to eat.

Cindy broke off from the others and came toward Faraz's table, with Amira trailing behind. "Mind if we join you, Karim?"

"Not at all," Faraz said.

Cindy sat directly across from him. Amira took the spot next to her and gave Faraz another demure smile.

"You two have any idea what's going on?" he asked.

Cindy responded. "What do you mean?"

"I mean the extra training, al-Jazar's mood. It seems like something is about to happen."

"Believe me, we'll be the last to know," Cindy said. "The guys used to complain that they could only work in the camp or be suicide bombers. Now, they complain that they're training to be fighters."

"It's just a bit of a surprise, I guess," Faraz said.

"Well—"

"Cindy!" came the call from the kitchen door. It was Katya, the German head of the kitchen crew. "I need you in here."

"She's a taskmaster, that one," Cindy whispered. She shrugged and got up with her tray. "See you later."

Faraz and Amira sat in uncomfortable silence. She was short, maybe five foot three, he estimated. From what he could tell from her untucked, long-sleeved shirt and calf-length dress, she was neither chubby nor thin, with large breasts that no amount of baggy shirt could hide. Her hair was covered, as always. He had thought she was pretty from the day he'd met her, but tonight her cheeks sagged and her brown eyes looked tired.

"Remind me, how long have you been here?"

"Couple of months now." Amira sounded unhappy.

"You don't seem all that pleased about it."

"I came here to be part of the jihad. It's not a vacation, is it?" Amira's South London accent gave her words a sense of irritation and ennui, like she was talking about work in a shop or a factory.

"No, it is not," Faraz said. "But I'm new. I'm still excited to be here. I already went out on an operation. But for the women . . ." He shrugged and tilted his head toward the kitchen.

Amira looked at him with a flash of anger. "Yes, for the women it's different. We are equal but different. They taught us how to shoot, but only to help defend the camp if we get attacked. Beyond that . . . well, don't ask me if I'm having fun cooking and cleaning for you."

"I didn't ask if you were having fun."

Amira paused, looking down at what was left of her food. Then she looked up at Faraz. "Well, you asked if I was happy. I'm not here to be happy. I'm here to work for the great cause."

She didn't sound sarcastic. But as Faraz studied her face, he could tell he had hit a nerve. "What do you really want to say?"

Amira sighed. "I have no right to complain."

"We all have the God-given right to complain. Well, that may not be in the Koran, but it's what we say in my neighborhood in Detroit."

That got a small smile from Amira, at least. "Even so, truly, I should not complain."

"And yet, you seem, well, I don't know you very well, but you seem sad, I guess."

She didn't deny it. Faraz let the silence linger until Amira said, "We should not talk about these things." She returned her attention to her dinner.

Faraz moved his hand closer to hers, but didn't touch her. "Please, Amira, tell me."

Amira looked at him, seeming to consider whether she wanted to confide in him, whether she could trust him. There was no reason to trust him, but she clearly had something to say. Amira looked back down at her plate and blurted it out. "I am to marry a fighter."

Faraz wasn't sure about her tone. Resignation? Anger? That sadness again. Definitely not the tone of a bride-to-be.

"Wow," he said. "Who is it?"

"He is a fighter from another camp. I have not met him yet."

"You haven't met him?" Faraz's surprise was genuine.

"That's the way it's done."

"Can you say no?"

Amira looked at him like he must be some kind of idiot. "Of course, I can say no under Allah's law. But then what? What sort of punishment would they give me? What sort of future would I have? When I came here, I was naive, but I was not as stupid as you are. I knew

I would marry a hero, provide a new generation for the jihad. But . . ." She continued staring at him, but stopped talking, as if she didn't know what she wanted to say. Or perhaps she did know, but wasn't sure she should.

"But what?"

"But nothing. Maybe you should mind your own business." Amira lifted her tray and started to slide her legs out from under the picnic table.

"Amira," Faraz said.

She stopped and looked at him with impatience bordering on disdain.

"I'm sorry if I was out of line. I promise, your secret is safe with me."

Amira finished the maneuver of disengaging from the picnic table. Faraz watched her skirt swing as she went through the kitchen door.

Chapter Twenty-eight

It was dinnertime in Baghdad, too. Bridget was eating at her desk—a container of yogurt and a bag of potato chips. She had little appetite after reading the detailed report on the hotel attack. A dozen American and European aid workers dead, more wounded, their program to teach young Syrians English and math destroyed. She read their bios, looked at their photos—smiling, hopeful. It was irredeemably sad.

Bridget switched her screen to the latest data on the sharp increase in terrorist chatter. The secure phone on her desk rang.

It was Liz Michaels at the Pentagon. "Any thoughts on the new data?"

"Well, hello to you, too."

"Sorry, I just came out of a meeting where everyone in the building called for more intel to explain the chatter."

"Good. More pressure. I was running low. And no, I don't have any particular insights. I was hoping the team had some."

"I can only tell you that the pattern is disturbingly

similar to what we saw, in retrospect, in the run-up to November, which is why paranoia is at an all-time high."

"An all-time high in your lengthy experience." It was an unnecessary jab that came from Bridget's own multi-pronged frustration.

It took Liz an extra second to respond. "Yeah, whatever, 'in my lengthy experience,' and seemingly everyone else's, too."

"Okay, sorry." Bridget took a breath. "How's Hadley taking it?"

"He was under control in this meeting, but I could see he was ready to blow. He doesn't want anything like November on his watch. He'd have called you himself, but he had to run to a meeting at the White House. I know you and Blowback have only been over there for two weeks, but I'm sure you'll be hearing from Hadley before long."

"Believe me, his desire for results is no greater than mine."

After the call, Bridget stared at the data and picked at her dinner. She found herself wishing Carter would come by and take her to the D-FAC. She needed the distraction. But he was away on a mission.

She should have been wishing Will was there. She did, up to a point. But that was impossible. Carter had the advantage of at least being in the same part of the world, and expected back within a few days. Any fantasy about a reunion with Will involved projecting months into the future. Carter also came with none of the long-term commitment she had never been good at.

Bridget put that out of her mind and thought about the third man in her life: Faraz. Just as she had been the key to getting him out of Gitmo a few weeks ago, now he was the key to getting her out of Baghdad.

And where the hell was he? Bridget threw the second half of the bag of chips into her trash can.

Al-Souri could tell that Nazim had bad news as soon as he came into the office. The man never met his eyes and stood at awkward attention in front of the desk.

"Tell me," al-Souri said.

"I am sorry to report, Commander . . ."

"Go on," al-Souri said, impatient now.

"Some of the faction leaders have agreed to meet, but several refuse, including al-Jazar. It seems he is intimidating the others. Already, one who agreed has changed his answer."

Al-Souri inhaled sharply. "Fools."

"Yes, *sahib*."

"Do they think they can defy me?" His voice was angry, but he kept his volume low.

"*Sahib*, I am sorry, but they still see you as new to this war and, in spite of your accomplishments in Afghanistan, as . . . how shall I say? Untested, perhaps."

"Untested?"

"*Sahib*, these are simple men. They must see power demonstrated in front of them. Stories from far away are, for them . . . well, just stories."

"And November? Is that just a story, too?"

Nazim did not respond, but the answer was clearly yes.

Al-Souri considered that. Years ago, he had not been so different from those men. They had been suffering here for decades, while he had been away. In recent years, they had taken up arms and suffered more, while he was still not with them. Now, he had returned and claimed to be their leader.

Up to a point, he could understand their doubts. But he was al-Souri, mastermind of attacks around the world, brother-in-arms to the great martyr Ibn Jihad. Now, although these men refused to accept it, he was taking their struggle to a new level, linking it to the global jihad, and to the money al-Malik could provide.

Al-Souri could not allow anyone to question his authority. "How many refuse to meet?"

Nazim swallowed hard. "About half, *sahib*."

Al-Souri stroked his beard. He looked out his window at the camp, its fence, and the desert hills beyond. Then he looked back at Nazim, still standing at attention. "Sit, please."

Nazim sat and leaned forward to wait for his commander's orders.

"Perhaps you are right," al-Souri said.

"*Sahib*?"

"They must see the power, as our foreign enemies saw it in November."

"We cannot defeat them all, Commander."

"Nor would we want to. We need those men. We must defeat them all by defeating one. In one stroke, we must end the doubt. And we must do it quickly."

Nazim's look changed from confusion to admiration.

"You wanted to attack al-Jazar's camp," al-Souri said. "I said no. But perhaps you understand these men better than I do, or better than I did before now."

Nazim smiled at the praise from his mentor.

"Al-Malik will not be happy," al-Souri continued. "But

I cannot do what he wants unless I unify the movement. You will get your wish."

"*Sahib*?"

"We will attack al-Jazar."

"Thank you, *sahib*."

"We will have one chance. Our attack must be decisive. We must have a victory, but more importantly, we must make a statement."

"Yes, Commander."

Al-Souri sighed. "Unfortunately, I cannot do it."

"You cannot?"

"No. I must go to meet with al-Malik and some men from . . . well, from outside. They want to meet al-Souri face-to-face before they will finance our plans. I will be away for two days, maybe three." Al-Souri paused, then looked directly at Nazim. "You will lead the attack."

Nazim smiled broadly now.

Chapter Twenty-nine

Faraz found it hard to focus on the next day's combat training or on his need to escape. He thought mostly about Amira.

When the men were dismissed, he ran to the showers. He was among the first in the food line, but Amira wasn't serving. She must be in the kitchen, cleaning up. He parked himself at his usual table and waited.

Amira did not appear.

"C'mon, Karim," Nic said as the area was emptying out. "Quick soccer game before bed?"

"No, thanks. I'm beat." Faraz walked with him to the center of camp, then headed toward the tents. He found a spot where he could lean on a building and keep an eye on most of the camp. If Amira came out of the women's area, he'd see her.

It was half an hour before dark when she appeared. She was walking the path that circled the camp inside the fence. She walked slowly, her shoulders hunched. She stopped and put her hand on the wall, as if for support.

Faraz moved to intercept her. He cut through the tents

and behind a storage building, doing his best to make it appear as if he had run into her by chance.

"Hi, Amira." Now he could see her wet cheeks framed by her hijab.

She looked at him, obviously irritated he had seen her like this.

"I won't ask how you are," he said.

Amira sighed. "Good." She walked past him, and he hurried to catch up.

"C'mon, Amira. Talk to me."

Amira stopped, and Faraz nearly ran into her. She looked both ways on the path. They were alone.

"I don't want to talk to you. I want to hit you right now," she said.

"Why?"

"I want to hit something, and you're here, annoying me."

"Well, if it will help." Faraz stood in front of her, ready to take the blow.

Amira balled her fists, but kept them by her sides. "Look, Karim, I want to be left alone. All right?"

"No. Sorry. Not all right. We're all in this together."

Amira glared at him.

"If you don't want to talk, at least let me walk with you."

Amira pursed her lips. But making a scene would only have drawn more people. "All right, if you must."

Faraz moved aside so she could pass. They walked in silence for a short distance and came to the side gate. Two fighters greeted them, AK-47s in hand. Faraz made a show of looking up toward the sky. "It will still be light for a while. Can we walk outside the walls?"

The fighters looked at each other, and one cocked his head. "Be back before dark."

Faraz led Amira out, then guided her to the left toward a small grove of parched trees.

"That was a good thought," she said, finally softening. "It's nice to be outside the camp."

Faraz took a chance and cast a line into uncertain water. "Yes. We're no closer to freedom, but it feels like we are."

Amira looked surprised. "You could be punished for saying such a thing."

"Well, now we each know something about the other that could lead to punishment."

"What do you know about me?"

"That you don't want to marry your fighter."

They entered the woods, where they could no longer be seen from the camp. "Let's sit for a while," Faraz said.

He picked a spot under one of the largest trees so they could both lean up against it, shoulder to shoulder, facing slightly away from each other. The ground was dry, although this was supposed to be the rainy season. The smells of the small wooded area were a welcome respite from the body odor, latrines, and weapons oil smells of the camp.

"So," Amira said, "you just got here, and you speak of freedom."

"You forget," Faraz said. "I went on an operation. They put a vest on me. I saw them mow down unarmed civilians—aid workers. I could see them. They looked like friends from back home. I was like them not long ago. Then al-Jazar humiliated Jamal. You were right in what you said. I didn't expect a vacation. But it's all a bit of a shock, to be honest."

"I'm surprised to hear you say that. You seemed like you were ready for jihad from the day you arrived."

"I was. But I don't have to tell you that the reality of jihad is pretty different from what I expected sitting back home in Detroit."

"It's not much like London, either."

Faraz thought Amira was making a joke. He smiled and turned toward her, but she was looking at the ground, upset.

"So, will you marry this fighter?" he asked.

The tears exploded from her eyes. She bent forward and put her face in her hands.

Faraz reached out with his left hand and touched her back. "Amira, I'm sorry. I shouldn't have mentioned it." He kept his hand where it was, surprised that she didn't object, prolonging the first real human contact he'd had in months.

"No," she said between sobs. "I need to get this out. I need to be ready when I meet him, the day after tomorrow. We are to be married next week."

She looked up at Faraz, her eyes wet, tears streaking her cheeks. She stared at him for several seconds, seeming to contemplate whether she could trust him further. She sighed, surrendering, as if she had nothing more to lose. Although they were well out of earshot of anyone else, she lowered her voice. "Honestly . . . Oh, dear God . . . Honestly, I think this was all a huge mistake." She burst into tears again. "I was living a comfortable life in London, having fun, clubbing. Then I decided that was all nonsense, which it was. But now . . ."

Amira twisted toward Faraz and put her head on his

shoulder, her left arm around his neck, her tears wetting his shirt.

It took Faraz a second to think what to do. "Amira, it's all right," he said. He put his right hand on her shoulder, almost hugging her now, but dared not pull her in closer.

She moved away a few inches, angry again, but apparently not from his touch. "It's not all right. Don't say it's all right. It's crap, and there's nothing I can do about it."

"Okay, okay. Sorry." Faraz kept his hand on her shoulder. "But maybe *we* can do something about it."

"What are you talking about?"

He was talking about escaping and rescuing Amira in the process. But he couldn't say that. Faraz played for time. "At least we can support each other. Maybe the two of us can make something happen."

"Make what happen?" She wiped her cheeks and sniffed, trying to stop the sobs. She sat back, breaking his light hold on her shoulder.

"I don't know. I don't know." Faraz was scrambling to find the right thing to say. "Maybe this is a start."

"What's a start? A start to what?"

"This. Talking. Honesty. Maybe a shared desire to do something."

He thought he saw a glimmer of hope on her face, but it faded quickly. She smiled a sort of resigned smile. "If you want honesty, Karim, I honestly think you're full of shit."

She let out a small giggle. It was the first time Faraz had heard her laugh. She dried her eyes with her sleeve. "You say do something. There's nothing we can do." After a short silence, she added, "But it sounds good." Her smile widened.

Faraz smiled back at her. "Maybe we can come up with a plan."

"What plan?"

He had run out things to say, so he blurted it out. "An escape plan."

"You are truly bonkers." She sniffed again, done with crying. "What do you think, we just walk down the road back to England? Or America?"

"No. We'd need a vehicle and—"

"Trying to get out, we would get ourselves killed. No, Karim, this is the life we chose, and we chose it for a reason. I'll be all right. I need to get my head 'round it, that's all." She stood.

Faraz hurried to stand, too. He reached out with his left hand and took her right. He looked into her eyes. "Listen, we have two days until you meet your fighter. Let's at least think about it."

Amira broke his gaze, staring off into the darkening sky, but she didn't pull away. After a few seconds, she looked down again. "I think false hope is worse than no hope. Let it go. This life is difficult, but it has meaning. I won't go back to clubbing and kebabs in South London."

Faraz smiled. "I have no desire to go back to video games in Detroit, either."

He got to hear her giggle again. Then she stopped. "Maybe he won't be so bad."

"Yeah," Faraz lied. "A lot of them are okay." He studied her face, framed by her hijab in the fading light. She was pretty when she didn't look sad. Her jawline was soft and her cheeks a bit wide. Her medium-brown skin was perfect, and Faraz had always found dark eyes intriguing.

He acted on instinct, desire, not calculation or mission requirements. He put two fingers of his right hand under Amira's chin. He lifted her head so she faced him, fresh tears forming in her eyes. Faraz leaned in, and she raised her lips to meet his.

The kiss was tender, innocent, too brief.

Amira put a hand on his chest. "We shouldn't."

"You're right, we shouldn't." But he kissed her again. He leaned in farther, and they kissed more deeply. Her hand moved from his chest to the back of his neck.

He eased them down onto the ground, and their bodies came together in a full embrace.

Darkness fell. The guards changed.

As quietly as they could, Faraz and Amira made love under the tree.

Faraz woke up first, freezing cold and half naked. He was instantly alert. If they'd been missed, there would be a search on. But he heard nothing. Praise Allah, the guards had forgotten them.

He didn't know the time, but it was late and very dark. Billions of stars twinkled in the desert sky.

Amira's blouse was open, and her skirt was rumpled around her thighs. He touched her shoulder. "Shhh."

Amira sat up, pulling the front of her blouse closed. She looked at him and giggled. "We have been very naughty. How long did we sleep?"

"I don't know, but it's late. The guards will be closing the side gate. We need to hurry."

She pulled him in for a long kiss.

"Amira," he said, "this was . . . I can't even begin . . . but we need to go, and we need a story for the guards."

"Right. Okay. We'll tell them I twisted my ankle. I'll lean on you, give them a smile. They'll buy it."

"All right. I don't have any better idea." He stood, put on his shirt, closed his pants, and offered Amira a hand. She stood and straightened her hijab and her clothes.

They kissed again—a deep, tender kiss—and they held each other in a long embrace. "Oh, Karim," she said. "We shouldn't fool ourselves."

"I'll figure something out."

Amira sighed and took half a step back. "No. You won't. There's nothing to figure out. This was . . . yeah, I can't even begin, either. It was beautiful. And thank you. It gave me some clarity. Now we both have to do what we have to do."

"I don't know . . ."

"Yes, you do. We both do. We'll always have this moment, but this has to be good-bye." She put her hands on his cheeks and kissed him, as if searing the memory into her brain. "Now come on. We have to go."

Amira took Faraz's hand and led him out of the trees.

He didn't argue, but inside he was screaming "no, this cannot be good-bye!"

Faraz hadn't made love to a woman in a long time, hadn't felt this way about a woman in a long time, maybe ever. It couldn't end this way. She couldn't go off to marry another man. He would come up with something. That was his mission now.

Amira went into the fake limp and put a hand on Faraz's shoulder for support.

Halfway to the side gate, they heard the first explosions.

Chapter Thirty

"Fire!" Nazim shouted at his men in a small grove of trees on the opposite side of the camp. Three teams dropped a second mortar round into their tubes, stepped back, and covered their ears.

Moments later, the fusillade landed in al-Jazar's camp.

"And again!" Nazim ordered. "Strike team, stand by."

A third volley of mortars flew as five drivers gunned the engines of their SUVs, ready to speed twenty of al-Souri's men to his opponent's camp.

Nazim moved toward the vehicles but stopped next to a fighter who was kneeling on the ground, a rocket-propelled grenade launcher on his shoulder, its targeting sight pressed to his right eye.

Nazim knelt next to the man and said, "Now."

The whoosh of the RPG sent the shooter teetering into Nazim, and they both nearly fell. As they steadied themselves, the camp's front gate exploded.

Nazim ran to the open door of the lead vehicle. "Go! Go! Go!"

* * *

The first mortar volley stopped Faraz and Amira in their tracks, and they both dove to the ground. After the second barrage, they started running toward the gate. They saw that the two new guards were pulling it closed.

"Wait! Wait!" Faraz shouted. "We are with you."

The guards looked at them and raised their weapons.

"No!" Amira said. "We are from the camp. It's me, Amira."

One of the guards seemed to recognize her. He lowered his weapon.

Faraz and Amira pushed past the guards. "Close the gate!" Faraz said, and he helped the men pull it shut and set the bolt and chain.

The guard said, "Why were you—" He was interrupted by the third salvo from Nazim's mortars.

"It doesn't matter," Faraz said. "We must defend the camp."

The two fighters ran for their duty stations.

Amira looked at Faraz. He could see she was scared. He wanted to comfort her, to say good night, but there was no time.

"The women have duties," she said. "I must go." She stroked his cheek, then turned and ran along the perimeter path toward the women's quarters.

Faraz didn't have a chance to say anything. He could only watch her go.

Then he turned and followed the guards the other way, toward the main gate, just as it blew to pieces barely forty meters ahead of him.

Faraz hit the ground, avoiding the shrapnel. He crawled off the main path, went behind a building, and emerged on the other side to see the attackers' SUVs speeding toward the opening where the gate used to be.

He ran behind another building toward the headquarters. He needed a weapon.

Gunfire sprayed in all directions as soon as the vehicles came into the camp. Faraz crouched at the edge of a storage building, waiting for a break so he could cross a small gap to the headquarters. Al-Jazar's fighters were starting to fire back. They had literally been caught sleeping, aside from the small guard contingent, several of whom had been killed by the mortars or the RPG.

One of al-Jazar's men ran out the back door of the headquarters building toward Faraz. As he crossed the gap, he was cut down by a hail of bullets. He fell, delivering his AK-47 at Faraz's feet.

Faraz took it, used the butt to break the lock on the back door of the storage building, and went inside for cover. The wooden structure didn't provide protection from the attackers' high-velocity ammunition, but at least he couldn't be seen.

It was dark inside. Faraz stumbled several times trying to get to the front of the building. He looked out a small window to see the devastation. Nazim's men had dismounted their vehicles and continued to fire. When several of al-Jazar's men mounted a counterattack from the rear of the camp, Nazim's team tossed grenades and finished off the survivors with bursts from their AKs.

Two groups of half a dozen men each fanned out to the right and left, shooting anything that moved and spraying tents and buildings at random. The main force stayed by the vehicles, with guns pointing in all directions.

Another SUV arrived. Several men helped take out the

grenade launcher and hefted it onto one man's shoulder. He took aim at the headquarters and fired.

The explosion destroyed most of the building, and a team of attackers stormed into the wreckage, guns on automatic.

Faraz had to get out of there. He went back to the rear door of the storage building, checked the path, and moved to his right, toward the side gate. The attacking teams had passed this area, and he was able to slip from cover to cover. The chains he had helped secure a few minutes earlier were gone and the gate was open. Outside, he found Nic, Jamal, Ismail, and Latif.

"What are you doing?" he asked.

"We don't know what to do," Nic said. "The camp is destroyed. Everyone is dead."

"The camp is not yet destroyed, and we are still alive," Faraz said. "So are others trapped inside. We have to attack."

"With what?" Nic asked. The other men looked scared, more likely to run into the woods than to reenter the camp.

"If you run, you'll be killed as soon as the attackers see you, or you'll die in the desert. Follow me. Take weapons from fallen fighters as we go."

Faraz turned and went in through the gate. Only Ismail followed. Faraz looked back at the others. "Now!" he shouted, raising his weapon. "Or I swear to God I'll shoot you myself." Nic and Jamal move slowly but came through the gate.

Al-Jazar's remaining men were fighting back now, and a battle raged near the kitchen. Faraz led the men in that direction. They took cover behind the building that housed the showers. There was a gap of several meters between their position and the next building.

"Follow me," Faraz said. "Stay low. Run fast. And keep firing."

Faraz stepped into the gap and opened up with his AK. Bent at the waist, he ran for the next bit of cover, then dove and rolled into a prone position behind the building. Nic, Ismail, and the teenager Latif ran with him, taking advantage of his cover fire.

Faraz saw that Jamal, the Kenyan who panicked during the attack on the aid workers, had stayed behind. "Come on," Faraz urged, "before they reload."

Jamal hesitated, frozen where he was.

"Now, Jamal. Now!" Faraz ordered.

Jamal ran, and a burst from an AK cut him down. Faraz fell to his knees, a few feet from Jamal but unable to help him.

Nic moved next to Faraz. "We have to do something."

"No," Faraz said, grabbing Nic's arm. "He's dead. If you go out there, you're dead, too."

"But—" Nic's argument was cut short by several more bullets hitting Jamal's body. "Oh my God." Nic's mouth opened in shock. "We're all dead."

"Stop that!" Faraz grabbed Nic's shirt. "Stay strong. Don't panic. We will get out of this. Now stay down."

Faraz peered around the edge of the building. He saw one of the attackers running away. He jumped back. "Take cover," he shouted.

A grenade exploded in the gap, tearing up Jamal's body and sending shrapnel flying into the team's hiding place. Several of them were wounded, including Nic, who took a piece of metal in his right thigh. Faraz had moved far enough away that he was okay.

He looked around the building again and saw the man who seemed to be in command of the attacking force take cover with some others behind one of the vehicles. Faraz caught a glimpse of his face before he turned the other way and shouted something in Arabic. He and his fighters covered their ears.

The RPG sailed over the attackers and hit the kitchen, killing or exposing most of al-Jazar's remaining fighters. The leader shouted again, and another RPG hit the women's barracks. Faraz gasped and got up to run toward the devastation.

Nic grabbed him. "Where are you going?"

"They hit the women's barracks."

"They hit everything. You just told me not to go out there."

Faraz shook him off. He looked at his small team cowering behind the building. He moved to the far edge and looked through the next gap. The attackers were firing toward what remained of the kitchen and the women's barracks. The leader rose from his crouch to move forward to another group of his fighters.

Faraz took half a step into the gap and raised his weapon. He got a bead on the leader and fired. The man fell, grabbing his left side. Faraz ducked back behind the building, half a second ahead of a hail of bullets.

Breathing heavily, Faraz moved back to his men. He was going to rally them for an assault when he heard shouting in Arabic. The attackers' gunfire stopped. There was more shouting. Then he heard vehicles moving.

Faraz took cover with his men as the attackers fired

several more rounds, seemingly at random. He heard no return fire.

Then there were shouts of "*Allahu akbar*," and the attackers fired into the air. Their vehicles threw up dirt as they sped out of camp.

Chapter Thirty-one

Faraz's ears were still ringing from the gunfire, but the camp was mercifully silent.

Then he heard the moans of the wounded and cries of "Allah!" and "No!" as the survivors tried to revive their fallen friends and realized they could not.

Faraz leaned out from behind the building to survey the ruins. All of the buildings and tents were damaged, and many had been destroyed. The electric generator had been blown to bits, so all the lights were out. The camp was lit only by the fires in several buildings, including the storage shed where he had hidden.

He went to the spot where the lead attacker had been standing when he was shot. There was a bloodstain on the ground. Faraz walked through the rubble, his AK at the ready. He saw a small tarp covering something.

"Move back! Move back!" he shouted. He ran to his left, grabbing Nic as he went and diving to the ground. He twisted his body around and yelled again at several people who had ignored his warning. "Take cover! There's a bomb!" He pointed to the tarp.

People scattered. The attackers' parting gift exploded

and threw nails and metal shards in all directions. A wall of shrapnel hit Ismail in the back, and he went down hard. Something hit Faraz in the right shoulder, spinning him around and sending a burning pain through his arm.

Faraz was angry at himself. He had pushed a little off the ground to issue his second warning, exposing his body to the shrapnel. He grunted from pain, got up slowly, and scanned the yard. He moved to Ismail. There were so many shrapnel holes in the back of his shirt and pants that Faraz couldn't count them. Ismail was clearly dead.

There was more shouting and moaning from the other side of the explosion. Faraz didn't see any more bombs, but he had no way to check thoroughly.

He ripped his right sleeve where the shrapnel had pierced it. He saw the head of a nail protruding from his arm. Army procedures said to leave it in until he got to a doctor, or at least a medic. Good luck. Faraz steadied himself, gripped the nail head with his left hand, and tugged on it.

The thing wouldn't move.

He twisted it. That worked better. He twisted and pulled, but the pain stopped him. He buckled to the ground, kneeling.

"You okay?" Nic came from behind him. He had a blood-soaked towel wrapped around his injured leg.

"Got this thing in my arm. Damn it."

"You should leave that. We'll see if the doctor survived."

"No time. He's probably dead, anyway." Faraz took hold of the nail again and pulled it out in one smooth, twisting motion. "Oh, damn that hurts." Blood oozed from the hole. "Take my ripped sleeve and tie it tight."

Nic took the sleeve and twisted it into position, wrapped it once around, and tied it.

"Tighter," Faraz said. "It's gotta hurt, or it's not doing its job." Nic pulled on the material. Faraz winced in pain. "That's better. It'll hold for a while, anyway. Thanks." He picked up his AK with his good arm.

"What now?" Nic asked.

"Now?" Faraz had only one thought. Amira. He said to Nic, "See who's alive. Post some guards. I gotta go."

Faraz took off at a run toward the women's part of camp. The kitchen was destroyed. He hoped she hadn't taken cover in there.

Beyond the kitchen, half the women's barracks was a pile of rubble, but the far side was still standing, its windows shattered and its wooden walls pockmarked with bullet holes. He ran up the three steps to the door and found it swinging on one hinge.

Inside, a woman's voice called for help. In the darkness, he could make out several bodies on the ground, some holding AK-47s in their hands. He crouched to check one of them, but she was dead.

"Karim." It was Cindy, sitting against the far wall. As he approached, he saw she was bleeding from a stomach wound. "Help me," she said, grabbing his leg with dwindling strength.

Faraz knelt down. "It's Okay. Let me look at it." He pulled away some of her ripped and bloodied shirt.

Cindy screamed. "Oh, shit that hurts!" Then she coughed hard, and blood spurted from her mouth. "I'm dying, Karim. Don't let me die."

Faraz saw that she was probably right. Even at a U.S. Army field hospital, she was likely a goner. Here, with no doctor and no supplies, there was nothing he could do.

He took a bedsheet from the floor, crumpled it into a ball, and pressed it to Cindy's wound. She screamed again.

"It's okay," he lied. "Press on this. Someone will come to help you. Have you seen Amira?"

Cindy took hold of the wadded sheet, but he could feel that she had little strength. Her eyes rolled back, her head flopped to the side, and she passed out. Her hands fell from the sheet, and the blood flowed again.

Faraz put the sheet back, put her limp right hand on top of it, and moved on. He checked each person on the floor. They were all dead, including the kitchen chief Katya. There was no sign of Amira.

Maybe she was farther back in the camp, in a safe place. Maybe she had gone out the back gate and fled to the woods. That would have been the smart move.

Through a gap in the damaged roof, Faraz saw the first hints of light in the sky. Outside, the crying and moaning continued. His view through the holes where the windows used to be showed some of the survivors trying to help the wounded. Others knelt on the ground and cried or wandered aimlessly, seemingly shell-shocked. People were calling the names of their friends, trying to find them amid the horror.

He turned back toward the room. "Amira," he said, hoping one of the still, dark shapes would answer. Then, louder, "Amira."

With the morning light growing stronger, he looked through a hole in the wall into what had been the other part of the barracks, the part that was little more than rubble. He moved to the opening.

That's when he saw her.

Amira was on her back under what was left of a

window, a rifle by her side. The wall was riddled with bullet holes. Her shirt and dress were covered with blood. Her hijab hung around her neck, exposing her short black hair.

"Amira!" Faraz screamed as he ran to her, fell to his knees, and dropped his weapon next to hers.

He checked her neck for a pulse. He slapped her face and shook her shoulders. He whispered a string of urgent requests: "Amira, wake up . . . Can you hear me? . . . Open your eyes . . . Amira, please . . . Please!"

But his tone was increasingly hopeless. He had known the truth as soon as he'd seen her. He sat back on his heels. There were four bullet holes in her clothes. Faraz looked at her face, undamaged, eyes closed, serene, beautiful. The lips he had kissed—minutes ago, it seemed—were slightly parted, as if ready for another.

He turned his gaze to the sky, toward Allah, and wailed, "Nooooo!" The sound surprised him. It came out not as a moan or cry. It was more of a howl, the noise an injured animal might make.

"No, No, No!" He stood, picked up the remains of a table, and threw it across the room. He grabbed a heavy beam that had fallen from the ceiling, but the weight of the thing put him off balance, and he fell next to it onto the floor, hitting his head on some debris.

Faraz ignored the pain. He looked at the brightening sky again. "No. Allah, please no," he said, but without conviction. His plea was more of a whimper. He knew it was no use.

He moved to Amira, cradled her head in his right hand, drew her close with his left. Faraz knelt there in the debris and blood, sobbing. He pulled her head to his chest, stroked her hair. His breath came in short gasps.

Faraz had experienced much death in the last year, but this was not like any of that. What he was feeling wasn't simple sadness or anger. It wasn't just revulsion, shock, or even despair. Surely, it was all of that. But there was something more. This was a crushing pain, a sharp, ripping, devastating blow to his body and spirit.

He should have kept her with him. Should have protected her. Should have run away with her, not taken her back into the kill zone. He should never have come here, never have taken this mission, never have met Amira.

As a soldier, Faraz had been trained to put his emotions aside in stressful situations, to focus on the mission. But as he held Amira amid the devastation, the emotions took over. The anger blew out of the box he'd put it in at Guantanamo.

They had taken everything from him. Now they'd taken Amira, too.

He eased her back onto the floor, fixed her hijab, closed her eyes with his fingers. He was almost in the Muslim prayer position. Allah, please, make it not so. Allah, please . . . He rocked forward and back. Allah, please take me, too. But he knew such a prayer was a sin.

Allah had left him alive for a reason. He would avenge Amira's death. He'd kill the men who attacked them. He'd destroy their organization so it couldn't hurt any more women like Amira. Then he would go home. He wouldn't let army or the DIA take anything more from him. There was nothing more to take.

A hand on his shoulder made Faraz jump and lunge for his gun.

"Easy, man," Nic said. "It's me."

Faraz relaxed, and turned his gaze back toward Amira.

"She's gone," Nic said. "Cindy, too. Lots of others."

Faraz didn't respond.

"You all right?" Nic pointed to the blood covering Faraz's shirt.

Faraz looked down. "Yeah. It's hers." He wiped his bloody hands on his pants.

"I can't believe this," Nic said.

"Yeah." They were silent for several seconds.

Nic took hold of Faraz's good arm. "Come on, Karim. We have to get out of here. The commander has called everyone to the headquarters."

Faraz didn't move.

"We'll come back for her. But we have to go now." Nic pulled on Faraz's arm to help him up, but Faraz pushed him off.

"Please, Karim, come with me."

Karim. Oh, Allah. In the midst of all this, Faraz had to be Karim.

Nic knelt next to him and whispered the *Shahada* for Amira.

The gesture penetrated Faraz's thoughts. He swallowed. "Thank you." He touched Amira's hand in farewell. Then he let Nic help him up.

They passed the bodies of several women, including Cindy, still posed as Faraz had left her. They took the path to the central road, past the blood of the attackers' leader, past the crater dug out by their bomb, past the tracks of their vehicles and more dead bodies.

The desert sun was up now, starting the quick process of baking the camp. Faraz and Nic joined the small group of foreign survivors in front of what was left of the headquarters—parts of two exterior walls and piles of broken furniture and other rubble. There were eight sand cats—seven men and Tasha, from LA—of the three dozen who had been in the camp.

"Is this all?" Faraz asked, the first words he had said since he'd left Amira's side.

"There are a few wounded in what's left of the clinic," Nic answered. "But most of the injured died. More will, too, I imagine. The doctor and his assistant are both dead. A couple of volunteers are doing what they can."

Faraz's arm ached. He rubbed it and tightened the bandage.

Al-Jazar emerged from the building with two fighters, the only Syrian survivors. One of them had his right arm in a large, blood-soaked bandage. The other fighter and al-Jazar were unscathed and carried their AKs pointed at the ground. They came down the building's front steps, and the survivors formed a semicircle in front of them.

"This is a dark day," the commander began. His clothes were caked with dirt on one side. "All of you, and our martyrs, fought bravely. This betrayal of jihad will not go unpunished."

Al-Jazar continued, but Faraz wasn't listening. He looked at the destruction. The camp gate was lying in pieces. Parts of the wall were down. All of the buildings were unusable. Most important, Amira was gone. It was as if she had only been there for a brief moment.

Faraz looked back at al-Jazar. The commander was dirty only on one side. Something was not right. The lieutenant's army brain was sluggish but starting to reassert itself. As the pieces came together, his anger surged.

"It was a difficult fight," the commander said.

"And where were you?" Faraz heard himself talking before he knew he had decided to say it.

Al-Jazar cocked his head and looked at Faraz. "I was fighting just as all of you were. I was behind the headquarters, firing all the time."

"You were not," Faraz said. He had him, now. Liar. "I was behind the storage building. I saw the back of the headquarters. I saw it twice. I never saw you."

"Do not question me, Karim. I know it is a difficult day, but be careful."

"Why are you covered with dirt on one side, while your other side is clean?"

"We are all dirty from the battle."

"But not like you." Faraz had no filter for this coward who had gotten Amira killed. "You did not come out of a fight looking like that. You came out of a hole. While we fought and our friends died, you hid in a hole in the ground."

"You make a serious charge," al-Jazar said. He started to raise his rifle.

Faraz moved more quickly. He lifted his AK and fired one round into al-Jazar's chest at a range of five meters. The bullet made a small hole to the left of the commander's breastbone and a huge crater as it exited his back, trailing blood and flesh that splattered on the stairs.

The force of the round threw al-Jazar backward. He was dead before he hit the ground.

The other armed fighter appeared frozen with shock for a split second, enough time for Faraz to hit him with two quick rounds before the man could raise his weapon. He fell next to his commander.

The wounded fighter collapsed to his knees, pressed his face to the ground, raised his hands, and begged in Arabic, "Please, my brother. Please!"

"Holy shit, Karim," Nic said. "What the hell are you doing?" He and some of the other foreigners had hit the ground when the shooting started. Others stood there, immobilized in disbelief.

"He hid in the ground," Faraz said. "Go inside the building. I'm sure you'll find his coward hole. We were not ready for this attack. All this . . ." He turned toward the camp, saw the smoldering women's barracks. His voice caught in his throat. "All this is his fault. Al-Jazar was willing to let us die while he hid from the fight. We already knew he was crazy. Today we saw he was a coward and a traitor."

Nic stood and looked at al-Jazar and the other dead man. "But this isn't a damn video game. You can't just kill him."

"I already did. He got what he deserved."

"What if you're wrong?" Nic asked.

"He's responsible for the deaths of our friends. I'm not wrong about that. Incompetent asshole. Go on. Go inside, check around the back, maybe. You'll find his hiding place."

Nic looked at the pool of blood growing around the two bodies. "I guess it doesn't matter now. But he was the only one who knew anything. What the hell are we supposed to do now?"

Faraz gestured toward the injured fighter. "Tie this man up. Collect the dead for burial. Tend to the wounded. Then we'll see."

"So, you're in command now?"

Faraz looked at him. "You have a different plan?"

Neither Nic nor anyone else had an answer.

"What if the attackers come back?" Nic asked.

"If they come back, we're all dead. But they won't. They accomplished their mission, and I wounded their leader."

"You did what?"

"Yes, shot him in the side just before they withdrew. Now go, all of you. We have lots of graves to dig."

"All right, all right," Nic said. He looked back at al-Jazar's body. "You've left us no choice."

Chapter Thirty-two

While the others went to work clearing debris and moving bodies, Faraz went into the ruins of the headquarters building to confirm his theory and see if he could find any useful information. In al-Jazar's office, the desk was moved to the side, papers and equipment were scattered, and half a dozen floorboards had been removed. The late commander hadn't bothered to replace them when he came out of his shelter, the crawl space between the floor and the ground—the right place for a rat to hide. Theory confirmed.

Faraz rummaged through the desk drawers. He didn't know what he was looking for until he found it. The old tourist brochure was from the years long past when adventure travelers would ride the desert roads, explore the market in Aleppo, and bargain with the Bedouin for camel rides. It had a map on the back.

A hand-drawn star several hundred kilometers northeast of Damascus was apparently their camp. West of it, maybe twenty kilometers, someone had drawn a small square and written something in Arabic. Faraz could read the letters from his Koran studies. It said, "*Al-Kufaar*." He knew that word. It meant "Infidels." Faraz stared at the square. The location seemed about right, based on his recollection of his briefings—one of the Syrian militia bases where U.S. troops had been deployed.

If he was right, he could lead his motley group to the Americans, surrender, make his report, and go home. But that's not what he had in mind.

Much of the area around the "Infidel" base was empty desert, with only a few small villages indicated. But farther northwest was another square. The handwriting next to it was hard to read, but after a struggle, Faraz figured it out. "Al-Souri," it said, and it was underlined three times.

Faraz folded the brochure and put it in his pocket.

By late afternoon, there was some semblance of order.

The bodies had been carried to the cemetery, each one lying next to a fresh grave, including two of the injured who had died during the day.

The survivors had cleaned each other's wounds and wrapped them with bandages salvaged from the clinic. The central road and main paths had been cleared of debris. Serviceable weapons and other equipment sat in neat piles.

Someone had gathered what was left of the food and set it out on a blanket on the ground in front of the headquarters building. There wasn't much—some bread, canned goods, vegetables, dried fruit.

The two injured foreigners were well enough to join them, making the team ten men, three women, and the wounded Syrian fighter, who had given them no trouble. They all sat on the ground for a solemn meal.

Faraz hardly ate. He felt sucker-punched, but his head was clear. He saw that Nic had changed out of his bloody pants. The bandage around his right leg formed a bulge under his new ones.

"This is all the food," reported Tasha. Her natural Afro was matted, her shirt was ripped, and her fingers were bloody from the day of work.

When most of the food was gone, Faraz said, "Save the rest. We'll bury our brothers and sisters, then sleep a few hours. We leave at two a.m."

"To go where?" Nic asked.

"To find food and shelter, and to kill the bastards who did this."

"To kill the bastards? Are you kidding me?"

Faraz glared at him. "You can assume I'm not joking."

"But, Karim, we have two working vehicles and a handful of people, all minimally trained. Maybe we should head for the border, back to the safe house, go—"

"Go home?" Faraz said. His anger flared.

"I was going to say, go get new assignments."

Faraz relaxed a bit. "No."

"No? That's it?" Nic looked toward Latif for support, but got none.

"Yeah. That's it. You want to argue with me?" He didn't reach for his weapon, but he was ready to. Faraz looked around the circle. "Listen, you think we'd make it? You know where to go? How to find the guides? We'd be shot up by the Syrian Army before we got to the border, or by the Turks if we crossed in the wrong place. There's nothing left for us but to take our revenge and then look for a new group to join."

Tasha spoke up. "Revenge? Revenge on who?" She sounded skeptical, but also interested.

"I know who did this."

"What are you talking about?" Nic asked.

Faraz had to be careful. "You heard al-Jazar speak of a usurper, someone who recently returned to Syria. I think our commander was in a power struggle with someone, and that person attacked our camp."

"And where do you get that from?"

"I read, a few weeks ago in the U.S., about a Syrian who fought in Afghanistan. The article said he had come home to lead a new phase in the jihad here. Al-Jazar was not the kind of guy to take orders from a newcomer."

"And now, we go find this guy—this experienced fighter who just crushed our camp—we find him in the middle of the desert and attack him?" Nic shrugged and pursed his lips. He looked at their assembled band of survivors. "With this?"

"We find a way to take our revenge."

"Makes more sense to surrender to him," Nic argued.

"I ain't surrendering to nobody," Tasha said. "If he was a real soldier for Allah, he wouldn't have done this."

"Sounds right." It was Latif, finally speaking up.

Nic took a deep breath and let it out. He scanned the others sitting around the blanket. No one looked him in the eye.

He turned back toward Faraz. "We should surrender to him, join his group."

"No."

"Why not?"

"He killed our friends."

"Which proves he's stronger than us. We have to join him, if he'll have us."

"Not happening."

"But—"

"Not happening!" Faraz put his hand on his AK. No one else moved.

"What are you doing?" Nic asked.

"I'm with Karim," Tasha said. Several of the others nodded.

"This is suicide." Nic was pleading, but no one seemed convinced. He sighed and shook his head. "I hope you know what you're doing, Commander Karim."

Faraz wanted to say, "I know exactly what I'm doing. I'm avenging Amira's death and going after the world's most wanted terrorist." Instead, he said, "Ease up, Nic. We're all in this together. We will find a way. Now, let's go. We have to bury our friends before it gets dark."

At the burial ground at twilight, the survivors arranged the dead alongside their graves—the Syrian fighters, including al-Jazar, in one row, the sand cats in another, separated into male and female groups. Jamal, "the coward," was among them. He was beside Ismail, who had wanted to wear the suicide vest. In the end, the one who had sought it and the one who had feared it both found martyrdom.

Faraz put his weapon on the ground, and the other survivors did the same. He led them in a grim procession from grave to grave, pausing to pay respects as each body was lowered. Except at al-Jazar's grave. Faraz spat into it and moved on.

Amira lay next to Cindy. Faraz knelt by her head and reached out, thinking he would open the shroud, see her face one more time. But he stopped himself. It wasn't proper. It wasn't what Amira would have wanted. He pulled his hand back and took hold of the sheet she was wrapped in. Nic helped him put her into her grave.

Faraz started to choke up, but he had no more tears, not even for Amira. His sadness fueled nothing but rage. He wanted to get this over with, get out of there, get to work punishing the men who did this.

He stood and moved to the area in front of the graves. The survivors gathered around him. "Anybody know the prayers?"

"I do," Latif said.

"Please . . ."

Latif chanted the prayers in Arabic. He scooped a double handful of dirt into each grave, then returned to the others and recited, "I seek refuge in Allah. All praise is due to Allah . . ."

When he finished, they stood in silence. It was a little cooler now. A breeze threw up some of the loose earth.

"Fill the graves," Faraz said. "Then sleep." His voice was hoarse. He turned away from the others, took a shovel, and went to personally fill Amira's grave. Then he handed the shovel to another man and picked up his rifle.

Faraz walked to the front of the camp, took a flashlight from the equipment pile, and turned toward the side gate. If he could sleep at all, it would be under their tree.

Chapter Thirty-three

Faraz reentered the compound around one a.m., his AK slung over his shoulder and the beam from the flashlight showing the way. He roused the others. "Gather all the explosives you can find, guns and ammo, too," he ordered. "Load it all into the vehicles."

He took several ammo clips and hand grenades for himself and put a hunting knife in a sheath on his belt. When they were finished, everyone gathered again in front of the headquarters for a meager breakfast of what little food remained.

Faraz unfolded the map and laid it on the blanket. "You see this? It says 'al-Souri.' That's the guy I was telling you about, the one who came from Afghanistan. We leave now, while it's still dark. We go there. We set up an ambush. We kill them all."

He looked around the circle of partially trained foreigners. Only two looked back at him. The rest avoided his eyes. It occurred to Faraz they must have talked after he had left them the night before.

Nic was their spokesman. "Karim, we heard you last

night, but you saw how strong they are. How can this group defeat them?"

"I have a plan." It was mostly a lie. At best, Faraz had an idea. But he didn't care. "I'll show you when we get there."

Faraz could sense the hesitation in the group. "Look, I know this guy." He corrected himself. "I know *about* him . . . from that article. We should be fighting Assad and the infidels, but he's making us fight each other. We take our revenge. Then we join another group. It's that or go back to . . . to whatever you left behind."

"I ain't doin' that," said Tasha. "I'm with you, Karim. We gotta do something."

Slowly, around the blanket, heads nodded. Faraz looked at Nic.

"Yeah, yeah," he said. "Might as well. What they did was wrong. We'll make them pay."

"What about this?" the teenager Latif asked. He pointed to the notation on the map. "It says 'Infidels.'"

"I know. It's probably a foreign outpost. We'll steer clear of it."

"What do we do with al-Jazar's man?" Nic asked, indicating the injured fighter.

"Tie his hands behind his back and put a two-foot rope on his feet. We'll point him toward the nearest village. He'll get there, but not very fast."

In the lead vehicle, Faraz took them on a circuitous route, avoiding villages, lights off, almost feeling his way in the dark. There were few road signs and not many hills or other features to guide them.

Faraz stopped at a crossroads and consulted the map. Ahead and to their right, they could see the lights of a village. On their left was a small sand dune. Other than that, the landscape offered no clues.

Nic limped over from the second SUV and spoke to Faraz through his open window. "Have you gotten us lost?" he said.

Faraz scowled at him and indicated a spot on the map. "I think we're here. Those lights are this village."

Nic pointed at the square on the map. "So we're close to the foreign outpost."

"Yeah." Faraz considered his options. "Let's check it out. The rest of you stay here."

Faraz got out of the vehicle, and he and Nic walked up the dune. Near the top, Faraz got on hands and knees, and Nic did the same. They crested the summit heads first. Nic lifted himself for a better view. Faraz grabbed him and pulled him back. "Stay down. They'll be watching."

The small base was only a few hundred meters away. Its lights were dimmed, but on the blank landscape it still stood out. Faraz saw the familiar HESCO barriers all around—four- by three-foot wire-mesh boxes, about two feet deep, filled with earth and rocks. There were guard towers on all four corners.

To the right, the road leading to the main gate was blocked by barriers, signs, and light towers. A similar arrangement guarded another gate to the left.

"Jeez," Nic said. "That's quite a little fortress. I hope we don't find anything like that at al-Souri's camp."

"It's American." Faraz caught himself. "I think so, anyway."

The two men lay there for a minute, staring at the base and scanning the area.

It would be so easy for Faraz to walk into the American camp—easy if they didn't shoot him on sight. He could report what he knew and go home, maybe all the way home to San Diego. Get the rest of these idiots arrested before they could cause any more damage.

But that wouldn't accomplish his mission—his mission, not Davenport's—to make al-Souri and the attack leader pay. To give up on that would betray Amira. After he killed them, he could go to the Americans. He wouldn't know anything about the big attack, the MTO, but eliminating al-Souri would count for something.

"No," he said out loud.

"What?"

"Nothing. Let's go." Faraz made one more scan of the base and its surroundings. That's when he saw something moving.

He had to look twice to be sure, but there was no mistake. It was a vehicle heading toward the barriers. "What the heck?" he said.

"What?"

Faraz pointed.

"Those morons will get themselves killed, whoever they are," Nic said.

"Could be."

They could see now that it was a pickup truck. It slowed as it approached the barriers. The cabin lights went on, and a man got out, gesturing wildly. They couldn't hear from this distance, but he seemed to be trying to explain something, maybe to ask for help.

Faraz saw the tiny shapes of American troops moving on the watchtowers to focus their attention, and their weapons, on the man and his vehicle.

Faraz and Nic looked that way, too, but they also had a wider view. Out of the corner of his eye, Faraz saw more vehicles approaching the outpost from the rear, lights off.

"Oh, shit," he said. "Look there. It's an attack."

"Oh, God. Well, this should be a good show."

Faraz felt nauseous. His thoughts pinged out of control. He needed to get out of there, to continue toward al-Souri's camp. But he couldn't let this happen.

The attacking force was larger than the one they had faced the night before. Faraz could see that the diversionary tactic was working. Most of the camp's attention was focused on the decoy and his truck. Faraz figured that such a small post would have a handful of Americans, along with an unknown number of Syrian militiamen with questionable skills.

If these were the same highly trained attackers from the night before, the Americans were in trouble. His rage told him to continue to al-Souri's camp. But his training overpowered it. Faraz didn't have much time, and his crew was weak. But he had to try. His revenge would have to wait. Or if these were al-Souri's men, maybe it would come right now.

"We have to get down there," Faraz said.

"Why?" Nic said. "That's a good-sized force come to attack the enemies of jihad."

"These could be the same guys who attacked us last night."

"Could be. Who cares? If they kill the Americans, we win. If the Americans kill them, we win. Anyway, we're no match for either one."

Faraz looked back toward the base. The sun was rising behind the attacking force on the left, which would make it hard for the Americans to see them. The attackers had stopped, possibly waiting for a signal. The man at the front gate seemed to be trying to convince the Americans to do something—open the gate, probably.

"I said we have to get down there," Faraz said, the anger rising in his voice. He turned to Nic lying next to him. "We're getting the others, and we're joining this fight."

"The hell we are. That's suicide."

"We all agreed I'm in charge, and I say we're going down there."

"Let's go and ask the others."

"No."

"No? You're crazy. How you gonna stop me?"

Faraz answered with his knife.

He reached under his body with his good left arm, pulled the knife from the right side of his belt, twisted for leverage, and drove the weapon into Nic's belly. Nic's eyes went wide. Faraz's right hand came up with a handful of sand and pressed it into Nic's open mouth, stifling his scream. Faraz moved the knife to Nic's throat and cut deeply in one smooth motion, putting as much of his weight into it as he could. The young man's body jerked and went limp.

Faraz was breathing heavily and sweating, despite the cool of the desert night. He held Nic until he was sure he was dead. Then, still prone, he pushed him away to bleed out into the sand.

Faraz looked back toward the camp. The attackers were still waiting, but he knew he didn't have much time. He wiped the knife on Nic's shirt and cleaned his hands with sand as well as he could. He'd have to hope the others wouldn't notice any bloodstains in the half-light. He crawled partway down the hill until he could stand and run back to the others.

"Quickly," he said. "Board the vehicles. There's a fight going on, and we're getting into it."

"What?" Tasha said.

"It's the guys who attacked us last night," Faraz said, although he didn't know that for sure. "This is our chance for revenge."

"Where's Nic?" Tasha asked.

"He's on the dune as a lookout. He'll come down the other side when we're in position. C'mon, move! Weapons ready!"

They sped to the next crossroads, where Faraz led them to the right toward the American base so they could come up behind the attacking force, using the sun to their advantage as the enemy had.

Faraz floored the accelerator and roared toward the rear of the attackers' convoy. A hundred meters out, he opened his window. Two seconds later, he hit the brakes, skidded to an angle, and started firing.

He killed two of the attackers before the rest of his force could get out of the vehicles and start shooting. The attackers spun around and returned fire.

A bullet grazed Faraz's right arm, above his wound. He fell back in pain and slumped onto the passenger seat.

Faraz's blood stained the seatback, but he saw that the wound wasn't too bad. As he lay there, a wave of bullets came through the windshield and open window, whizzing above him.

Faraz crawled across the seat and exited the vehicle through the passenger door, away from the fight. Two members of his team were already dead. He crouched behind the engine and put a fresh ammo clip on his gun. Faraz leaned out in front of the vehicle and emptied the clip, strafing the opposing force.

He got a glimpse of the base. All its lights were on now, most of them pointing in his direction. If nothing else, he had exposed the position of the attackers.

His comrades were firing, but not effectively. Several of them had been killed. He turned toward the second vehicle. "Take aim!" he shouted. "Don't waste ammo!"

If he hadn't turned his head, he might have seen the fighter mount the RPG launcher on his shoulder. As it was, he only saw it when he turned back, and then it was too late.

The grenade blew the second SUV into a million pieces and killed the four foreigners who were taking cover behind it. Faraz saw Tasha launched into the air. She landed in a lifeless heap by the side of the road.

"Oh, this is not good," Latif said, kneeling next to Faraz.

"Damn," Faraz said. "Follow me." Bent over, he led Latif to the shallow gully at the side of the road. He pushed him down just as their SUV exploded from another RPG shot.

When the debris settled, Faraz heard shouting in Arabic.

"They want us to surrender," Latif said. "We must run."

Before Faraz could respond, Latif took off. He ran along the gully, away from the outpost. When the road turned, giving the shooters a clearer view past the burning wreckage of the SUVs, they hit him with a short burst.

Nic had been right. This was suicide.

There was more shouting in Arabic. Faraz didn't understand, but if it had been him, he would have been saying something like, "Stand up slowly and keep your hands where I can see them." It was no better than fifty-fifty that they'd kill him anyway. But what choice did he have? At least he'd alerted the Americans. His other missions were impossible now.

Faraz had to assume this was his last chance. He threw his AK out of the gully, raised his hands, and searched his memory for the right words.

"*La tutliq alnaar*," he shouted. Don't shoot.

As he climbed out of the gully, Faraz could see that his assault had killed several of the attackers and their advance toward the Americans had been stopped.

The Americans would likely launch a counterattack at any moment.

Someone barked an order in Arabic. Two men ran at Faraz and tackled him. They pinned his arms behind his back and punched him repeatedly. One of them took his knife and grenades.

The voice in the darkness shouted more orders.

They pulled Faraz to his feet and dragged him toward their vehicles. They pushed him onto the floor of the back seat of a pickup truck. He lay on his bad arm as the men piled in. Someone kicked him in the head.

Faraz felt the vehicle turn in a tight half circle on the narrow road and take off at high speed.

Chapter Thirty-four

When they came to a stop, one of the men took Faraz by the collar and dragged him out onto the ground. The men kicked and cursed him, and he curled into a ball.

A two-word order interrupted them.

Someone pulled him to his feet, and he found himself face-to-face with an angry man whose shirt was soaked with blood on the left side. The man grabbed Faraz by the neck and shouted a question in Arabic.

When there was no response, he squeezed tighter and shouted louder.

"*La 'atahadath al-Arabia*," Faraz said. I don't speak Arabic.

The man cursed and slapped Faraz hard across the side of his head. Faraz fell to his knees.

"Commander," another man said. Faraz didn't understand the rest of what the fighter said, but he was pointing at the commander's bloody shirt.

Faraz's gaze went from the blood to the commander's face. He had a flash of recognition. It was the attack leader he had wounded the night before—the man responsible for Amira's death.

This was the reason Faraz had led his "brothers and sisters" to their deaths in a futile tribute to his own anger, guilt, and lust for revenge.

From his knees, Faraz launched himself upward at the commander, tackled him like he'd been taught when he tried out, unsuccessfully, for the high school football team back in San Diego. His legs kept moving until he had knocked the commander down and driven him into the ground.

Faraz felt a fresh surge of warm blood from the man's wound. He cocked his fist, but someone caught his arm. An instant later, two men threw him off their boss. At least five of them pummeled him with their fists and feet. Faraz caught a glimpse of two others tending to the commander before a fist hit his face so squarely that all he saw were stars.

He woke up in the dark, blood caked on his face, his hands and feet tied together. He struggled to open his eyes. The lid of his right eye wouldn't budge, but he got the left one open halfway.

Faraz was in a narrow room with wooden walls, possibly a shed. There was a small window to his left, covered with dark paper or cloth. A shard of light came through one edge, and another through a rip near the center.

He pushed himself into a sitting position and scooted backward so he could lean against the wall. The door was in front of him, maybe ten feet away.

Faraz licked his lips and felt something caked on them. He tasted blood and spat it out onto the floor. He hurt everywhere, and his throat was so dry he could barely swallow.

The room smelled of stale body odor and urine, suggesting he was not the first man to have been held there.

He closed his one usable eye and thought about how stupid he was.

Part of Faraz's brain was trying to access his POW training. But most of it was berating himself, telling him what he should have done and not done. He should have listened to Nic and taken his band of wannabe jihadists back to Turkey. He should have protected Amira. He should have surrendered to the Americans. He should have never taken this mission.

That attack leader was no doubt planning his interrogation, torture, and death.

Faraz leaned his head back against the wall and thought about Amira. He wanted to picture their time under the tree. But all he saw was her lying in the rubble, eyes closed, chest riddled with bullets.

The door opened with such force that Faraz thought it would fly off its hinges. It banged against the wall and nearly bounced shut.

A man stomped in and picked Faraz up by his hair. He winced and used his good eye to look into that same angry face.

"I am Nazim, deputy to Commander al-Souri. Who are you, traitor?" he said through gritted teeth, still holding Faraz by the hair.

That much Arabic, Faraz could understand. His suspicions were all confirmed in that one statement. His fate likely sealed, as well. If this man didn't kill him, al-Souri surely would.

"I am Karim—" he croaked out, before the man pulled his hair harder and threw his head against the wall.

Faraz crumpled to the floor. His teeth caught a lip, and he spat out fresh blood.

Nazim pushed him over and placed a foot on Faraz's neck. Then came a stream of angry Arabic questions.

Faraz could barely breathe to answer, if he'd understood. "*La*," he said. "*La al-Arabia.*" No Arabic. Then, through the fog of pain, Faraz had a thought. "*Pashto*," he said. "*Ana 'atahadath Pashto.*" I speak Pashto.

"Aach," Nazim said in evident frustration. He reached behind his back. When his hand reappeared, it was holding a knife.

Nazim knelt down, his knee on Faraz's injured right arm. The pain was excruciating. Nazim brought the knife to Faraz's throat. He stared at Faraz from a foot away. The man's eyes were wide with fury.

Nazim pulled the knife back, out of Faraz's field of vision. Faraz expected it to return and slice his throat. He said the *Shahada*.

But when Nazim's hand came toward him, Faraz saw that he had flipped the knife. He hit Faraz square in the face with the handle and knocked him unconscious.

Chapter Thirty-five

With the buzz of Saddam's former dining room swirling around her, Bridget read the details of the outpost attack and the desperate requests for the intel side to provide some sort of explanation. An unknown force had basically saved the outpost, and the troops had no idea what it was or why it had intervened. She couldn't provide a definitive answer, but she had an idea.

They had reports of a jihadi-on-jihadi battle the night before, an attack on a terrorist camp that had not been done by any coalition force. They had attributed it, tentatively and without hard evidence, to the growing feud among anti-Assad groups.

Now, maybe, with two possible intra-jihadist fights in two days, they could begin to figure it out.

But that was only her second problem. The top priority was to figure out why terrorist chatter was still up and why money was flowing out of suspected terrorist financing accounts to unknown destinations. It was like a Category 5 hurricane warning, but she had no idea where it would hit, or when.

Her phone rang.

"Davenport."

"Good morning." Hadley's voice sounded tired.

"Hello, sir. Three a.m. in D.C. Are you just getting up or have you not yet gone to bed?"

"Who can tell, these days?"

"You're calling about the outpost attack?"

"And everything else."

"Yes, sir. We're working it. Seems to be more of the rivalry we saw yesterday."

"I barely care about that. What I care about is that they were attacking another of our bases, and we had no warning. Meanwhile, they're planning something bigger, probably much bigger. This can't go on."

"All our best people are working the numbers and all the inputs. The incident at the outpost is another data point, but really we don't have any better analysis than we had yesterday."

"We don't have an analysis problem. We have a facts problem. And without facts, we have an action problem. We can't stop what we can't see. Blowback has got to know something about this. He's in a jihadi camp, for God's sake. We need to know whatever he knows."

"I've been thinking the same thing. But as you know, any attempt to contact him is extremely dangerous."

"It's war, Bridget. It's dangerous. If you need to drive across the desert and call his name through a megaphone, that's what you need to do."

Bridget took a beat, wheeled her chair to the right, and leaned into the corner of her cubicle to make it harder for anyone to hear what she said. "Short of that, sir, as we discussed, we do have some Syrian assets. We could send one of them to try to find him, get a message to him."

"Now you're talking. You have someone in mind?"

"Not yet. I'll review the files. But even if we send someone, it's a long shot."

"Might be our only shot. You're in theater to make things happen. Get someone out there, and soon. We need to know what these guys are up to. There will not be an MTO on my watch. Are we clear?"

"Yes, sir."

"Good. Get on it." He hung up.

Bridget tapped her keyboard to access a secure file and reviewed the operational profiles of half a dozen U.S. intelligence assets in northern Syria. None of them were very good options, but one seemed to be at least reasonably well-positioned to make a trip into the wild northeast without raising suspicions.

He was largely untested, but they all were. These people could only be called upon for one significant mission. Anything more would create suspicion, move their danger factor from high to unacceptable.

Bridget read the man's profile a second time. All right, sir, good luck out there.

She opened a secure form and created a mission. The operations center would contact operative #SN247.

A few hours later, Bridget's phone rang again.

"Any plans for the evening at HQ?" It was Will, apparently working to sound cheery but coming off as checking up on her.

"Thought I might hit the disco."

The joke fell flat.

"Same here." Will sounded deflated.

Bridget put on a brighter tone. "How's the leg?"

"About the same, honestly. PT guy is all positive vibes, but I still can't get far without the cane. How's the mission?"

"Things are happening. Can't say much."

They went silent.

"But, speaking of the mission, I just got an email from the general, so I better get on it." That was a lie. Truth was, they didn't have much to talk about. Bridget was falling deeper and deeper into the Black Hole.

"Okay. Take care."

"Talk soon, okay?" She made a point of not saying "tomorrow." Maybe letting a day or two go by would help.

"Sure. Bye, babe."

"Bye."

Bridget turned to a long list of things Liz had sent her, then stared at the spreadsheets some more.

With the windows all covered, she didn't realize how late it was. As soon as she hit Send on her last email, she saw Carter making his way through the cubicles from across the room. Even in this place packed with large men, he stood out—tall, broad, and freshly shaved, including his head, and sporting a broad smile.

Two opposing reactions fought for her attention. She was surprised at the brief but undeniable tingle she felt, as if the quarterback was heading to the nerdy girls' table. But at the same time, she felt something in the pit of her stomach, a mix of guilt and dread.

Before she could choose which way to feel, he was there.

"Good evening, Bridget. How is the DIA today?"

"We're fine, Carter. I see you're back and all cleaned up."

"Good of you to notice. We Georgia boys can clean up fairly well when we have a mind to."

Bridget looked back at her computer.

"Matters of concern?" Carter asked.

"Always. That's my job."

"And I'm guessing that your job has kept you from suppah, even at this late houah."

Bridget was getting used to his accent, which allowed it to sound charming. "As a matter of fact, yes," she allowed. There wasn't anything more she could do tonight, and she was hungry.

"Well, I was about to see what's on offer in the chow hall. This is supposed to be a twenty-four-houah war."

"Yeah. Okay. Sure."

She thought her ambivalence was clear, but Carter ignored it. "Excellent," he said, as if she'd just agreed to go to the prom. He stood aside and held out his hand, indicating that she should go first.

Bridget locked her computer, took her small pack, and led him through the cubicles toward the D-FAC.

Dinner was more pleasant than Bridget had expected or wanted or was ready to admit. Carter's stories about life in Georgia were entertaining, his laugh was infectious, and his crow's-feet pointed invitingly to those pale gray eyes.

When they finished, Bridget agreed to let him walk her to her trailer. The night air was cool, and without the glare of the sun, the stone-lined paths and occasional trees with hanging lights could have been anywhere.

“How much longer do you have here?” Carter asked.

“Until the mission’s done,” she answered. “It’s open-ended. How about you?”

“I’m getting short on this contract. A few more weeks, unless they extend us.”

“You must be eager to get home.”

“Yes. And no. See the parents and a few folks, sure. But there’s nothing to keep me there. This is my life. I’ll be back before long.”

“You don’t think you could give it up?”

“Like you did?”

“Yeah.”

“I admire that you changed direction. Truly, I do. You did your time—more than your time—and found something else that makes you happy. But I’m not there, not yet, anyway. There are still bad guys to fight. I have no interest in sitting on the sidelines.”

“That’s real commitment. Sometimes, I wish I had it.”

“You’re still in the fight, but with your brain instead of . . . you know . . . what I bring to the battle.” He flexed his arm muscle, barely contained by his short-sleeved shirt.

Bridget chuckled. “This is me,” she said, stopping at her trailer door. They were in the half-light between two lampposts. She put on a Southern accent. “Why, thank you for a lovely evening, Mistah Holloway.” Her self-imposed prohibition against flirting had apparently been lifted.

Carter laughed out loud. “Well, you are most welcome, Ms. Davenport.” He made a quarter-bow. When he stood, he stepped toward her, put his hands on her shoulders, and leaned in.

Bridget went for a friends' air kiss, but he moved his head to make clear he wanted more. She stopped. She had been here before, in the other war, with no good outcomes. This was totally unfair to Will. But he hadn't been himself lately, maybe never would be. And he was far away. She likely wouldn't see him for months. Who knew what they'd have by then?

Meanwhile, Carter was right here. She gave him a half smile. They kissed, a warm, gentle first kiss. Then he put his big arms around her and pulled her in for a deep, romantic one and a full-body hug. It felt so good.

When the kiss ended, Bridget put her hands on Carter's shoulders. She looked down, avoiding his gaze, trying to decide in a second or two whether to say good night or invite him in.

Her phone buzzed in her pack. The spell was broken.

"I should check that," she said.

He released her. She fished the phone out, read the text, and said, "I have to go back to the office."

Carter's disappointment was clear. Bridget gave him a sympathetic smile. Now that the opportunity was gone, she was disappointed, too. And relieved.

"What's happening?" he asked.

"Just more questions we can't answer. It's not yet 'suppah' time in Washington."

Carter smiled.

"But I have to go deal with it. Sorry."

"I'm sorry, too."

"Um, bye." Bridget gave him a peck on the cheek—an implied rain check, maybe. She turned and headed off on the path.

"Bye," she heard him say from behind her.

Chapter Thirty-six

"Madam," the shopkeeper said to the elderly woman he'd been haggling with, "look to the quality. You will not find any like this in all Aleppo, nor in Damascus." He spread the sheer pink scarf across his arms for her to see.

Rasheed Abu-Ramzi still managed to make a living at his small store in Aleppo's ancient market. The tourists were long gone, but his reputation and the quality of his goods brought in enough local business to keep his wife and baby fed. He wasn't even worried about the extra expenses he would soon have. He was joyous about them. His wife was six months pregnant.

"Yes," the woman acknowledged. "It is good. But the price is too high."

"Madam, three and a half dinar is truly my best price." Rasheed feigned insult. "This is the price I would give to my own mother, may Allah protect her. She is the one who gave me my name, to keep me on the right path." Rasheed meant Righteous One.

His customer snorted her doubt and continued to study the fabric.

Thanks to his late father, who had opened the shop fifty years earlier, Rasheed knew all the best artisans, craftsmen, and manufacturers of northern Syria personally, and he was able to buy their best work at their best prices, especially during these troubled times, when there were not so many buyers. The eclectic collection of inlaid boxes, decorative macramé, metal bowls, women's scarves, and other items sold well, in spite of the war. He had added some small electronics items—flip phones, chargers, cables, and the like.

And he had a sideline that enabled him to feel good about himself and also bring in some extra cash.

The woman caressed the fabric between her thumb and forefinger. At length, she shrugged and reached into her purse.

As he counted out her change, Rasheed said, "You have made an excellent choice, madam, and an excellent bargain."

Rasheed's phone buzzed on the counter. "Thank you, madam. A thousand blessings upon you."

The woman put the scarf in her bag and left.

"Yes," Rasheed said into the phone.

"Your mother is ill and needs to see you," said a male voice.

Rasheed's shoulders sagged. He let out a breath. "Thank you," he said. "I understand."

He closed the phone and frowned. His relatively good day had gone bad. His mother was not ill. But his easy, lucrative sideline was about to become more difficult.

For him, it had been the occasional phone call, a tidbit of information here and there, and a promise of further cooperation at some undefined time in the future. For his employers, he was operative #SN247, and the time for further cooperation was now.

Rasheed took a new flip phone from the wall-mounted display, inserted its battery and a SIM card, and plugged it in to charge.

Rasheed closed the shop at six p.m., as usual, and set off in the general direction of his apartment with that new cell phone and all the money from the cash box in his pocket. He walked north and east, zigging and zagging through the market's narrow lanes, doubling back as he had been taught, to ensure he was not followed. There was no reason he would be. But he had been warned to follow the procedures. And they could be watching, testing. Yes, maybe this was only a test. All he had to do was make a phone call, and the payments would continue. Please, Allah.

Along the way, Rasheed greeted many of the merchants by name. If asked, they would testify that they saw him walking in different directions at about the same time.

It was getting dark now, which was good. He stopped in a back alley, with no windows or doors nearby for eavesdroppers. He took out the new phone, turned it on, and dialed the local number he had memorized months ago. A series of clicks and beeps sent the call to a phone far away.

On the first ring, a man's voice said, "*Aywah.*" Yes.

Rasheed gave the name he had been told to give. He answered the questions as he had been instructed. By the time the call was finished, he had his mission.

* * *

Walking home on another indirect route, Rasheed's mood was sour. He was committed to his path, and he knew it came with responsibilities. He had also known that the easy money would not be easy forever. But, why now? Oh, Allah, not now.

He threw the phone into a reeking dumpster behind a restaurant and made the last turn for home.

"You are late," his wife Nur admonished when he came through the door. Their two-year-old son ran to greet him and wrapped his little arms around Rasheed's right leg.

"I am sorry, my love. Late customers." He hugged the boy and mussed his hair.

"You do not look like you are late for happy reasons," Nur said.

"Truly. I was only upset to keep you waiting."

"Did you lose your phone, too?"

Rasheed gave a sheepish smile. "I am sorry. I should have called."

"Sit," Nur said. "Your dinner is getting cold."

As Rasheed ate, he watched Nur tidy up the kitchen and listened to his son laughing in the next room, watching a cartoon on TV. Rasheed reminded himself that he was the luckiest man in the world. He was a simple merchant. He made a decent living, nothing more. He was short and thin. His dark hair seemed to be perpetually greasy. Yet he had married this beautiful woman, surprising all his friends, and they had that wonderful son, with another on the way, *inshallah*.

Nur's anger would fade. He would do this little job, collect his bonus, and buy her a new dress. In her eyes, and in his own, he would be as rich and noble as a prince.

* * *

When they had put the boy to sleep and gotten into their small bed, Rasheed snuggled up behind Nur, kissed her gently on the neck, and wrapped his arm around her round belly.

"You know me too well," he said.

"Of course I do," she replied, twisting her neck so he could see her smile. "But you have still not told me why you were in a sour mood, especially if you had customers. Did they keep you and then not buy?"

"No. But supplies in the shop are low. I must go to the north tomorrow to buy more."

"It is dangerous in the north."

"I know. That is why I was troubled when I returned home. But life goes on. To sell, I must buy. And those old friends in the countryside, who are worse off than we are, they must sometimes sell."

"Can you not send someone?"

"Who would I send? The cost would erase my profit."

"I know. But I must ask." She took his hand from her belly and kissed it.

He pulled her tight and rubbed against her. Nur reached back to touch him. He reached under her nightshirt.

They made gentle love and succeeded in not waking the boy, who snoozed in his crib in the same room.

Rasheed slipped out of bed before dawn. He washed and dressed, then said his prayers in the kitchen. He returned to the bedroom to kiss Nur and their son.

Nur woke briefly, and he patted her belly. She squeezed his hand and went back to sleep.

Rasheed pulled his jacket tight in the predawn chill as he made his way to his friend Ibrahim's car lot.

He found Ibrahim praying the early prayers in the small trailer that served as his office and bedroom. Ibrahim greeted him with a two-fisted handshake and a triple kiss, left-right-left. He led Rasheed to a small pickup truck. It was badly dented. As far as Rasheed could tell through the caked-on desert sand, the truck was gray, and there was rust around the wheel wells. But Ibrahim assured him it ran well and, of course, came at a special price for his good friend.

"It will not leave me stranded in the desert?" Rashid asked.

"Impossible," Ibrahim said. "And to prove it, I will take no money for the rental until you return."

"Thank you, my friend."

Rasheed drove northeast out of the city, roughly paralleling the Turkish border, as the sun rose over the dunes. He was pleased that the truck's radio worked, and he hummed along to classical Arabic tunes as the kilometers sped by.

He cleared two government checkpoints without any problems. He had the proper identification and the proper bribes.

The truck performed as Ibrahim had promised, and by midday Rasheed had stopped to purchase some goods so that his cover story would hold up with Nur and anyone else who asked why he had traveled to the war zone. He also bought some men's clothes, which he normally didn't carry.

He thought they might be helpful for the real purpose of the trip.

After midday prayers at a village mosque, he bought a deep-fried meat pie from a vendor and sat at a picnic table to eat it. He struck up a conversation with a large man sporting a bushy moustache and a Western-style vest.

"Have you traveled the road between here and the Iraqi border?" Rasheed asked. "I know a village there where I can buy some excellent handicrafts."

"Dangerous," the man said. "Much fighting these days."

"Assad's men this far north?"

"No," the man said with evident disdain. "Infidels. And brothers fighting brothers." He ate the last bite of his meat pie.

"Ach, terrible," Rasheed said. "Where is that?"

"Not far from here. Near Dawaniya village."

"I shall be careful."

"To be careful, you should return to the south. *Ma'a salaama, akhooee*." Go in peace, my brother.

Back in his truck, Rasheed thought of Nur. She would be worried, even though she knew there was no cell service in much of the area where he was traveling. If he continued, he would not get home before dark. It would not be the first time he had stayed away overnight on a buying trip. But she didn't like it. He didn't like it, either.

He could go home, call the number, tell them he had failed. But they would be angry. Surely, the money would stop. Also, Rasheed believed in what he was doing. He was not the type of man to join a militia, but he could do this. He could go for a drive through his own country. He could talk to people. He could pass on a message, if he got the chance. He could make a phone call and report what he learned. Someday, he would be able to tell his son he had not sat idly by while the tyrant and the Iranians tried to destroy his country, that he had done what he could for the cause of a free Syria.

Rasheed started the truck and swung southeast toward Dawaniya, across the narrow triangle of Syria that separated Turkey from Iraq.

Rasheed stopped at a local gas station—a crossroads collection of jerry cans manned by a teenager. The boy pointed him toward the site of the brother-on-brother battle a few nights earlier.

Rasheed arrived at the still-smoldering ruins of al-Jazar's camp ten minutes later. He eyed the damage from the gate, afraid to go inside. He said a prayer for the dead and continued along the road. If the man he was looking for had been there, he might well be dead. But having come this far with no problems, Rasheed decided to explore farther toward the border and take a different road home.

He passed a dune, not knowing Nic lay dead near the top under a thin blanket of blown sand. He didn't see the American outpost on the other side. He went through the intersection where Faraz had stopped and followed the road around to the right. A short time later, he came upon a proper gas station—one real gas pump and a shack.

Rasheed slowed the truck but decided not to stop. He saw a thin old man struggle up from a broken wicker chair, hopeful of making a sale. Rasheed gave him a wave and got a disappointed shrug in return.

The road wound between dunes until it brought Rasheed

to a small rise. He stopped to take in the view. Ahead and to his left was a lonely grove of desert trees. A short distance beyond, he saw a camp of some sort. There were men on guard duty outside the gate and more looking over the wall, presumably standing on some sort of platform behind it. They all had guns, and even at that distance they looked fearsome.

In the distance were the hills of Iraq.

Normally, Rasheed would have turned back, avoided going anywhere near the camp. But this was not a normal trip. He should approach, see what he could learn. It would be dangerous, but they had no reason to think he was anything other than what he was, a merchant with goods to sell.

The vehicles came from behind Rasheed so quickly that they were upon him before he could react. They skidded to a halt, one ahead, one beside, and one behind. The men got out quickly and pointed their weapons at him.

"Who are you?" the man in charge asked. "What are you doing here?"

Rasheed raised his hands and reached through the window to be sure they could be seen. "I am Rasheed Abu-Ramzi, a merchant from Aleppo. I have wares to sell. Please, look in the truck."

The leader cocked his head. One of the fighters lifted the tarp that covered the goods, jumped into the truck, and rummaged through to be sure there were no weapons or other contraband.

"You are foolish to come here for a few dinar," the leader said. "Get out of the truck."

Rasheed complied, and the commander searched him and the cab.

"What shall I do with you?" the man asked.

"Please, my brother, is that your camp? I have clothing and cigarettes and other items for your men. Best prices in all of Syria."

The man snorted. He looked Rasheed up and down. Rasheed hadn't needed any disguise to appear to be a simple merchant. After several tense seconds, the commander shrugged. He ordered one of his men to drive Rasheed's truck and put the merchant in the back of his SUV between two fighters.

The vehicles kicked up a cloud of sand as they sped the few hundred meters to the camp.

Chapter Thirty-seven

When they dismounted, the commander introduced himself. "I am Nazim. You are welcome here. I will send my men to look at what you have brought. I warn you, do not cheat them."

"Never, *sahib*. Never would I cheat our brave mujahideen."

As Nazim walked away, Rasheed noticed the bloodstain on his shirt.

Once Rasheed was no longer seen as a threat, he was welcomed, in keeping with Syrian tradition. The men were respectful. One brought him a glass of tea. Most of them bought a shirt or pair of pants or sandals. This was turning out to be a surprisingly profitable stop, in spite of the "special discounts" he was giving them.

After an hour, Nazim came out of the headquarters building. "You will eat with us," he said as he passed by, without waiting for a response.

Rasheed would rather have gone back to the town where he'd had lunch. But the commander did not leave any room for discussion. The merchant packed up, and one of the men led him to an outdoor seating area, where Nazim gestured for him to sit at his table.

Over a meal of rice, chicken, and vegetables, with yesterday's pita, Nazim pumped Rasheed for news from Aleppo and Damascus, and from his trip through the northeast. Rasheed was a font of information, providing insights from news he was able to access that the fighters could not get in the middle of the desert.

When the conversation finally lagged, it was Rasheed's turn to get some information. "I have heard about brother-on-brother fighting. Is this true?"

Nazim frowned. "Yes, it is true. There are some who want to fight their own wars. Assad can win a dozen small wars, but he will lose one big one. That is why we must unify all the brothers."

Rasheed nodded, as if that were the wisest analysis he had ever heard. "What you say is true, my brother. That is why the war has gone on so long."

"Indeed." Nazim gnawed on a piece of bread. "We were in one such battle." He snorted. "Two, actually."

"Your injury?" Rasheed asked.

"Yes."

"May Allah restore your health."

"We captured one fighter, one of those who refuses unity. The coward attacked us from behind. Foiled my strike on the infidels."

"Your strike?"

"Yes. I saw an opportunity to strike at the infidels and took it. This man intervened, killed several of my men, the dog. Now, the infidels have increased their defenses, and I will have to explain to my commander."

"Disgraceful."

"Yes. And, like the infidels, he came from far away to fight us."

"What do you mean?"

"He is from Afghanistan, *ibn zina*." Son of a whore.

Rasheed couldn't believe his luck. He had been sent to find a sand cat, an American operative from Afghan parents who had infiltrated the mujahideen and gotten involved with their feud. It seemed strange to him. When the contact on the phone first said it, Rasheed had asked him to repeat the information.

Now, he couldn't believe he had found this sand cat. Maybe. Surely, there couldn't be more than one Afghan who fit that description.

"I want to interrogate him," Nazim continued. "But he claims to speak only Pashto. Our commander, the esteemed al-Souri, speaks the language, but he is away. The traitor will live another day or two, until he returns."

"I used to speak a little Pashto," Rasheed offered.

"Why is that?"

"I used to speak a little bit of many languages, from when traders and tourists came to Aleppo."

Nazim's expression brightened for the first time since Rasheed had arrived. "You must try to speak to him."

"Oh, Commander. I only spoke a few words. I may not remember—"

"Nonsense. You will speak to him." Nazim got up, their dinners only half eaten. "Come," he said to Rasheed. "I will take you to the prisoner."

Rasheed recoiled when Nazim pushed open the door to Faraz's shed. First, it was the smell that shocked him. Then it was the sight of the man.

He was bruised and bloodied, curled up in a corner, surrounded by urine stains and feces. His hands were tied in front of him. The man drew himself tighter into the fetal position and covered his head when Nazim approached.

Rasheed stayed outside, but one of the fighters pushed him forward. He stood behind Nazim, trying not to look at the prisoner and taking shallow breaths to avoid the stench.

"Up!" Nazim shouted.

The man moved slowly, in evident pain. Nazim grabbed him by the hair and pulled him to a kneeling position.

Faraz kept his eyes down. His hands protected his crotch.

Nazim let go of the hair and wiped his now bloody and greasy hand on Faraz's shirt. He stepped aside and said to Rasheed, "Ask him why he attacked us."

"I am sorry, Commander. I am not sure my Pashto is good enough." Rasheed coughed and turned away. He felt sick to his stomach but controlled the urge to vomit.

"Ask him!" Nazim ordered.

Rasheed turned back and forced himself to look at Faraz. "Yes, sir," he said. He switched to Pashto, racking his brain for every one of the maybe two dozen words of the language he had ever learned. "Why," he said. "Why, um, hit them?"

Faraz looked up at Rasheed. His hesitation cost him. Nazim slapped him hard with the back of his hand. Fresh blood flew out of Faraz's mouth, and he nearly fell over.

"Answer!" Nazim screamed in Arabic.

"My commander's orders," Faraz lied in Pashto.

"Orders," Rasheed translated.

"From who?" Nazim boomed.

Rasheed translated, and added, "I am with you."

Faraz let surprise flash on his face. Rasheed hoped Nazim didn't notice.

"Commander al-Jazar," Faraz said.

Nazim understood that. "Liar!" he shouted. "That dog is dead, killed when I destroyed his camp."

Rasheed translated what he could.

Faraz shook his head. "Injured. He gave the command before he died." It was close enough to the truth.

Rasheed translated the basics again.

Nazim kicked Faraz in the chest and sent him falling back onto the floor. "The coward!" Nazim exploded.

Rasheed didn't translate that. Instead, he said, "Message. Big danger coming. Call your mother." His limited Pashto was a hinderance. He couldn't say "intelligence reports indicate a major terrorist attack is imminent. Call headquarters ASAP," or anything close to that. He could only hope Faraz understood, and that the Syrians around him didn't notice that his Pashto translations weren't matching Nazim's Arabic.

From the floor, Faraz made a sort of half nod. Rasheed hoped that meant he had received the message.

Rasheed couldn't imagine what a man in Faraz's position could do with the order to call headquarters, or what "big danger" could possibly concern him as he appeared on the verge of death himself. But as badly as Rasheed felt to see someone in such a situation—particularly someone on his side of the conflict—there was nothing he could do about it.

It wasn't his job to save the man, anyway. His job was to find him, pass on the message, and perhaps receive a message in return. That last part was impossible, but to his great surprise and relief, the rest of his mission was almost completed. All Rasheed had to do now was make a phone call. Then he could go home to Nur and his son.

Soon, a bonus would be delivered to his shop, and he'd be welcoming his second son into the world with money to spend on the celebration.

Even in that awful, stinking shed, with a man on the floor barely alive, Rasheed had to suppress a smile.

Back outside, Nazim turned to Rasheed. "You did well, my friend. A few words can make a big difference." Nazim looked at the sky. "The roads are not safe at night. You will stay here. My men will take you to the crossroads in the morning." Without waiting for a reply, Nazim walked away toward the headquarters.

Later, lying on a thin mat in a room with three of Nazim's men, Rasheed couldn't stop thinking about Faraz. The man was a few dozen meters away, but there was no way to help him. It was a shame. It was also a shame that Rasheed had risked his life, and left his wife frantic, for nothing, in the end—only to tell the Americans their man could not help them.

In the morning, Nazim was true to his word. After prayers, and tea and bread, he ordered three of his men to fetch a vehicle so they could escort Rasheed to the main road. Rasheed thanked Nazim for his hospitality and said he was happy to have been of some small service to the jihad.

Rasheed got into his truck, and while waiting for the escort vehicle to come to the gate, he saw Nazim speaking to one of his men. The fighter was pointing toward Rasheed, and Nazim appeared to be at first surprised, then distressed.

When the other vehicle arrived, Rasheed followed it out of the camp. At the crossroads, he bid the men farewell and headed southwest. He opened his phone and kept an eye on it to see when he might catch some signal. He had been trained to report any information as soon as possible. When Rasheed had two bars—the most he could hope for out here—he pulled to the side of the road and dialed.

His report was short—he had found a Pashto-speaking man, badly beaten and held prisoner at al-Souri's camp. The man appeared to understand the message he delivered but offered no intelligence in return. How could he? Rasheed gave the location and said he had nothing more.

That was when he heard the vehicles approaching. He looked at his side-view mirror and saw the sand they were kicking up. They were beside him before he could think of any way to dispose of the phone.

Nazim got out of the lead vehicle. "Problem with your truck?" he asked through Rasheed's open window.

"No, Commander. Thank you for your concern. I only stopped to drink water." Rasheed knew it was a bad lie as soon as he said it.

"You cannot drink water while driving?" Nazim asked. His eyes moved to the phone, still in Rasheed's hand.

"I also called my wife," Rasheed said, pleased that a better lie had come to him. "She was worried."

"Is that so?" Nazim said. He reached in and took the phone. "One of my men is good with languages. He does not speak Pashto, but he says you used too many words speaking to the prisoner. A few of the words he recognized from other languages. He thinks maybe you were not making an honest translation."

"Commander, I'm sure your man is sincere, but he is wrong. Pashto is a difficult language, different from Arabic. I assure you, my translation was as good as I could do with my poor Pashto."

Nazim seemed unconvinced. He opened the phone. "This is your wife's number?" he asked, looking at the screen.

Rasheed felt sick to his stomach. He wiped the sweat from his forehead. "Yes," he said, barely audible. Then he had a thought. "But she has gone out now."

Nazim pushed the button to redial and activated the speaker. "What is your wife's name, my brother?"

Before Rasheed could come up with a fake name, he heard a man's voice answer the phone. They all heard it.

"Is this the wife of Rasheed Abu-Ramzi?" Nazim asked.

There was no response.

Rasheed could not hide his panic. "Commander, I can explain—"

"No. I can explain. You are a spy and a liar."

"No, Commander, please. I have a son. My wife is preg—"

By then, Nazim had raised his AK. Through the truck's open window, he shot Rasheed in the face.

Bridget sat wide-eyed, staring at a secure email with the verbatim translation of Rasheed's first call. Faraz held prisoner by al-Souri's men. Near death. Her left hand came up to cover her face.

Another message alert sounded, and Bridget leaned in

to read it. It was a transcript of the second call, including the conversation between operative #SN247 and an "unknown male," and the dry notation that the call ended with the sound of gunfire and someone apparently destroying the phone.

Bridget's stomach turned. She had never met Rasheed, didn't even know his name. She hadn't known about his wife or his son, or the baby who would be born, until he mentioned them. But she'd always known there was a man behind the number, a man who pledged loyalty to the cause of freedom and took an assignment in dangerous territory—from her. He completed his mission and died for it.

And it looked like Faraz could be next.

Bridget picked up her phone and dialed the ops center. General Hadley, Liz, and several other folks in Washington were about to get wake-up calls.

"No," Hadley said. "I'm sorry, Bridget, but no."

His voice sounded strained—some combination of distance and having been awakened at two a.m. Or maybe he felt some of the angst Bridget felt.

"But sir, we sent him out there, we—"

"I know. I feel as bad about it as you do. But at best, he's being held inside a terrorist camp. If we attack, they'll kill him before the choppers land. At worst, he's already dead, and honestly, after they cracked our agent, you know that's the more likely scenario."

"We have to try, General."

Hadley took a moment. "The lieutenant knew what he was getting into. We're not risking a dozen men on the small chance he's still there and the smaller chance we can get him out alive. Whoever we heard on that call knows the agent called in. He also knows we won't bomb him in case our man is still alive. He'll have his defenses up, maybe bring in extra men. We'd have to do an air-ground assault against heavy resistance. And probably just to recover a body, if that. So, no. I'm sorry, but no."

Chapter Thirty-eight

Nazim blasted through the door to Faraz's cell breathing hard, sweating, and screaming Arabic curse words.

Lying on the floor, Faraz tried to crawl away.

Nazim kicked him hard in the belly. "You are a spy!"

Faraz knew that word. "No, Commander, please," he coughed.

Nazim kicked him again, sending Faraz twisting backward in agony. Nazim grabbed the waistband of Faraz's pants and flung him toward the middle of the room, forcing two of his men to jump out of the way. Faraz landed facedown.

"Hold him," Nazim ordered.

The fighters pinned his arms. The pain was intense. He was weak from loss of blood.

Nazim put a knee in the small of Faraz's back and pulled his hair to lift his head and extend his neck. Faraz looked through the open door. He saw two more fighters holding Rasheed's body between them, his face a mangled mass of blood and flesh.

Faraz's breath caught.

"This is what we do to spies," Nazim said. "You are next."

The men threw Rasheed's body into the cell. The two agents lay side by side.

Faraz whispered the *Shahada*.

"You do not deserve to pray to the one true God!" Nazim shouted, jerking Faraz's head farther back. "This time, I will not change my mind."

Faraz heard Nazim remove his knife from its sheath. He thought of his mother. No matter. She thought he was dead, anyway. How did he allow himself to get talked into this mission? Damn them. Damn them all!

He felt the blade on his neck. He closed his eyes. He had no idea why he said what he said.

"Al-Souri."

His voice was hoarse and faint. He wasn't sure whether he'd actually said it.

"What did you say?" Nazim asked. He kept the knife against Faraz's neck.

"Al-Souri," Faraz said again, a little louder. Then he used two more of his Arabic words. "*Hua sadiqqi*." He is my friend.

"Al-Souri . . ." Nazim went on in a furious stream, but Faraz didn't understand it. When Nazim finished, he glared at Faraz from above, knife still poised.

"*Hua sadiqqi*," Faraz repeated. He choked on a bit of his blood. Then he said slowly, struggling with the language. "*Akhbarah al-Souri, Hamed fi hon. Hamed Anwali. Min Afghanistan.*"

Tell al-Souri, Hamed is here. Hamed Anwali. From Afghanistan.

Part Three

Chapter Thirty-nine

In the small, wood-paneled ceremonial room in the Navy wedge of the Pentagon, several dozen people sat on straight-backed wood and leather chairs chatting amiably until the master chief came in. "Attention to orders."

Everyone stood, and the military members snapped to attention. Lieutenant Commander Will Jackson and Rear Admiral Jeffery "Lumberjack" Kowalski came through the door and climbed the two steps to the stage. Will used the handrail and made it up without too much trouble.

The recessed spotlights glared off Will's impeccable summer white uniform as he stood at a slight angle, leaning on his cane to ease the pressure on his bad leg. He was working hard to suppress a smile.

Lumberjack stepped to the lectern. "By order of the Chief, Naval Operations . . ." The admiral read the document promoting Will to commander, then executed a sharp turn to the right to face Will. They exchanged crisp salutes.

Admiral Kowalski gestured toward Will's parents in the front row. Will's father, the six-foot-five great-grandson of Swedish immigrants who settled in Minnesota, wore a beige Western shirt and a bolo tie. He offered a hand to his petite Jamaican-born wife in a blue and white navy-themed dress, and they stepped onto the stage. Standing on each side of their son, they removed his lieutenant commander shoulder boards. The master chief handed them Will's new boards, with the three wide stripes of a full commander, and they struggled to thread them onto his shoulder straps.

"I'm just too short," his mom said, getting a friendly laugh from the crowd.

Cameras clicked, and a young seaman got it all on video. When they finished, Will's father stepped back and gave him a salute, then a hug, drawing more applause. Will kissed his mom and shooed his parents back to their seats so Lumberjack could make his speech.

Will scanned the crowd, acknowledging friends and colleagues who had come from as far away as Naval Station Norfolk in southern Virginia. It was gratifying to get the promotion. He had worked hard, been injured twice—in Afghanistan and again in Bethesda—and had earned the respect of his men, his colleagues, and his superiors.

But his joy was tempered. He was being promoted into a desk job, thanks to his bad leg. And the person he most wanted to be there to share the bittersweet experience and help him navigate it was in stuck in Baghdad, babysitting some poor bastard on a top-secret mission somewhere in Jihadiland.

An hour later, Will insisted on walking his parents to the exit in spite of his limp and his mother's protests. He was glad to do it for them and to fill a few minutes of his day with something other than sitting behind that desk.

After kissing his parents goodbye at the Metro exit, Will and his cane worked their way back through the long, wide corridors to the SEAL Operational Support Center, a war room of sorts, where updates on SEAL activities arrived in close to real time, along with routine requests for supplies, personnel, and other support. It was irritatingly close to the action he wanted to be part of.

His new rank got him a small office on the edge of a workroom filled with cubicles. Will would be spending the next who knew how long making sure other people did their jobs providing needed services to still other people, who would distribute it to more other people, who were the people actually doing what SEALs were supposed to do.

Will sat in his chair and leaned his cane against the wall. It was a gift from his parents, with a BUD, the SEAL symbol, hammered into its handle. The BUD signifies that a SEAL has passed the Basic Underwater Demolition course. The insignia is a golden eagle perched on an anchor holding a trident and a flintlock pistol. Will had earned the right to display it more than ten years ago, but he wasn't sure whether it was relevant anymore. He didn't need a BUD to do a desk job.

He rubbed his bad leg. It ached from the long walk, and he had an hour until he could take another pill. Will stared out his window into an air shaft. Do this for now, he said to himself. Be the best damn support supervisor the navy has ever seen. Take the time. Do the physical therapy. Then get back into the field, or get the heck out.

"Yes, sir, Commander," he whispered. Then he turned to his computer, logged on, and started supervising.

* * *

That afternoon, Lumberjack knocked on Will's open door. "How's it going?"

"Great, Admiral. Getting the hang of it, I think." Will was trying not to sound sarcastic.

"Well, you might not want to get too comfortable."

"Sir?"

"Will, I've got a problem, and I think you can solve it, if the docs will clear you for travel."

"I'll take it, sir, whatever it is." Will's enthusiasm was obvious, but he also knew he wouldn't be joining an operational team anytime soon. At least maybe he could be a support supervisor someplace other than the Pentagon.

"You know Tim Miller from Team Two?"

"Sure, sir, good man."

"Yes, well, he was supposed to take this post, but he has a health issue and the docs pulled his clearance."

"I hope Tim's okay."

"He will be, but he can't deploy this week. Can you?"

"Um, yes, sure sir. But I don't know if I can pass the physical, either."

"You're healthy except for the leg, as far as I know."

"Yes, sir."

"Shouldn't be a problem, then. This will be a desk job—Mission Coordinator. You'll be the touch point for this office, ops, command, other branches—making sure our teams are ready to go, that missions and rules of engagements are clear, areas of operation are deconflicted. You know the drill."

"Yes, sir. I worked with MCs all the time."

"Still lots of reports to write and paper to push, but at least you'd be out of here. You up for that?"

"Oh yes, sir. Assuming the docs clear me, where am I going?"

"Baghdad."

Chapter Forty

After seventy-two hours, the air in Faraz's prison shack was barely breathable. His hands and legs were in shackles, with chains that allowed him some movement, but not enough to have any chance of escaping. His leg chain was bolted to the floor. Nazim's men had fixed most of the gaps in the window covering, so it was almost totally dark.

Faraz was weak from the skimpy rations they gave him—little more than scraps, much of it inedible—and the frequent beatings by Nazim, who still didn't believe this traitor knew al-Souri, but seemed unwilling to take a chance and kill him before the commander got back from his trip.

The small building was piled with junk and supplies. Faraz kept his corner as clean as he could. It was the corner as far from the door as possible, which gave him a second or two of warning when Nazim came in for another session. Faraz divided his time between sleeping, little bits of painful exercise, and preparing for what was to come.

He was going to see al-Souri. The prospect scared him

and excited him. The man was the key to both of Faraz's goals—the one Bridget had given him and the one he gave himself after al-Souri's men killed Amira. In his weakened state, it was difficult to focus, impossible to separate duty from emotion. Faraz knew he had to be very careful or he would fail at both.

The door flew open, and the flood of light blinded Faraz. This was the usual prelude to another beating. He shielded his eyes with one hand, put the other between his legs, and pressed himself into his corner. His breath quickened.

But this time, he did not hear the usual sound of Nazim's approach or feel the pain of the first blow. Faraz peeked through his fingers as his eyes adjusted to the light. He saw a figure silhouetted in the doorway, with another just behind.

"Lower your hand," a voice said. A familiar voice, but not Nazim's. It took Faraz's brain a split second to realize the voice was speaking Pashto.

"Lower your hand," the voice repeated, more insistent.

Faraz complied. He blinked his eyes a few times, still adjusting to the light.

"Leave us," the voice said, now in Arabic.

From behind, Nazim objected. "Commander—" But the man waved a hand to cut him off. Nazim left, and the man stepped into the shack, moving to the side, away from the glare of light from outside.

Now Faraz could see him. He looked like he had aged more than the three months they'd been apart, perhaps because he had nearly died that night Faraz saved his life. The lines on his face seemed deeper. His beard was longer and grayer. But he stood straight, close to six feet tall, and had the same aura of quiet authority Faraz remembered, enhanced by the imam's skullcap he now wore in place of his Afghan turban.

"*Qomandan*," Faraz said, using the Pashto title. Commander.

"Hamed," al-Souri replied. He knew Faraz only in his Afghan cover identity. "I did not believe them when they told me."

"Yes. I can understand."

Al-Souri crossed the small room and slapped Faraz hard with the back of his right hand. Faraz's head jerked to the side and he fell onto all fours, tasting his own blood yet again.

"*Qomandan*, please," he said.

"Traitor," al-Souri whispered, with more venom than Faraz had ever heard him express, even toward the infidels. The commander stood over him and took a knife out of a holder strapped to his waist.

Faraz turned his head up. "Please, *Qomandan*, let me explain."

Al-Souri brandished the knife, ready to strike. "Explain? Explain how you gave our location in Afghanistan to the infidels? Explain how you helped them kill my friend and our leader, Ibn Jihad? Explain how you got away? Explain how even here, you led a spy into our midst?"

"I saved your life, *sayyid*. Would a traitor do that? I was almost killed setting a bomb for you. Would a spy do that? You were my *qomandan*, my imam. You were my father in jihad. And *sayyid*, I was like a son to you, was I not?"

Al-Souri seemed to back off slightly.

"*Qomandan*, please. Allow me to live a few minutes,

to tell you what really happened. Then, if you want to kill me, I will accept it as Allah's will."

Al-Souri kicked Faraz in the ribs, knocking the wind out of him. He fell over, gasping for air.

"Talk," al-Souri said.

While he waited for the prisoner to catch his breath, al-Souri stared at Faraz. The commander's thoughts wandered to the young man he had met in Afghanistan, the one who had gone from doubting his role in jihad to being the hero of an operation, and later, a trusted member of his personal security detail.

Al-Souri had thought of Hamed as a protégé. He defended him when Ibn Jihad had doubted his loyalty. Then, when Hamed fled and the bombs came, al-Souri beat himself up for having allowed a traitor into his inner circle.

But maybe there was a different explanation. If Hamed was loyal, that would mean that he, the great al-Souri, had not been fooled by an infidel spy, that he had, as he had always thought, turned a naïve country boy from the refugee camps into a skilled and loyal fighter in Allah's jihad.

This was the story he wanted to believe. It was so good he had dared not pray for it to be true. And he never thought he would have the opportunity to get the full story of what happened that night in Afghanistan.

Now, here was Hamed in front of him, bent forward, trying to breathe. Hamed was the same age his own sons had been when they were killed in the early years of the jihad. His new sons were still too young for the struggle, so his fighters were his family—boys he turned into men and sent to do Allah's work, perhaps even to have the highest honor, to meet Him as martyrs. Hamed had been among the best of them until, well . . .

Al-Souri lowered his knife but kept it in his hand. He took two crates from the far corner of the shack, sat on one, and gestured for Faraz to sit on the other.

"So, tell me this story, Hamed. Tell me how you were not a traitor, tell me how the infidels found us, where you learned the medical skills to save me, why you killed your brothers in jihad—may Allah protect them—and why you fled the camp even though you were 'not a traitor.' And tell me how you came to be here, three thousand kilometers away, in Syria, with an infidel spy coming to find you. I always enjoy a good story."

Faraz struggled to his feet and sat on the crate. He pushed his hair off his face and stared at his old boss, teacher, mentor . . . target. Faraz was amazed to still be alive, to still have a chance to accomplish both his missions—perhaps a better chance than he'd ever had.

All he had to do was convince al-Souri not to kill him.

Chapter Forty-one

The story Faraz told was a corker.

In it, he was a simple orphan from a refugee camp again. He found meaning and direction through the benevolent hand of al-Souri, the famed fighter, leader and teacher of Allah's Holy War.

But when al-Souri fell out of Ibn Jihad's good graces and his favored one, Hamed, was accused of being a traitor, he had had no choice but to run, to kill the men who had been his brothers in order to save his own life, to seek safety in the mountains. He had not called in the air strike. He loved Allah's jihad. And he was there, in the compound, when the missile hit. He could have been killed along with the others.

Later, in hiding, when he heard al-Souri had returned to Syria, his only goal was to find a way to reach him, to explain, to apologize, to rejoin the jihad.

That is why he had gone to Syria as a foreign fighter. He hadn't known, he said, that the group he joined was opposed to al-Souri's leadership, and when he realized the situation, he had personally killed the traitor al-Jazar. Faraz said he foiled the attack on the outpost out of rage and selfishness, that he hadn't known Nazim was working under al-Souri's orders until after he was captured.

Surely, it was Allah's hand that had brought him, in spite of his own stupidity and incompetence, once again into the presence of al-Souri to beg for his understanding and forgiveness.

Whatever Nazim thought had passed between the visitor and himself was wrong. The man's Pashto was terrible. They were barely able to communicate.

Faraz had rehearsed the story for twenty-four hours. The DIA team would have been proud.

When he finished, al-Souri stood. "You tell an interesting story, Hamed. Only you and Allah know whether it is true."

"It is true, *Qomandan*."

"We shall see."

Al-Souri left and closed the door behind him, plunging Faraz back into darkness.

Over dinner, al-Souri told the story to Nazim, who didn't believe a word of it.

"He attacked us. He fought with the traitor al-Jazar. He gave signals to the spy who came to our camp. And in Afghanistan, he surely betrayed you and ran away and killed many fighters. He cannot be trusted."

Al-Souri did not reply, chewing on a piece of pita.

"Commander, you cannot be considering this."

"Are you telling me now what I can consider and what I cannot consider?"

Nazim looked down at his empty plate. "No, Commander, of course not."

"Good." Al-Souri thought some more. "This man spoiled your attack on the Americans."

"Yes, Commander, and he must be punished."

"If he deserves punishment, it will be provided. But perhaps he can correct his mistake, and in the process convince us he is on the right path."

"I do not trust him."

"I know. I am also not sure whether to trust him. But perhaps a test will convince us both."

"What test?"

Al-Souri laid out his plan. Nazim scratched his head. "He could betray us, reveal our location, destroy everything we have built."

"We will be ready. At the first sign of trouble, we will kill them all."

Nazim sighed. He seemed unconvinced, but that didn't matter. "Yes, Commander," was all he could say.

"Nazim," al-Souri said. "I need you to be with me."

"Of course, Commander."

"I am glad to hear it. There are few I can trust as I trust you. But we need all our resources, all our brothers. And perhaps Hamed, too. I have been busy these last days planning our next operations with our friends from the Gulf. They are impressed with the plan and will provide the money. We will break the infidels' resolve and begin to build our Caliphate."

"I am with you, Commander."

Al-Souri smiled. "Now, bring me one of the phones from the safe. I must make a call to set the plan in motion."

The burner phone's vibration hit Mahmoud's leg as he was handing a plate of baklava to a woman and her boyfriend, who had somehow wandered into Abu-Tawfiq's coffee shop on Edgware Road.

"I will bring your coffees in a moment," he said.

It was near closing time, and Mahmoud had been watching the clock, eager to get home to his real job running comms for the organization now known as the Muslim Caliphate of the Levant.

A call at this time of day was unusual, and must be urgent. Mahmoud hurried through the beaded curtain, went to the back corner of the storage room, and took out the phone.

The screen read "Unknown Caller." He pressed the green button. "Yes."

"Do you know my voice?" The question was in Syrian-accented Arabic, with a hint of something else, as if the speaker had spent many years abroad.

Mahmoud involuntarily snapped to attention, all his senses alert. It was rare that he received a call directly from the commander. He knew better than to say his name. "Yes, I do."

"Good."

"It is an honor, *sahib*."

"Are you well?"

"Praise be to Allah. And you, *sahib*?"

"Praise *al-Jabbar*."

Al-Jabbar was one of the ninety-nine ways to refer to Allah. "Praise al-Jabbar" was a perfectly acceptable way to answer the question "how are you?" but it was unusual enough that it had been chosen as a code word. *Al-Jabbar* meant "The Compeller"—He who compels His faithful to righteousness. It was also the name of one of the missions that the operatives were prepping—the attack that would compel Allah's enemies to surrender. This was the order to set other operations aside and make final preparations for Operation al-Jabbar.

"Praise *al-Jabbar*, indeed," Mahmoud responded, confirming he had understood. And he added a message of his own. "Although He prefers me as a poor man." He was saying that there was not enough money in the accounts to do what al-Souri was asking.

"Surely, Allah will provide very soon," al-Souri said.

Mahmoud broke into a broad smile. "*Allahu akbar.*"

"Be well, my brother," al-Souri said, and he ended the call. It had lasted maybe thirty seconds.

Mahmoud went out the back door without so much as a glance at the couple waiting for their coffee. He destroyed the SIM card and the phone as he walked. He wanted to get to his flat as quickly as possible, but he took a circuitous route. Security was more important now than ever.

The next morning, Faraz was taken out of the shack for the first time since he'd arrived. His chains were removed, and he was allowed to wash. He had a normal breakfast at a table outside the shack, all the time surrounded by armed fighters.

After the meal, Nazim appeared. Faraz stood, ready to defend himself, but Nazim kept his distance. Al-Souri arrived a few seconds later.

"Sit," he ordered.

The two men joined al-Souri at the table. Faraz could see Nazim staring at him, ready to pounce at any sign of hesitation or betrayal.

"In two nights, when the moon is dark, you will prove your loyalty or die the death of a traitor. I will give you the opportunity to correct your mistake. You will join us attacking the American outpost. You will carry a bomb, plant it as close as possible, and when it explodes, you will join us in finishing them."

Faraz swallowed hard. "Yes, *Qomandan*. I will do this for jihad, and for you."

"We will be nearby, with all our firepower," Nazim said. "If you betray us, you will die along with your friends in a great inferno."

"They are not my friends."

"We shall see."

Faraz slept that night in shackles in a tent with armed men outside. He needed a plan.

If he could approach the outpost without being shot, he could have them call in an air strike. But watching al-Souri and Nazim go up in a ball of fire felt too impersonal. He wanted to look into their eyes when he took his revenge. And an air strike wouldn't get the intel Washington needed on the MTO and the financing.

This was going to be complicated, and he only had until tomorrow night to figure it out.

Chapter Forty-two

Commander Will Jackson, wearing desert camo with his new rank insignia, had his cane in his left hand, his duffel in his right, and his carry-on on his back.

He had shaved on the plane, and his tight-coiled black hair was trimmed to the standard quarter-inch length. His leg ached from the long flight, but he was as ready for a combat zone tour as he could be. Less ready for what he was about to do.

Will hadn't bothered to find his billet and drop his things, but rather headed straight for Saddam's ballroom, as directed by the young soldier at the check-in desk. He'd been fantasizing about this for a week, ever since Lumberjack offered him the assignment.

Bridget had been harder to reach lately, no doubt busy, but also likely becoming detached from her stateside life, as always happened. When the transfer orders came, he had decided to surprise her.

Will scanned the cavernous room, its broad columns interrupting the sea of cubicles. In the far corner, on an extra-tall partition, he saw the handwritten DIA sign. He moved toward it, dodging desks like a slalom skier in spite of his cane, picking up speed as he went.

When he reached his destination, he stopped, put down his duffel, straightened his uniform, and knocked on the partition's plastic edge. He poked his head around it. "Is Ms. Davenport here?"

Bridget turned from her screen and gasped. "Will!"

To him, she sounded more surprised than delighted. But she recovered quickly, jumping out of her chair and embracing him.

The words poured out. "Oh my God, Will. What the hell are you doing here? I mean, it's great to see you. I never imagined. Christ, Will, you nearly gave me a heart attack." Then she hugged him again and pulled him into the relative privacy of the cubicle to give him a proper welcome kiss.

"Now, that's a welcome worth flying halfway around the world for," Will said. "For a second there, I wasn't sure."

"Well, you could have sent me an email or something." She smacked his chest, then stood back at arm's length and looked him over, from his cane to his new rank insignia. "The silver leaf looks good on you, Will." She touched the commander's patch and kissed him again. "Wish I could have been there. So, how are you? What, why, how?"

Will dragged his bags into the cubicle and sat in the guest chair to tell her, resting his hand on his cane—his new standard position. He took in the sight of her—hair pulled back in a ponytail, white blouse, khaki slacks over combat boots. Yeah, more than worth flying halfway around the world for.

"That's amazing," Bridget said when he finished the

story. "It's great to have you here, and you must be thrilled to be out of the Pentagon. I guess this means your leg is doing okay."

"Better every day," he said, which was more or less true. "Not quite ready for action—I mean, military action." He raised his eyebrows.

Bridget laughed. "I know what you meant." She blushed a little.

It was good to hear her laugh. They'd both been under so much stress, it seemed like it had been a long time. "Anyway, no military action for me, but it feels good to be closer to the fight. They say I can continue my physical therapy here. How's your mission going? You ready to leave, now that I'm here?"

"No. It's a mess, though. Can't say much about it, but it's, yeah, awful."

Will knew better than to ask any more questions.

Carter's voice came around the partition before he did. "Ms. Davenport, I do believe this is the time of your suppah reservation, and I'm sure the maître d' has your table r . . . I am sorry. I didn't know you had a guest."

Will looked at the tall, muscular man with the shaved head, blond eyelashes, impeccable nonmilitary khakis, amusing accent, and no cane, who, it seemed, had come to take his girlfriend to dinner. Carter looked back with a "what's your problem?" expression.

Bridget interrupted their moment. "Carter, this is Will Jackson, fresh off the boat. Will, Carter Holloway of Spotlight Security."

Will leaned on his cane to stand and extended his right hand.

Carter shook it. "Oh, please, Commander, no need to stand."

To Will, it sounded patronizing, like just about anything anyone said these days. He stood anyway.

"Carter, let's do that dinner another time. Will and I have a lot of catching up to do." Bridget stared at Carter in a way that made Will think there was more meaning in her look than in her words.

Will glanced at Carter for a reaction. The guy's gaze lingered on Bridget half a second longer than Will would have liked.

"Of course. Not a problem," Carter said. He turned toward Will. "Commander, it was good to meet you. Do let me know if Spotlight can be of any service. Bridget, I'll hope to see you soon." He gave a head bow and backed out of the cubicle.

"Interesting character," Will said.

"Yeah, but not a bad guy. You'll like him, I think."

Will wasn't sure which one of them she was trying to convince.

"Let's get you settled and get some chow," she said.

"Some 'suppah,' you mean?"

Bridget rolled her eyes. "Whatever." She put her right hand on his arm, and with her left brushed a nonexistent strand of hair from her face. "Let's go celebrate your arrival."

She took one step and stopped. "Wait. You called the cat sitter, right?"

Will laughed and picked up his bags. "Yes, ma'am. Sarge's board and billeting are fully organized and funded."

"All right. Good job, sailor."

* * *

After dinner in the D-FAC, Bridget walked Will to his trailer. Sitting on his bed, they kissed, and Bridget relaxed into his familiar embrace. She thought about Carter and his very different embrace. There's nothing quite so titillating as being with someone for the first time. But this . . . this was what she had been missing.

She went to kiss him again, but Will pulled away. His hand was on the cane, with the BUD at eye level. The golden eagle seemed to be mocking him—a man who couldn't walk properly, claiming to be something he wasn't.

"Tell me about Carter," he said.

"About Carter? There's nothing to tell about Carter." But then she did tell him, part of the story, anyway. "He's a war-zone friend, someone to have dinner with now and then. That's all. You know how it is."

"No, I don't. I never spent more than a few days at HQ in Kabul, but it seemed like quite the dating scene. Here, too, I imagine."

"Really, Will? Really? You're going to hit me with this?"

"I felt like I was hit with something back in your cubicle."

"Oh, Will. You blast in here, and you're shocked I'm friends with a man you haven't met? You and I, we have something special. Is it this fragile?"

"I don't know. Maybe so. It's been a long road for me, while you've been where the action is—dodging my calls, I'm guessing—and doing dinner and God knows what with Mr. Spotlight."

Bridget stood up. "You've got a lot of goddamn nerve." She towered above him, red-faced. "I've been working my ass off trying to keep people alive, and frankly, not doing a very good job of it." She paused, but composed herself.

Will started to speak, but she cut him off. "All kinds of shit is coming down. You show up . . . Surprise! And you expect me to drop everything to welcome you—which I do, with pleasure—and then some guy I barely know comes to have dinner with me—in the D-FAC—and you, you accuse me of . . . Jesus, Will. I know you've had a tough time, but . . . damn." She walked the two steps to the door, then turned toward him and brought her voice under control. "Let me know when . . . I don't know . . . when you're you again."

She opened the door and left without closing it or looking back.

Will stood and hobbled to the door in time to see Bridget turn a corner and disappear.

This was not the reunion he had hoped for, but it was probably the one he deserved. His wick was short. His expectations were high. And his decision to surprise her was bush-league.

Bridget wasn't the only one who wanted to know when he'd be himself again. He had been wondering about that for a long time. He smacked his right hand against the trailer wall, then reached to slam the door with his left, lifting the cane off the floor and nearly toppling over.

* * *

Speed-walking toward her trailer, Bridget was livid. Why did Will have to show up unannounced? Why did Carter have to come by? Why the hell was she so, so angry?

That was a good question. She could blame the stress of work and the shock of Will's arrival. The truth was—guilt. It was only a kiss, but . . .

Still, damn Will for assuming the worst. Maybe she was overreacting, but she didn't need this right now. She had one operative dead and another in imminent danger, maybe also dead by now. If they confirmed that—please God, no—she'd be out of there, back home without Will or Carter.

She diverted her route to head for the office. She certainly couldn't sleep now, and maybe the experts in Washington had something, anything, on the fate of a prisoner held in a terrorist camp somewhere in northeastern Syria.

Chapter Forty-three

Faraz, Nazim, and al-Souri crawled up the same hill where Faraz had killed Nic. He was afraid they would come upon the rotting corpse, but the desert sands had covered it, or maybe someone else had found it and given the guy a decent burial.

Lying flat under the moonless sky, they surveyed the scene. After Nazim's failed attack, the Americans had added more lights and more lookouts. It was going to be difficult to approach the outpost without being seen.

Faraz knew that from his previous visit to the hill. He had built his plan around it. "Perhaps from the other side," he said.

"No," Nazim said. "You will not be out of my sight."

Al-Souri overruled him. "Hamed is right. There is no other way. Send one man with him."

"Why not fire our missiles now and be done with it?"

"Because it will take all our ammunition to defeat them, and we need it for what lies ahead. We will not spend it all tonight unless we have to. And Nazim, you know victory in such a battle is not assured."

Faraz could see Nazim's face redden even in the darkness.

"We will do this my way," al-Souri said. "And perhaps we will also learn whether a traitor or a fighter has arrived in our camp."

Faraz walked unarmed ahead of Bassem, the man Nazim had assigned to accompany him. Bassem had a finger on the trigger of his AK, the weapon raised slightly so he could shoot Faraz quickly if he had to. Nazim had chosen well. Bassem was among his most able fighters, and he was over six feet tall with the body of an offensive lineman.

They took a long route, behind the hill, across the road, and into some trees to come up on the other side of the outpost. Faraz carried the bomb in a shoulder bag. From the edge of the trees, they were closer to the outpost than the hill was, but there was no cover to protect the last thirty meters Faraz would have to cross to plant the bomb against the wall.

"This is not good," Bassem said as they reached a spot opposite the midpoint of the far side of the base.

"Yes," Faraz replied. "Come here. Look at this." Faraz led Bassem a few steps into the woods. He put the bag on the ground, turned quickly, and took a step toward Bassem, forcing him to move his gun aside. "Listen," he said, but he followed it with a knee to Bassem's testicles.

Bassem doubled over. Faraz pushed the rifle aside and dove into Bassem, throwing the big man off balance and pushing him to the ground. Faraz pummeled his face with punches. With his man momentarily disabled, Faraz grabbed the gun and drove the bayonet into Bassem's side.

He cried out in pain, but Faraz cut off the sound with a hand to his mouth, at the same time pulling the blade out, raising it, and driving it into Bassem's throat. Faraz lay on him while he died, hoping the fight had not drawn the Americans' attention or triggered the bomb's timer.

Faraz got up slowly. He unzipped the bag and inspected the digital clock strapped to the top of the cluster of plastic explosives and the sack of shrapnel. It seemed to be intact, and the countdown clock still read 5:00.

He breathed a sigh of relief and sat down on the ground. He looked out through the trees and could see no change. It seemed their scuffle was deep enough in the trees that they were out of sight of the Americans, and certainly of al-Souri's men on the hill beyond.

Part one of Faraz's plan had worked. Now for the hard part.

Faraz walked through the trees, staying in shadow, looking for somewhere his approach to the base could not be seen from the hill beyond. There was no perfect spot, but he found a place where he thought they would see him only briefly before he was obscured by the outpost's walls.

He took a breath, looked at the fortified outpost. This was a terrible plan. Worst case, the Americans would shoot him, and al-Souri would launch his attack. Second-worst case, al-Souri would see what he was doing and launch the attack anyway. Success was the least likely outcome. But it was the best he could come up with, and there was no turning back now.

Faraz crouched at the tree line, put the shoulder bag on the ground, waited for the guards on the wall to turn the other way, and ran.

He only had a few seconds, but that was all he needed to get out of al-Souri and Nazim's sightline. Then he dove to the ground, his hands and feet spread. He needed to shout, but he had to find the right volume level—loud enough for the Americans to hear, but soft enough that his voice wouldn't carry across the hard ground to the hill.

He saw half a dozen American M4 rifles turn toward him.

"I'm an American! U.S. Army. Undercover. Don't shoot. Don't use a loudspeaker. Please help me."

A voice came over a megaphone. "Take off your jacket, slowly."

"Yes. I will do it. Please, stay quiet. No alarm. No loudspeaker. I'm undercover. Hostiles are nearby."

The voice on the megaphone came again, but more quietly. "Take off the jacket."

Faraz complied, showing that he was not wearing a bomb.

Three men came out of a side gate and moved toward him, their weapons pointed at his head. One of the men frisked him. Then the same voice spoke, but without the megaphone. "Who the fuck are you?"

Faraz looked up, saw the captain's bars on the man's desert camouflage uniform. "Lieutenant Faraz Abdallah, sir, 101st Airborne, on assignment for the DIA."

Still lying on the sand and rocks of the Syrian desert—under the lights of the outpost and, he hoped, outside the view of al-Souri and Nazim—Faraz told a short version of his story. He gave the captain his code name, his security code, and the phone number of the ops center.

"Ask for Bridget Davenport," he said. "She'll vouch for me. And Captain, I led the attack that saved the outpost a week ago."

"Sit up," the captain said. The man shined a light in Faraz's eyes and studied him.

Faraz raised himself off the ground, exposing his shirt stained with Bassem's blood.

"You injured?"

"No. The guy's in the woods, dead."

The captain lowered his weapon. "That's a helluva story."

"I know. But it's true. And we don't have much time until their leader assumes I ran or got caught and decides to send his full force at us. We have to move fast."

"We?"

"Sorry, sir, but my mission is high priority. We can't blow my cover. We need to set off an explosion in the next few minutes that causes some damage but, obviously, doesn't kill anyone. Then I need to go back to them."

"Back to them?"

"Yes, sir. This will prove my bona fides. Please, we need to go inside and get started. Oh, and one more thing."

"What's that?"

"There's a bomb in a bag at the tree line. Your men will have to deal with it later."

"A bomb? You brought a bomb to my camp?"

"It's far enough away that it's not a threat. Please, sir, we need to move. Your men need to plan a devastating attack. On themselves."

* * *

Captain Jamie Anthony couldn't believe what he was doing. He had a man in his office who looked for all the world like a terrorist but talked like an American and knew all the right things to say. He had his men putting together a bogus bomb that would make a lot of noise and scatter a lot of sand. He had his medical staff setting up half his men with phony injuries, like they did in a medevac exercise. And he was sitting on hold with some number in D.C. that claimed to be the DIA ops center.

The allegedly fake jihadi at his desk was sucking on his second bottle of water and looking more nervous by the second. The guy kept telling Captain Anthony how much he had to hurry. But he wasn't going to do anything irreversible until someone picked up the goddamn phone.

Anthony was under orders to be extra careful after the attack on Outpost Brennan. He still wasn't a hundred percent sure whether he'd end up arresting this guy or implementing his lunatic plan.

Bridget was still fuming about Will as she sat at her desk in Baghdad trying to convince herself to go get some sleep. Her call with Liz Michaels at the Pentagon had contained no new information and no new ideas for how to find Faraz. There was also the bad but not unexpected news that terrorist chatter was up again, sparking fears that the next attack was imminent.

It was after midnight now, and she needed to get some sleep. She entered the code to lock her computer and jumped when the phone rang.

"Davenport."

"Ma'am, this is the ops center. I have a call for you

from a Captain Anthony at FOB Pierce. He used code word Blowback."

Bridget bolted upright in her chair. For a second, she couldn't speak. Finally, she got out, "Put him through."

The call from northern Syria to Washington and back to Baghdad covered more than ten thousand miles, even though Bridget was only about three hundred miles from Forward Operating Base Pierce, as the crow flies.

Captain Anthony had just started to explain the situation when he stopped. Faraz could hear Bridget interrupt him.

"Yes, ma'am," the captain said. Then he listened. "Yes, ma'am, all possible assistance." Then he turned to Faraz. "She wants to speak to you."

Faraz took the receiver. "Ms. Davenport?"

"Yes. Faraz, thank God you're alive. How are you? Do you have anything on an MTO?"

"No, ma'am, but I'm okay. I'm back with al-Souri and hope to find out what he's up to soon. Right now, I have to go. The captain will fill you in on the rest."

"But, Faraz—"

"Sorry, no time. I'll be in touch when I have something." Faraz looked at Anthony. "We good?"

"Yes. We're good."

Anthony reached for the phone, but Faraz put it back in its cradle. "Time to go."

Less than two minutes later, the captain was shaking Faraz's hand as they said goodbye at the side gate.

Anthony's team had their "explosion" ready. The "victims" and the medical staff were poised to spring into action.

"Goodbye, sir, and thank you."

"Good luck, Lieutenant. We're here if you need us."

"Thanks. Um, there is one thing." Faraz leaned in and spoke softly to Captain Anthony.

"How will we know when and where?" Anthony asked.

"Keep your patrols out as usual, southwest of here. If we get lucky, you'll see us and have a chance to, um, further boost my credibility. I'll try to signal you. If it doesn't work out, I'll handle things on my own."

"Seems like you do a lot of that."

"Yes, sir."

"Okay, Lieutenant. We'll be watching."

"Thank you, sir. Are the men ready?"

"When you are. Good luck out there."

Faraz turned toward the trees and took off running.

On the hill, Nazim had already twice told al-Souri he thought Hamed had fled, that they needed to go after him and to launch their attack on the outpost. His doubts, and al-Souri's own, were trying the commander's patience.

Al-Souri saw Nazim was about to speak again. He held up his hand. "A few more minutes," he said."

"We are exposed here. If he sends the infidels—"

"Do not teach me tactics! I was fighting infidels when you were sucking your mother's teat. Now, quiet!"

Al-Souri's anger was intended to mask his own doubt. He wanted to be right about Hamed, but his confidence was waning. He turned back toward the outpost.

"Look! There!" he said, pointing to the far side of the base. "There he is."

They saw Faraz running toward the trees. The Americans opened fire on him, a fierce fusillade, but it looked like Faraz made it to the cover of the woods.

Then an explosion rocked the base, and a fire broke out.

Al-Souri smiled.

The base alarm went off, a low siren that rose and fell in rhythm. They could see a frenzy of activity. They could hear shouting. But they were too far to make out the details.

"He did it," al-Souri said.

"Yes. It seems he did," Nazim acknowledged without enthusiasm.

"Look. They are running inside, carrying a wounded man, I think."

"Shall we attack now, Commander, finish them all?"

Al-Souri thought before answering. "No. We must save our ammunition, and our men. We have struck a strong blow and learned what we needed to learn. We return to base as soon as Hamed and Bassem reach us."

Back at the camp, Faraz and al-Souri had tea in the commander's office. It reminded Faraz of the room in Afghanistan where they'd studied Koran together—the desk cluttered, the windows dirty, no place comfortable to sit.

On the hill, al-Souri and Nazim had believed Faraz's story that the infidels' gunfire killed Bassem, who had been waiting among the trees, and that Bassem's blood was on Faraz's clothes because he had tried to revive him.

It was not hard to convince them that it was too dangerous to go back to retrieve the body. Al-Souri ordered a ceremony for the martyr in the morning. Now was the time for a quiet celebration, a recommitment, a reunion of father and son.

"You did well, Hamed," al-Souri said.

"Thank you, *Qomandan*."

"Already the radio is reporting on our victory. Many dead and injured. We have again shown the infidels they cannot come to our land without consequences."

"*Allahu akbar*."

"It is unfortunate that we lost Bassem. We need all our fighters for the work to come. This now includes you. The dictator must fall, and the infidels must be expelled."

"Yes, *Qomandan*." Faraz decided to see whether al-Souri's good mood would loosen his tongue. "And around the world, as well, no? The November attacks were a great victory."

Al-Souri seemed surprised by the question. "Your role is here, Hamed. Do not worry about what is not your affair."

Faraz clearly had some work to do to further regain al-Souri's trust if he was going to get the intel he needed.

Chapter Forty-four

Bridget debriefed Captain Anthony on a secure conference call, with Liz and General Hadley listening. She wrote up her report and caught a few hours of sleep.

When she woke up, her first thought was about Will. Here she was in a war zone, and her boyfriend shows up. How many times had she fantasized about that? He'd been through a lot. She should go find him, cut him some slack.

But his jump to the wrong conclusion upset her, despite the fact that it had almost been the right conclusion. And she didn't want to deal with all that right now. She had a ton of work to do. She'd find Will later.

Back at her desk, Bridget saw that news of the attack on FOB Pierce was all over the Afghan and international outlets—three Americans and seven Syrian militiamen "dead," a dozen more "injured." There were photos taken by one of the troops. There was blood everywhere. There was even a video clip of a memorial service. With a little coaching from Liz and her team, Captain Anthony and his men had done an excellent job protecting Faraz's cover.

Hadley had fired off a rare congratulatory email. No doubt he'd get the story into the president's morning intel brief. This was big. They were back in business, although Faraz was still in extreme danger, and she was painfully aware that the last time he had seemed to succeed, they'd been hit with the November attacks.

Satellite photos of the area around FOB Pierce gave them their best indication yet of exactly where al-Souri's headquarters was, where Faraz was. They could start making plans for attack or extraction. But they couldn't move on, either, not until Faraz got what they needed and sent them some sort of signal.

After a few hours at her desk, running some contingency scenarios and dealing with other issues Liz threw at her, Bridget needed some lunch. She left her desk and decided to treat herself to an Iraqi kebab from the vendors who were allowed to set up in the parking lot that separated Saddam's palace from the building being used as the commissary. Maybe she'd do a little shopping while she was over there. Fight with the boyfriend—retail therapy. Seemed logical, even in a war zone. Maybe especially in a war zone.

Bridget put on her sunglasses as she emerged into the midday glare and walked along a path toward the base's main road. As she was about to cross it, she heard the emergency medical alarm.

To her left, she saw the main gate slide open and medics running toward it from several directions. Bridget stopped to watch the drama unfold.

Five armored vehicles sped through the gate. The lead one stopped about twenty meters from where she was standing. Two of the trucks were damaged. Men jumped from their seats and ran to help unload their injured colleagues.

Bridget saw Castillo and some of the other Spotlight guys she had met. But where was Carter?

"What happened?" she shouted.

"IED," came the response. Improvised Explosive Device, the military's designation for a roadside bomb.

Memories flashed of her own IED experience in Afghanistan years ago, and of the carnage at Bethesda. She put her right hand on her stomach, losing her appetite for kebabs.

That's when she saw Carter. He came from the back of the convoy covered with blood and dirt. He was helping to carry a casualty onto a gurney. Bridget took off at a run.

She reached Carter in a few seconds, as he relinquished his hold on the injured man. Bridget grabbed his arm.

"Oh my God, Carter!" She raised her voice, "Hey, we need another litter over here!"

"No, Bridget. It's okay. It's not my blood. It's his." Carter gestured toward the man now being rushed away by the medics.

"Oh, thank God," Bridget said. She embraced Carter, ignoring the blood.

Will's new office was some distance away, and his bad leg made him a slow walker. He'd come out to see what the emergency was and arrived within sight of the convoy just in time to see Bridget holding Carter.

He stopped and stared, at first not sure of what he was seeing. It was only a brief hug, but when it ended, she held Carter's arm as they walked toward the aid station. Will felt the heat rise on his face. He gripped his cane hard, and he felt as if everyone was staring at him.

His body slumped. He turned and limped back toward his office. People still running toward the convoy made way for the cripple.

Will thought about little else all afternoon. He considered going to see Bridget, but he was too angry. He was sure he was right about her and Carter. There was no choice but to accept the new reality of his injured leg, but he'd be damned if he was going to accept this. Damn her. Damn Carter. Damn this life.

Hours later, Will came upon Carter sitting with Castillo and some of his Spotlight team members in the D-FAC.

"I guess that wasn't your blood, then," Will said, standing at their table.

Carter's eyebrows came together. "No, Commander. It was not. And thankfully, my colleague is going to be all right."

"And what about Bridget? Is she going to be all right, too?"

"Excuse me?"

"I saw you two together when the convoy came in."

"She was kind enough to come over and express concern for me, and she was relieved that it was, as you noted, not my blood."

"Very pleased, from what I could tell."

Carter's colleagues chuckled, but he gave them a look that shut them up.

Will mumbled, "Son of a bitch."

"Pardon me?"

Will raised his voice. "I said you're a son of a fucking bitch."

"Commander, normally we could step outside to determine that, but in your condition . . . "

Will dropped his cane and dove at Carter, getting in the first punch to the big man's jaw. Still in his chair, Carter threw Will off, and he fell to the wooden floor next to his cane. Carter stood and held out an open palm toward the Spotlight guys. They stayed where they were, but he couldn't prevent them from whooping and hollering.

Two MPs were moving fast, zigzagging between tables in their direction.

Carter loomed over Will. "Let's not, shall we?"

"We will one day," Will said. Carter reached down to help Will stand, but he slapped his hand away. The MPs arrived, and each of them grabbed one of Will's arms.

"Let us help you, sir," one of them said.

Will tried to shake them off, but they held firm. He surrendered, putting his weight on them so he could get to his feet. Carter picked up Will's cane and handed it to the MP.

"Now, let's get you out of here, Commander," the MP said.

Will limped away, still held between the MPs, finally shaking them off at the exit door.

He grabbed his cane, walked two steps, and fell. His leg hurt like hell. The MPs picked him up again and half carried him to the aid station.

* * *

After spending the night in the clinic on some serious pain meds, Will was summoned to the Joint Special Ops command HQ, where an army brigadier general named Bigelow made him wait an hour on a metal folding chair in a tiny hallway. Bigelow worked for the three-star who commanded Special Ops by all services throughout Iraq.

Finally ushered into the office, Will found Bigelow standing behind his desk, feet apart, hands on hips. Will stood at attention as best he could, staring straight ahead at the star on Bigelow's chest.

The general leaned forward over the desk and looked at Will's rank insignia. "I was just checking."

"Sir?"

"I couldn't believe that a navy commander would start a brawl in the D-FAC. What the hell is your problem?"

"I apologize, sir. I—"

"You're damned right you apologize, and you will apologize to the man you attacked, and the D-FAC boss, and me and anybody else I tell you to."

"Yes, sir."

Bigelow stood up straight, framed by columns on either side with wood paneling behind, in what must have once been the office of one of Saddam's cronies. His salt-and-pepper hair was trimmed short. A Ranger tab on the left arm of his camo jacket identified him as one of the army's elite, definitely not someone to be messed with.

"Is this going to be a problem going forward?"

"No, sir. It was a personal matter. I lost my composure. It won't happen again." Will still stood at attention, hand on cane.

"Commander, that better be your solemn promise. One

more incident—of any kind—and you will spend the rest of your tour behind bars, followed by a navy brig back home. And that promotion you just got will be long gone."

"Yes, sir. I understand. You have my word."

"You're damn lucky the Spotlight guy didn't want to make an issue of it. I was afraid you'd have to be on the next plane out of here. We can't afford to lose you, and we can't afford any more crap like this. Do I make myself clear?"

"Yes, sir."

"How's the leg?"

"Better than it's been in weeks, with the extra meds they gave me last night."

"Good. Now, get back to work. And I strongly urge you not to end up back here on any disciplinary matter."

"Yes, sir."

Chapter Forty-five

There were no more armed guards watching Faraz, but he felt Nazim's eyes on him all the time. The man worked him hard, ordering him to do extra runs with heavy packs—simulating the weight of bombs. Whenever Faraz didn't understand an order, he got a smack in the back of the head. More memories of Afghanistan, when he was a fresh terrorist recruit.

After several days of such treatment, Faraz confronted his tormentor. "I am not your prisoner anymore," he shouted in halting Arabic.

Nazim exploded with a tirade Faraz didn't fully understand.

Faraz responded with a screed of his own in Pashto. Nazim hit Faraz in the chest with both hands, knocking him down, and spat on him. Then he turned his back and walked away, daring Faraz to attack him.

The next day, al-Souri called Faraz into his office. "Nazim is not happy with you."

"He cannot accept that I am a fighter."

"I have spoken to him, but you must also show him the respect he deserves."

"Yes, *Qomandan*."

"You will go on the supply run to the market today."

"Nazim will not want it."

"I have spoken to him."

"Thank you, *Qomandan*."

They took two vehicles, an SUV and a pickup truck, with three men in each. The truck had the lead. Faraz and Nazim were in the SUV with a fighter named Khalil driving. Nazim still refused to let Faraz carry a weapon.

They were heading northeast toward open desert. Nazim must know a market town Faraz hadn't been to. Or maybe he was taking Faraz to a remote area to kill him. Still, Faraz was happy about the direction they were going, and that the vehicles kicked up large clouds of dust as they sped along the road.

Faraz was alone in the back seat. He put his arm out the open window and let it hang down toward the road. He waved it casually back and forth, like a pendulum. To anyone in the other vehicle who saw him, it would look like a silly, childish move.

They drove for about ten minutes, and Faraz's arm got tired from repeating his signal over and over. He was about to give up when an explosion flipped the pickup truck in front of them onto its side.

Khalil barely managed to avoid the wreck, turning the SUV's wheel and sending it off the road. They hit a hole and bounced hard. The engine died. Khalil banged his head on the ceiling and passed out.

Faraz held onto the front seat and prayed. Through the windshield, he saw a dozen militiamen running down a dune, firing AKs as they went, strafing the pickup truck but not the SUV.

Nice job.

Nazim threw the door open. “Out! Out!” he shouted. Faraz followed him, and they crouched behind the engine for maximum cover.

Faraz looked around the vehicle. “Careful!” Nazim pulled him back. But Faraz had seen what he needed to see. Captain Anthony was looking back at him through field glasses from the top of the hill.

“Come, Hamed!” Nazim ordered. “We go to the pickup!” He started to pull Faraz toward the other vehicle, where the men were trying to climb out through a window.

“No!” Faraz shouted, tackling Nazim as a flying 40-milimeter grenade obliterated the truck and its occupants.

Faraz and Nazim lay flat and covered their heads against the debris. Faraz saw the shock on Nazim’s face. He grabbed Khalil’s AK from the front seat and went to the edge of the pickup to fire toward the militiamen. Several of the them went down, perhaps a bit too fast. Faraz ducked back behind the engine as a hail of gunfire went high and wide.

Nazim moved to the spot Faraz had used and fired. Watching from under the vehicle, Faraz saw two militiamen fall. He couldn’t be sure whether they had actually been hit.

Then the militiamen’s return fire came again, closer this time. Faraz pressed his body to the ground.

“Aaach!” Nazim yelled. He fell backward, wounded on his left arm, nearly landing on Faraz.

“Commander, stay down,” Faraz said. His Arabic had improved enough that he knew basic commands, and he’d been rehearsing this scene in his mind since his last words with Captain Anthony at the outpost.

Faraz grabbed the AK and took his place at the firing position. He fired high and waved his weapon left and right.

The militiamen turned and ran back up the hill, leaving their "casualties" behind.

"We must go," Faraz said. "They are breaking off their attack. Can you get in?"

"Of course. It is nothing."

Faraz helped Nazim up and boosted him into the back seat of the SUV, then went to the other side, opened the door, and pushed the still-unconscious driver to the middle seat. Blood from Khalil's head dripped down the window. Faraz got in and praised Allah when the vehicle started.

He also praised Allah that the attack had gone better than he expected. Not only had he come under fire and performed well, he had saved Nazim's life. If this didn't convince him of "Hamed's" commitment to jihad, nothing would.

Faraz turned the wheel hard and hit the gas, skidding around into the direction he wanted. He got the vehicle back up onto the road, skirted the burning pickup truck, and sped back toward camp.

The guards opened the gate to let Faraz's vehicle slip through and skid to a stop. A fighter ran up to them. "Where is the other vehicle?"

Nazim got down from the SUV, holding his injured left arm with his right hand. "We were hit. They are gone. Martyrs. Take care of Khalil." Nazim went directly into the headquarters building, leaving Faraz to help the others with Khalil.

As they approached the clinic, Faraz noticed two SUVs he didn't recognize parked near the back of the camp. One of them had blackout windows and a phone antenna on top. Security men he also didn't know guarded the SUVs.

Once Khalil was settled in the clinic, Faraz walked to one of the outdoor sinks to wash, then went to the headquarters.

As he approached, al-Souri emerged with two men. One appeared to be in his fifties, portly and wearing a Western-style suit coat. The other was much younger and stayed a step behind. Nazim came out after them and waited by the door. Al-Souri was speaking and gesturing. When the older man spoke, al-Souri made a show of agreeing.

"It is unfortunate," Faraz heard al-Souri say. "Three martyrs. But many more of the traitors were killed."

Faraz had rarely seen the *Qomandan* act so solicitously toward anyone.

Al-Souri and the others walked past Faraz like he didn't exist. At the vehicles, al-Souri made a half bow and kissed his visitor on both cheeks. He waved as they drove away.

Nazim came up to Faraz from behind. "Khalil is in the clinic?"

"Yes."

Nazim looked Faraz up and down. "You did well today," he said, seeming to be rather unhappy to have to say it.

"Who was with the commander?"

Nazim snorted with evident disdain. "They call him al-Malik." The king.

Before Faraz could ask anything more, Nazim walked

on toward the clinic. Faraz watched the gate close behind the visitors' vehicles.

After their near-death experience, Nazim seemed more inclined to accept Faraz as a member of the team.

"You will come on the tax run," Nazim said. "Bring your sleeping pad."

Nazim's injured arm was bandaged and lashed to his body. Faraz could see he was eager to continue operations as usual, not to show any weakness in front of his men.

The "tax run" provided some income for al-Souri. Nazim was good at convincing local merchants to support the jihad, particularly with Faraz and three other fighters to back him up. They made several stops on the first day, then had dinner courtesy of a village elder.

In the evening, the visiting fighters bedded down for the night in a small empty house, and Nazim regaled them with war stories by the light of a small kerosene lantern. Faraz and the other men made a point of being duly impressed.

"Those are great victories," Faraz said. "But what of the future? When will we strike the infidels again?" He still spoke haltingly, but his Arabic was starting to flow.

"Do not worry, Hamed, our leader has plans. The world will soon know that November was not our last operation."

"Tell us, Nazim," one of the fighters begged. "A great blow to America, perhaps?"

Faraz was grateful for the unwitting help with the interrogation. The men leaned in to hear the answer.

Nazim held up a hand. "I cannot tell you much, my

brothers. But yes, America will feel our wrath. You saw our visitor yesterday?"

The men nodded.

"You saw his vehicle, smelled his cigars and his whiskey? Maybe you smelled his women, too." Nazim spat on the floor.

The men gave an awkward laugh.

"You called him al-Malik," Faraz said.

"Ha! We should call him al-Meḥfaza." The Wallet.

The men laughed again.

"He is a messenger named Assali, nothing more." Nazim sighed. "He gives us scraps from the wallets of his masters, but we must accept him. We need a king's wallet for what the commander has planned. I assure you, my brothers, the infidels will pay a much higher price."

"Tell us," one of the men urged.

Nazim paused for dramatic effect. "My brothers, what do you think the Americans value above all—except money, of course?"

"Above money?" Faraz asked in mock bewilderment. "I do not know." The men laughed again, and turned to Nazim for the answer.

Nazim scanned their faces, clearly reveling in his superior understanding of the enemy and his inside knowledge of the strategy to defeat it.

The arrogance disgusted Faraz, even as he used it to get what he needed. "Please, Commander, do not keep us waiting any longer."

Nazim smiled. "Americans love their money, but they will spend it on one thing without end. They will buy only the best, provide only the highest quality, ensure only the finest outcome for one thing."

"Their women?" one of the fighters guessed.

"No, my brother. Not their women."

"What, then?" Faraz asked. He was not going to let this opportunity pass.

Nazim surveyed the fighters in the half-light. "My brothers, our goal is to make the cost of the infidel occupation so high that they leave our lands. We have killed their soldiers. We have attacked their cities. We have damaged their oil supply and their banking system. And still they persist."

"What is it?" Faraz asked. "What is their weak point?"

Nazim smiled.

"Their children."

He let the words hang in the stale air.

Faraz started sweating. He was glad it was dark, because he was sure his face was turning red.

"Their children?" he asked. His voice revealed his shock. He cleared his throat. "How will we attack their children?"

"That I cannot tell you, but be assured the scope will be broad. The Americans are soft. They do not protect their families. The opportunities are many. The three targets of November were nothing compared to what is to come."

What could Nazim be talking about? Schools? Universities? Day-care centers?

"But does the Noble Koran allow such a thing?" Faraz knew the answer to his question—at least, the answer al-Souri would provide—but he needed to keep Nazim talking.

"Of course it does. They teach blasphemy and hatred of Islam from kindergarten to universities. They pervert

Allah's teaching, make whores of their women. Most important, these attacks will break the infidels' will to fight us. They must see that we will stop at nothing to bring Allah's light to the world."

The men were silent.

Faraz's mind was racing. "And that is why that man, Assali, came to the camp?"

"Yes. These things do not come cheap. But when his masters heard our leader's plan, they could not say no. And now . . . well, preparations are already being made. We do not have long to wait. But, my brothers, I have said too much. We must sleep now."

Nazim turned off the lantern and laid down on his mat.

Faraz wanted to press for details, but he dared not.

"*Allahu akbar*," one of the fighters whispered in evident awe. Faraz joined the others in echoing the sentiment.

Chapter Forty-six

Faraz hardly slept, and throughout the following morning of village visits he couldn't focus on his duties. He had no reason to doubt Nazim's words. He was desperate to find out the details. But he knew that might never happen. What was most important now was to get out of there, to make contact with Washington.

Nazim's words echoed in his brain. "We do not have long to wait."

On the way back at midday, they stopped at the gas station near the camp. The rickety building looked like it might fall down at any moment. The owner, his skin darkened by long days in the sun and etched by years of hard work for little pay, bowed to Nazim. He rushed to fill the vehicles and half a dozen jerry cans.

Faraz and the other fighters stood guard. Nazim paid the man, who made a show of not wanting to accept money from the defenders of Allah. But he took it anyway.

As they boarded the vehicles, Faraz saw the gas station owner finish counting the money, and then, with a big smile on his face, take out his phone, apparently to tell someone about the large sale he had made.

* * *

Back at the camp in early afternoon, dismissed from duties to wash and eat lunch, Faraz started to formulate a plan. There was no more waiting now. He had to make his way to the American outpost.

He'd have to get past the guards somehow. The outpost was a long walk, and if they were chasing him, he'd never make it. Ideally, he'd steal a vehicle, but that would be impossible without raising an alarm.

His plan was not coming together. Every time he thought it through, it ended with him dead by the side of the road.

Crossing the camp from the showers to his tent, he berated himself, pushed himself to come up with something. From the corner of his eye, he saw al-Souri emerge from the headquarters building onto the porch. The commander shouted, "Nazim!"

Faraz turned to see Nazim come out of his own tent shirtless.

"Come here!" al-Souri shouted, and he went back inside.

That was unusual. Normally, al-Souri would send someone to retrieve whoever he wanted to see. Faraz was trained not to ignore anything, to focus on what was not usual and find out why. Rarely was a departure from habit or protocol irrelevant.

Nazim disappeared back into his tent and came out again, buttoning up his shirt. He must have also sensed the urgency of the summons because he jogged to the headquarters building—another thing Faraz had never seen.

Faraz ducked into his tent and dressed. Then he made his way toward the headquarters along a side path behind some tents. He came up alongside the building, under al-Souri's office window.

The window was closed, muffling the conversation inside. But Faraz could hear someone shouting. He realized it was Nazim shouting at al-Souri. Another departure from the usual. Why would he do that? Al-Souri would not tolerate such disrespect. Faraz expected Nazim to be marched out of the building and punished.

He caught a few words of Nazim's tirade. "*Qiltilak haik!*" I told you so.

What? What had Nazim told al-Souri?

Faraz heard al-Souri speaking, but couldn't make out the words. He was not shouting back at Nazim. Rather, his tone sounded subdued, defeated.

Then Nazim spoke again, louder. "*Sawf 'aslahah.*" I will take care of it. Or maybe, I will take care of *him*. In Arabic, it was impossible to know without hearing what came before.

A million questions flew through Faraz's mind as he stood there, frozen in place against the wall. But he had no time for questions. He had to assume they were talking about him—that Nazim had been right about *him*, that Nazim would take care of *him*.

He had to get out of there. Now.

Faraz couldn't take the chance that he could convince al-Souri again that whatever information he had was wrong. Not with what he knew, what he had to report.

He moved to the rear corner of the building. The side gate was in front of him, but it was locked. He was sweating. His heart rate spiked, and he was breathing fast. His fight-or-flight instinct took over, and he knew he would not win a fight against Nazim and the whole camp.

Faraz turned right into the alleyway along the wall and walked quickly toward the back of the camp. He didn't want to draw attention by running.

He came around a corner and saw his destination, the refueling area. Two men were refilling an old, rusted pickup truck from a jerry can. One of them had leaned his AK-47 against the side of the vehicle.

The men took no note of Faraz as he moved toward them. He grabbed the AK and hit the nearest fighter in the back of the head. The man fell, dropping the jerry can on its side and starting a flow of gasoline into the dirt. His colleague froze in place long enough for Faraz to flip the rifle and kill him with one pull of the trigger. The shot drew the kind of attention Faraz didn't want, but he had no other options.

He jumped into the truck. The key was in the ignition. He started the engine and stepped on the accelerator. Faraz held the rifle out the window. He fired at the puddle of gasoline, setting it on fire.

As he brought the truck onto the camp's main road heading for the gate, he saw two things. He saw that the gate was closed, and he saw Nazim come out of the headquarters building and take an AK from one of the guards.

"Hamed! Where is Hamed?" Nazim yelled.

"There!" shouted one of the guards, pointing at the vehicle.

"Stop him!"

Behind Faraz, the open jerry can exploded. With his left hand out the truck window, he turned his gun toward the front of the camp, firing at random, scattering two fighters who were running to follow Nazim's order.

Faraz floored the accelerator and turned the AK toward

the passenger side of the pickup, firing through the open window toward the headquarters. Nazim and the guards dove for cover. Faraz sped past them and hit the gate at high speed, breaking it open.

The truck's bumper caught on the left side of the gate, swinging the vehicle around. Faraz found himself facing Nazim, who was running at him from the headquarters. He threw the truck into reverse and ducked his head as Nazim strafed the windshield. The ancient transmission screamed in protest.

Faraz turned the wheel to spin the vehicle again, shifted gears, and pressed the pedal to the floor. Dirt flew, but the truck jumped forward. He looked up to see the road, then lowered his head again as gunfire shattered his rear window.

The vehicle went into an open field. Faraz had to raise his head again to get back onto the road, but now he was far enough that their bullets couldn't reach him. He held on tight and leaned in hard, trying to coax more speed from the straining engine.

In the rearview mirror, just before the road turned and the camp went out of sight, Faraz saw Nazim gesturing wildly, issuing orders. Faraz assumed he was calling for vehicles. The camp's SUVs had big engines. He'd never make it all the way to the outpost.

He could think of only one option. It wouldn't save him, but it might enable him to complete his mission.

At the first intersection, he went right. The road took him past a grove of trees, which would obscure Nazim's view. Maybe he'd guess wrong at the crossroads. Faraz needed more time than he had.

He arrived at the gas station less than two minutes later, slamming on the brakes and startling the owner, who came running outside.

"What is it? What is it?" the man asked in a panic.

"Inside!" Faraz ordered, emerging from the truck AK-first and pushing the man backward into the one-room building—part office, part bedroom. It stank of gasoline and dirty sheets. "Give me your phone."

"My brother—"

"Now!" Faraz screamed, leaning in close and pushing the rifle's barrel into the man's chest.

"Yes, yes," the owner said, reaching into his pocket. His hand shook as he handed over an old flip phone. Faraz took it, turned the gun, and hit the man in the face. He went down hard.

Faraz went out the back door, leaned against the wall, and opened the phone. His adrenaline was surging. This is what he had trained for, to do his job under unimaginable stress. A few months ago, stress had almost killed him. Now, it fueled his determination.

The phone had plenty of battery power but only one bar of service. Faraz forced his shaking fingers to dial the number.

The call seemed to take forever to go through. Praise Allah, it was answered on the first ring.

"Operator."

Chapter Forty-seven

Bridget was at her desk, searching the intercept logs for anything that could refer to a jihadi prisoner. She hadn't seen Will since his fight with Carter except for one quick visit to the clinic to tell him he was an asshole.

So much for cutting him some slack.

She felt bad about it afterward. He was at least a chivalrous asshole. *Her* chivalrous asshole, if he was still hers. Maybe that should count for something. Damn. Would she ever get this right?

Carter had sent an email, apologizing for pushing Will to the floor and saying his unit was on standby duty all week, so he would not be able to see her. Just as well.

Her phone rang.

"Davenport."

"Ma'am, this is the ops center. We've had a call, code word Blowback. Recording is on the secure server. Transcript is in the works."

Bridget dropped the handset on her desk and typed her password so fast that she got it wrong. Finally, she had the file. She heard Faraz's voice, breathless, scared, speaking quickly. He must have been in imminent danger because he didn't go through the authentication codes.

He said only, "Blowback. The target is ch—"

Faraz was interrupted by a thud, perhaps a punch. She heard the phone clatter to the ground. There was angry shouting in Arabic. Then it sounded like something hit the phone, and it went dead.

Bridget put her hand over her open mouth. She got the chills. She might have just heard the final seconds of the life of the young lieutenant she met a year and a half ago, the guy who was so green, so fresh-faced, that he could hardly comprehend what she was asking him to do—that young man who had reminded her of herself. She had convinced him to accept not one but two incredibly dangerous missions. Incredibly important missions. He was the only person who had any chance of accomplishing either one of them.

She knew him at his best. She had seen him at his worst at Gitmo. And she had seen him come back from that to fool the world's top terrorist a second time and have a chance to stop his next vile attack.

Faraz's death was too awful to contemplate. But beyond that, if Faraz was dead, she was sure a lot of other people would also die soon. And it would be on her.

Bridget listened again. Faraz had come frustratingly close to telling them what they needed to know. But what was "ch," and when was the attack coming? She picked up her phone and dialed the ops center.

Within two minutes, she had General Hadley and Liz Michaels on the line from Washington, along with

General Bigelow at the Baghdad Special Ops HQ, a few buildings over from where she was sitting.

"This is not the same as last time, sir," Bridget said. "If he's alive, he has vital intel. If he's not alive, we must hit these guys now to have a chance of blocking the MTO."

"I agree," Hadley said. "But we can't be sure where he is."

"We have to assume he called from the camp we've seen on the sat photos, or that they would have taken him there. I'm betting it's al-Souri's headquarters."

"Bit of a leap, but I'd make the same bet. We need that intel. Just have to hope that's where they took our man."

"And that he's still alive."

"Right. General Bigelow, we need an op in the air ASAP to the location Ms. Davenport will give you. Bring our agent home alive if at all possible, gather all intel material, lethal force authorized, expect heavy resistance."

Bridget heard Bigelow say, "Yes, sir. I will activate the team, but we'll need clearance through the regular chain before departure."

"You'll have it," Hadley said.

Bridget said, "Thank you, General." Then she hung up and sent the info on al-Souri's suspected location to Bigelow.

Bridget turned to the cabinet next to her desk and unlocked it. She took out a classified file and put it into her small backpack. She grabbed her body armor and helmet from under her desk.

Was there was anything else she needed? What she needed was an M16, but as a civilian, she hadn't been issued one.

She slipped into the vest and took off at a sprint for

the Special Ops HQ, dodging pedestrians on the narrow walkways.

She was winded when she came around a corner to find Carter in full battle gear, yelling, "Move, move, move!" His fifteen-man Spotlight crew trotted in rough formation toward a row of vehicles.

"Carter! What are you doing?" Bridget asked.

"Doing your mission, it seems. As I told you, we are the standby unit."

"Oh, shit."

"You want to wait for someone else?"

"No, no. We gotta go."

"We?"

"Yes, we. This is my op, my man out there, vital intel on the line. You know I have the training, and I'm going"

"We will need authorization."

"Then I'll get it. Meanwhile, load 'em up."

"Yes, ma'am," he said, with evident sarcasm. But he stepped back to let Bridget board the lead vehicle. He hefted himself in after her and shut the door.

"This is not a good idea," he said.

As the vehicles started moving, Bridget called Bigelow. A few seconds later, she handed the phone to Carter.

He listened. "Yes, sir, General, if that's what you want." He listened some more. "Yes, sir, understood, mission has a green light." Carter handed back the phone. "Welcome to Spotlight, Ms. Davenport."

It was a short ride to the helicopter landing field, where the twin overhead rotors of a huge Chinook were already turning at idle speed and waiting for them.

"Not that thing," Bridget said.

"It's all we have for the first leg," Carter told her. "We'll get Black Hawks at al-Asad." Al-Asad was the Iraqis' desert air base in Anbar Province, a hundred miles west of Baghdad and about halfway to the Syrian border.

Bridget was not happy with the extra time it would take, but with the priority Hadley had given the mission, she had to assume this was the best option available. At least they were on the move. She stepped onto a milk crate provided by the aircrew and boarded the chopper, taking a canvas seat along the wall, with one of the team members on her left and Carter on her right.

His second-in-command, Castillo, walked the length of the cabin, checking equipment and getting a thumbs-up from each man. Castillo gave a final thumbs-up to Carter, who turned toward the pilots and shouted over the rotor noise, "We are good to go. You boys know how to fly this thing?"

"I guess we'll find out," came the muffled reply from behind the pilot's oxygen mask. In the same second, something like twenty-five thousand pounds of machine and men lifted off the ground. And one woman.

Bridget turned to Carter and shouted into his ear. "You got the brief?"

"Yes. We are to get an agent out alive. Expect heavy resistance."

Bridget shrugged. "That about covers it."

"And we are crossing a border we're not supposed to cross, to go where exactly?"

"Heart of the beast."

"Pardon?"

"Al-Souri's HQ. The agent has been undercover."

"You know where al-Souri's HQ is?"

"Pretty good idea," she said, pulling a satellite image out of her pack. "We've been holding off, waiting for our man to get the info and call it in. Now, if he's still alive, he won't be for much longer. We need to get him out, or a lot of people are going to die."

Carter studied the photo. It showed the camp, the grove of trees, the gas station, the roads, and lots of nothing around them. "Your man, he's an Arab?"

"Afghan American. Army lieutenant."

"But . . . never mind. Okay. How will we know him?"

"Here." Bridget took a picture of Faraz out of the file. It showed him shortly after his return from Afghanistan, in full jihadi mode. "Pass this around. Code name Blowback."

Carter looked at the back of the photo, saw Faraz's real name, age, rank, and serial number. He flipped it again to memorize the face, then passed it down the line. "Just another day at the office, then."

Bridget didn't laugh.

"Listen, Bridget, you stay on board when we get there." She started to object, but Carter cut her off. "My guys know what they're doing. One wrong step and you're in the cross fire."

Her shoulders sagged, but she knew he was right.

"Hey, I have a present for you," Carter said. He reached into a supply duffel and took out an M4, the smaller version of the U.S. combat rifle, and a couple of magazines of ammo. "I assume you know how to work one of these."

Bridget took the weapon and gave it a quick inspection. "Well enough. And thanks."

"That's for self-protection only. Don't go all army crazy on me."

Bridget pursed her lips.

"And this." Carter gave her a handheld radio the size of a brick with a long retractable antenna. "It's set to our frequency."

"Thanks." She clipped the radio to her belt. "What's your call sign, anyway?"

"Bulldog."

Bridget smiled and tilted her head toward the cockpit. "See if this crate has afterburners, will ya, Bulldog?"

She twisted her body to look out a small porthole. The crowded streets of Baghdad gave way to scattered villages and farms. They passed towns made famous by the war—Fallujah and Ramadi—heading for open desert.

Bridget sat back in her seat and fought off the anxiety that came with going on any kind of war zone mission. Call it what it is—fear. But she knew a little fear was a good thing. It kept people from doing anything stupid. Mostly.

Al-Asad Airbase came into view, and the pilots banked left to approach. The chopper door opened before Bridget knew they had landed. It always amazed her that they could bring such a big beast down so gently.

She followed Carter out and stood with him to watch his men unload the gear and carry it toward two waiting Black Hawks. They were smaller than the Chinook and sported an impressive array of guns and rocket launchers, along with auxiliary fuel tanks mounted on small wings near the top of the fuselage. They were spun up and ready to go.

It took two trips for the team to move the equipment.

As they were finishing, they stopped to turn away from the backwash of another arriving helicopter—a Marine Corps UH-1Y Venom.

Once it landed, Carter and Bridget moved toward the Black Hawks. Before stepping on, Bridget turned to look at the Venom and grabbed Carter's arm. "Holy shit," she said.

Will Jackson was limping toward them in full battle gear, plus one customized SEAL emblem cane.

Bridget had to shout to be heard over the roar of the choppers. "Will, you can't be serious."

"Oh, I am," Will yelled back, now standing right in front of her. "They asked for a SEAL unit, but we didn't have one. The Spotlight guys were on call. When I heard you went along, well, I have enough juice to get these guys to give me a ride."

"No way." Carter's voice boomed over them both. "We are not taking an injured man on this mission."

"I think you are," Will said. He pushed past them and boarded their helicopter.

"Get off my chopper, Jackson. Don't make me throw you off."

"It's not your call, Holloway. This is Bridget's mission."

Both men looked at her.

"Goddamn it, Will!"

"Look, I'll stay on the chopper. Guard the rear. Handle comms. Whatever. I know I can't run with these guys. But if you're going, I'm not staying behind."

Carter objected. "Bridget, you cannot—"

"Seems you were happy enough to have *her* come along," Will jabbed.

Carter moved toward him, apparently ready to throw him off the helicopter.

Bridget raised a hand to stop him. "All right. No time to argue. Will and I will stay on the chopper. Let's go."

Bridget grabbed a handhold and pulled herself on board. Carter stood there looking at her.

"This isn't a damn tourist flight!"

Bridget hadn't seen Carter angry before, and he did a good job of it. His eyes went wide, and his pale skin turned light red. He seemed to stand taller than his already impressive height. But she was not going to be intimidated.

"Will and I are both qualified. I have a man in imminent danger and lifesaving intel on the line. Get your ass on this thing, and let's go."

Carter fumed a few seconds longer, then came back down to normal size. "This is not supposed to happen," he said. But he stepped onto the aircraft. He turned to the ground controller, raised his right hand, forefinger pointing upward, and twirled it around. "Let's fly," he said. And he sat down heavily in his seat.

"This is not okay, Bridget. Anything goes wrong, it's on you. And on you, Jackson." Carter looked at Will, then at his cane. "Jesus." He turned away.

Bridget was wedged between Will and Carter, hips and legs unavoidably touching on the narrow, straight-backed seat of the Black Hawk. Its sliding doors had been removed to save weight and facilitate entry and exit.

When they reached altitude, the temperature in the chopper fell to match the atmosphere. Bridget reached into her pack and gave Will the folder with the camp image and Faraz's picture. "You might as well know what we're doing," she shouted.

"This guy? I met this guy. He's here, now?"

"Yup."

Bridget looked at her watch. Too much time had passed since Faraz's call. Damn. Why couldn't these things go faster?

It was a full excruciating hour before the pilot's voice crackled in their headsets. "Two minutes."

Chapter Forty-eight

Nazim's sucker punch behind the gas station flattened Faraz. The kicks that followed reinjured his ribs. When the men pulled him to his feet, Nazim kicked him hard in the groin.

They dragged him, doubled over, into their SUV and sped back to camp.

In front of the headquarters building, they pulled him out of the vehicle and threw him to the ground. He curled up in a protective fetal position. He couldn't stop shaking. Fear? Adrenaline? Certainly anger that he hadn't gotten his message out, and crushing guilt about his failure to prevent the attacks that would now happen.

Al-Souri towered over him. "Hamed. Oh, Hamed," was all he said.

"He was making a call, but he only spoke for a second or two," Nazim reported. "Now he must die the death of a traitor."

Al-Souri sighed. "And he will. We shall make an example of him. Put him in the shed. At sunset, we will gather the men. We will summon others to join us, to see what happens to traitors."

"Please, *Qomandan*," Faraz pleaded in Pashto. "I was only—"

A kick to the ribs from Nazim silenced him.

"You were only calling your American friends," al-Souri said with remarkable calm. "You were only betraying Allah and His jihad."

"No, *Qomandan*." Faraz struggled to speak. "Please, let me explain."

"You are very good at 'explaining,' Hamed. Very good at lying. And sadly, very good at fooling me."

"I proved myself to you many times, *Qomandan*. I saved Nazim's life. I attacked the Americans."

Al-Souri spat at him. "You did not. We are not so naïve as you think. There was a large explosion, much chaos in their camp, but no casualties. Seems odd, does it not?"

"Casualties? Many were killed and injured. You told me about the news reports."

"Lies. We checked their announcements. The Americans report all their casualties to the media, first the numbers, then later the names. That day, there were numbers, but no names ever came. There were no photos of the dead. No families cried before the television cameras. Do you think we are so stupid, Hamed? Do you think we do not follow these things? You betrayed me in Afghanistan. You betrayed me here. You will not betray me again."

Al-Souri kicked Faraz in the back, then turned to Nazim. "Summon as many men as you can, but they must get here quickly. We will show the infidels the price of opposing us."

* * *

For the rest of the afternoon, Faraz lay in the same hot, reeking corner where Nazim had first imprisoned him, held by the same chains. This time, they gave him no food or water.

He wiped the sweat from his face with his dirty hands. He cataloged his life. He had been a good son, until he had abandoned his parents for . . . for this, as it turned out. He had volunteered to defend his country. He had done his best.

That would have to do.

In an hour or so, he would find out the answers to life's great questions. Is there a God? Is there an afterlife? Perhaps he would see Amira again, and his father. No. Stupid. No.

Bile rose in Faraz's throat, and he spat it out. If this is the end, let it happen already. He gave himself credit for trying, but in this moment, he should be honest with himself. He had failed.

An attack on children. There had been others by terrorists perverting Islam, but not on the scale al-Souri contemplated. Even knowing the man's philosophy, having been tutored in it, he would never understand how he could do it. Faraz had seen al-Souri playing with his own children in Afghanistan. Now he would kill other men's children and say it was for Allah. Well, al-Souri wouldn't be doing it. He'd be ordering others to do it. Just as bad, if not worse, but far easier. A couple of phone calls. A bank transfer. Say a prayer, and it's done. *Allahu akbar*.

Faraz had been so close to stopping it. But close was not good enough.

He jerked his chains, tried to dislodge them from the bolt that held them to the floor. It was no use. Hearing the effort, a guard came in and hit him in the stomach with his rifle butt.

Faraz slumped to the floor, heaving for breath.

He must have passed out, because the next thing he knew, he was hit with a bucketload of cold water. Faraz sputtered and retreated into his corner, his knees up, his legs protecting his midsection. Two men lifted him to his feet, unlocked the leg chain from its anchor, and force-marched him out of the shed.

He went limp. He was not going to help them execute him.

The men had gathered in the clearing in front of the headquarters. It was a large group, maybe double the number usually in the camp. Faraz had never seen some of them before. Their vehicles were crowded into the back of the compound, where damage from the fire Faraz had started was clearly visible. Al-Souri had apparently gathered men from nearby camps to witness the lesson he was about to teach.

The *Qomandan* stood on the landing at the top of the building's steps wearing a clean white tunic and white pants with a white *takkiye*. He was the image of purity, preparing to root out the evil of apostasy.

His feet still in irons and his hands chained in front of him, Faraz was forced to stand on a wooden crate facing the crowd. Now that he was there, at the place of his execution, Faraz let go of Hamed. He stood tall, as a U.S. Army officer should. He was proud of his small role in fighting the evil he knew better than most. If he was going to die, they would see him with his head high, shoulders squared.

Nazim smacked the back of Faraz's head to make him lower his gaze. But he still stood as straight as he could.

"My brothers," al-Souri began. "Before us stands a traitor, a spy, a betrayer of Allah."

The men grumbled, and Faraz heard shouts of "Kill him!" and "Death to traitors!"

Al-Souri launched into a sermon. He quoted the Koran and ancient scholars. He talked about the importance of Allah's jihad. And he spoke with passion about the sin of betrayal and Muslims who collude with the enemy.

"So, what punishment does Allah decree for such a man?" he asked.

"Death!" came the replies. "Death now!"

"It is the will of Allah," Nazim shouted. "*Allahu akbar*!"

"*Allahu akbar*," the men repeated. Some fired weapons into the air.

In Afghanistan, Faraz would have expected a wooden block and a hooded executioner, with a ceremonial sword if one was available. Here, out of the corner of his eye, he saw Nazim approach with a pistol in his right hand.

Faraz wanted to stand strong. He was ready to accept his fate, but he could not stop his body from shaking. Two fighters came from each side, knelt down to be out of the line of fire, and held his wrists

Nazim spat into Faraz's face. The crowd cheered. Nazim stepped back and started to raise his weapon.

That's when Faraz heard the choppers.

He raised his eyes toward the sky. He saw the men in

the audience do the same, almost in unison. Faraz turned his head toward the sound and saw al-Souri come down the steps to get a view to the west, toward the setting sun.

They couldn't see anything in the glare, but the sound was getting louder.

Nazim shouted, "It is an attack! Defensive positions! Board the vehicles!" The men holding Faraz let go and ran toward their assigned stations. Nazim turned away and issued more orders. Men were running in all directions.

Faraz jumped down from the box and shuffled toward the shed as quickly as his chains would allow. He could only hope Nazim was too busy to shoot him. Faraz went through the shed's open door and took cover behind the wall.

When no one followed, he peered out. He saw Nazim in the middle of the compound giving orders, still holding the pistol, red-faced and gesturing wildly. He had a lot of men to command, with all the visitors who came for the execution.

Faraz looked toward the headquarters. Al-Souri was gone, presumably hiding inside the building, maybe crawling into a hole like the one al-Jazar had used.

Faraz expected the helicopters to come in low, strafing, dropping explosives. But they didn't. Instead, looking through the gap where the gate used to be, he saw them make hard combat landings just outside the range of the terrorists' AK-47s. The troops came out fast, firing toward the men on the wall.

Nazim came in Faraz's direction, running toward a line of vehicles that were ready to attack the invaders. As Nazim passed the shed, Faraz jumped him. Pain shot through Faraz's rib, but Nazim fell. Faraz wrapped his handcuff chain around Nazim's throat and pulled him into the shed facedown.

Nazim squirmed hard and flailed his arms, trying to get the chain off his neck or get ahold of Faraz. Al-Souri's deputy got his knees under himself and tried to stand. Faraz pulled on the chain to choke him and body-slammed him back to the ground.

Faraz put his foot on the back of Nazim's neck and pulled on the chain. "This . . . is . . . for . . . Amira," he said, increasing the pressure with each word.

Nazim's hands came to his throat, desperately trying to stop the choking. Faraz leaned in, putting all his body weight on Nazim's neck. Then he jerked the chain.

Nazim's neck snapped, and his body went limp.

Faraz lunged for Nazim's pistol as two fighters came in to rescue their commander. Faraz killed them with two shots.

The vehicles sped past the shed's open door to launch the counterattack. Faraz took a few seconds to catch his breath. He looked at Nazim. The man's eyes were open, his mouth was twisted into a look of agony. Faraz spat. At least this one would hurt no children.

Faraz searched Nazim's pockets to find the key to his handcuffs and leg irons. He freed himself and moved to the doorway. Faraz took an AK from one of the dead fighters, stepped over them, and looked out the doorway to assess the battle.

Chapter Forty-nine

Carter was among the first out of the choppers. His only words were, “You two stay here.”

It was a difficult situation. He would have liked to bomb the hell out of the camp, or at least hit it with some RPGs. But the priority was to get the agent out alive, and putting a whole lot of metal and explosives into the area was not a good way to do that.

His men were under orders to aim carefully and hit only targets that were shooting at them.

Carter took cover with half his men behind a small sand berm. The others ran right, toward a gully by the side of the camp’s access road.

“We’re taking fire from the wall to the left,” Castillo said.

Carter considered his options. He had to reduce the incoming fire, or they’d never get into the camp to look for the agent. If he took too long, they might kill the man, if they hadn’t already. He had to take the chance that Faraz was not on the wall with their first line defenders.

“Hit it,” Carter ordered. Castillo loaded a grenade into the launcher under his M4, checked the safety, and waited for a lull in the shooting. When it came, he lifted himself up onto his knees, his head and the weapon coming over the berm. He fired and dropped back down within three seconds. The left side of the camp wall exploded in a shower of wood, blood, and bodies.

"Let's move," Carter said. He led his men out of cover toward the gap in the wall, running as fast as he could and leading with his M16 on automatic.

He entered the camp still shooting. He killed two more terrorists and carved out a small safe area behind some debris, where they could take cover and reload.

The move drew fire from the men on the other section of wall, creating an opening for Carter's second unit to fire an RPG and make their advance. Their aim wasn't quite as good as Castillo's, but it got the job done.

Carter was about to lead an advance when three vehicles came from the back of the camp and sped out through the gate. Two turned left, toward Team Two, the other went right, effectively placing Carter's unit between hostile forces front and rear.

"How many fucking jihadis they got in this camp?" Castillo asked.

"Too many," Carter said.

They hunkered down, returning fire as best they could.

As soon as Carter's team left the choppers, they lifted off for a short hop to a safer distance. Bridget and Will crouched on the floor, frustrated to be another hundred meters from the fight. The helicopters' security teams had taken up defensive positions in case the enemy turned its attention in their direction. But they were not going to get into the battle unless ordered. More likely, if things got desperate, the choppers would lift off and fire from the air.

Bridget knew there would be a drone somewhere above them, sending live video back to Baghdad and D.C. and watching for approaching threats. The drone's missiles could make a decisive difference in the battle, but protecting Faraz was paramount.

For now, Carter and his men were on their own.

Bridget and Will watched the battle develop. "This is bad," Will said when the vehicles came around behind Carter's men. "Look at the size of that force." He picked up his rifle, as if he was going to go do something about it.

"Stay down, Will."

"They need some rear fire."

"Not from you. Look at you."

"Bridget—"

"Listen, you said it's my mission, and it is. And you are staying down, or I swear to God I will have you cleaning latrines on a rust bucket for the rest of your career."

Will was taken aback, but he recovered.

"Heads," he said.

"What?"

"We call them 'heads' in the navy." Will's lips curled into his trademark smile, and his dimple made its first appearance since he'd arrived in the war zone.

Bridget was both disarmed and infuriated.

"Look at that," she said. To the far left, they saw a man running. He wasn't dressed like a fighter, but he seemed to have come from the camp. He was tall, wearing a white tunic and skullcap. He was fleeing the fight.

Bridget grabbed the radio Carter had given her and pushed the Transmit key. "Bulldog, you have a man escaping out the north side." She adjusted the squelch to minimize the static.

It took Carter a few seconds to answer. "We're pinned down. Can't help. If it's your man, he should head for the choppers. Let me know if that happens."

"Roger," Bridget replied. She put down the radio and stared at the runner. "That's not Faraz. Too tall, moving too slowly, not coming to us."

"So what if one jihadi gets away? Eye on the ball, Bridge."

"Al-Souri's tall. Could be dressed that way. This guy's moving slower than a young man would. We're gonna lose sight of him in those trees in a second."

"Bridget . . ." Will gave his voice an upward inflection, implying a warning not to get any ideas.

She ignored him.

Bridget picked up the M4, jumped down from the chopper, and took off running to intercept the mystery man. She bent at the waist to make a smaller target, but as her angle took her closer to the camp, she drew fire from one of the SUVs.

She dove to the ground, twisted her body so she faced the battle, and found the guy who was shooting at her. Bridget fired a burst, forcing him to take cover behind the vehicles.

But the shooter and another man emerged and fired back.

Bridget had no cover. She buried her face in the ground, trying to show the shooters the smallest target possible.

With luck, they weren't good enough to hit her at that range.

Another burst of gunfire came from a different direction. Bridget turned her head enough to see that Will and one of the chopper guys were targeting the men who were shooting at her. They were too far for high-percentage shots, but close enough to make the men take cover.

Bridget lifted her torso into prone firing position. When one of the terrorists peeked out from behind the SUV, she took aim and fired. He fell backward. She had a split second to take pride in her shooting skills before his comrade stepped out and fired a furious barrage, trying to sweep both Bridget's and Will's position.

That was a mistake.

As Bridget moved to press her body to the ground again, she saw Will cut the man down. Nothing like having a SEAL for cover fire.

Their corner of the battle went quiet. They seemed to have accomplished what Will had wanted to do—providing rear cover for Carter's team and eliminating the threat from one vehicle.

But that hadn't been Bridget's goal. She wanted to stop that runner. She looked toward his last location just in time to see him disappear into the trees.

"Bridget," Will shouted.

She saw him gesturing for her to come back to the chopper. She scanned the battle. As far as she could tell, there was no one left in the SUV to threaten her. Bridget stood and bolted for the woods.

"Bridget!" Will screamed it this time, but she didn't look back.

* * *

Will jumped out of the helicopter onto the ground. He collapsed in pain, holding his leg.

"You okay, sir?" asked a chopper crewman.

"Yes, damn it. I'm okay." Will stood and leaned on the aircraft. He watched Bridget run a zigzag course toward the trees.

Then he heard a single rifle shot, and he saw her fall.

Will moved by instinct, but he only got one step before he had to admit he'd never make it in the middle of a gunfight. He lunged back into the chopper for the radio. "Holloway, this is Jackson. Davenport is down, northwest of your position. She went after the escapee."

"Damn. What the hell is the problem with you people and orders?"

"I tried to stop her."

"Okay, you stay there. I mean it, or I will shoot you myself."

"Roger that, but hurry."

Carter and his team were still taking fire from inside the camp. They had some cover in their small, improvised bunker of debris, but they couldn't stay there.

"We gotta break out," Carter said.

"Right. RPG?" Castillo asked.

"Big risk for our agent, but yeah, we can't sit here."

"On it." Castillo loaded another grenade and set his feet, ready to stand and shoot.

"You gonna fire that thing?" Carter asked.

"You gonna lay down some cover?"

Carter raised his rifle above the debris and let loose a

fusillade of automatic fire into the camp. Two of his men did the same, forcing the terrorists to stop shooting and dive for cover.

Castillo stood to fire his RPG, but a short burst came from his left. He and his weapon fell hard onto Carter.

"Casty! Goddamn it!" Carter twisted out from under Castillo.

He saw his eyes first, staring at the sky. Then Carter saw the line of impact marks on Castillo's body armor. That would have hurt but not killed him. One bullet got his exposed shoulder, which was bleeding onto the ground. Also not a big deal. The last bullet in the trail was the fatal one. It hit his neck and came out the other side, creating a stomach-turning maw of flesh.

"Oh, Casty, man." Carter bent over him, ready to rip off his body armor and start first aid. But he could see it was no use. Half of Castillo's neck was gone. His body was limp.

Carter's formidable frame sagged. He reached over and closed Castillo's eyes. The other men watched, their looks blending fear and shock. But there was no time to mourn. They were under fire, and Carter had a dozen other men to worry about.

Carter turned to his team. "Hit that shooter." He gestured in the direction of whoever had killed Castillo. The men laid down covering fire. Carter grabbed Castillo's weapon and rose up onto his knees.

"Cease firing," he ordered.

When the gunfire stopped, the shooter poked his head out to find a new target. Carter's grenade devastated the man's hiding place.

Carter took cover again and listened. There was no

more shooting from inside the camp. Maybe they were all dead. Or maybe they were regrouping. The only way to find out was to advance and clear the area.

Carter turned to the next most senior man on the team. "Ferguson, you're in charge. Secure the camp. Link up with Team Two. Find our man." He looked down at his dead friend. "Take care of Casty and meet me back at the choppers."

"Roger that, chief."

"I gotta run a rescue." Carter assessed his team. "Barrett, Lesher, with me. Ferguson, you've got the rest."

Carter led the two men back to the gap in the wall. To his left, he saw that Team Two was still engaged with the terrorists who had gone in their direction.

He keyed his radio. "Team Two, report."

"Taking fire, but we got this," came the reply.

"Roger."

Carter led Barrett and Lesher to the northwest. Twenty seconds later, he saw Bridget lying on the ground. Not moving.

He ran directly to her. She was facedown, hands on her head in a protective position, one knee raised to waist level. Her right side was soaked with blood.

"Bridget!" Carter shouted.

"Yeah," she grunted. "I'm hit. Stomach, below the armor."

"Don't move."

Carter's men took up positions to protect them, but too late. A hail of gunfire came in. Carter grunted and fell on top of Bridget. Lesher and Barrett returned fire.

"You hit, boss?" Lesher asked.

"On the armor," Carter said. "Damn, that hurts." He rolled over. "You okay, Bridget?"

"Yeah." Her voice was weak.

"There he is," Barrett shouted, gesturing with his rifle.

Carter rolled over into firing position, facing back toward the camp.

"Next to that piece of wall," Barrett said, pointing.

"Got him," Carter said. They both took aim and fired short bursts. The man fell. They waited. There was another burst of gunfire from inside the camp. "That's Ferguson doing his job. Keep your eyes open."

Carter moved back to Bridget. He ripped the side of her shirt where the bullet had made a small entry wound, which was oozing blood. He rolled her onto her good side, and she cried out in pain. He tore at the Velcro strips of Bridget's bulletproof vest and laid it open.

The exit wound was uglier. The high-powered 7.62-millimeter round from the AK blew out a significant chunk of Bridget's skin. The good news was that the wound was close to her side. The bullet had spent only a split second inside her, and if it had hit anything important, she probably wouldn't be talking to him.

Carter pulled a package of quick-clotting gauze from a pouch on his belt and ripped it open. "This is gonna hurt." He pressed the clotting agent into the exit hole.

Bridget suppressed a scream. "Damn it."

"Gotta do it." He pressed more gauze inside, took out a large bandage, and covered it. He eased her over onto her back.

Carter looked up to see his second team advancing on the camp, keeping the few remaining terrorists busy while he worked.

"They okay?" Bridget asked.

"They're securing the camp."

"You find my agent?"

"No, not yet. I have a man down."

"Oh, Jesus. Who?"

"Castillo."

"Oh, Carter. I'm so sorry."

"Yeah, me, too. I worked with him for a long time."

Carter took another pack out of his pouch. "Gauze for the front now."

Bridget gritted her teeth. Carter pushed a wad of gauze into the wound. Bridget stifled another scream and squeezed Carter's arm. "Oh, sweet Jesus." She dug her nails into his bicep.

Carter reached into the medical bag again and took out an injection pen.

"No, I don't want that shit," Bridget said, gasping for air.

"You need it."

"Carter—"

"Stop arguing!" His anger flared. "This is my show now. That wound will hurt even more when we move you." He used his teeth to pull the cover off the needle and delivered ten milligrams of morphine through her pants leg into her left thigh. Then he recapped the pen and dropped it onto the ground.

"Ouch. Damn. You done?" Bridget was sweating and still panting.

"Yeah, for now. You'll be all right." Carter wiped her forehead with his hand. "Bleeding's under control. Seems like a pretty lucky spot for an abdominal wound. What the hell were you doing?"

"Going after that runner. I think it was al-Souri, top of our terrorist list. But Carter, you've got to find my agent."

Chapter Fifty

Faraz saw al-Souri run, too.

After the vehicles left, the back of the camp was deserted. He moved carefully, making sure no one stayed behind who could kill him. Faraz needed to live long enough to pass his intel to someone who could do something about it.

He saw the twin gun battles, one on each side of the gate. He could have reached Carter's group, but they'd have probably shot him on sight. So he turned into the alley behind the tents. He came within sight of the rear door of the headquarters just as al-Souri came out. Faraz ducked for cover. When he emerged, the *Qomandan* was gone, and the camp's side gate was open.

Faraz moved as quickly as he dared to the opening. He looked outside and scanned left and right with his rifle. He caught a glimpse of al-Souri disappearing into the trees in the distance.

Damn. He was not going to let the man get away again. Even if Faraz's intel stopped this attack, al-Souri would regroup and hit them again.

But Faraz couldn't take a direct route to intercept him,

either. He'd be exposed to fire from both the Americans and the jihadis.

Faraz went east to enter the wooded area away from the battle. The setting sun cast a long shadow in front of him. He would have to circle around and catch al-Souri on the road. The *Qomandan* undoubtedly had plenty of "friends" who would take the risk of hiding him in return for a substantial reward, or in return for not being killed.

Faraz's injuries slowed him down, but he had to reach al-Souri before he got to someplace he could hide.

Carter was still kneeling over Bridget, putting pressure on her wound with his right hand. He saw her eyes go wide as she looked at something over his shoulder.

He turned to see Will hobbling toward them, his cane in his left hand and his rifle in his right.

"Damn it, man!" Carter said.

Will ignored him, falling to his knees on the other side of Bridget. "You okay?"

"I'll live, but you should have stayed at the chopper."

"I couldn't leave you out here. Shooting stopped, so I came."

Carter turned to look back toward the camp. Jackson was right. The men of Team Two were heading for the gate. They had won their battle against the terrorists who came out of the camp to confront them and were joining up with Ferguson's group inside.

"Sir," Lesher said. He pointed with his rifle to a figure running toward the trees.

Bridget twisted her body to see and grunted in pain. "What is it?"

"Another runner," Carter said.

"Could be your man," Will said.

"What?" Carter was skeptical.

"Why do you say that?" Bridget asked.

"I met the guy, remember? I mean, this was just a quick look from, what, a hundred meters, but yeah, could have been him."

Carter was not convinced. "Why would he run? Why wouldn't he come to us?"

"Chasing al-Souri," Bridget said. "Makes sense."

Carter looked toward the camp again. There was a short burst of gunfire. He keyed his radio. "Ferguson, report."

"Linked up with Team Two. Still clearing the camp, but we appear to be secure."

"Any sign of the man we came to get?"

"Negative."

"Keep looking, and commence intel gathering. Grab everything you can, but quickly. When possible, send two men to my location for wounded evac to chopper. Davenport and Jackson go out ASAP. Second bird and rest of the men wait for me. Copy?"

"Gotcha, Bulldog."

Carter turned to his team. "Barrett, wrap this." Carter removed his hand from Bridget's side. It still let out a trickle of blood, but nothing compared to before. "And top it off with more clotting stuff, front and rear."

"Yes, sir."

"We should get her out of here," Will said. "Abdominal wound. Standard protocol."

"We will, as soon as I have men to take her. She's stable for now."

"Listen, Holloway—"

"I am in command of this mission, and I will have these men restrain you if I have to."

"It's all right, Will," Bridget said.

"No, it's not."

"The mission is . . ." Bridget's head rolled to the side. A second later, she seemed to revive. "The mission is the priority," she said. Her words were starting to slur.

"This is not a committee meeting," Carter said. "We will get Bridget out as soon as the area is secure. Meanwhile, I will take these two men and go after the runners. And you, Commander Jackson, will stay here to protect Bridget in case there are any jihadis on the loose." He looked from Will to Bridget, then back to Will. "There will not be a vote on this. The men will help you get her back to the chopper ASAP. Or I can cuff you, and I'll have to leave an extra man here."

"All right, all right," Will said. "I'll watch Bridget. You do what you have to do."

"Commander, I'll ask for your word that you won't follow us," Carter said, looking him in the eye, appealing to his integrity as an officer and his loyalty to his girlfriend, or whatever she was. "I don't need an injured man lost somewhere in Syria."

Will glared at him. "I said all right." He checked his weapon and took up a firing stance on his right knee, which took most of the weight off his bad leg.

Barrett was tying off the bandage. "You should be okay for a while, ma'am."

"Thanks." Bridget's voice was soft. The morphine seemed to be hitting her.

Carter touched her arm. "We'll get you some real medical attention as soon as we can. Barrett, Lesher, let's go.

Jackson, remember your promise. And when Ferguson gets here, he's in charge. We have protocols. Don't mess us up."

Will nodded.

Carter and his two men took off at a run for the woods.

Bridget lay on her back and watched Will scan the area for hostiles, training his rifle back and forth across the area between their spot and the camp, then turning to check his rear. She had never seen him in SEAL mode before.

The sun had set, and she felt cold. Bridget shifted her position, moving closer to him. The air smelled like men, gunpowder, and blood. Her blood.

"I'm glad you're here," Bridget said, her voice still weak.

"A few minutes ago, you didn't seem so glad to see me. Before that, you were ready to have me busted."

"I didn't say I was glad you left the chopper against orders. I only said I'm glad you're here."

Will gestured toward the injector still lying next to Bridget. "You sure it's not the morphine talking?"

Bridget sighed. "No. It's not." It was hard getting through to him when he couldn't look at her. His eyes stayed focused on the battlefield.

She felt dizzy again, but it passed. Bridget swallowed. Her throat was dry, but she knew she shouldn't have any water until a doctor said she could. She struggled to talk, reached out to touch his good leg. "Listen to what I'm saying, Will. I'm glad you're here."

Will waited a moment, then stole a quick look at her.

“Thanks for saying that. I wasn’t going to let you come out here on your own.” He paused. “Sorry I’ve been such a jerk. It’s just—”

“I know.” She squeezed his leg. “Don’t worry about it. And I’m sorry I was such a b . . .” Bridget’s voice trailed off, and her eyes closed.

“Stay with me, Bridge.” He shook her shoulder. “Hey! Where’s the rest of that apology?”

“Bitch,” she managed. Then her hand fell from his leg.

He shook her again. “Bridget! Wake up. Don’t make me tell them your last words were ‘I was such a bitch.’”

She snorted. He’d actually made her laugh as she lay wounded in the middle of a battlefield. Maybe it *was* the morphine.

Bridget heard him talking as if from far away.

“Eyes open, Army. You do not have permission to lose consciousness until we reach base.”

She couldn’t open her eyes, but she felt his hand on her shoulder. She put her hand on top of it. Her words were slurred. “Yes, sir, Navy.”

Chapter Fifty-one

Faraz came to the edge of the small wooded area and looked out into the twilight. He couldn't see much. He figured al-Souri faced the same decision he had faced during his escape that afternoon—which way to turn. The nearest bit of civilization was the gas station, and there was a village not far beyond. The other direction had nothing but desert for a dozen kilometers.

He climbed up the embankment to the road and turned right. His ribs hurt with every step, but he ignored the pain.

After two hundred meters, Faraz got a split second of warning—some movement from the edge of his peripheral vision—but not enough to avoid the blow across his back. Whatever hit him was heavy and had been swung with considerable speed.

Faraz fell headlong into the ditch by the side of the road. His rifle flew well ahead of him. His hands broke his fall, but he was dazed and in pain.

"Infidel!"

Faraz heard al-Souri's curse and turned his head in time

to see the man rear back and raise a large tree branch above his head with both hands.

Instinct took over. Adrenaline defeated pain. Faraz twisted his body out of the way just before al-Souri would have struck him again. The branch hit the ground where Faraz's head had been. The force of the blow pushed it into the ground, and al-Souri had trouble lifting it for another swing.

That gave Faraz the time he needed to shift his position. He got a good look at his attacker for the first time. Al-Souri carried a leather satchel over his left shoulder, with the strap crossing his chest so the bag sat on his right hip. But what impacted Faraz most was al-Souri's face. The man's skullcap had flown off. What little gray hair he had flew wildly, his cheeks were flushed under his beard, and his eyes showed an intense rage that further spiked Faraz's fear.

Faraz lifted himself onto one knee and tried to jump at al-Souri, but the pain in his ribs stopped him. Now, al-Souri had the advantage again. He reversed the branch, lifted it, and let out a grunt of effort as he swung it toward Faraz's head.

It would have been a death blow, but the aim was off. Al-Souri hit Faraz in the right shoulder. Faraz reached for the branch with both hands and knocked it out of the *Qomandan*'s grip. It flew off to the side, out of reach for both of them.

Lying on his back, Faraz spun a quarter turn and caught al-Souri's feet with his legs, bringing the man to the ground. Faraz made it to his knees and had a chance to land a punch. He aimed for al-Souri's jaw, but the *Qomandan* turned his head to absorb the blow, then raised himself up on one elbow. Al-Souri swung a kick into Faraz's stomach. The man might be old, but he hadn't forgotten how to fight.

Faraz fell forward onto all fours. His injured shoulder collapsed from the weight. Al-Souri went for the branch and came around swinging. This time, he hit Faraz on the right side of his head, spinning him around and knocking him onto his back.

Al-Souri stood and raised the branch for a final blow. Faraz barely saw it coming, but even though his head throbbed and his ribs felt like they would push out of his chest, he launched himself at al-Souri's midsection, tackling him as the branch swung too high. They hit the ground, and al-Souri lost his grip on the weapon.

Faraz was dizzy. He felt blood dripping into his right ear. But he was on top of al-Souri. If he didn't finish him now, he might not have another chance. Faraz used all his weight to pin al-Souri's arms to the ground. He put a knee on the man's crotch. Faraz gulped for air to clear his head.

Al-Souri's white tunic and trousers were soiled with mud and blood. Faraz's blood. The *Qomandan* was struggling, cursing Faraz in Pashto and Arabic.

Faraz saw the branch. To get it, he'd have to release al-Souri's right arm, but he had to take the chance. Faraz couldn't hold him much longer. He feared he might pass out.

Faraz lunged for the weapon. Al-Souri used his free hand to grab Faraz's face. He pressed hard, digging his nails into Faraz's left cheek and pushing with surprising strength. His index finger searched for an eyeball.

Faraz reached the branch, but it was too big to pick up with one hand. He pulled it along the ground as hard as he could and landed a sharp blow directly on the top of al-Souri's head. That stopped the pushing. Al-Souri's hand fell from Faraz's face. Faraz used both hands now to raise the branch and bring it down onto al-Souri's forehead with all the strength he could muster.

Al-Souri grunted and his body went limp. Faraz raised the branch again, then pushed it down hard. "*You* are the traitor to the true will of Allah," he screamed. "Murderer, murderer, murderer!" With each word, Faraz brought down the branch again. And with each blow, he smashed open the box of emotions he had so carefully built at Guantanamo. The grief, anger, and guilt poured out of him. And his strength, too.

When Faraz stopped, he was exhausted and dizzy. Tears streaked the blood and dirt on his face, stinging the cuts al-Souri's fingernails had made. Faraz dropped the branch and sat back to steady himself.

Underneath him, the global jihad leader, terrorist mastermind, and radical spiritual icon was still. His eyes were closed. His nose and cheeks were broken. Blood gushed from his head, stained the leather strap he still wore, and soaked the ground.

Faraz wiped his hands on his shirt, then ran them through his hair. He felt blood on the right side where al-Souri had struck his most effective blow. Faraz felt shaky. He reached to the right to steady himself against the ground. A wave of nausea came, and he vomited.

He wiped his lips with his sleeve and looked back at al-Souri. The man was surely dead. But Faraz's mission was not over. He had to make his report. He needed to get back to the Americans. He tried to stand, but he felt light-headed and suddenly very cold. Faraz tipped forward, his chest landing on al-Souri's fractured face.

* * *

Carter, Lesher, and Barrett came to the edge of the woods. They saw nothing. Heard nothing. The daylight was all but gone.

"Which way, Bulldog?" Lesher asked.

"Nearest village is that way." Carter pointed to the right. "Gas station, too, according to the sat photo. If this was the jihadi leader, he'd go there."

"All right. That way, then." Lesher took point without being told, walking in the gully by the side of the road.

Carter was in the rear, straining to see anything he could, forward or back.

"Lights?" Lesher asked.

"Night vision," Carter said.

The men stopped to take their goggles from the containers on their belts and mount them on their helmets.

They walked a hundred meters, until Lesher stopped short. He had nearly stumbled over the two bodies in the gully.

Carter rushed up from the rear position. His men were pulling one man off the other.

"Lights," Carter said. All three flipped the goggles up off their eyes and turned on their gun-mounted beacons.

The man on the bottom in the bloodstained white tunic had almost no face. It had been smashed in, apparently with the large, bloody branch lying by his side. The other man was younger and dressed like a jihadi. They laid him on his back.

Carter knelt next to the younger man. He also had a head wound and blood on his face. His hair was matted, and his beard was longer than in the photo Bridget had showed them.

"Abdallah?" Carter leaned in to try to feel his breath. "He's breathing, I think." Carter rubbed two knuckles against Faraz's breastbone. "Abdallah! Can you hear me, man?" No response. Carter checked for a pulse on Faraz's neck.

"Is he alive?" Lesher asked, kneeling on the other side of al-Souri's body.

"Yes. Barely. Other guy?"

"No way."

Barrett stood above them, doing a constant 360-degree scan.

Carter took the canteen off his belt and poured water on Faraz's face.

Faraz moaned.

"There you go, son," Carter said. He wiped Faraz's face and gently slapped his cheek. "You with me?'

Faraz stiffened and raised a hand to defend himself.

"Hey, it's okay. We're the good guys, come to take you home."

Faraz had heard that before, with a not-altogether good outcome. But he lowered his hand. He blinked, trying to focus.

"Can you give me your name and code name?" Carter asked.

Faraz swallowed, grabbed Carter's arm, and pulled him close. He felt weak. His head hurt. Everything hurt. He didn't know how much time he had left. The guy seemed to be American. He would have to trust him.

"Lieutenant . . ." Faraz winced as his broken ribs shot pain through his chest. "Faraz Abdallah. Code name Blowback."

"Now you're talking. Let's get you out of here." Carter took Faraz's injured right shoulder and helped him sit up.

Faraz cried out in pain.

"Sorry, but we gotta get you, and us, back to the choppers."

Lesher came around behind Faraz, put some gauze on his head wound, and wrapped it.

"We'll carry you," Carter said. "Choppers aren't far. But we gotta move."

Faraz grabbed Carter's shirt. "Okay, but . . ." His hand fell from the shirt. His eyes closed, and his head lolled to the side.

Carter took hold of Faraz's cheeks and slapped him gently. "But what, Lieutenant? Come back to me, now."

Faraz opened his eyes. "MTO." He stopped to breathe. "Children are the target. Unknown multiple locations." His voice was raspy, his words slurred. "Timing uncertain. Financing from A . . ." He faded again, then came back. "Assali." Faraz swallowed. "They call him al-Malik."

"Children?"

"Yes." Faraz stopped to take several breaths. "Schools, colleges, like that."

"Has it been launched?"

Faraz leaned forward onto Carter's shoulder, panting. "Don't . . . think so. Not sure . . ."

Now that he'd made his report, Faraz felt drained. Out of energy. Maybe out of time.

"Okay, Lieutenant. I got it." Carter looked up at his men. "Lift him up, guys, nice and easy."

Barrett and Lesher got Faraz into a two-man carry. Barrett had his legs. Lesher was behind, his arms under Faraz's, trying not to put too much pressure on the bad shoulder. Faraz's chin rested on his chest. His eyes were half closed.

"We got you, sir," Lesher said. "Try to stay awake."

Faraz heard him but couldn't answer.

Carter took out a phone and snapped a couple of pictures of al-Souri. He reached down, lifted the strap over the dead man's head, and put the satchel on himself.

"You guys ready?" They nodded. "I've got the lead."

Chapter Fifty-two

Will sat on a white plastic chair next to Bridget's clinic bed.

She was sleeping, still feeling the effects of the anesthetic. She had a couple of dozen stitches total, front and rear, under her hospital gown and the crisp white sheets. A tangle of tubes and wires connected her to several machines monitoring her progress.

In a few hours, she would be on a medevac flight to the U.S. military hospital in Germany, the same one where Will was treated after he was wounded a few months earlier.

Bridget's bed, machines, and visitor's chair were surrounded by green curtains hung from tracks on the ceiling. The white-painted walls, clean windows, and freshly mopped floor resembled not at all the battleground she'd been lying on the previous evening when she'd violated Will's order to remain conscious.

Will wore a camo jacket against the breeze from the wall-mounted air conditioner. He had showered and changed at the nurse's insistence while Bridget was in surgery.

"You won't be visiting my clinic with all that mess,"

she had said, hands on hips, barring the door. The doctor had read him the riot act about the extra stress he had put on his leg, which continued to ache in spite of a heavy-duty shot of painkillers.

Bigelow reamed him out, restricted him to his quarters and the clinic, and assigned another SEAL to his duties. Lumberjack, in Washington, had sent him a WTF email that included a threat to recall him to the Pentagon. It would be okay with Will if that was where Bridget was going. But he doubted it would happen. If you're going to go rogue, it always helps to be part of a successful mission.

Bridget opened her eyes. "Hi." Her voice was soft and hoarse. She cleared her throat. Then coughed.

"Hi," Will said, leaning closer. "Howya feeling?"

"Like I was hit by a truck."

Will smiled. "Not quite. An AK round, but same difference, I guess."

"Wait. Where am I? What happened? Is Faraz okay? Did he have intel?"

Will put a hand on her shoulder. "Take it easy. Everything's okay." He told her what he knew about what had happened after Ferguson hustled them onto the chopper with Castillo's body and four Spotlight guys. "I don't know about the intel. All I know is Abdallah made it out alive, gave his report, and is on an urgent medevac to Germany."

Bridget let out a breath. "I need a phone, Will. I need to know what's going on. There could be an attack—"

"Knock, knock," came a voice from outside the curtain. It sounded more like "Knawk, knawk."

Will tensed. Bridget held up a finger, signaling for him to stop whatever he was going to do or say.

"Come in," she said.

Carter pushed the curtain aside and came into the cubicle. He, too, was cleaned up, wearing camo pants and a dark green T-shirt. "How's the patient?"

"I'm okay. And thanks, um, for everything. But how's Faraz?"

"I am told that Lieutenant Abdallah had emergency surgery and will have more when he gets to a larger facility. The doc said he's unconscious but stable."

"Did you speak to him?"

"Yes. He gave me some info, which I would describe as fragmentary but useful, broad strokes on an MTO."

"Have they launched?" Bridget tried to sit up.

"Easy now. He wasn't sure, but thought not. I'm certain your agency and others are all over it. I understand the lieutenant came around and gave a fuller report later."

Bridget eased back onto her pillow.

"And I must say, my men gathered quite a trove of material in the jihadi camp."

"That's great news," Bridget said. "Please make sure they pass it to my office."

"That has already been done."

"Good. Thanks. What about al-Souri?"

"Abdallah took care of that. I'll show you the pictures when you're feeling better."

Bridget smiled and closed her eyes.

Carter spoke to Will. "Thank you for your assistance, Commander. Turned out you were in the right place at the right time, enabled me to take both my men with me to do what we needed to do."

"You and your men did a good job out there. Impressive unit."

"Truly, sir, that means a lot coming from a SEAL."

"And my condolences on the loss of your colleague. I know how hard that is. He seemed like a good man."

"The best. Thank you, Commander."

Bridget spoke without opening her eyes. "You guys gonna kiss and make up now, or what?"

The men didn't answer.

"Because if you are, I'm keeping my eyes closed."

"I think it's safe to open them," Carter said. "But . . ."

Bridget opened her eyes in time to see him hold out his right hand. Will stood, leaned on his cane, and shook it.

In the White House Situation Room, President Martelli read the transcript of Faraz's report for the third time, shaking his head. "Astounding. Even with everything we know about these terrorists, it is astounding."

Defense Secretary Marty Jacobs sat to his right. Jay Pruitt of the NSC and General Hadley of the DIA were among the many officials arrayed around the conference table. It was a rare day of good news in the war on terror, and it came just in time for the presidential primary season.

"Marty, what's the update?"

"Mr. President, the nationwide State of Emergency you ordered last night is being implemented by all security agencies working with our local government counterparts. All schools, universities, day-care centers, and similar locations have been secured, with help from the National Guard. The military is on high alert worldwide and is assisting Homeland Security with transport hubs."

Jacobs gestured toward large screens on the far wall showing a color-coded spreadsheet of key U.S. military installations. "Those columns turn red as the emergency orders are implemented."

"No one wants to live in an armed camp," Martelli said. "But we'll have to until we crack the terror cells and find any bombs they already planted."

"Sniffer dogs and bomb robots are searching every facility," Jacobs reported. "Intel and law enforcement agencies are using the info gathered in Syria to track down the operatives."

"What about the money trail?"

Jay took that one. "Sir, the treasury secretary is on a call now with major bank chairs, and has EU finance ministers next. FBI is scanning the account numbers the team provided. They're scattered all over the world, but we should get them locked down within a few hours. This Assali guy had his fingers in a lot of pots."

"Let's be sure we find them all."

"Yes, sir. Finding the man himself may be more difficult, but he has expensive tastes, which should narrow it down. Unclear whether he's a messenger or a real player."

"And he works for some of our so-called friends?"

"It seems that way."

"That's another thing that's astounding when it's staring you in the face, even though we sort of knew it already. Well, keep at it. I want to shut these guys down for good."

"We will, sir."

Martelli turned to Hadley. "General, my congratulations to Task Force Epsilon. Please wish Ms. Davenport a speedy recovery for me."

"Yes, sir."

"Let's arrange a call when she's feeling up to it."

"I'm sure she would appreciate that very much, Mr. President."

Martelli pushed out his chair, and they all stood. He offered a hand to Hadley. "And your man, the young lieutenant, he did an unbelievable job . . . again, I should say."

"Thank you, Mr. President."

"Killed their top guy and several others, reported the plan, exposed their financier. That's the kind of Blowback I'm talking about."

Chapter Fifty-three

A week later, Faraz sat in the back seat of a black sedan idling in front of a nondescript brownstone apartment building a few minutes before one o'clock in the morning.

Faraz leaned forward and craned his neck to see the fourth-floor window. "You sure your men can handle this?" he asked.

Sitting next to him, Carter said, "Our last mission was to pull you out of a terrorist base in the middle of the Syrian desert. I think we can handle one man sleeping in an apartment in London."

"Right." The bandage on Faraz's head, which once resembled an Afghan turban, was now a couple of square inches of gauze held on by two strips of white tape. It was covered by a black wool cap. He also wore black jeans and a black jacket. Under his T-shirt, his ribs were still wrapped, but the pain was tolerable thanks to some good meds, which also had his injured shoulder under control. He had three scabs on his left cheek from al-Souri's fingernails. Faraz looked like a boxer, a bad one, who had a jihadi beard and needed a haircut.

"And we won't be bothered by local law enforcement?"

"Oh, no, sir. Our Spotlight team here is first rate and fully coordinated with the bobbies. We do what the locals can't and the U.S. military won't. It's all in a day's work, except that you're here."

"Yeah, well, this one's mine."

"Understood."

"Zero one hundred, sir," the driver reported. His British accent made him sound incongruously genteel for the task at hand. "Are we a Go?"

"It's up to the lieutenant," Carter said.

Faraz looked up at the window one more time. From what he could see, there was no light on behind the closed curtains. "Yes. Let's do this."

The driver touched his earpiece and said, "Initiate."

Carter's men, Barrett and Lesher, also dressed in black, emerged from a van parked a few meters ahead. They went up the five steps outside the building and through the unlocked outer door.

Faraz and Carter followed.

At the same time, eight Turkish military vehicles used no stealth whatsoever as they covered the last few hundred meters to the farmhouse. The surveillance cameras detected their arrival and set off an alarm.

Trevor and Melissa bolted out of bed and ran in different directions, as they had practiced. They didn't say a word or spare a glance.

Wearing only boxer shorts, Trevor went down the hall and opened the front door. By then, the soldiers were pointing automatic weapons at him.

Trevor raised his arms. "Don't shoot!" he shouted,

buying a few extra seconds for Melissa to key in the code on the digital lock and take the detonator out of the safe. He wished they'd said good-bye.

Two soldiers mounted the steps.

"Melissa!" Trevor shouted over his shoulder. "Jig's up, love. *Allahu akbar*."

He heard her repeat the blessing. A moment later, a rapid series of explosions destroyed the house and killed them both, along with several of the Turkish soldiers.

As Faraz went up the steps, he saw Barrett and Lesher break the lock on the inner door with a small battering ram. He and Carter went past them into the building's ground floor hallway, drew their weapons, and waited.

No one responded to the noise.

Two more men came up behind them to guard the entrance while Faraz, Carter, and the others went up the stairs.

At the apartment door, they listened. There was no sound, and no light came through the space at the bottom of the door.

The Turkish civilian police were busy that night, too. Faraz's description had confirmed their suspicions from long-term surveillance of the mosque in Diyarbakir.

A SWAT team crashed through the door of the young man's father's house and tossed in a stun grenade. The old man shouted in protest and staggered toward them in a nightshirt, his gray hair in disarray, his hands up.

"On the floor," the team leader ordered.

"No, please," the man pleaded, falling to his knees.

There was a burst of gunfire from the backyard.

"Murderers!" the man screamed. Tears welled in his eyes, and he crumpled to the floor and said the *Shahada*.

"Take him," the commander ordered.

As his men took hold of the old man, the commander moved along the hallway. The man's wife jumped him from the bedroom doorway, digging her nails into his neck. The officer threw her off. She hit the floor and collapsed in tears. One of the policemen pointed his weapon at her.

The team leader wiped his neck and went out the back door.

The couple's son lay facedown on the ground in a growing pool of blood, surrounded by members of the team.

Faraz and Carter took positions on either side of the apartment door. Barrett and Lesher stood between them. Carter nodded. The two men broke through the door with one swing of the ram.

Carter went in first and scanned the living room and kitchen to the left. Faraz went the other way toward the bedroom. He was there inside of two seconds.

Faraz turned on the high-powered flashlight in his left hand as he raised a pistol fitted with a silencer.

Mahmoud was fumbling to grab a gun from his night table.

"*La*," Faraz said. No. He blinded him with the light.

Mahmoud froze and closed his eyes, his hand inches from the weapon.

"Leave the gun," Faraz said, switching to English. Then he added in Arabic, "*Akhooee*." My brother.

Mahmoud withdrew his hand, and Faraz moved to the side of the bed and kicked the night table so the gun fell out of reach.

"*Meen inta?*" Mahmoud asked, blinking and shading his eyes with his left hand. Who are you?

"A friend," Faraz answered. "*Min Soorya.*" From Syria. "Do you remember me?"

Faraz moved the light so Mahmoud could see his face.

"Yes!" Mahmoud's voice brightened and he relaxed, as they wanted him to. "You came through here a couple of months ago. Karim, is it?"

"Right. Why have you not launched the operation?" They were pretty sure no one had been in touch with Mahmoud since al-Souri's death, that he hadn't received or passed on any commands. It was Faraz's job to confirm it

"Do you have the orders?" Mahmoud asked. "With the new security in the United States, I thought the operation was canceled."

"Have you not already been given the Go command?"

Mahmoud looked confused. "No, no, *akhooee*. Truly. I have sat by the phones every night, as always. Since the tragic martyrdom of our leader, Commander al-Souri, the phones have been silent. Please, look in the desk. You will find the codes."

Faraz took two steps to his right, keeping his gun pointed at Mahmoud. He opened a desk drawer and glanced down long enough to see half a dozen flip phones and a notebook exactly like the one al-Souri had been carrying.

"You see, my brother," Mahmoud said, "there is no need for the weapon. I know my job."

"Yes, I'm sure you do." Faraz kept the gun pointed at

Mahmoud. "You prepare the teams, provide the money, and convey the orders."

Mahmoud smiled.

"You send naïve foreigners to die in the desert, and dispatch your teams to kill children."

"It will be the most devastating attack in the history of jihad."

"Against the children. Shame on you. Allah would not approve."

"It is necessary, *akhooee*."

"I am not your brother." Faraz took a step toward Mahmoud.

"No!" Mahmoud held out his hands toward the gun.

Faraz's finger tightened on the trigger. His hand shook a little, but he restrained himself. He raised his voice. "Come in here and take this guy."

Carter's men came into the room, wrestled Mahmoud off the bed, and forced him to kneel. Barrett put a gag on the prisoner. Lesher cuffed him. They stood him up and marched him into the living room.

"I guess we're done, then," Carter said from the bedroom doorway.

"Almost." Faraz found Mahmoud's backpack on the floor, took the phones and notebook from the desk, and stuffed them in. Then he turned and led the team out of the building.

One other security unit was active that night.

Members of an elite Jordanian paramilitary force with several American "observers" infiltrated a five-star Amman hotel one by one, convening in a room down the hall from their target. As the chief American's digital watch turned over to 0300 local time, two hours ahead of London, he opened the door and let the Jordanians take the lead as they moved in single file along the hallway.

A colonel used an electronic passkey to unlock a door, then stepped aside as his men ran past, American M4 machine guns at the ready.

The colonel followed with the lead observer. There was no one in the suite's large living room, only the remains of dinner for two, an overflowing ashtray, and some empty hard candy wrappers.

Two soldiers moved to the bedroom on the left, where they startled a young blonde who had been sleeping. She screamed and covered herself with the sheets, pushing up against the headboard away from the men.

"Don't shoot! Don't shoot!" she begged in British-accented English. "I don't speak Arabic."

"Hands up!" the colonel shouted as he moved past his men.

The American watched from the doorway as the woman complied, dropping the sheet and exposing herself from the waist up. She was shaking. Her sequined red minidress and underwear lay on the floor. Her hair fell across her shoulders. There was a fresh bruise on her left cheek. The room smelled of expensive whiskey, cigars, and perfume.

"Where is he?" the colonel demanded.

The woman looked around. "I don't know. I swear. He was here when I fell asleep. Please, sir."

"A fat man? Balding?" the American asked.

"Yes."

"He gave you that?" The American gestured toward her cheek.

The woman touched the bruise and winced. "Yes."

"What was his name?"

"He didn't tell me his name," she said, seeming to relax a bit. "They never do."

The colonel threw the sheet over her. "Watch her," he ordered. He pushed past the American as he left the room.

The team searched the suite, but the woman was alone.

The American keyed his radio. "Negative acquisition. Repeat, negative acquisition. The target is not on-site."

Back in the car in London, Faraz handed the backpack to Carter, took out his phone, and dialed the ops center. After reciting the codes, he said, "It's done. No orders conveyed. Suspect in custody. Further intel material en route via our friends."

He ended the call and turned to Carter. "Thanks for your help."

"Our pleasure, Lieutenant. Really. Good working with you."

"And you. Mind if I borrow your car?"

"Not at all. I'll ride with the team." Carter opened the car door. "See you again, I hope."

"Me, too. And thanks again for the rescue."

"That? That was the most fun I've had on the job in years."

They shook hands. Carter got out of the car and walked toward the other vehicle. Faraz sat back in the seat and said one word to the driver.

"Heathrow."

Chapter Fifty-four

Faraz peered through the window but couldn't quite make out his old neighborhood as the big jet descended across the always-blue San Diego sky.

He had dumped his ops outfit at the airport and put on jeans, a blue T-shirt, and a cotton sweater he'd gotten at the hospital in Germany. He had a toothbrush, a razor, and some pain pills in his backpack, and little else.

His reflection in the airplane window showed a different man than he'd been for the last year and a half. A barber at Heathrow had taken off his beard and brought his hair under control. He had that feeling of seeing someone you might recognize but not quite remember—perhaps a long-lost acquaintance who looked older now.

He wondered whether his mother would recognize him. But that was silly. Of course she would. He was her son, Faraz Abdallah. Definitely not Karim Niazi or Hamed Anwali.

Faraz had spent much of the flight trying to figure out how to handle his homecoming. His mother thought he had died over a year ago. Should he just knock on her door? Davenport was right. That was probably not a good idea. A phone call? Also bad.

He thought maybe he'd go see his aunt, his mom's sister. Then she and her husband could go to mom's house with him. That was as close to a strategy as he had come up with. But he still wasn't sure.

Bridget had called him after the London op and told him to meet her in D.C. She said they had to talk. There were things she had to tell him that she couldn't say on the phone. She spoke of new threats and other "developments." But Faraz was done taking orders from Bridget. He had hung up and thrown the phone away.

He had a brand-new military ID, a passport, a credit card, and some cash they'd given him for the London mission. He was going to use them to take advantage of this probably brief period of freedom.

After California, he would go back to his unit. Or maybe he'd leave the army. He needed some time to think about that. But first, he needed to see his mom. Ease her burden. And try not to give her a heart attack in the process.

The immigration officer said, "Welcome home, sir," and gave Faraz a casual salute.

"Thanks," he said.

By the time he came out through customs, he felt like he was on another planet. Even though he had spent five days at the hospital in Germany and forty-eight hours in London, the crowd, the noise, the gaudy advertisements hit Faraz hard. It had been a long time—more than a year and a half—since he'd been on his own in America. He felt at home in a terrorist camp, but here, a few miles from his actual home, he was an alien.

Outside the terminal, Faraz stood on the sidewalk, breathing the exhaust from the cars and buses, and didn't know what to do. He got in the taxi line, still not sure what he'd say to the driver. But once in the cab, Faraz thought of a place he should go before doing anything else. It was the right thing to do, and it would give him more time to work on his homecoming plan.

He told the driver to take him to Oceanside. He didn't know the exact address, but it was off El Camino Real, across the street from a church, oddly enough.

His memory served him well. As they approached, the red-roofed white buildings came into view, like an idyllic village opposite the stark landscape of scrubland and power lines. When they made the turn, the church spire topped by a giant cross was on the left. A particularly tall pole with an American flag stood next to a parking lot on the right.

They went in past the flag, and Faraz told the driver to wait. He walked through the Eternal Hills Memorial Park to the Muslim section. He stopped at a freestanding gateway and took off his shoes. It was hot and getting hotter as the sun rose toward midday.

Walking among the graves was strangely comforting. He stopped at the marker over his cousin Johnny's grave. That was where it had all started for Faraz—his decision to be a soldier, to honor Johnny's memory. Johnny's funeral was the first time Faraz had been to this cemetery.

That was early 2002, and the family had visited at least once a year after that.

Faraz said a blessing for Johnny, then moved on, wiping the sweat off his face. Two rows over, he found what he was looking for.

"Oh, *fahr*," he said out loud as he went down on one knee. He caressed the grass.

Faraz admired the flowing golden Arabic script at the top of the black marble slab, a verse from the Koran. Below it were his father's name in English, the dates of his life, spanning only fifty-eight years, and the Koran translation. "Indeed we belong to Allah, and indeed to Him we will return."

He knew the phrase well from the many martyr funerals he had attended.

After what seemed like a long time, but also too short, he stood. He looked around to get a sense of exactly where the grave was so he could remember for next time.

That's when he realized what he was looking at. Next to his father's grave was his own—the final resting place of the sandbag-filled casket that his parents had cried over last year. They had sat on folding chairs on the path where he stood now, surrounded by family and friends. He stepped back as if to watch.

The honor guard removed the flag from the coffin and folded it. The squad leader knelt and presented it to his mother. She sobbed, unable even to thank the young man.

Faraz got a chill. The misery he caused had played out right here. The guilt and shame returned.

He looked away.

His eyes fell on a fresh grave on the other side of his

father's, recently shoveled dirt matted down, with no grass yet growing on it, no granite marker yet installed.

At the foot of the grave was a small sign stuck into the ground, like a gardener might use. The piece of paper in its holder had a name scrawled in Pashto and English: Faiza Abdallah.

"What?" Faraz said, too loudly for a cemetery. He fell onto both knees in front of the little sign and read it again. He could not believe it. His mother's name, and a date—one month ago.

Faraz knelt there, frozen, his mouth open. His mother had died, too? Oh, Allah!

Still kneeling, he stretched his body toward the sky. He let out a scream. Angry. Pitiful. Primal. "*Mohr*!"

A family across the cemetery turned and looked at him but kept its distance.

Faraz sat back on his heels, his shoulders slumped. He felt the anger rise inside him, the anger he had felt at Guantanamo, and in Nazim's shed, and when Amira died. The anger that had nearly killed him.

He put his hands on his face and dug in his nails, much as al-Souri had done. He wanted to feel the pain, and he did.

Faraz's mother had died not long after losing her husband and, she believed, her only child. He bore responsibility for that. He wanted to throw something, to hit someone. But there was nothing and no one.

A month ago. Where had he been a month ago? Living in a terrorist camp, making love to Amira, holding her lifeless body in his arms.

That's why they hadn't told him. This was what Bridget wanted to tell him in person.

He pounded his fist into the ground until it came up bloody. There were tears in his eyes, and a few escaped when he blinked. He thought he should cry more. But he couldn't.

Faraz wiped his cheek. What he had accomplished was important, world saving. But the cost was higher than it should have been, higher than he had ever imagined. Too high. His parents. Amira. So many others.

He looked at the graves and imagined what his parents would say, what Johnny would say. For Johnny, it would be, "What ya gonna do now, little man?" Johnny was always great at cutting through whatever intractable problems confronted young Faraz.

"What now?" indeed.

One of the pearls of wisdom Johnny had taught Faraz was that he couldn't do anything about the past, only the future. That's why Johnny had enlisted straight out of high school, with plans to go to college on the G.I. Bill.

Faraz took some airline napkins out of his backpack and dabbed the blood from his hand. He stood, brushed off his clothes, bowed his head, and for the first time in a long time, he prayed. Faraz prayed. Not Hamed or Karim.

When he finished, he stared at his parents' graves, and his own. Nothing was left but the question. What now?

Faraz didn't know how long he stood over the graves, but it was so long that the taxi driver came to look for him.

"There you are. I thought maybe you slipped out the back or something."

"No. Sorry." Faraz reached into his pocket and counted out a hundred dollars for the man.

Faraz looked back at the graves.

There was only one answer to Johnny's question, the same answer Johnny had had all those years ago. Faraz didn't like it, but he couldn't think of anything else that might someday, in some way, justify the cost.

Faraz had expected to be home about now, having tea and sweets with mother. Instead, he had no mother, and no home to go to. No home except one.

He took a deep breath and let it out, then touched two fingers to his lips for a farewell kiss.

Faraz turned and walked toward the parking lot. "Come on," he said.

At the taxi, Faraz turned to the driver and spoke in a voice that sounded more confident than he felt. "Take me back to the airport."

He would catch a flight to Washington and see what Bridget and the major had in store for him.

ACKNOWLEDGMENTS

They say that for a writer, Book Two is always more difficult than Book One. I was very fortunate to have my support system well established.

My wife, Audrey, is my first reader, critiquing my books part by part and encouraging me to forge ahead. Her support is invaluable.

The next reader is Lourdes Venard of Comma Sense Editing. Her experience, honesty, and skill were again crucial in shaping this story and its telling.

Also subjected to early drafts are the intrepid members of my critique group. We cheer each other's successes, deliver praise and tough love as appropriate, and always provide a friendly and supportive eye. Thank you, dear friends, Porter Beermann, Caryn DeVincenti (Dana Ross), Jane Kelly Amerson Lopez, Marcie Tau, and Lou Ann Williams.

For me, beta readers are essential. I have many friends in the military, the media, and academia who are more expert than I on a variety of subjects that make their way into my novels. They help me infuse the books with authenticity and save me from many errors. Many thanks to Robert Burns, Steve Boylan, Tom Collins, Marvin

Diogenes, Greg Hicks, Joyce Karam, Vince O'Neil, and Thom Shanker.

My thanks also to the terrific authors who have been gracious enough to take the time to read advance copies of my books and provide endorsements. Their kind words were like gold, and their willingness to put their names next to mine in asking you, the readers, to buy my books is humbling. Thank you, Steve Berry, John Gilstrap, Ali Ahmad Jalali, Jon Land, Ward Larsen, Daphne Nikolopoulus (D. J. Niko), Vince O'Neil (Henry V. O'Neil), Alan Orloff, Tony Park, T. Jefferson Parker, Hank Phillippi Ryan, Les Standiford, Admiral (Ret.) James Stavridis, and Tom Straw (Richard Castle).

The team at Kensington Publishing has been great to work with, supportive, responsive, warm, and professional. It's worth noting that we finished *Blowback* in the throes of the coronavirus pandemic and stay-at-home orders. But somehow they managed not to miss a beat. The Task Force Epsilon team is led by editor Michaela Hamilton, and also includes Lauren Jernigan, Alexandra Kenney, Arthur Maisel, Crystal McCoy, and Alexandra Nikolajsen. I am also eternally grateful to the boss, Steve Zacharius, for his faith in this series and his support for the effort to bring it to print.

The characters and events in *Blowback* are fictional, but many grew out of people I knew and experiences I had during my time covering the Pentagon, the White House, the Middle East, and South Asia. My thanks to the many people over the years who facilitated my reporting, and to those on various sides of many issues who gave their time to provide me with some understanding of who they are, what they do, and why they do it.

Finally, I must thank you, the readers, for trying this series. I hope you enjoyed *Blowback* and the first book, *Sandblast*. Please write to me through my website, alpessin.com, and let me know what you thought. If you feel motivated to tweet or write an online review on one of the bookselling websites or reader forums, that would be much appreciated. You can also find me on Twitter @apessin, Instagram @alpessinauthor, and Facebook at the Al Pessin Author page.

I look forward to being in touch and to keeping you informed about the next book in the series, *Shock Wave*, scheduled for release in the spring of 2022.

Stay safe.

—Al Pessin, "Staying at Home"
in Delray Beach, Florida,
August 2020

Don't miss the next exciting thriller from Al Pessin

SHOCK WAVE

A TASK FORCE EPSILON THRILLER

Coming soon from Kensington Publishing Corp.

Keep reading to enjoy a preview excerpt . . .

Chapter One

The lone passenger felt every whitecap as the small boat crept toward the desert shore. He thought he might be sick. But he was determined not to show any weakness.

He looked out the porthole but saw nothing. It was a moonless night.

The man was sweating in the stale, hot air of the small forward cabin. The old, rusting bench with thin, plastic-covered cushions provided none of the creature comforts to which his unique capabilities had entitled him these many years.

The cabin brought to mind the tiny apartment where he'd grown up, where he'd learned of his father's murder, where his mother had died for lack of medical care. He had worked hard to forget that apartment through the decades of plush furnishings and air-conditioning. He shook off the memory.

A swell hit the boat and nearly knocked him from his seat. He put a hand on the bench to steady himself and let another wave of nausea pass.

How had he come to this—on this scow, hat in hand,

virtually on his knees begging for the seeds to regrow his operation? Begging for his life.

Not long ago, this all would have been done with a phone call and an electronic transfer. Now, calls were more dangerous than ever. Moving money was impossible. Damn them!

Assali's anger and shame fueled a new determination to succeed, to impress his masters, to get back to the air-conditioning. If they let him live.

A member of the crew opened the cabin door. "Two minutes, *sahib*," the man said in Arabic, then retreated without waiting for an answer.

Still clinging to the bench, Saddiq Mohammed al-Assali thanked God that he had survived the voyage. "*Allahu akbar*," he whispered. God is great. But his tone was more sarcastic than reverent. Surviving this far was a victory, but perhaps a fleeting one.

Assali stood, something a taller man would not have been able to do in the low-ceilinged cabin. His ample belly made it hard to balance in the rolling sea and strained the fabric of his sweat-stained traditional Arab *qamis*, an untucked long-sleeved white shirt that reached his knees and was buttoned all the way to his neck.

He wiped his face and felt the three-day stubble. He ran a hand through his hair. It came out greasy. Disgraceful. But such was life on the run. He had only his small travel case, half a bottle of water, and an empty plastic bag that once held German pretzels. He wished he hadn't eaten them.

Assali put on the suit jacket he'd bought not long ago at the priciest men's tailor shop in Amman. He picked up the carry-on, put the water bottle in a side pocket, and stepped to the cabin door, crushing discarded candy wrappers and cigarette butts as he went. For the first time he could remember, he had smoked his last. Perhaps, if this was the end, they'd at least give him one before the execution.

Mounting two of the three steps to the deck, his face caught the breeze. It blew away some of the humidity and refreshed him.

They called this the Red Sea, but all he could see was black. The small cabin cruiser was painted black. The three-man crew all wore black, and they had turned off the running lights. Looking toward the rear of the boat, he could hardly see anything.

They had engaged the electric motor and so were running almost silently. They were invisible and inaudible. At least, that was the theory. Who really knew what technology the enemy might have?

Assali mounted the final step onto the deck and turned to look around. His fist closed on a rail, and he peered into the darkness. In the distance to his left, there was a glow in the sky—the lights of Eilat and Aqaba, he reasoned. Staring ahead and trying not to blink, he forced his pupils to dilate. The shoreline appeared, dark gray against the blackness, maybe a kilometer away.

"How can you be sure this is the place?" he asked.

"From the satellite, *sahib*," the man at the controls assured him.

Assali looked toward the shore again and shrugged. He could only hope these men knew what they were doing.

The next wave tossed the boat and splashed over the rail.

Assali turned away but tasted the salt as water crashed onto the deck. He had two hands on the rail now, and was more concerned about going overboard than about vomiting. This had to be the longest kilometer in the world.

Finally cresting the last wave, the boat surfed down to the shore and ran aground.

This time, Assali's "*Allahu akbar*" was sarcasm-free.

"Here, *sahib*," the crewman said, indicating a small ladder he had lowered over the stern.

"Into the water?" Assali asked. This would be the final indignity. Final for now, anyway.

"It is only half a meter," the man said, barely concealing a derisive smile.

Assali pursed his lips and moved toward the ladder.

The sky brightened for a split second, as if from a distant bolt of lightning. All eyes turned north, toward the glow of the cities, in time to see a second flash. Then the sound reached them—a low rumble, barely audible. They felt it as much as heard it. The boat bobbed in the surf.

Assali snorted at the irony that he was close enough to actually feel the impact of what he'd done. That would be a first. And also a last, he hoped. He preferred to run his operations from a safer distance.

"It is done, then," the crewman said.

"Yes. So it would seem."

"*Allahu akbar*," the man said.

Assali did not repeat the blessing. His look said, "Give God credit if you want. This was my doing."

He took a deep breath and tried to shake off the last of the claustrophobia and nausea. He might yet survive this night.

Assali took hold of the ladder's handles and hefted himself over the rail. He pursed his lips and let out a curse, then stepped down into the warm water. His designer leather loafers hit the sand, and his gaberdine dress pants were wet past the knees. The hem of his *qamis* touched the water, but, praise God, his suit coat was spared. He held his bag high on his shoulder.

As he made awkward steps toward dry land, the dimmed headlights of three vehicles blinked from behind the mangroves at the edge of the beach.

Assali did not turn to wave or thank the crew. He climbed the beach incline and walked toward the cars with as much dignity as he could muster, his pants dripping, his shoes and socks caked with sand, and his heart pounding.

He was sweating again, but not from the heat. A week ago, he would have been welcomed as an honored guest. Now, even after what he had just done, he wasn't sure whether he would make it off the beach alive.